Johan Wilhelm van Hulst

January 28, 1911–March 22, 2018

A Humble Servant of God, Guided by His Grace

Susie Joy Oertli Stewart

April 6, 1968–March 7, 2018

Warrior Princess and Treasured Friend

Daughter of the King

Praise for *Memories of Glass* and other novels by Melanie Dobson

Memories of Glass

"*Memories of Glass* is a remarkable, multi-layered novel that weaves stories of friendship and faith in wartime Holland together with a modern-day orphanage in Africa. Memorable characters portray the complexity of human relationships and reveal the lasting consequences of our choices, whether cowardly or courageous, and the mysteries kept me turning pages, leaving me with much to ponder."

LYNN AUSTIN, BESTSELLING AUTHOR OF *LEGACY OF MERCY*

"Like colored shards in sunlight, Melanie Dobson once again shines her light of truth in this elegantly complex and gripping tale of the hidden terrors of the Netherlands during WWII. *Memories of Glass* is a remarkable story, and one that will linger in the hearts of readers long after the last page."

KATE BRESLIN, BESTSELLING AUTHOR OF *FOR SUCH A TIME*

"Breathtaking, heartbreaking, and ultimately uplifting, *Memories of Glass* shows the beauty of helping others, the ugliness of people helping only themselves, and the destructive power of secrets through the generations. Melanie Dobson's memorable characters and fine eye for detail bring the danger of the Netherlands under Nazi occupation to life. This novel will stay with you."

SARAH SUNDIN, AWARD-WINNING, BESTSELLING AUTHOR OF *THE SKY ABOVE US*

"Heart-wrenching history combines with gripping characters and Melanie Dobson's signature gorgeous writing to create a tale you won't be able to put down—and won't want to. *Memories of Glass* is an amazing, intricately woven story of finding light in the least likely of places."

ROSEANNA M. WHITE, BESTSELLING AUTHOR OF THE SHADOWS OVER ENGLAND SERIES

"I couldn't stop turning the pages of Melanie Dobson's *Memories of Glass*. Drawn from history to highlight the Dutch resistance to Hitler's Nazi regime, the story is sweeping in its scope of setting, each vividly alive on the page, and its pace felt like a snowball rolling downhill, gaining in suspense as the life-and-death stakes mounted. Peopled with characters heroic, flawed, and unforgettable, *Memories of Glass* is sure to please longtime fans of Melanie Dobson's books as well as readers new to her novels."

LORI BENTON, AUTHOR OF *THE KING'S MERCY*

Hidden Among the Stars

"This exciting tale will please fans of time-jump inspirational fiction."
PUBLISHERS WEEKLY

"A romantic tale of castles, lost dreams, and hidden treasures wrapped inside a captivating and suspenseful mystery complete with an unpredictable, unforeseen, and unexpected ending. Not a book to miss!"
MIDWEST BOOK REVIEWS

"Star-crossed, forbidden love and the disappearance of family members and hidden treasure make a compelling WWII story and set the stage for modern-day detective work in Dobson's latest time-slip novel. . . . *Hidden Among the Stars* is Dobson at her best."
CATHY GOHLKE, CHRISTY AWARD–WINNING AUTHOR OF *UNTIL WE FIND HOME*

"*Hidden Among the Stars* is a glorious treasure hunt, uniting past and present with each delightful revelation. It's must-read historical fiction that left me pondering well-crafted twists for days."
MESU ANDREWS, AWARD-WINNING AUTHOR OF *ISAIAH'S DAUGHTER*

Catching the Wind

"Dobson creates a labyrinth of intrigue, expertly weaving a World War II drama with a present-day mystery to create an unforgettable story. This is a must-read for fans of historical time-slip fiction."
PUBLISHERS WEEKLY, STARRED REVIEW

"Dobson skillfully interweaves three separate lives as she joins the past and present in an uplifting tale of courage, love, and enduring hope."
LIBRARY JOURNAL

"A beautiful and captivating novel with compelling characters, intriguing mystery, and true friendship. The story slips flawlessly between present day and WWII, the author's sense of timing and place contributing to the reader's urge to devour the book in one sitting yet simultaneously savor its poignancy."
ROMANTIC TIMES

"Readers will delight in this story that illustrates how the past can change the present."
LISA WINGATE, NATIONAL BESTSELLING AUTHOR OF *BEFORE WE WERE YOURS*

MEMORIES
OF
GLASS

A NOVEL

MELANIE DOBSON

Tyndale House Publishers, Inc.
Carol Stream, Illinois

Visit Tyndale online at www.tyndale.com.

Visit Melanie Dobson's website at www.melaniedobson.com.

TYNDALE and Tyndale's quill logo are registered trademarks of Tyndale House Publishers, Inc.

Memories of Glass

Designed by Jennifer Phelps

Edited by Kathryn S. Olson

Published in association with the literary agency of Natasha Kern Literary Agency, Inc., P.O. Box 1069, White Salmon, WA 98672.

Scripture taken from the Holy Bible, *New International Version*,® *NIV*.® Copyright © 1973, 1978, 1984, 2011 by Biblica, Inc.® Used by permission. All rights reserved worldwide.

Memories of Glass is a work of fiction. Where real people, events, establishments, organizations, or locales appear, they are used fictitiously. All other elements of the novel are drawn from the author's imagination.

For information about special discounts for bulk purchases, please contact Tyndale House Publishers at csresponse@tyndale.com, or call 1-800-323-9400.

Library of Congress Cataloging-in-Publication Data
Names: Dobson, Melanie, author.
Title: Memories of glass / Melanie Dobson.
Description: Carol Stream, Illinois : Tyndale House Publishers, Inc., [2019]
Identifiers: LCCN 2019006670| ISBN 9781496434180 (hc) | ISBN 9781496417367 (sc)
Subjects: LCSH: World War, 1939-1945—Underground movements—Netherlands—Amsterdam— Fiction. | Jewish children in the Holocaust—Netherlands—Amsterdam—Fiction. | GSAFD: Historical fiction.
Classification: LCC PS3604.O25 M46 2019 | DDC 813/.6—dc23 LC record available at https:// lccn.loc.gov/2019006670

Printed in the United States of America

25	24	23	22	21	
7	6	5	4	3	2

Brilliant color flickered across her canvas of wall. Sunflower yellow and luster of orange. Violet folded into crimson. A shimmer like the North Sea with its greens and blues.

Most of the walls in her bungalow were filled with treasures of artwork and photographs and books, but this pale-cream plaster was reserved solely for the light, a grand display cast through the prisms of antique bottles that once held perfume or bitters or medicine from long ago.

The colors reminded her of the tulip fields back home, their magnificent hues blossoming in sunlight, filling the depths of her soul with the brilliance of the artist's brush. Spring sunshine was rare in Oregon, but when it came, she slipped quietly into this room to watch the dance of light.

Sixty-eight bottles glowed light from shelves around her den, their glass stained emerald or amber or Holland's Delft blue. Or transparent with tiny cuts detailing the crystal.

These wounds of an engraver—the master of all craftsmen with his diamond tools—made the prettiest colors of all.

Only one of the bottles was crimson. She lifted it carefully off the shelf and traced the initials etched on the silver lid, the ridges molded down each side, as she lowered herself back into her upholstered chair.

All of them she treasured, but this one . . .

This bottle held a special place in her heart.

Her fingers no longer worked like they used to. They were stiff and curled and sore. But her mind was as sharp as a burnishing tool. Perhaps even sharper than when she was a girl.

She held this bottle to her heart, leaning her head back against the pillow.

No matter what happened, she wouldn't forget.

Couldn't forget.

A cloud passed over the sun, darkening the room for a moment, and she felt the keen coldness of the shadow. The memories.

Some memories she clung to, but others she wished she could lock away in one of the vaults under Amsterdam's banks. Or a tunnel carved into the depths of the old country.

Closing her eyes, she remembered the darkness, the chill of air deep underground seeping back into her skin. The memory of it—of all she'd lost in Holland, of the terrible mistakes she'd made—had haunted her for more than seventy years.

Shivering, she pulled the afghan above her chest.

Seconds ticked past, time lost in the cold, before sunlight crossed over her face again, color glittering in the gaps of darkness. When she opened her eyes, the light returned to illuminate the wall.

Slowly she stood, balancing against the lip of wainscoting that rounded the room until she placed the bottle back on the shelf. Her legs felt as if they might give way, just for a moment, but she regained her balance long enough to find the sturdy legs of her chair. A front-row seat for her memories.

"Oma?" her great-granddaughter called from the hallway, on the other side of the door.

Her children and their children all worried about her, but they needn't worry. Even in her heart sadness, even when her body tripped over itself, all was well with her soul.

Her family, they knew about her Savior, but they didn't know all she had done. No one who remained in this world knew. It was her secret to harbor, for the safety of them all.

"Come in," she said softly, her gaze back on the glass.

Even if her mind began to slip like her feet, this room would always remind her of the ones she'd lost.

And the one she had to leave behind.

I hope I will be able to confide everything to you,
as I have never been able to confide in anyone.

ANNE FRANK

THE DIARY OF A YOUNG GIRL

ONE

JOSIE

GIETHOORN, HOLLAND
JUNE 1933

Flower petals clung like scraps of wet silk on Josie's toes as she ducked alongside the village canal. Klaas Schoght could search all afternoon if he wanted. As long as she and her brother stuck to their plan, he would never find them or the red, white, and blue flag they'd sworn to protect.

Klaas's hair, shimmering like golden frost, bobbed above his family's neatly trimmed hedge across the canal from her. She watched the sprig of sunlit hair as Klaas combed through the shrubs, then between two punts tied up to a piling, before he turned toward the wooden bridge.

There were no roads in Giethoorn—only narrow footpaths

and canals that connected the checkered plots. Most of the village children spent their time swimming, boating, and skating the waterways, but her brother preferred playing this game of resistance on land.

"Jozefien?" Klaas called as he crossed over to the small island her family shared with a neighbor.

She ducked between the waxy leaves of her mother's prized hydrangea bushes, the blossoms spilling pale-purple and magenta petals into a *slootje*—one of the many threads of water that stitched together the islands. Her brother had taught her how to hide well in the village gardens and trees and wooden slips. Even on the rooftops. She could disappear for hours, if necessary, into one of her secret spaces.

"Samuel?" Klaas was shouting now, but Josie's brother didn't respond either.

All the children learned about the Geuzen—Dutch Resistance—at school, their people fighting for freedom from Spain during the Eighty Years' War. Her brother was a master of hide-and-seek, like he was one of the covert Geuzen members fighting for freedom centuries ago.

In their game with Klaas, neither she nor Samuel could be tagged before her brother pinned the Dutch flag onto the Schoght family's front door. Klaas didn't really care whose team he was on, as long as he won.

Between the flowers and leaves, Josie saw the hem of Samuel's breeches disappear up into a fortress of horse-chestnut leaves. They had a plan, the two of them. Now all she had to do was hide until her brother signaled her to dive.

It wasn't the doing, Samuel liked to tell her, that was key to resisting their enemy. It was the waiting.

And Klaas hated to wait.

The boy wore a black cape over his Boy Scout uniform, but she could see the white rings around the top of his kneesocks as he searched one of her family's boats.

This afternoon he wasn't Klaas Schoght, proud scout, tenacious son of their village doctor. This afternoon he was the pompous Fernando Álvarez de Toledo, the Spanish governor over Holland, trying to capture the Dutch resisters and their flag made from the fabric of one of Mama's old dresses that was, thankfully, too threadbare to remake into a shift for her only daughter.

Josie much preferred wearing the long shorts and blouses that her mother reluctantly allowed during the summer so she wouldn't keep ruining her dresses. And even more, the Brownie uniform she wore today—a light-brown dress that hung inches below her knee. Her knit beret and brown shoes and long socks were tucked away in the house behind her.

The three of them had developed the rules for this game, but she and her brother kept their own names—Josie and Samuel van Rees, the children of a teacher and a housewife who sometimes helped at the kinderschool.

Klaas didn't know that the Dutch flag had climbed the tree with Samuel this afternoon. When her brother gave the signal, Josie would distract Klaas so Samuel could hang the stripes of red, white, and blue on the door.

Water lapped against the bank, and she glanced again between a web of white blossoms and waxy leaves to see if Klaas had jumped into the water. Instead of Klaas, she saw a neighbor pushing his punt down the canal with a pole.

Her knee scraped on one of the branches, and she pulled

it back, wiping the glaze of blood on a leaf before it stained the hem of her uniform.

The injuries from their battles were frequent, but now that she was nine, she tended to them on her own. Once, a year or so back, she'd run inside with a battle wound. Mama took one look and fainted onto the kitchen floor.

Ever since, Josie visited Klaas's father if she had a serious wound.

When the punt was gone, she listened for the thud of Klaas's boots along the bank, but all she heard was the cackling of a greylag, irritated at Josie for venturing too close to the seven goslings paddling behind her in a neat row. They looked like Dutch soldiers following their orange-billed colonel, each one uniformed in a fuzzy yellow coat and decorated with brown stripes earned perhaps for braving the canals all the way to the nearby lake called Belterwijde.

If only she could reach out and snatch one of the goslings, snuggle with it while she waited in her hiding spot, but the mother colonel would honk, giving away her location to the governor of Spain. And Fernando Álvarez de Toledo would brag for days about his triumph. Again.

This time, she and Samuel were determined to be the victors.

Long live the resistance!

The battalion of geese swam around the punt below her and disappeared.

"Jozefien!" Klaas was much closer now, though she didn't dare look out again to see where he was.

Did he know Samuel was up in the tree behind her? Klaas

didn't like climbing trees, but his fear of heights would be overpowered by his resolve to win.

A stone splashed into the canal, rocking the boat, and her heart felt as if it might crash through her chest. Operation van Rees was about to begin. While Klaas was searching for whoever threw the stone, she would hide on the other side of the bridge.

She shed her dress and slipped into the cool water in her shift like her brother had instructed, holding her breath as she kicked under the surface like a marsh frog escaping from a heron. Six long kicks and she emerged under the wood bridge, her long knickers and undershirt sticking to her skin, the water cold in the shadow. From the canal she could see Klaas rummaging through Mama's flowers, and above him, Samuel descending from the tree, ready to race across the bridge.

Beside her, carved into the wood, were three sets of initials.

S.v.R.   J.v.R.   K.S.

The boys didn't know that she'd carved their initials here, but this recording of their names made it feel permanent. As if nothing could ever change between them. Often she, Samuel, and Klaas were the worst of enemies in their play, but in reality, they were the best of friends.

Josie inched away from the bridge, toward the narrow pilings behind her that kept the bank from sliding into the canal. Something moved on her left, and she turned toward the house of Mr. and Mrs. Pon. The Pons didn't have any children, but an older girl was watching Klaas from the porch.

A German Jewish man and his daughter—refugees, Mama had said—were moving in with the Pon family. Josie had learned German, along with English, at school. Tomorrow, perhaps, she would ask the German girl to play. They could resist Spain together.

Samuel's bare feet padded across the bridge; Klaas would be close behind. She dove back under the surface and emerged once again, this time in her secret hiding space between the moss-covered pilings, tucked back far enough under the quay so Klaas couldn't see her chestnut-colored hair.

She couldn't touch the bottom in the middle of the canal, but it was shallow under the wood awning. Her toes sank into the mud as her chin rested an inch or two above the surface, and she waited patiently between the pilings, like Samuel had instructed, until he hung the flag on Klaas's door.

One of the goslings, a renegade like her, paddled by without his fleet. Then he turned around to study her.

"*Ga weg,*" she whispered, rippling the water with her hands. The gosling rode the tiny waves, but he didn't leave.

She pressed through the water again, the ripples stronger this time, but the gosling moved closer to her as if she were his mother. As if she could rescue him. She reached out a few inches, just far enough to pet the creature but not so far that anyone could see.

The moment her hand slipped out from under the platform, a face leaned over the ledge, lips widening into a smile when he saw her. Then his fingers sliced across his throat.

"Klaas!" she screamed, her heart pounding.

He laughed. "You have to find another hiding place."

She huffed. "Samuel told me to hide here."

Klaas jumped off the bank in a giant flip, knees clutched to his chest, and when he landed, water flooded over her nose and mouth. She swam out into the center, splashing him back as he circled her. He might be four years older, but neither he nor his impersonation of Fernando frightened her.

"You don't always have to listen to Samuel," he said.

"Yes, I do." Klaas didn't know anything about having a brother, or a sister for that matter. Nor did he listen to much of what anyone told him, including his father. Sometimes it seemed that he believed he was governor of Giethoorn instead of the make-believe Spanish general.

"The Dutch have won!" Samuel exclaimed triumphantly from the opposite bank.

Klaas shook his head. "I found Jozefien before you pinned the flag."

"I pinned it five minutes ago."

Klaas lifted himself up onto the bank, facing Samuel. They were the same age, but her brother was an inch taller.

"It's been at least six minutes since I found her," Klaas said, hands on his hips, the black cape showering a puddle around him.

"You did not!" She whirled her arms through the water, attempting to splash him again, but the canal water rained back down on her instead.

"I did."

The two boys faced off, and for a moment, she thought Klaas might throw a punch. Maybe then Samuel would fight for what was right instead of letting Klaas win again.

"I suppose you won," Samuel said, surrendering once more.

She groaned. Her brother always let Klaas win whenever his friend claimed victory. Why wouldn't he stand up for himself and for her? For Holland?

Klaas raised both fists in the air. "To Spain!"

"To the resistance," she yelled as the boys turned toward Klaas's house.

Fuming, she swam back toward the bridge, to the underwater steps built for those who didn't want to hop up on the planks as Klaas had done. When she passed by the cropping of initials, she rapped them with her knuckles.

The best of friends, perhaps, but some days Klaas made her so mad. And Samuel, too, for not fighting back when Klaas lied to him.

The next time they played, the resistance would win.

As Josie climbed the mossy steps out of the water, the German girl inched closer to the canal. She had dark-brown hair, draped rather short around her head, and her brown eyes seemed to catch the light on the canal, reflecting back.

"I'm Anneliese," the girl said in German. "But my friends call me Eliese. I'm ten."

Josie introduced herself, speaking in the German language that her father had taught all the village children.

The girl sat on the grass, pulling the skirt of her jumper over her knees. "Would you like to be friends?"

Josie smiled—another girl, a friend, living right next door. They would be friends for life.

"I'm Klaas."

Josie turned to the opposite bank to see both boys

standing there, Samuel with his mouth draped open as if he might swallow the light.

Josie waited for Samuel to introduce himself, but when he didn't speak, Josie waved toward him. "That's my brother standing beside Klaas. He'll come to his senses soon."

Samuel glared at Josie before introducing himself. And when he did, Eliese smiled at him.

Samuel didn't speak again, just stared at the girl. And in the stillness of that awkward moment, with her brother utterly entranced, Josie knew.

Nothing in her world would be the same again.

TWO

AVA

Memories are curious things. Some I want to remember, and others . . . well, I simply don't. Most of my memories—at least the ones from childhood—are curdled into lumps anyway. No amount of stirring will separate them.

But today my family and I are remembering together. Not the twenty-seven years of my life, but the legacy of William Kingston, my great-grandfather. A legend of a man who built a glass kingdom around the world more than seventy years ago, the profits trickling down generations into a significant fortune for his son, Randolph, and daughter-in-law, Marcella, and then eventually my two uncles and myself and Marcella's other five grandchildren who are still alive.

Whispers filter from the rows behind me, but my eyes are

fixed straight ahead on the podium. Marcella Kingston, my grandmother, is standing on the platform near the enormous front door of this renovated library, talking with the mayor of Amsterdam and Paul Epker, the new library director. Above the door, painted in an elegant golden script, is one of her favorite proverbs in Dutch.

Kennis is macht.

Knowledge is power.

Dressed in a tailored black suit and Gucci pumps, the toe of each one adorned with a crystal bow, Marcella exudes the perfect mix of elegance and dignity— a gracious hostess and powerful business leader—as she waits for the ceremony to begin. Her sons don't always like what she says, but they respect her. As does every vice president employed by the Kingston Corporation and a multitude of government officials across party lines.

Since no one is speaking to me, I twirl one of my strappy heels in circles, trying to pretend I'm running barefoot across a sandy beach back home, the golden retriever I had as a girl splashing in the waves beside me. Wishing I could breathe in the salty breeze on the shores of North Carolina, where I was born.

In a blink, that lump of memory is gone.

Sawdust, that's what I smell now, along with musty leather and expensive fragrances worn by those seated in the rows behind me.

It's Remembrance Day in the Netherlands, the Dutch honoring all the people they lost during World War II. My family is here to celebrate the grand opening of Kingston Bibliotheek, a research library in Amsterdam for those who want to remember by studying European history, business, and culture.

This row house in Amsterdam's Jewish Quarter is centuries old, one of the many elaborate merchant homes built tall and thin like a ladder since Dutch taxes were once based on the width of one's residence. William Kingston bought it seventy years ago and renovated what had been vandalized during the war, using the space as a home and office when America first launched its European Recovery Program. Eventually he began providing Kingston Windows to people across Europe.

My uncles—Carlton and Will—and five cousins are all quiet now in their chairs, staring at the back of my head as we wait for the ceremony to begin. Or I guess they're staring. It's purely speculation on my part since I'm seated in the front row. Alone.

I don't dare turn around to confirm whether or not they are looking back at me, but if eyes could shoot bullets, I suspect my body would be riddled with holes. And so would every book—forty thousand of them—on the shelves that circle this library and climb two stories above my head.

The Kingston family paid for a restoration of this house during the past year. Or at least, the Kingston Family Foundation financed the restoration. Neither of my uncles wanted the family's money to fund this library, and they despised the fact that their mother, Marcella, had the audacity to appoint me as director of the foundation.

In the eyes of the law, Marcella can appoint me to serve however she sees fit; but in their eyes, I'm an outsider who weaseled her way into Marcella's good graces twelve years ago to steal part of their fortune. Nothing I do will convince them that I simply want to be part of the family.

The Kingstons may be broken, but they're all the family I have left.

I pluck at a thread on my wine-colored wrap dress, both my gloves and dress purchased from a ritzy shop in New York by a woman named Claire, Marcella's personal assistant for the past thirty-plus years.

Claire has coordinated all the details for this dedication, including what I'm wearing, the precise seat where I'm sitting, and who will attend the luncheon that follows, but Claire is nowhere in sight now. She probably snuck into a reading room to chug down one of the energy shots stashed away in her leather briefcase beside her iPad, medications for Marcella, and who knows what else. I don't need a jolt of caffeine to wake up. Adrenaline has been shooting through every nerve in my body since I walked into this room, like a surge of electricity through faulty wiring.

Red lights glow from video cameras focused on the podium, prepared to record every detail this morning so Marcella's publicist can distribute the footage online and to news outlets around the world. Will and Carlton and their children and all the significant others will smile politely for the cameras after the ceremony, but this afternoon all hell will break loose behind closed doors. The Kingstons are rapidly losing their fortune, and while they blame some of this loss on me, they keep it a secret from the rest of the world.

"Why is she here?" one of my cousins—Austin, I think— whispers from somewhere behind me, as if I can't hear him.

I never felt much like an outsider until, ironically, a case-worker found my mother's family in New York.

Clutching the ivory handbag in my lap, I wait for a response. Perhaps this time one of my uncles will actually stand up for me.

"Marcella wants her to participate in all the family functions," my uncle Will—a senator from New York—says.

"But Ava's not really family—"

I strain my good ear, trying to hear what else they say, but the Dutch official is introducing Marcella now, prattling on about her achievements and the esteemed Kingston Family Foundation that finances good work around the world. Then he begins extolling William's achievements.

As valuable minutes slip by, even Marcella starts to become agitated. I can always tell by the way her lips press closer together, shooting tiny lines up her cheeks that her dermatologist hasn't been able to laser away. *Laugh lines*, most people call them, except Marcella Kingston never laughs. These lines are more like the trail of a shooting star about to explode.

Marcella stands before the man finishes his intro, inching gingerly toward him until he relinquishes the podium. Smiling graciously, she welcomes the small crowd and begins to honor the legacy of William Kingston—her father-in-law—for them and the cameras. My lips are set in a semi-permanent smile, and I nod periodically as if I haven't heard this speech a hundred times.

Glancing up, I scan the balconies on three upper floors for Claire, but she seems to be gone. Wrought iron railings cage in the balconies, and a trio of ornate windows filter light into the library. Between the shelves of books is an impressive array of Dutch art, some of it recovered from an old mine after the war.

My phone blinks, and I glance down at the screen, thinking Claire is sending me another text, telling me to fix the tie on my dress or smooth my hair.

Are they all glaring at you?

I almost laugh out loud at my best friend's message. While I guard the details of my life like a Doberman, Victoria can talk about almost anything without blushing. Victoria-can't-keep-a-secret, I started calling her when we were thirteen and she told me that Brian Webster was going to ask me to our seventh-grade dance. She hadn't meant to ruin his plans— or my surprise. She just didn't believe in secrets.

Now I just call her Vi, and I love her for allowing me to be just who God made me to be.

My handbag partially covering my phone, my eyes focused back on Marcella, I type out a text that I hope is coherent.

I'm not giving them the pleasure of turning around.

Vi texts again. Class is ranked solely in one's heart and mind.

Brilliant. Where did you hear that?

From a deep wellspring of wisdom.

I glance up at Marcella before looking back at my phone. Your yoga instructor?

A fortune cookie.

A laugh escapes my lips this time, and I try to cover it with a cough.

True class . . . I tuck my cell into my handbag before she replies again, lest I really do ruin the ceremony.

"My father-in-law partnered with the Dutch people after

the Second World War," Marcella says. "He built businesses specifically in the interest of providing jobs, and his investments began to multiply. He was committed to working alongside the citizens of this great country as they recovered from the war, and his selflessness helped educate and provide for people across Europe."

I never met my great-grandfather, but I've memorized his carefully choreographed legacy. William and Abigail Kingston had one son, Randolph, in 1938. William's business partner was a German man named Peter Ziegler, who had one daughter, Marcella, two years after Randolph was born.

According to Marcella, Peter and William had schemed since the birth of their two children to seal the Kingston-Ziegler business partnership through Randolph and Marcella. Their marriage took place on June 12, 1965, on the lawn of the Kingston estate in New York.

Randolph died more than a decade ago, not long after I arrived in New York. He and Marcella had been married forty-five years, birthing two boys and adopting my mom when she was a baby.

William lived until he was eighty-two and managed to acquire enough money to catapult his family into the top one percent before his death. A coveted position, but I'm not convinced that it's an enviable one for his descendants. Before he died, he set up a foundation to give away a percentage of his fortune to educate and provide good jobs for those who wanted to work. None of his heirs except Marcella seemed to be pleased about giving money away.

My grandmother's eyes skirt over me as she speaks, settling

on the row behind me. My mom was the hardest working person I've ever known—helping care for our little family by working as a server, administrative assistant at our church, and part-time gardener. A landscape artist really, creating masterpieces in North Carolina's sandy soil.

Sadly, Marcella's sons haven't seemed to embrace the same work ethic as their sister . . . or their grandfather.

"William Kingston invested in people first," Marcella says, quoting the familiar Kingston business creed passed down through the generations. "And these people became masters of their craft. They changed the world with their innovation and ability to make it a better place."

William sought knowledge from the time he was a child, I've been told, growing up as a banker's son in New Jersey, throughout his years at Cambridge, and then during the Great Depression, when he began snatching up stock at rock-bottom prices, the return on his investments later rivaling the worth of men like Joe Kennedy and Howard Hughes.

No one's past is perfect, but I've yet to hear anyone mention any major glitches in our family's journey.

"Through this library, we envision a continued return on William's investment in people and knowledge so generations after us will learn from the past as they fight against evil and pour their lives into all that is good."

Marcella's gaze travels down the row of her grandchildren and several of their spouses as she speaks about how William planted seed money in the Netherlands and around the world to inspire innovation and help others grow.

And now the Kingston legacy will continue on in this library.

Claire appears on the stage with a pair of giant scissors, and Marcella turns toward the white ribbon strung across the library's front door. A camera flashes behind me, capturing this moment, and after Marcella clips through the ribbon, I reach for my purse.

I should keep my gaze forward—I know this—but my eyes seem to act of their own accord. Both uncles are sitting right behind me, along with Will's third wife and Carlton's current girlfriend. Lined up to their left are the cousins who talk plenty about me but refuse to speak directly to my face.

I want them to like me, but nothing I can do, besides running away like my mother, will make them happy. According to Marcella, I don't need their friendship or their money—each cousin has a trust fund with their name on it. While none of the family dares question Marcella, they hate me for every dollar she's invested in me and my education.

Much of the family, it seems, is simply waiting for Marcella to die so they can begin living their lives. But Marcella, at seventy-nine years old, isn't planning to die anytime soon. And this woman plans *everything*.

As the crowd disperses, I walk up the platform steps and kiss Marcella carefully on the cheek so I won't leave an imprint on her coating of powder. She directs me to Paul Epker.

"This is my granddaughter Ava Drake." She scoots me toward him with a nudge on my back. "She helps me with research for the foundation."

Research is my specialty, along with the gut instinct my mom once said was a gift.

"It's very nice to meet you." He picks a piece of lint off one of the stripes on his suit jacket. "I hope you will do some of your research right here."

As Marcella turns to speak to someone else, I glance up again at the thousands of books in this space, most of them written ages ago. "All my research is about contemporary organizations."

"The past often has a way of creeping into our present," Paul says, the word *way* sounding like "vay," and I stare at him, surprised, wondering if he somehow managed to uncover part of my story, pre–Kingston family.

But he just smiles kindly at me, waiting for me to speak.

"Do you have anything about the Kingston family history on your shelves?"

"I've ordered several books with information about William Kingston and Peter Ziegler." He looks up at the loft. "I will find one for you."

"Thank you." The history I know about the Kingston family is an oral one from Marcella and a biography about William that I borrowed from her personal library.

"Did you attend Yale like your grandmother?" he asks.

"No, I went to—"

Marcella steps back into our conversation, interrupting me. "She attended a prestigious university in North Carolina."

Paul smiles again; whether it's genuine or not, I wouldn't know. Years ago, before high school, when someone smiled at me, it usually meant they were being friendly, no strings attached, because I had nothing of value to offer. Now I'm never certain if someone actually enjoys my company or if they see dollar signs floating in some kind of aura above my head.

Strange how my own insecurities swell in the face of wealth while I'd bloomed just fine growing up on a much-lower economic plane.

Paul says something else, but with the pattering of voices, I can't make out the words.

I turn my head. "I'm sorry?"

"Which university?"

"It was called—"

"Thank you for your work today," Marcella says to him. "It was exactly as I'd envisioned."

When she directs me off the platform, I flash an apologetic smile, but Paul doesn't seem frustrated at our abrupt departure. When you manage millions, I've discovered, people are much more likely to forgive any trespass. I could stomp all over certain individuals with my spiked heels, and they'd say I missed a spot.

Marcella doesn't want Paul, or anyone, to know that I attended a state school, as if that would somehow taint the facade that she's invented for me. All of my cousins were educated in the halls of the Ivy League, but after three years at a private high school in Connecticut, I wanted nothing to do with the invasive destruction of ivy, no matter how Marcella tried to convince me otherwise. I'd insisted on getting both my bachelor's and master's degrees in business back home.

The front door is propped open in front of us, and after Marcella steps outside, Claire leans down toward my right ear so I can hear. "A storm is brewing."

The sky has indeed darkened, but that's not the storm she's referring to. It's the somber faces glaring back at us.

"Lunch is scheduled for noon," Claire says, "at a place called Merkelbach. I've reserved the entire place in case of . . ."

I sigh. "Thunder."

"And lightning." She nudges me, nodding that someone is behind us, probably trying to talk with me. I turn to see Paul Epker, a book in his hand.

Darkest Before Dawn—the title is stamped in gold foil on the dark-green cover.

"This book mentions both of your great-grandfathers."

I tuck it under my arm, thanking him for the loan.

"Mrs. Kingston asked me to order another book that, according to the catalog description, talks more specifically about the Kingstons' business before World War II. I could only find one copy still in existence, so it's taken a bit of finagling . . ."

"Will you let me know when it arrives?"

He nods. "I'll overnight it to you."

Water splashes from the faucet of sky outside, a raindrop sliding across my bare shoulder and streaming down my arm. More drops follow at a rapid pace, and Claire snaps open the leather case, shooting up an umbrella in record time to rescue Marcella from disaster.

As black umbrellas mushroom across the sidewalk, I reach into my purse and pull out my compact one, strewn with butterflies. Then I spring it open above my head.

"I'll meet you at the restaurant," I tell Marcella and Claire, wanting a few minutes to explore on my own before I face the angry tribe.

Claire glances up. "But the rain?"

"A little water won't hurt me."

Marcella scans the crowd one more time, and I see something new in her eyes, a look that passes so quickly that I must be mistaken because Marcella never looks scared.

"You'd better ride to lunch with Claire," she says.

I almost balk, but if Marcella is concerned . . .

I follow Claire to a waiting car near the sidewalk, and I wonder why everything of use in the Kingston family must be black. Almost as if we're all supposed to live our lives in mourning.

Some nights I curl up on my bed, mourning the loss of those I've loved, but no one has told me why this family—my family—is grieving.

THREE

JOSIE

"Dinner, Jozefien, that's all I ask." Klaas dug his hands into the pockets of his trousers, wagging his head as if she'd wounded him with her refusal. "I'll take you to Café Royale."

Schutterijweg 265.

Each letter, number, clicked like a typewriter key in her brain, making an imprint before she forgot the address.

"I can't," Josie said, trying to focus on the man standing beside her, the woven handle of the basket seeming to burn her hand. "At least, not tomorrow night."

It seemed innocent enough, this basket. A bouquet of purple and orange tulips, two glass jars, and a lining of gingham napkins. But her brother had hidden an envelope in the bottom, under the gingham. And no one, including Klaas, could find out what she was delivering to Maastricht tomorrow.

Schutterijweg 265.

Klaas fingered the tulip petals. "Orange is supposed to be banned."

"Fortunately no one told the flowers."

Klaas leaned against a marble column of the expansive lobby, his blond hair combed neatly back, the knot of his plum-colored tie bunched up above his waistcoat. He wrapped his arms across the breast of his gray-striped coat. "What's more important than dinner?"

"I'm helping Keet with her children."

His eyebrows arched up, his handsome blue eyes studying her. "She only has two *kinderen.*"

"She's had another since you visited," Josie said. "And now there's a fourth on the way."

An older couple scooted past them, and the yellow stars stitched to their clothing seemed to glimmer in the chandelier light and ripple across the long marble countertop in the lobby, trying to penetrate the milky glass that separated the bank tellers and managers from their Jewish patrons. The woman clutched the man's arm with one hand and the other was gripped around the strap of a fashionable shoulder bag. He carried a tan attaché case that, Josie assumed, was filled with money and jewelry and perhaps the title to their house. Everything valuable they owned.

The bank of Lippmann, Rosenthal & Co. had been formed almost a hundred years ago by two Jewish men and had been well-respected until the occupation. This new branch, called Liro by Amsterdammers, was designed by the Germans to secure all the valuables of Dutch Jewry. The securing of property became mandatory with yet another regulation by occupiers who'd vehemently promised they wouldn't persecute the Jewish people in Holland.

Then again, the Germans had promised they would never bomb the Dutch, hours before they crushed the grand city of Rotterdam into dust. Now Holland was being assaulted from inside and out. An onslaught of German soldiers, Gestapo, local police, and NSB—Dutch Nazis—who were all implementing what Hitler demanded of them.

Josie switched the basket to her other hand. "Samuel will go to dinner with you tomorrow."

He eyed the basket. "Did he bring you another gift?"

"Jam." She lifted the flowers to show him the two amber-colored jars. "Golden raspberry from home."

She was fairly certain that her brother had purchased it at the market—he hadn't been back to Giethoorn in weeks—but Samuel often called her from the bank these days, saying he had a gift from home. Better, he'd once told her, for them to make their exchanges in public than attempt to do so in secret.

Klaas reached for one of the jars, and she held her breath as he examined it, hoping he wouldn't find the envelope.

Schutterijweg 265.

She couldn't allow him to blur a single one of these letters or numbers in her mind. The smallest of details meant life or death in their work.

Klaas placed the jar back onto the napkin, and she swung the basket casually to her side. "How's Sylvia?"

"Sylvia and I are no longer together." He gave her that sly smile he liked to use when they were children. "She said I was much too interested in someone else."

Josie hugged the basket to her chest, not certain how to reply. Klaas had never treated her as anything more than Samuel's little sister. Someone he had to tolerate even when she annoyed him, a responsibility she'd taken quite seriously until Eliese arrived in Giethoorn.

They were all grown up now, Eliese safe in England while Josie, Samuel, and Klaas had moved to Amsterdam. It was her first year in the city, studying at the Reformed Teacher Training College, but Samuel had worked for several years at the Holland Trade Bank before transferring to Liro, and Klaas was employed at an architectural firm. Unlike her, Klaas managed to pretend that nothing in Holland had changed in the past two years, that their future was as promising as it had ever been.

He glanced at his watch. "I must return to the office or my boss might decide to lock the door." He tweaked her chin like she was a child again and they were skating along the canals back home. "I wish I could go back to Maastricht with you."

"Perhaps one day . . ."

"Perhaps." He smiled again before he left.

Josie glanced at the partially caged window where her brother sat, helping another Jewish customer entrust his worldly goods into the care of the regime. A *roofbank*—that's what this new branch of the respected institution was called. A pirate ship ready to plunder. The Nazis never planned to return anything they stole, but her brother kept pretending that all the gold and diamonds and certificates of stock were simply being stored here.

If only Samuel could have remained at the Holland Trade Bank with Eliese's father and their investors. Instead, the occupiers shuttered the bank's door months ago because of Mr. Linden's Jewish heritage. Last she had heard, Eliese's father was cooperating with the Germans.

The rain had stopped, but Josie still tied her red scarf under her chin, wishing it were a brilliant orange. Klaas didn't think she knew much, but she was well aware of the ban on her favorite color.

In the early weeks of the occupation, she had worn her orange sweater—the color of Dutch royalty—to classes each day until Dr. van Hulst, the headmaster at her college, quietly pulled her aside and handed her a blue cardigan, saying there were much more productive ways for her to rebel against the unwelcome guests who'd taken up residence in their city.

She'd found a bracelet in the pocket of that cardigan, and she'd worn it every day since, hiding the silver links and orange lion under her sleeve.

A row of green-uniformed guards stood outside the rain-soaked windows; their honey-brown hair reminded her of the yellow pollen produced from ragweed, infiltrating every inch of this bank's plaza. She rushed out past them, toward the bike rack, before someone stopped to search the contents of her basket more thoroughly than Klaas had done.

The road followed the river back toward the college, located at the edge of Amsterdam's Jewish Quarter. The handle of the basket looped over one arm, the glass jars jostled as she bumped along the cobbles, trying to avoid the puddles. On a normal day, she would slow down to protect her wares, but today she wanted to deliver this envelope back to the safety of her room.

In a year, she hoped she would be ready to teach on her own. In a year . . . if the Allied troops prevailed and the Jewish children in their country were once again allowed to attend school.

She hated this feeling of being caught in the enemy's web. Stuck. Of only being a courier for her brother with letters he said were making a difference, yet she didn't know if they were doing anything at all. People whispered about resisting this enemy, as her country had done so long ago with Spain, but they needed—she needed—to do more.

Someone cried out nearby, and her heels dropped to the ground. It was a little girl, standing on the stoop of one of the row houses, a stuffed bunny clutched to her chest.

Josie pedaled beside the parked automobiles in the alley and leaned her bicycle against the stoop. In the windows she could see faces of other people, watching the child, but no one came outside to help.

She rushed up three steps with her basket and knelt beside the girl, her heart sinking when she saw the yellow star on her cardigan. She must be at least seven. The younger children weren't set apart by the stars.

"What's wrong?" Josie spoke quietly lest she frighten the child even more.

"They're taking us away."

"Who is taking you away?" she asked.

The girl pointed toward a blue automobile that waited at

the opposite end of the narrow lane, a capped driver inside. "The police."

Something rumbled inside the house, thunder echoing between the walls, the sound of heavy boots pounding down the steps.

Would this girl's parents want Josie to steal her away before the police did? Surely one of the neighbors would open up their door if she knocked, hide the girl inside.

But when Josie reached out her arm to take the girl's hand, she shrieked in terror. A woman rushed out the door and held her close, glaring as if Josie were the one threatening their family.

Two Dutch policemen stomped out behind her, grim shadows in their black shirts and boots like the fabled Ossaert, a clawed monster who searched for innocent victims in the night. The agents were gripping the arms of a disheveled man wearing a tailored suit coat with a torn star and a swollen bump on his head.

Had they beaten this poor man in front of his wife?

"What are you doing?" Josie demanded.

The sergeant's gray eyes, dual blades, pierced through her. She took a deep breath, the blaze of her anger dying down into embers of fear.

"Are you a neighbor?" He scrutinized her skirt and jacket as if searching for a star.

She shook her head. "I was worried about the girl."

"You needn't worry," he said stiffly. "We're relocating her and her parents to a safer place."

The terror in the girl's face shredded Josie's heart. If only she could still steal her away . . .

"Please let the woman take her!" the father pleaded.

"*Stilte!*" the sergeant barked.

Silence.

The second policeman, the one who refused to look at Josie, shoved the father toward the car. The look in the mother's eyes had changed, pleading now for Josie to help.

"Please . . . ," Josie begged the sergeant.

He grasped Josie's wrist, and the teeth of the orange lion bored into her skin. If he pushed back her sleeve and saw the bracelet, he'd arrest her right there.

Then again, he might arrest her anyway.

"I didn't realize you were taking her to safety," she said, relenting under the pain. And she hated herself for letting him bully her, cowering while this family was dragged away.

"Go home, Fräulein." He pointed. "Is that your bicycle?"

She reached for the handlebars. "It is."

Several people had stopped along the sidewalk, gazing at the family as if they were a parade of animals being led to the Artis Royal Zoo.

"What do you have in your basket?" He swept it out of her hands and threw her tulips on the wet sidewalk, the purple and orange petals wilting in the puddled raindrops.

"Diederik!" he called before tossing a jar of jam. The other officer tried to catch it, but the glass shattered against the cobblestone, spraying shards and raspberries across the pavers. The sergeant lifted the second jar, studying it as Klaas had done earlier. Then he turned over her basket, and the two cloth napkins slipped to the ground, red-and-white checkers bleeding on the ground.

She held her breath, waiting for the envelope to fall out, but no envelope appeared.

Had Samuel forgotten to hide it in the basket?

The sergeant ground his heel into the orange flower petals before turning to leave.

She slid down to the ground, wrapping her arms around her knees. Her entire body was trembling. She reached for the crushed flowers first, as if she could somehow recover their beauty, as if the brilliant color of their petals could soak up the darkness suffocating her.

As if the flowers could help her breathe again.

Then she picked up the napkins.

The bottom napkin felt stiff. Someone had stitched the fabric of two napkins together, concealing what must be Samuel's envelope.

Schutterijweg 265.

The face of the little girl haunted her as she clutched the napkin to her chest, tears welling in her eyes. She'd deliver this message to Maastricht for this girl and her parents and all who were being tormented by the Nazis.

An elderly gentleman seemed to appear out of nowhere, wearing a black raincoat and hat.

She stood beside him. "Do you know this family?"

"As well as any of us can know each other these days."

"Do you know where the police are taking them?"

"To one of the camps, I fear."

"What happens at the camps?" she asked.

He took a step away as if he'd already stayed too long. "None of us know for certain."

She glanced back toward the end of the alley. "What are their names?"

"Van Gelder," he said. "Werner, Hanneke, and Esther van Gelder."

"I only wanted to help," she whispered.

"It's too late to help them. Too late for any of us now."

FOUR

Jagged light cuts through the muddy sky above Merkelbach, thunder shaking the walls of the old manor house near Amsterdam's center. Marcella hasn't arrived yet, but Claire positions herself inside the arched doorway, a basket in hand for collecting cell phones and electronic devices from each Kingston before the thunder from our family's storm echoes on their screens.

I drop my phone into Claire's basket and step toward a window overlooking the expanse of terraced gardens, all being pummeled with rain. Austin, the thirty-year-old son of my uncle Will, walks into the house behind me, clutching his phone as if it's life support.

Claire inches the basket toward him. "Phone, please."

He shakes his head. "This is ridiculous."

Claire just smiles at him, her perfectly glossed lips pinned together as Austin scans the dining room behind her, the dark wood floors and freshly cut flowers and family members standing in small circles, nursing their drinks.

"You can't fault Claire," I say, stepping to her side. "Marcella won't begin the meeting until everyone cooperates."

A black Mercedes-Benz pulls up beside the house, and the chauffeur opens an umbrella for Marcella before she climbs out of the backseat.

Austin doesn't notice; his eyes are focused on Claire. "So you're adding your phone to this pool?"

Her smile doesn't waver. "I will do exactly what Marcella asks me—"

"Only because she's paying you."

"Hello, Austin." Marcella sweeps into the entryway, removing her black gloves. "I wasn't planning to talk about money until after our first course."

He blinks, his hands smoothing the burgundy tie around his neck before he turns toward our grandmother. "We need to reevaluate the no-electronics policy."

Marcella takes the basket from Claire's hands and holds it out to him. "I will take that into consideration."

He slowly lowers his phone into the pool.

"I'm expecting a call," he tells Claire, but she doesn't reply.

Claire's devotion is to Marcella alone, and my grandmother doesn't allow anyone except her assistant to have a cell phone during her meetings. Nor does she communicate via text or email. She prefers to have her attorney review every one of her written words before distribution.

Marcella doesn't have a phone to deposit in the basket—if she needs something, she calls for Claire.

The heels of her pumps clap across the floor, marching toward a staircase. "Come with me, Ava."

I follow her quickly, not daring to glance over my shoulder.

Upstairs we step into a parlor with a pale-peach couch and two antique chairs. Marcella closes the door and sits on one of the chairs. "Vultures, every one of them."

"You'll outlive all of us." I collapse into the second chair and kick off my shoes, one of them hitting the vintage screen that shields a fireplace.

The sharp lines around her eyes soften into a narrow chasm, the underbelly of her armor. This family that she's worked so hard to hold together for more than fifty years keeps boxing each other inside—and sometimes outside— their ring.

"My sons might poison my coffee if I live much longer."

"So start drinking tea."

"Never." Reaching inside her handbag, she removes three file folders—red, blue, and green—and places the green one in her lap. "Speaking of coffee . . ."

I'm quite familiar with Marcella's file system. The Kingston Family Foundation extends about two dozen grants each year from the more than hundred million dollars in its coffers. For the past three years I've been helping her research applicants while I completed my MBA, but after my graduation in December, Marcella offered me the volunteer role of director.

Now when we receive grant requests, I determine which ones meet the initial qualifications, and then Marcella and I pore over the qualifying proposals as we narrow down those that best fit our mission. I spend weeks partnering with a research firm to write up a full report—a dossier, we call it—and if Marcella is still interested, she files it in a green-means-go folder and hands it back to me.

This is the part of my job that I enjoy most of all: interviewing the grant writer and principal members of the organization for a final confirmation that what they've written is true. Since December, I've visited almost twenty organizations around the world. Most of them have portrayed themselves accurately on paper, but those who haven't . . .

Marcella tolerates deception as much as she tolerates cell phones.

As Marcella hands me the green folder, I read the printed label on its tab.

Bishara Coffee & Café.

And I smile.

I don't like coffee, but I handpicked this nonprofit from our applications because my mother would have liked their faith-inspired work. Bishara's coffee plantation in Uganda partners with a roaster and three coffee shops in the Pacific Northwest to provide a sustainable income for all of its workers. *Good news*, the name means in Swahili, and as the grant writer noted in the application, the Kingston foundation is trying to bring good back into the world.

"I can't guarantee anything," Marcella says. "But I want you to vet it."

"Of course." Opening the folder, I skim the fact sheet one more time.

Five years ago a man named Landon West and his sister, Kendall, started the first Bishara coffee shop in Portland, Oregon. According to our research firm, Landon had been working full-time as a tech analyst when he went on a mission trip to Uganda. After building a dormitory for orphaned kids, he decided that he wanted to do more than just offer housing for these children; he wanted to offer them a future.

His fiancée at the time had other plans.

After they broke up, Landon decided to use his MBA and technology experience to provide an education and eventually jobs for Uganda's children and offer them hope through faith in Christ. Marcella doesn't put any stock in what she terms religion, but she champions both innovative jobs and education. Even though my own faith has been shaken, I understand this hope that my mother clung to in her last years.

A self-proclaimed coffee snob, Landon invested his savings to create a nonprofit organization that would provide jobs in both Oregon and Africa, the income from their coffee harvests supporting a school for the workers' children in Uganda and a home for orphans in their community. Now Landon and Kendall want to build a clinic to provide medical care and to offer even more jobs by expanding their distribution.

Under the application section about inspiration, the brother-sister team noted that they have a Dutch great-grandmother who'd spent a lifetime inspiring them to love others. Between the café's mission and the Dutch heritage of its owners, I'd hoped to convince Marcella that Bishara would be a good fit for our grant.

I turn the page. "Should I go to Portland next week?" Marcella drums her nails on the armrest.

I glance up. "Is something wrong?"

"I need you to leave right away."

I tilt my good ear toward her, confused. We are supposed to fly home to New York later today, after lunch. Next week I'm planning to travel for the foundation, but this weekend, I'm supposed to be eating steamed shrimp in North Carolina and walking the beach with Victoria. My first time home since graduation. I can almost feel the sand between my toes.

"You want me to fly out tomorrow?" I ask.

"No . . ."

I study her face. "What is it?"

She reaches for the folder and tucks the paperwork back inside. "You're flying out now."

"But we're supposed to have a family meeting."

"Exactly."

That sinking feeling, like an anchor plummeting inside my chest, settles in my gut. Marcella has always assured me that, in spite of all the turmoil, I'm still a valued member of the family. She thinks her sons' animosity is rooted in their anger at my mother—their sister—for running away years ago to marry the Kingston stable boy, but it seems to me their hatred is rooted in something deeper: the fear that they'll lose a chunk of their fortune to me.

"It's corporate business we have to discuss," Marcella says. "And they won't be happy. I don't want to parade you in front of that firing line."

"They're already angry about the library."

She doesn't sigh exactly, more like a deep breath that

screams disappointment. "The money we spent for restoration wasn't earmarked for any of their pockets."

"They think all the Kingston money is earmarked for them."

"Yes, well—" She stops herself. "You are different, Ava. You know how important family is. Much more than money."

If only this knowledge could bring resolution. For more than a decade, I've longed for a family who loves each other, but the only thing that seems to bond this family is their insatiable greed.

She pats my hand. "I don't know what I'd do without you."

My anxiety begins to subside when she folds her fingers over mine.

On her good days, and even her bad days, Marcella reminds me of my mom. I don't know what I would do if I lost Marcella as well, through death or if she decided to knock me out of the Kingston ring.

"Did Claire already book me on a flight to Portland?"

Marcella squirms, although not in a traditional, fidgety sort of way. She shifts her legs, tucks one of her pumps under the other, and scratches the tip of her nose. This bit of choreography, I've learned, means something is very wrong.

I lean back in my chair. "I'm not going to Portland either."

"I took the liberty of contacting the Portland offices last night. Mr. West wasn't available."

I feel queasy, the faux sand on my feet rinsing away in the tide. "Where exactly is Mr. West?"

"Working with their partner company in Uganda."

I slowly process her words. "You want me to fly to Africa?"

The lines fan out from her eyes again. "You're already halfway there."

I stand and move toward the rain-streaked window. The black Mercedes-Benz is waiting in the looped driveway, the chauffeur smoking a cigarette in the front seat. I've been to Africa only once, and even though I am advocating for Bishara, I'd hoped my time in Kenya would be the last time that I ever needed to travel there.

"I'm flying to North Carolina on Friday." Six days from now.

"You'll be back before Friday," Marcella says. "All you need to do is tour the plantation and interview Mr. West."

The Kenyan organization that I vetted three months ago had proved to be a farce, but my vaccines are up-to-date. Anything I don't have packed, I can buy at the airport in Amsterdam with my corporate credit card or perhaps at a shopping mall in Kampala, Uganda's capital.

I turn back. "I need malaria medication."

"Claire already bought it for you."

I don't have a choice; I know that. As the foundation's director, I report to Marcella, and I believe in the mission of our work. The foundation money, when used well, has enormous power to do good, and more than anything, I want to do something good with my life.

"Claire and I will be taking the Global back to New York, but there's a commercial flight leaving from Schiphol in—" she glances at her watch—"two hours. You'll have a driver waiting for you on the other side."

I reach for my handbag.

"Call Claire when you land." Marcella kisses my cheek before opening the door.

The crowd turns to stare when I step back into the dining room alone, my pair of heels in one hand, purse in the other. I slip on my heels and head for the door.

Austin steps up beside me. "You're leaving already?"

"I have to make a trip for the foundation."

"You'd do anything for Marcella, wouldn't you?"

I cringe at the tone of his voice. "Within reason."

When he snorts, I scan the crowd behind him. The heat in Uganda will seem arctic compared with the blaze scorching this dining room. No matter how much I want peace, there seems to be no negotiating it with this family.

He stops beside the front door. "At least Claire gets a salary."

"It's none of your business—"

He holds the door open. "Everyone else in the family gets paid for something."

"All my expenses are covered."

"Which means you can't ever leave her."

"I don't want to leave her," I insist before stepping out into the rain.

"But one day you will, just like your mother."

I face him again. "You don't know anything about me or my mom."

"You and Marcella can pretend you're a Kingston, but no matter how much money she throws your way, you don't belong."

I don't wait for the chauffeur to close the door. I slam it shut and lean my head back against the seat, rainwater trickling down my shoulders. If my uncles treated my mother with the same disdain, she must have fled from this family.

I wish I could cry, release my sadness in the saltiness of tears. But I don't cry, haven't cried since November 3, 2006.

Nothing I can do will ever make any of the Kingstons—other than Marcella—like me.

FIVE

JOSIE

MAASTRICHT
MAY 1942

As the train traveled south through Holland, Josie pressed her nose against the window and studied the mosaic of tulip blossoms and sugar-beet sprouts, colorful fields stitched together by silver threads of canal. As the fields were replaced by birch woods and loping hills and medieval towns with endless hiding spaces, she silently repeated the address on Schutterijweg.

The ancient city of Maastricht dipped like a toe into the waters between Belgium and Germany, the river Meuse separating medieval cathedrals and Roman walls on this sliver of Dutch land. A bus transported her across the river from the train station, above the town on the winding country road called *Ganzendries*.

Hills were rare in Holland, and the treed ones surrounding Maastricht were especially unique, the ground blotted with dozens of holes like pats of butter on brown bread. More than twenty thousand tunnels, Keet once told her, created a labyrinth underneath these hills, the corridors connected yet poorly planned as farmers and monks spent centuries mining their land for marlstone.

Her cousin's farmhouse was tucked behind a fortress of trees, two of the mine openings scarring the hillside of their property. Both were gated and locked so Erik and Keet's children wouldn't stumble inside.

If only she'd been able to bring Esther van Gelder with her this morning, hidden her away until her parents returned. The local police wouldn't even suspect Keet was hiding a Jewish child. After the bombing in Rotterdam, families across Holland had taken in orphaned children who needed homes.

"Josie!" Her cousin was a decade older than her, but Keet's energy was as endless as the passages under her and her husband's farm.

Three children, two girls and a boy, came running out to greet her, kissing Josie on both cheeks. The sisters twirled around her as if they were chimes blowing in the wind, just as she and Eliese used to do when they were girls. When friendship was more important than anything else in this life.

Josie blinked. She and Eliese were no longer girls who twirled in circles. They'd released each other's hands before the occupation and spun in entirely different directions.

"Come inside before you're overrun." Keet laughed, strands of her curly hair escaping from its pins.

Josie ducked under the low-hanging beam across the front door and stepped over piles of boots and knapsacks and a cat that wouldn't budge. The house smelled like gingerbread and mint tea, underlined with a suspicious aroma coming from a pair of wool socks clumped on the floor.

"How's your brother?" Keet asked as Josie pulled back a chair from the breakfast table.

"Okay, I suppose. He changed banks a few months ago."

Keet set two cups on the table and lifted the teapot from the stove. "I never thought he'd leave Mr. Linden's bank."

"The Nazis didn't give him a choice."

"They never ask our opinion, do they?" Keet poured them both a cup of tea. "How are Klaas and Eliese?"

"Klaas is apprenticing at an architectural firm. And Eliese . . ." Sadness welled inside her. She hated nothing more than saying goodbye to the people she loved. "I haven't heard from her since her father sent her to England. As long as the Nazis are in Holland—"

An airplane flew low over the house, shaking their table.

Eliese and her father had moved to Amsterdam six years ago, and Samuel followed soon after to work with Mr. Linden. Before the Nazis arrived, an American and a German had swept into Amsterdam and invested an enormous amount of money into Holland Trade Bank. Samuel didn't like the American, but Eliese was quite enamored. Josie couldn't tell her cousin that Eliese had gone to England with him.

"What is the news from Amsterdam?" Keet asked.

"The German and Allied planes are flying over every night, but they're not dropping bombs."

"They're not dropping bombs here either, but the Germans watch our land closely."

Josie's fingers traveled over the damp envelope hidden under her girdle. She needed to deliver it before sunset, without her suitcase in hand.

"How are the people holding up?" Keet asked.

"I suppose it depends who you are," she said. "Most are trying to pretend the Nazis aren't there, but it's getting harder every day. They're stealing the male students away to work in German factories, and now the Jewish people have to wear yellow stars on their clothing and deposit all their valuables in Samuel's new bank."

"They are wearing the stars in Maastricht as well."

Josie's mind flashed back to the van Gelders. "Some of those with stars are being forced out of their homes."

Keet leaned forward. "What do you mean?"

As she poured out her story, tears poured as well, about the girl who'd looked so sad, about the father who'd begged for her help.

And Josie had done nothing.

"You can cry all you want at this table, but not out there." Keet nodded toward the window. "Out there we have to be strong. Fight them with our hearts along with our heads."

"I wanted to sweep up that little girl and run away."

"They would have shot you and then her."

Still she hated her cowardice. "If only I knew where they were taking her . . ."

Keet's little Nelle ran into the room, a squirming cat in her arms. "Will you come play with us?"

"Soon," she promised. "First I was hoping to borrow a bicycle and get some fresh air."

Nelle wrinkled her nose. "We have plenty of fresh air right—"

"I won't be long," Josie said, the lump of envelope pressing against her skin.

After Nelle left, Keet eyed her curiously. "A bicycle ride?"

"Just to visit a friend."

Josie found the designated cottage on Schutterijweg a short distance from Keet's house, surrounded by oak trees and wildflowers that bloomed in the wheat-colored soil. A flock of bluebirds, printed on the curtains, framed the front window. Partially drawn curtains would have signaled danger, but they were wide open this afternoon and the strains of classical music from a gramophone drifted outside.

She'd delivered dozens of these letters for Samuel in the past year, but she still held her breath after she knocked, waiting for someone to answer.

Moments later the face of a middle-aged man appeared at the window, and he scanned the empty lane behind her before he slid the bolt to unlock the door.

"My favorite niece," he exclaimed. They'd never met, but Samuel had been very clear: if the man didn't refer to her as his niece, she should keep the envelope hidden away.

"I've missed you, Uncle," she said, loud enough so anyone

who happened to be in the woods would hear. "Father sends his greetings."

"He must visit soon as well."

The exact response she'd expected.

When the man waved her inside, Josie stepped into the linoleum entryway, hemmed in between two closed doors and a set of stairs. Her nerves shuddered like they always did on these deliveries, uncertain of what awaited her.

The man didn't introduce himself. If he did, he would use a fake name anyway. Her current name, according to the identity card in her pocket, was Laurina de Jong. Not that he would ask for her name either. Better that they remained simply uncle and niece.

She glanced at one of the doors. "I need a private place to retrieve my father's gift."

He opened the door on his right. "In here will do."

Quickly she moved into the formal room and pulled the curtains closed. She draped her blue sweater over a chair, untucked her blouse, and retrieved the envelope. The door at the opposite side of the room squeaked, and Josie gasped when it began to open, stuffing the envelope into the pocket of her skirt. "Who's there?"

A woman slipped through the doorway, her black hair coiled above her ears, her lips pinched together. "Are you from Amsterdam?" she whispered.

Josie opened the door into the entry, preparing to run if she must. She wasn't supposed to speak to anyone in this house except the man pretending to be her uncle.

The man's eyes grew wide when he saw the woman behind her. "Go back to your room," he commanded.

"I just wanted to find out what is happening. My husband—"

"This isn't the time," he said, directing Josie back out into the entry hall, slamming the door behind them.

Shaken, Josie set the damp envelope on the newel post.

The man picked it up. "Why is it wet?"

"I—I dropped it in a puddle."

He ripped open the top and pulled out a stack of paper money, clotted together from the dampness. Josie stared at the guilders. Hundreds of them.

Delivering correspondence for the resistance was one thing, but this . . .

Her mind wandered to the image of her brother in Amsterdam, a manager working with the bank's Jewish customers to store their things. Surely Samuel wouldn't have taken their money, even to invest back into the resistance.

"You must leave." The man opened the front door. "If someone asks why you were here, you lost your way. I've given you directions into town."

"Of course."

"And if someone asks—"

Josie finished for him. "No one else was in your home."

The number nine tram stopped on Plantage Middenlaan minutes before curfew, between the Reformed Teacher Training College and the vacant theater across the street called Hollandsche Schouwburg. Josie drummed her fingers against the handles of her bicycle, which she'd stored for the weekend at Amsterdam's train station, as she waited for the engineer to open the door.

Streetlamps along Plantage Middenlaan once flickered on after dark, illuminating the theater and dozens of stately buildings that lined this street, but the Nazis had extinguished the lights two years ago so Allied airmen wouldn't know they were flying over the city.

The tram rumbled away as Josie stepped into the refuge of shadows and rang the bell beside the college's wrought-iron gate before leaning back against a brick wall. The envelope in her girdle was gone now, but the weight of it still pressed against her skin. Her brother had said that she was delivering letters for the resistance, but it seemed she might have been delivering money all along.

Samuel had to be honest with her. Next weekend, when they went home together, they would talk. She wouldn't deliver another envelope until he told her where he'd gotten those guilders.

The side door to the college opened, and light sparked in the alleyway between the brick college and the children's crèche housed next door. Johan van Hulst, the college headmaster, stepped outside with a flashlight in hand, his black-framed reading glasses shoved back over unruly hair. He was only about a decade older than her, joining the school as a teacher four years ago. Then the college lost their funding, and he stepped in to keep it open. The eighty students currently enrolled, both male and female, admired him greatly for it.

"I was worried," he said through the widely spaced spindles of the gate, his keys rattling as he unlocked the latch.

"My train was late."

She secured her bicycle on a rack before retrieving her satchel. As he locked the gate behind her, she hurried inside.

The teaching college was made up of two buildings. In this building were the offices, classrooms, dining hall, and a corridor on the top floor with rooms that some students, including her, called home. In the back, across a courtyard, was the second building with a chapel and library. The courtyard was walled off by hedges, but the college shared outdoor space with the crèche and more than a dozen other buildings that made up their city block.

Dr. van Hulst locked the door behind them and turned on the light in the stairwell. "I've been wanting to speak with you, Josie."

She braced herself. Dr. van Hulst didn't seem to sympathize with the Nazis, but what if he'd found out she'd spent the weekend in Maastricht, delivering money for the resistance? He could have her dismissed from college—or worse.

"Miss Pimentel needs an extra caregiver at the crèche," he said.

She sighed. Nothing made her happier than spending time with kids. "When does she need help?"

"In the mornings," he said. "Would you like to assist her?"

"Very much, but . . ."

He pushed his glasses back up the bridge of his nose. "What's wrong, Josie?"

"I have theology class at ten o'clock."

She followed him up the steps, to the dark landing on the first floor. He peeled back a curtain made from brown velvet to look out at the Hollandsche Schouwburg across the street. In the silky gray of dusk, she could see the needled pillars on the elegant theater, the Greek muses in statue form that gazed down from its roof. This place had once hosted some of the best productions in Amsterdam, but most of the performers had been Jewish. The Nazis had closed down this theater in the past year, canceling all further productions so the performers couldn't work.

A spark of light seemed to float in front of the main door, the glowing cigarette of a soldier patrolling Plantage Middenlaan and the entrance to the Jewish Quarter, across a canal to their west. Then an army truck stopped in front of the theater, a dark-green canopy masking whatever was hidden in its bed.

"Trucks have been coming and going all day," he said.

"What are they doing?"

"I'm not certain." He resealed the blackout curtain before turning on a lamp that made the paneled walls glow. "These days, perhaps, it is better to practice our theology than listen to lectures about it."

She nodded.

"I will make sure your schedule is rearranged."

The headmaster bid her a good night, and with her satchel in hand, Josie climbed up to the top floor. God, she suspected, would want the theology she'd spent a lifetime learning to siphon down into her hands and feet. Share His love with those who needed a glimpse of it during this dark season.

Perhaps she could help her country most by caring for its children.

SIX

ELIESE

AMSTERDAM
JUNE 1942

Eliese lifted her pen off the dining room table, a warm breeze stealing through the open window as she began transcribing her father's accounts into the ledger. He'd given her dozens of numbers, along with the names of the oil, metal, and chemical companies where he'd invested the money for Holland Trade Bank.

She recorded the words and correlating numbers carefully as Samuel van Rees had done when he worked with her father. Everything had to be secret now, the ledgers hidden away each night under their house as collateral so Hitler would remember to keep his promise of clemency to the

Linden family. So that the chancellor of Germany wouldn't forget her father's generosity.

Gerrit Linden had begun investing in German companies more than a decade ago, but when the Nazi Party started threatening the Jewish people, he feared staying in Berlin, so they'd traveled to Holland with the masses.

Then the shadows of Fascism began creeping over their new country. When they did, Gerrit created a safety net of his own, investing heavily in the enemy so the enemy wouldn't come after him. The investment in Hitler had made her family quite wealthy, but they couldn't enjoy their wealth in the midst of a war. Much of their money had been reinvested in Sweden's gold or deposited in banks outside Holland and Germany, beyond Hitler's reach.

Days after the Nazis invaded Holland, her father had sent Samuel, his only clerk, in search of another position, but he never liquidated the investments. Unlike her father, Eliese doubted Hitler would let the Linden family spend their Reichsmarks or guilders.

Numbers and letters—those were easy to change when necessary; but people . . . people didn't cooperate like the laws of mathematics or grammar. They were difficult to analyze, even more difficult to understand.

None of them knew what Hitler would do next.

"Hein play?"

Her two-year-old son bounced along the edge of the wooden playpen that she'd set up in the sitting area, in view of the dining room. Hein didn't want to nap on the pillow beside him. He wanted to play and play while she was so tired, she could easily sleep the rest of the day and perhaps even the night right here at the table.

She loved her son, but some days it ached to look at the winsome smile that he'd inherited from his father. His Aryan blond hair, so different from her dark brown.

She missed William dreadfully. When this war was over, she and Hein would take the first ship leaving for New York, reuniting with his father at the harbor.

Hein pointed at his chest. "Spelen?"

Eliese sighed. "I can't play."

He didn't know many words yet in his first two years of life, but the ones he did know, he knew in three languages— the English of his father, his mother's German, and the Dutch language of this country where she and William had been destined to meet. She spoke to Hein mainly in English to prepare him for America.

"Mama?"

Eliese couldn't play right now, rarely played at all these days, no matter what language he asked. Instead she had to huddle over this table for hours, working on her father's books. They weren't allowed to leave this old canal house anymore lest an old friend or acquaintance see them. A handful of people knew she'd returned from England, but only her father and their household staff knew about her son.

Now, thanks to the Nazis, their staff had been dismissed. No Aryan was allowed to work for a Jew.

Hein threw his ball, slamming it into the hutch on the other side of the room. The doors shuddered, protecting the china and a domed mantel clock with pink rosebuds painted under the glass. The clock had been her mother's, and it made her think of the fragile, beautiful woman who'd died when Eliese was a week old.

Her father had packed the clock carefully when they'd fled from Germany, one of the few heirlooms he'd been able to keep. He'd also managed to bring enough of their financial assets to set up HTB in Amsterdam, a sister bank to the one that he and his Aryan partner operated in Berlin. And later, the partner bank William had opened in New York with one of her father's German friends named Peter Ziegler.

Hein shook the wall of the playpen. "Please, Mama."

"Soon, sweetheart." She returned to the book in her hands, to transcribe her father's numbers.

Hein should be playing right now with other children in a crèche, but the Nazi Party had mandated that all Jewish children stop schooling with Aryans, even if Hein's father wasn't Jewish.

When he began crying, she hopped up to close the windows. The neighbors knew Hein was here, but she didn't need to remind them or anyone outside on the sidewalk or along the canal. She sat back down at the table, her eyes blurring as she struggled to refocus on the numbers.

Oh, for those carefree days back in Giethoorn when she could play games with Josie and the boys for hours upon hours. If only she could take her son back to that village of islands, stay with Mrs. Pon for the summer like she used to do. They could play and play.

She should have found a way to stay in London after William left for New York. If she'd begged, the Zieglers might have found her and Hein another place to stay.

Peter and his wife, Trudy, no longer lived in Germany. They owned homes in both New York and London, and they'd let her use their terrace house in England for a year while they were in America. She and William were supposed to marry the summer of 1939, but the New York bank had called him back in May. He'd promised to return to her soon, promised they would marry by Christmas instead.

She blamed Hitler personally for making William break his promise.

William didn't know about the baby when he left London, but the Zieglers learned soon enough. When they arrived back in England, they'd been shocked to find her in an expectant state.

She'd sent multiple telegrams to the Kingston home in New York, inquiring about William, but never received a response. No matter how loyal the Zieglers were to William, Trudy was expecting as well, and they didn't want two babies in their house. The first of September, they managed to find a seat for her on one of the last civilian boats traveling back to Amsterdam with a promise that William would come for her soon.

She'd told her father that she and William had married in England, and she now wore his surname with pride. Eliese Kingston. She liked the metropolitan sound of it, the English name that deemed her different. Chosen. Even if she was no longer allowed to leave the house.

Father didn't believe she'd married—she knew that—but this purported union was advantageous for both of them. Neither William nor Peter had visited Amsterdam since the war began—the Holland Trade Bank shuttered—but the

American money was heavily invested under her father's management for the sole purpose of unifying his beloved Germany and pouring American capital into their economy.

Interest from the bank's investments had flooded back to Amsterdam, especially what they'd put into a corporation called I. G. Farben that produced more than forty German products, some of which were critical to the German armed forces. This she knew from the many late-night meetings between her father and William. Before the war began, she'd brought them glasses filled with *oude jenever* and soaked up their conversation like the sponge her former maid had used to clean up spills.

Geld, her father had called the investments in I. G. Farben. They and their investors had received a small fortune in returns.

When the Nazis requisitioned the bank building, her father moved the records of his investments to their rambling home in the heart of Amsterdam. And he secured his collection of diamonds—much more valuable these days than guilders—into the cellar so he wouldn't have to turn them over to the Nazis.

"Mama!" Hein shouted again.

She turned and this time she saw clumps of his blond hair on the floor.

"Stop pulling out your hair," she reprimanded.

"No pull." He shook his head solemnly before he smiled. "Play?"

She put down her pen. When she wasn't wretched with worry, the smile of his captured her heart.

Oh, why hadn't she stayed with Hein in England?

William would have sent for her as soon as he was able. They would have traveled back to New York together, the three of them, and—after their wedding—spent these past two years visiting all the places he'd told her about: the Empire State Building, Radio City Music Hall, St. Regis Hotel. They would have been living as a family instead of being divided by an ocean that only played host these days to military vessels.

One day, they would all be a family again, and Hein would grow up to be as smart and handsome as his father.

He shook the sides of his playpen, saying her name over and over, but when Eliese finally pushed back her chair, her father walked through the door.

"Anneliese can't play today," he said.

Hein sat back in the pen. He might not listen to her, but he always listened to Opa.

Eliese picked up her pen again.

"Have you finished the accounts?" Papa asked.

She nodded. "Everything is in order."

Her father tucked the book and papers under his arm.

As long as he kept investing in the German companies—and kept their money tucked away—Hitler would protect them. The man only disdained the Jews that he didn't need. Or at least that's what Papa thought.

Sometimes she wondered if Hitler might hate them even more because he needed them.

Her father nodded at Hein. "We have to find another place for him to live."

She shook her head. "Hein needs to stay with me."

"It's too dangerous—"

MELANIE DOBSON

"What will William say if he finds out that you shipped off his son?"

"Oh, Anneliese . . ." His eyes, they said everything. Her father thought William didn't care about her or their son, that he wasn't coming back even after this war. Papa thought she was no different from one of the women who rented herself out in De Wallen—the walled district.

But William had loved her. Papa simply looked the other way in 1937 when she and William began seeing each other, enamored by the flood of cash that William and Peter brought to his bank as silent partners in Germany's growing economy.

"We won't be keeping books anymore for our accounts," her father said.

"How will we keep track of them?"

"All the important ones are in here." He tapped his head. "As long as I'm alive, Hitler will get his money."

"But we're on Puttkammer's list." Papa had paid thirty thousand guilders—another fortune—to add them both to this elite listing that a fellow banker named Puttkammer had created. The list—along with the signed stamp on their identity cards—guaranteed their freedom, just in case the Nazis forgot about all Gerrit Linden and his bank had done.

Hein didn't need a Puttkammer stamp. None of the Jewish or Aryan children were required to have identity cards.

"The money is still our collateral," he said slowly. "And your work."

She glanced at the ledger under his arm. "My work?"

"Walter Süskind needs your help."

She stood up. "What sort of help?"

Her father paused, seeming to consider his words. She knew Mr. Süskind, but not well. The Unilever salesman and her father had been acquaintances for almost a decade, both of them Jewish businessmen who'd emigrated from Germany.

Her father stepped toward the back door. "The Jewish Council is setting up a deportation center at Hollandsche Schouwburg. He wants you to assist him with registration."

Goose bumps flooded her arms. "I want no part of that."

"You don't have a choice. The Jewish Council has commissioned him, and he has commissioned you."

She lifted Hein from the playpen, resting him on the shelf of her hip. "Puttkammer will protect us."

"And so will your job with Süskind."

The door slammed, shaking the hutch again when her father stomped outside, into the overgrown courtyard behind their house. The entrance into the cellar had been covered with new flooring inside their home, but Papa had built a separate entrance to access the cellar—and his safe—through the gardener's shed.

She lifted a lock of Hein's blond hair from the floor and slipped it into a pocket in his baby book. Then she picked up the ball from the floor and sat down beside him, rolling it to the wall.

Her son smiled again. "Play."

SEVEN

Sunshine seeps through dust-smeared windows as Willie, my Ugandan driver, attempts to maneuver his Land Rover around craterlike holes on what he calls a road. The vehicle dips down into a crevice, jarring every one of my bones, and when our back tire slams through it, I feel like we're astronauts trapped inside one of those old space modules, attempting reentry for the first time.

You don't belong.

Austin's words flare in my head, taunting me hours after I left him behind. Words that hurt worse than sticks and stones.

But this trip isn't about me. It's about funding an organization to help children who no longer have parents to support them. Orphans who don't feel as if they belong.

This Bishara organization, I hope, is truly helping them find family in their children's home.

Willie and I have been driving more than two hours now, first on a highway and then deep into the heart of this country. The dry grass that hedges both sides of our vehicle stands almost as tall as my five feet, six inches, brushing against my door whenever Willie swerves to miss a pothole.

If something happened out here, I don't know who I'd call. My cell phone, I realized en route to the Amsterdam airport, was still in Claire's basket with the rest of the Kingston phones. The only contact I have in my new prepaid phone is Willie's—I called him after finding an itinerary with his number stapled to the dossier.

When he first picked me up from my hotel in Entebbe, Willie regaled me with stories about his childhood along Lake Victoria, but now all of his stories are about the diverse residents of what he calls elephant grass, the kind of residents who slither across the ground.

The takeaway: No matter what happens during my trip, stay out of the grass.

"Your plantation should be at the end of this road," Willie says, though his tone doesn't inspire much confidence that we'll find it.

According to the grant proposal, Bishara Coffee Plantation is located three miles outside the city of Mityana, and I hope it's true. Months ago, I'd bumped along a similar clay path in Kenya to vet another NGO, but all the driver and I found at the end was a field and a brick hut with a resident who'd never heard of Nairobi Kids International or the campus that was supposed to be located on her sweet potato farm.

I traveled to three other places, the purported locations across Kenya, and found all but Nairobi's main campus vacant of a school or children's home. Apparently, the organization never imagined that someone from Kingston Family Foundation or any of its donors would actually visit a school outside the one they showcased for sponsors.

In lieu of notifying the organization about our findings, Marcella phoned a friend—the attorney general of New York. Within days, the Brooklyn office for Nairobi Kids closed its doors, and the case against them is now pending in court. Marcella is generous with the foundation money, but she doesn't tolerate frauds.

Today I'll verify the validity of this coffee plantation, then catch the midnight flight back to the Netherlands and ultimately New York. At least, that's my plan. Only one flight leaves each day from Entebbe to Amsterdam. This morning I tried to confirm my flight reservations, but so far Internet access on this phone has proved to be as sketchy as the roads.

Willie drives under an arch that clearly states we've arrived at Bishara Coffee Plantation. Lush hills, emblazoned with a thousand shades of green, circle the plantation, and I'm relieved. All I need to do is meet Landon, take a tour, and then ride back to the hotel. After a late dinner, I'll check in for the midnight flight.

A large courtyard stands at the entrance of the plantation, flanked by three tin-roofed buildings. Long tables divide the courtyard into neat columns, each one filled with bright-red cherries ready to be processed, I assume, into beans. On the hillside to our right, behind the long building, is a cluster of what looks like houses and farm buildings—a small village in this remote place.

By all appearances, at least, this coffee plantation appears to be exactly what it purports on the grant paperwork. Now to find the man who partners with Ugandans to run it.

Willie parks the Land Rover beside the courtyard, and my heels poke holes into the red clay when I step outside, my handbag strung over my shoulder. A brew of smells hits me: farm animals, diesel fuel, the sweetness of berries.

"Should I wait?" he asks.

I check my phone. Just a few hours, four at the most, to interview Landon and his team. Nine hours until I'm jetting back to the States.

"Why don't you return at three? I'll call if I need you earlier."

"No problem, *Mzungu*."

"Ava," I remind him, but he just shrugs.

I changed out of my expensive dress and strappy shoes back in Amsterdam, but my jeans and white blouse and heeled sandals still feel quite out of place, especially when I see an African woman rushing toward me in a traditional lavender-and-yellow dress with pointed shoulders and a wide sash, her hair pinned back in a loose bun.

"Welcome to Bishara," the woman says warmly, both hands outstretched to shake mine.

"Thank you." I shift the handbag on my shoulder. "I'm looking for Landon West."

Willie reverses his Land Rover and flies back through the open gate. The woman glances at the retreating vehicle, then down the road. "Where is your team?"

"It's just me," I say, trying to sound casual. Just an American woman, dropping by a remote plantation in the middle of Africa. Alone.

Nothing really casual about it.

The woman's smile fades. "We were expecting fifteen people."

"I'm not with a group," I explain.

A tractor chugs through the columns of tables behind her, stirring up a cloud of red dust.

"Are you from England?" she asks.

"No, the United States."

She studies me again. "We don't usually have Americans visit without a volunteer team."

"I'm just here to meet with Mr. West."

The woman points to the east side of the complex. "Last I saw him, he was in the nursery."

I'm envisioning a place to nurture seedlings and such until she explains that he's helping with the children.

I glance at the tables loaded with coffee cherries. "Shouldn't he be managing the harvest?"

"He works wherever he's needed." She begins lumbering across the courtyard with a slight limp, and I follow her.

Something else rumbles on the narrow road behind us, and we both turn to see two white vans bouncing toward us. The expected team, I imagine.

She glances between me and the vans, torn as to how to proceed.

"I can find Mr. West on my own," I assure her.

She points toward the building on the right of the

courtyard, the brick side marked by two large sets of doors. "The nursery is on the other side of the storehouse."

Dozens of African men are working inside this building, moving heavy burlap bags onto a truck trailer. They nod toward me as I cross the floor, as if it's perfectly normal to see a white woman wandering around the property alone. My heels wobble on the packed dirt, but I hurry to an open door on the other side, wanting to meet Landon West before this team arrives.

The nursery itself is easy to locate, the cry of a distraught child flooding out an open window. The bricks on this two-story building are a rusty orange, and beside the open door is an array of brightly-colored Crocs, all different sizes, waiting for feet to ignite them.

Inside, a woven rug covers most of the cement floor to my right. A bin of toys and two rocking chairs sit near a screened window, and on the opposite side of the large room, a young woman is scooping beans from a cast-iron pot and something that looks like oatmeal onto the tin plates of about twenty children lined up on benches.

Seconds after I arrive, several children jump down from their seats, plates clattering against the benches as they surround me. I should have brought gifts, pieces of candy or something. Empty-handed, I smile awkwardly at them.

The woman in charge smiles back at me but doesn't seem to think I need rescuing. "You are most welcome," she says, dishing up another ladle of beans.

One of the girls reaches for my hand, startling me.

"Hello," I say.

She ducks behind my arm before peeking out again.

A little boy kneels on the floor to examine my painted toenails and another tugs on my elbow. "Most welcome," he says, trying to coax me toward the benches for lunch.

"Oh no." I shake my head slowly so he understands. "I need to find Landon West."

The caregiver nods toward the door. "He's outside."

I sigh, not ready to trek across the plantation in my heeled sandals, when a tall, light-skinned man—Mr. West, I assume—steps through the door, a girl about two or three years old wailing in his arms. He's wearing faded jeans and a bleached flannel shirt, the girl clinging to one of his sleeves. He bounces her like she's a baby, but the movement doesn't seem to be helping.

"I'm Ava," I begin, "from—"

"Am I glad to see you, Miss Ava." Long bangs drift over his eyes as he speaks, and he clears them with a shake of his head. I'm expecting surprise, frustration even at the interruption, but all I see is relief in his eyes.

I trail him as he paces across the rug in his bare feet. "You knew I was coming?"

"Of course." His brown eyes flash when he looks back at me. "We've been planning on it all week."

Usually Marcella keeps these visits secret, but she said she'd called the Portland office. I just didn't know that she'd left a message for Landon. He's probably spent his week preparing the plantation and his paperwork for my review.

"She needs—" He holds the girl out toward me, and for a moment, she stops crying, her eyes wide. She looks just as concerned about the exchange as I am. "Well, I'm not sure exactly what she needs. I'm hoping you'll be able to figure it out."

"Oh no." My hands splay out in front of me. I want to help children, but I haven't actually held one since the night my brother died.

Landon inches the girl back toward his chest, but he doesn't step away. "Her English name is Faith."

More tears spill down the girl's cheeks, soaking the collar of her blue dress. "What's wrong with her?"

"I don't know. Her stomach has been hurting all morning, and our nurse doesn't return until Friday." He reaches for a cup of milk and holds it to her lips, but she refuses to drink it. "Is there a doctor or nurse on the team?"

"I don't know—"

"If not, I'll take her to the clinic."

I eye the woman who's feeding the other children. "Can't someone take her right now?"

"We're a bit short-staffed," he explains. "Makes us all the more grateful for people like you who come to help."

I'm not entirely sure why it's taken me so long to realize that Landon thinks I'm a volunteer, here to hold babies in lieu of interviewing him. Perhaps it's the jet lag—or because I've been living inside the Kingston bubble for so long.

Marcella would be properly appalled, but it feels strangely comforting to be treated as a member of this unknown team instead of Marcella's granddaughter, a member who doesn't know anything about caring for kids.

"Please, Ava," he begs, holding the girl out again. "She just needs someone to love on her."

My brain is screaming for me to resist, but my arms refuse

to cooperate. At this moment, it seems, Landon West doesn't need five million dollars from the Kingston foundation. He needs someone to care for this child.

Faith starts crying again when I take her, and I feel like crying as well as I place her awkwardly on my hip, my face turned away in case she sneezes. "Where can I find a Kleenex?"

Landon smiles. "In Kampala."

Two hours east of here.

When Faith reaches for him, he kisses her on the forehead. "I'll be back soon, Mirembe. Miss Ava will take good care of you."

If only I were that confident in my abilities . . .

After he welcomes the team and someone else takes Faith, I will speak with him about the mission of Bishara.

Before he steps outside, Landon turns back, appraising me briefly before he speaks again. "Have you spent much time in Uganda?"

Faith is still crying, but I've placed her on my left hip so the noise doesn't muffle my good ear. "Eleven hours, most of them in a hotel."

He laughs as if I'm making a joke. "We always take our shoes off before walking into a home."

I stare at him, dumbfounded, and the rebel inside me roars. I've traveled thousands of miles, across a hellish path called a road, with a potential offer of millions at his disposal. And he has the audacity to critique my feet!

In that moment, I want to aim one of my heels straight into a kneecap, either one will do.

But then again, he doesn't know I'm with the foundation,

and when I glance at the female caregiver and then the children, I see that all of their feet are bare. My nerves feel as if they might fray, but I'm certainly not here to be disrespectful of them or their culture.

Landon waits as I slide my shoes off and hand them over. Then he tosses the three-hundred-dollar sandals on top of the Crocs.

"You can borrow a pair later, if you'd like," he says, pointing at the Crocs. "We have all sizes."

"No thank you."

"You might want to wear something else tomorrow to cover your feet, in case you end up working outside."

A swarm of creepy things—spiders and snakes—infiltrates my mind, and I cringe at the thought of them stealing over my toes.

Turning away, I drum on Faith's back as we walk toward a window on the other side of the room. I don't dare tell Landon that I won't be here in the morning.

EIGHT

JOSIE

GIETHOORN
JUNE 1942

Clouds swept over the village canal below the van Rees home, a stormy blue rippling across the surface and splashing against timbered walls. A cup of surrogate coffee in hand, Josie looked out at the bridge between their home and the thatched cottage where Klaas's parents lived.

It had been ten years since Eliese arrived from Germany. Ten years since Mrs. Pon had welcomed her as a daughter into her home next door—for a year at first and then each summer until Eliese moved to London.

A mosquito landed on Josie's arm, a renegade that had slipped through the tiny hole on their screen porch, and she slapped it.

After Eliese arrived in Giethoorn, things changed among all of them. Often, when they were skating or swimming, Mrs. Schoght wouldn't let Klaas join them. She thought Eliese, along with all the other Jewish immigrants, should return to Germany for good, but Dr. Schoght held no animosity against his neighbors. When Mrs. Schoght was gone, Klaas was allowed to play.

Mother stepped onto the screened porch, carrying a knapsack she'd prepared with Josie and Samuel's lunch. She'd been disappointed when Josie asked to take a canoe ride before it rained, but she and Samuel hadn't been able to speak on the train to Giethoorn, at least not about anything of consequence. She was anxious to ask him about the guilders.

"How is Mrs. Pon?" Samuel nodded toward the cottage where Eliese and her father had stayed, the only house that shared their little island.

Mother sighed. "She's left Giethoorn."

Samuel set his coffee cup on its saucer. "Where did she go?"

"Kamp Westerbork. She received a notice . . ."

Westerbork was located fifty kilometers northeast of their home, an internment camp built initially to house German Jewish refugees who were fleeing from Hitler. Three years later, Hitler's soldiers followed them across the border.

Samuel's shoulders dropped. "She shouldn't have gone."

"It will only be temporary," Mother said, "until the Nazis leave. Then she'll return home."

"The Nazis aren't planning to leave anytime soon."

Mother patted his hand. "She won't be far away. We can visit her whenever we'd like."

"It's still a trap," Samuel insisted.

"If she didn't go, they would have sent her back to Germany."

The face of Mrs. van Gelder flashed in Josie's mind. The terrible fear in her eyes. Would the van Gelders be sent to Westerbork or shipped off to Germany?

Mother slipped onto the wicker sofa, taking a sip of the coffee that she'd left to cool. "Westerbork has the best hospital in all of Holland, and the employees are Jewish. Mrs. Pon has a good job as a nurse, and she won't have to worry about those NSB men who've been harassing the Jewish people. There are rules for the refugees at Westerbork. Protection for those who aren't trying to hide."

Kamp Westerbork was a village for immigrants, not a prison camp like Amersfoort. Perhaps Mrs. Pon would be content working in the hospital. She'd been lonely, it seemed, since Mr. Pon passed away.

Samuel stirred another spoonful of sugar into his coffee. "The hospital is a ruse."

Mother didn't seem to hear him. "It's run by the Jewish people, not the Nazis."

"But they still must answer to Hitler!"

"The accommodations may not be plush, but Mrs. Pon said she'll make do."

Samuel looked out the window at the pink hydrangeas that bloomed around the Pon cottage, as if Eliese might come skipping across the well-worn path between their homes as she used to do. And Josie knew exactly where he went in that moment. To the years when he'd fallen in love with a woman who, long after she'd left Holland, still held his heart.

Samuel turned his gaze away from the cottage. "We'd best go canoeing before it rains."

Josie kissed her mother's cheek and then joined her brother at the covered slip beside the house, the knapsack with their lunch over her shoulder. Mother once hoped she could transform Josie into a bona fide lady, one fit to dine in the Royal Palace, but Josie had dashed her dreams by being more interested in accumulating camping and hiking badges instead of ones the other Girl Guides earned in the kitchen or with their sewing machines. Her mother no longer critiqued her. In fact, she almost seemed to appreciate the woman Josie had become.

Samuel untied their canoe as she climbed down four rungs to join him. Then he handed her a paddle. It was cold for June, and when the clouds poured out, it would be frigid. But they couldn't risk talking about the resistance at home.

Josie untied the sweater from around her waist and pulled it over her head. Then she dipped her paddle into the water, synchronizing with Samuel as they moved up the narrow waterway, waving to neighbors along the footpath.

The waterway emptied into a quiet lake, surrounded by wooden punts grounded on the peatland, birds watching them from the grass. They followed the perimeter, and then Samuel guided them down another canal, this one walled in by reeds.

On their right was the abandoned windmill where the local Girl Guides once met for their weekly meetings. They'd all paddle here in groups, she and Eliese and about ten others, claiming this old place as their clubhouse.

How she missed those times with her friends.

After the Nazis infiltrated the country, they banned both the Girl Guide and Boy Scout troops. As long as they kept people isolated, their enemies thought they held all the power. But the Dutch continued to meet in secret, like she and Samuel in these wetlands. The Dutch feared the men who occupied their country, but it seemed to her that the Nazis feared the Dutch people as well, or at least they were afraid when they partnered together. No Nazi—Dutch or German—could stop them from talking with each other.

Samuel paddled toward the reeds, pushing the boat up on the soft peatland so they could climb out. They hiked through the grass until they reached the windmill, five floors chock-full of some of her best memories.

Inside the main room were the crates and chairs they'd once used when they met to learn all manner of things like how to light a fire, care for a wound, knit the woolen swimming costumes they wore on hot summer days. They also launched their boat races here, races that would last all day as they traversed wetlands across the countryside. The last time she and Eliese raced as a team, they'd won.

Instead of using the dusty chairs, she and Samuel sat on the old planks in front of the door, legs outstretched onto the grassland, the bog in front of them—a peatery—framed by the sky and water and reeds. He leaned back on his elbows, looking for the briefest of moments like the boy who used to compete with Klaas.

A century ago, a peat digger had lived here with his family, and in those years before electricity, the man and his workers would have dried the messy soil—fen—to make fuel. Simpler times, some called them.

How she longed for the simplicity of her youth instead of the tangle of knots that seemed to bind her wrists and feet, knots that even the smartest Girl Guide couldn't untie.

Wooden sails shuddered in the breeze overhead, and Samuel glanced around as if checking to see if someone was out here, listening to them. "Did you deliver the letter to Maastricht?"

"Yes." She tore the paraffin crust off a ball of cheese, splitting the Edam with her brother. "The recipient was upset because the contents were wet."

Samuel leaned forward. He wore glasses like their father, brown frames sketching squares around eyes that diligently counted and recorded money at the bank, eyes that sparked a fierce blue when someone threatened those he loved. "How wet?"

"An NSB officer dumped the contents of your basket into a puddle. Fortunately, the envelope stayed hidden, but it was soaked."

He groaned. "You could have been hurt."

She brushed her hand over the tall grass that had grown through the planks. "I'm worried, Samuel."

"We're all worried—"

"The man in Maastricht opened the envelope."

His eyes narrowed.

"Inside was—"

"Don't say it, Josie."

She squirmed, the fabric of her trousers snagging on the planks. "You know exactly what was inside."

"Of course."

"All along I thought I was delivering letters for the resistance. To stop the Nazis—"

"Many of them were letters."

She unwrapped a packet of zwieback and ate the sweet toast. "Where did you get the money?"

"I can't tell you that."

"Why not?" she asked.

"It would ruin everything."

"I'm risking my life to help you, and I don't even know what you're doing." She sounded like a child, pouting when a parent said no, but it truly wasn't fair. "Are you stealing from the Jewish people?"

"No—"

"But you are stealing."

"From the rich, I suppose. To give to the poor."

"It's not a game, Samuel."

He flushed. "We've taken money that was meant to destroy and turned it into something good."

She leaned back against the doorpost, wrestling with his words. Was it right to steal money from the enemy, funds meant to destroy the Jewish people?

"I can't tell you where the money is coming from, but it's meant to help people like Mrs. Pon hide away."

"And Eliese?"

"If she were still in Holland . . ."

The wooden sails shook again. "The last time I was here," she said, "Eliese and I were celebrating our big win."

He took off his glasses and cleaned them on his shirt. "I miss the way Holland used to be."

"I think you still care for Eliese."

He wiped away the perspiration beading along the line of his short blond hair. "I want every Jewish person to be safe."

"But Eliese is different."

"She's our friend, and thankfully she is safe in London."

Josie sighed, drumming her heels against the planks. "It's getting worse for the Jewish people, isn't it?"

He nodded slowly. "The Nazis have been biding their time, but it's all a show. They're just waiting until the Dutch have let down their guard. Then, I fear, they'll release Hitler's fury on all of us."

A cormorant swept down and glided across the channel before diving under the surface. Seconds later, it reappeared with a fish in its bill.

"Last week, I watched a Jewish family being taken away from their home. They had a little girl. . . ."

"The Jews in Amsterdam are all being relocated to the Jewish Quarter."

The bridge into the Jewish district was only blocks from her school, the perimeter around it cordoned off with wire. "Perhaps I could visit."

He shook his head. "They only let Jewish people in . . . and then they won't let them back out."

"I only want to help."

"You are helping, Josie, and not just me," he said quietly. "Hundreds, perhaps thousands, are hiding now. The resistance is calling them *Onderduikers*."

Underdivers. Like the woman in Maastricht.

"The less you know, the safer you will be. If anything happened to you . . ." He stopped. "We need your help, but I can't bear the thought of anyone harming you."

"No one's going to harm me. They think I'm a silly Dutch girl."

"You're the smartest silly girl that I know."

"Except Eliese," she added.

"Eliese is not the least bit silly."

Josie slugged his arm, and he laughed before his lips pressed together again.

"Thank you for helping," he said. "It's people like us, the students and teachers and bookkeepers, who will win this war."

Later that night, after she'd settled into her bed, Samuel knocked on her door. "Josie?"

She turned on her lamp and scooted up against the pillows. "What is it?"

He shut the door. "I have to go away for a while."

She cringed. One by one, those she cared about were slipping away. "As an underdiver?"

"More like an undermover, I suppose."

"Do Mother and Father know?"

"No, but Father won't be surprised."

"I want to keep helping those who are hiding," she said.

"I have one more envelope to deliver. It needs to go to a friend in Amersfoort, and the—" he paused, slipping an envelope out of his coat—"the contents will be distributed from there."

She eyed the envelope. "How many guilders are inside?"

"Twenty thousand."

She shivered. "I've never even seen that much money."

His gaze wandered to the window. "It's enough to provide

for many who are hiding now and extra to make them new identity cards."

"Did you steal it from the Nazis?"

"I've never stolen anyone's money."

She took the envelope from his hands. "I'll deliver it."

He gave her the address and specific instructions on what to say when she arrived, confirmation that the right person received this extraordinary amount to help with their resistance. She repeated the words back several times until she had them memorized.

"Don't trust anyone else," he said, "not until you hear from me."

"What about Klaas?"

He kissed her cheek. "No one."

How she hated this war, stealing away their trust of neighbors.

"I will see you soon." He kissed her forehead. "Long live the resistance!"

"Long live—" But her brother was gone, an apparition stealing out the door.

Tying her cotton robe around her nightgown, she slipped into the corridor, desperate to say goodbye to this brother that she loved, but in the room next to hers, the bed was neatly made, Samuel's suitcase already gone.

Outside she rushed across the grass, the dew seeping between her bare toes as she hurried toward the canal, the night air stealing through her robe.

Through the darkness, she heard a motor, and when she reached their slip, she realized the family boat was gone.

Josie sank to the edge of the *slootje*, her legs dangling into the water. She and Samuel had been on the same team for as long as she could remember. He didn't tell her everything, for her own good, but he had always trusted her with exactly what she needed.

But now, she suspected, Samuel wasn't coming back, at least for a while. These threads of canal could take him all the way across Holland, wherever he need to go until their country prevailed.

Long live the resistance.

And long live—she prayed—Samuel van Rees.

NINE

Sing. That's what my mom used to do when I couldn't sleep. An old song about rainbows, all the colors threading together in my mind as she tucked me into bed.

I sing the lyrics softly to Faith as we rock in a chair, the ones about listening to her heart, singing exactly what she feels. Instead of singing, Faith cries what she's feeling, clutching my finger as if I might be able to take away the pain.

I wish I could take away whatever is hurting her. Wish I could take away pain from children around the world.

Landon's promise to return soon has turned into hours. I've spent all afternoon trying to comfort Faith, but she refused to eat her lunch of *posha* and beans, refused to join the other children upstairs for a nap.

Faith's cries slowly soften into a whimper as I begin singing the colors again, her hand starting to relax its grip on mine. I keep rocking. Keep whispering this song.

Before she went upstairs, Ruth, one of the two caregivers in this home, offered me a lunch of the porridge mixture, sharing her story as I ate. Ruth's mother had died when she was eleven, the third wife of a man who already had all the children he wanted with his other wives. Years later, Landon hired her to help care for the children at Bishara—some of them orphans who live here, others who return home with their parents each night after the coffee harvest.

My singing stops when Faith closes her eyes, but I continue to rock, bare heels pressing against the coarse rug. Her breathing has slowed, her cry silent now.

Ruth said that Landon is usually the only one who can stop her crying. No one's here to see my accomplishment, but as I lean my head back against the chair, settling into the carved slats, I feel a little proud that she's stopped her crying for me as well.

My gaze wanders toward the smeared glass on a window. Clothes flutter on a line outside, bright skirts and blouses and shorts for a child. On the hill behind it, plantation workers water rows of shrubs, red clusters of cherries dangling off each one.

My toes burrowing into the rug, I listen to the laughter of a child upstairs, footsteps padding across the floor as Ruth and the other caregiver, I assume, try to corral the children for their naps. And I marvel at the simplicity of this place. Revel in it, really. Just yesterday, I was surrounded by immeasurable wealth, but instead of gratefulness, this wealth bred discontent. Anger. No one would have appreciated the cuisine for their lunch or the expensive wines or their elegant surroundings, just like they didn't appreciate each other.

The pillar of a legacy—and the persistence of Marcella—are the only things that unite the Kingston family. And the money. Once the business is divided, I suspect not even a legacy will keep them together.

What would William Kingston think, I wonder, if he looked down and saw the mess of his family? That the wealth he and Peter Ziegler had worked so hard to obtain, money to set up a secure position for his family, had almost destroyed it instead? Both he and Peter, I suspect, would be devastated to see the aftermath.

I glance at the benches, all the plates and food cleared away now by Ruth and the older children. My uncles and Austin and the others would revolt if they were fed *posha* and beans every day, but I can't criticize them for it. I'm caught up in this wealth as well. On one hand, I don't want to be treated differently, and yet I've come to expect people to treat me and my pricey shoes with respect instead of considering how I can respect them. In those moments, I'm like my cousin Austin clinging to his cell phone, the item more important than the people around me.

With Faith asleep, I retrieve the book that Paul Epker gave me. The library in Amsterdam has been a dream of Marcella's for decades. Books, she once said, are the best legacy. They outlast one's life and shed light on the past when truth is hard to find.

Perhaps this book, *Darkest Before Dawn*, will shed some light on my family.

Gently shifting Faith into my left arm, I balance the book's spine on my knee and begin to read the prologue. Written in the 1960s, it's a historical account of Americans who invested in Europe before World War II, an analysis of how these moderately wealthy men accumulated an enormous fortune after the tumultuous years of the Great Depression.

Skimming through the pages, I find the chapter about my two great-grandfathers—Randolph's father, William Kingston; and Peter Ziegler, the father of Marcella. The section is only nine pages, but I'm intrigued to read Peter's story since Marcella hasn't told me much about him.

William and Peter both attended Cambridge in England. According to the author, they met after initiation into a secret society called Memento Mori, shortened to the Mori Men. The oath my great-grandfathers took in this brotherhood lasted a lifetime.

On the next page are photographs of William and Peter, in the decade after Cambridge. William is wearing a hat over his dark hair, a tie and jacket to accompany the determination in his eyes, the laser focus of success. I've seen his likeness many times, on the walls of the Kingston home and in the faces of my two uncles.

But I've never seen a portrait of Peter Ziegler. His face is thinner than William's, and he is smiling in this photograph. In lieu of a hat, his hair is combed straight up at his forehead, falling over to the side before fanning back. I see Marcella in him—the brown eyes and thin, pallid face—though she has the Kingston determination in her gaze.

Peter was Jewish. A German Jew.

This surprises me. I knew William spent some time in

Europe before World War II, but I didn't know about Peter's heritage. After graduation, the author says, William went home to New York, but instead of returning to Germany, Peter and his wife, Trudy, built houses in both London and New York.

I rock the chair as I turn the page, not wanting to waken Faith.

The author lists four of the companies that William and Peter invested in, none that I have heard of, but William joined the board of directors in several of these companies. Before World War II, the two men expanded their empire by opening a private bank in New York to partner with one in Amsterdam.

After the war, my great-grandfathers started Kingston Windows and invested in a number of other companies that crossed borders. By the early 1950s, both men were worth millions. In 1962, Peter was hospitalized in a sanatorium in New York called the Craig House, while William's son, Randolph, continued growing their business.

That was the end. The last paragraph about the Kingston-Ziegler dynasty.

Is this why Marcella refuses to talk about her father? Did he become ill or somehow dent the Kingston veneer?

When I return to New York, I'll ask her again to tell me his story.

A clock on the wall ticks past one. Willie is supposed to take me back to the hotel at three, but I can't leave Faith until Landon returns, and I can't leave Uganda until I'm able to ask him some questions about Bishara.

I glance down at the girl sleeping in my lap, at the

pockmarks scarring her cheeks, the patches of hair sprouting on her scalp. I've been so relieved that she stopped crying, I didn't stop to study her face. Appreciate who she is. So focused on the outcome of my meeting with Landon that I almost plowed right over this girl in the middle.

What does Faith's future look like in Uganda? With Landon's leadership, and perhaps a scholarship from the foundation, she won't have to become a second or third wife like Ruth's mother to survive. In that way, the grant money could truly be used for good.

The warmth of the room lures my eyes closed, Faith continuing to rest against my chest, and I stay here, contented, until I hear voices outside the window. Landon sticks his head through the front door and scans the room until his gaze lands on me. Then he whispers something that I can't hear.

I turn my head. "What did you say?"

"I'm sorry it took so long." He steps toward us, his eyes on Faith. "How's my girl doing?"

"She's been asleep for over an hour."

"That's great news. No one on the team works in medicine, and I've been worried about her." He pulls up a second rocker and sits beside me, sweeping his light-brown bangs back out of his eyes. "Oddly enough, no one on the team knows about an American woman who works with kids either."

I look down at the girl again, at her hand dangling over my arm. "That's because I'm not on their team, and for the record, I have no experience working with children."

"Well, you've been a saint to help today." He eyes me with curiosity. "But why exactly did you come to Bishara?"

Feet pound down the steps, and when two kids peek around the corner at us, I nod toward the door. "Perhaps we can talk someplace else."

"Of course," he says. "Did Faith drink anything before she fell asleep?"

"No, she wouldn't take the milk." As I shift her to my other arm, her free hand falls to my lap. "I checked for a fever, but her skin isn't hot."

At least not considering the warm temperature in this room. I don't know much about caring for a child, but I know that hot skin is a bad sign for anyone, young or old.

"When she wakes up, she'll be ready to eat." He reaches for Faith's hand, to tuck it close beside her, but then he stops, the smile on his face devolving quickly into concern.

Landon slips out of his chair and kneels beside us, feeling her head, her cheeks.

"She's not hot," I reiterate.

He says something in response, his voice low. I turn my head, leaning closer to capture his words. "I'm sorry?"

"Her skin's not supposed to be this cold."

I search the room for a blanket, but it's much too warm for blankets here.

When he starts to lift her from my lap, I protest. "It took forever for her to fall asleep."

The look in his eyes, I can't read it exactly, but it's something like pity. Why does he feel sorry for me?

"She's not asleep, Ava." He lifts Faith up. "She's unconscious."

My arms drop to my sides, the weight of his words pressing into my chest, and the room seems to spin around me before I catch my breath.

How did I not know? I should have tried to awaken her, found help, but I'd been relieved instead . . . proud of my work.

He cradles her to his chest. "I have to get her to the clinic in Mityana."

In that moment, I wish I hadn't sent Willie into town. "Can we take one of your trucks?"

"You don't need to go—"

"I want to help." And this time I really do.

My handbag over my shoulder, I follow Landon outside as he straps on a pair of Tevas. Then he tosses me a pair of lime-green Crocs, adult size.

I leave them on the grass and reach for my sandals instead, quickly slipping them on. With Faith in his arms, we jog through the storehouse and into a smaller brick building that houses a beat-up motorcycle.

He hands Faith back to me. "You'll need to hold her as close as possible to keep the road from jarring her."

I stare at the motorcycle. "We're taking this?"

"With all the potholes in the road, it'll take us at least an hour to get to the clinic by truck, and I'm afraid we don't have that long. The motorcycle will get us there in twenty minutes."

Landon secures a child-size helmet over Faith's head, then hands me a helmet sans visor. Either he snubs a helmet for himself or I'm wearing the only adult one he owns.

In college, I dated a guy who was an avid biker. I rode

with him enough times to appreciate his passion for motor-cycles even as I had a much firmer appreciation for the convertible that Marcella had given me. But I remember how to lean as Landon speeds through the columns of tables in the courtyard, clinging to Faith with my left arm even as I clench Landon's chest with my right, Faith and my handbag sandwiched between us.

Grass lashes against my bare arms as he swerves around the potholes, the motor of the bike roaring in my good ear. My arms ache, but I don't dare release my grasp on either of them.

I pray as we rush toward Mityana, asking God to save this child from whatever has overtaken her. If only I'd known she was so ill. I would have found Landon right away so we could take her to the clinic.

As we sweep around a narrow curve, Landon shouts something back to me, something I can't hear.

A thin black tower emerges on the road, a thread as tall as the grass. Underneath it, coiled on the clay path, is a dark spool.

My scream echoes through the helmet as the head of the snake flares, a black cape mottled with yellow, and in that instant I know my skinny jeans, my open sandals, will do nothing to protect against its fangs.

I scream again as Landon tears to the right, through the depths of grass. The strands lash against my face, my arms, my feet. And I close my eyes, cocooning myself over Faith's limp body. All I can see, in the wildness of my mind, is the snake chasing after us as if we're a matador with a red cape.

I won't let this snake have her.

Landon whips back onto the path, swerving slowly around another hole so we don't overturn.

Clearly he's driven this stretch of road many times. How often has he been fleeing from a snake?

"Hold on," he shouts above the motor, but I'm already clenching him like the barb of a fishhook, afraid the motorcycle might swim off without me.

Over my shoulder I see a black ribbon streaming toward us at a frightening pace.

How fast can a snake run? Or crawl. Or whatever it's called.

"Hurry!" I yell, but Landon doesn't need my urging. I lean into him again as he bends over the handlebars, pressing us forward, Faith clutched to my chest. In that moment, I'm glad she doesn't awaken to struggle against me. If I had to let go of Landon to settle her—

I can't let go of him.

We bounce over the small holes, and ahead I see several cars, crossing the road. The holes begin to diminish, and when I turn back again, the snake seems to be gone. The sound of honking horns breaks through the motorcycle's roar, and I take a deep breath, six counts, eight, trying to calm my racing heart and mind.

Landon turns onto a road crowded with trucks and motorbikes carrying multiple people, the sides of this road lined with shacks that display signs for Coca-Cola and Airtel, long-horned cows tied to posts out front.

People turn to stare at the spectacle of us, and in that moment, I'm extremely glad to be parading through a crowd.

Releasing my grasp on Landon, I shift Faith on the seat.

She feels limp, like one of the dolls that I had as a child. Like my brother long ago when I tried to rescue him.

I blink at the thought, surprised.

Had I been holding Andrew that night?

I remember so little from the fire, and the things I do remember, I'm never sure if they're accurate or not. I'm alone in my scattered, scarred memories. Not knowing what is real and what my brain has concocted to cope with the truth.

Landon turns again, this time onto a quieter road, and parks his motorcycle in front of a cement building with a red cross on its flag.

When I step onto the dirt drive, he takes Faith from my arms, cradling her again. "How is she?"

"The same, I think."

But what do I know? I proved to be an expert on absolutely nothing today.

Inside the clinic is a waiting room, two people sitting in plastic chairs by a window. A dark-skinned man in scrubs meets us at the front desk. Dr. Daniel, that's what Landon calls the man. When he sees Faith's limp body, Dr. Daniel takes her from Landon and rushes her right back into an examination room, telling us with a British accent to wait in the lobby.

Landon sits in a chair beside me. The doctor, he says, comes twice a year from England to work at this clinic, but my mind is still swarming with snake. "What was that on the road?"

"A spitting cobra."

My arms begin to shake. I don't need to watch National

Geographic to know that a cobra can kill. And that one had wanted us for its lunch.

"Why was it chasing us?"

"It wasn't chasing us, Ava. It was trying to get away."

"It sure felt like it was chasing us."

"I've only seen snakes a few times in Uganda," he says, tapping his feet on the cement floor. "Each time, it was going the opposite direction."

"That snake wasn't headed the other way, at least not at first."

"We startled it." Landon stands beside me. "It was probably afraid of us too."

I can't imagine how that snake would act if it weren't afraid.

Landon paces to a window as I check my phone. A quarter after three. I shoot Willie a text, telling him that I'm in Mityana. Then I rub the muscles in one of my arms before switching to the other, trying to calm the adrenaline coursing through my skin.

When Landon sits again, he rakes his fingers through his bangs. "I should have brought her earlier."

My gaze moves past him to the narrow hallway where the doctor has taken Faith, the words *Hakuna Matata* painted in a cheerful orange overhead. "Neither of us knew she was sick."

"Ava—" he leans forward, clasping his hands in his lap—"why exactly are you in Uganda?"

"I work with Kingston Family Foundation. We received your grant proposal."

He looks confused. "I didn't submit a grant proposal."

My visit to Kenya was prompted by a grant proposal for

work that wasn't really being done. But who would falsify a grant proposal for an authentic organization?

Reaching for my handbag, I pull out the folder with a copy of the proposal and find the signature at the back of the application. Kendall West Stafford signed it. Landon's sister.

As I hand him the proposal, I lower my voice so those sitting nearby won't hear our conversation. "Your sister asked for five million dollars to expand your operations and hire more employees here and in Portland. While I can't extend you a grant on my own, I have to say, I agree with her. To start, you could use several more workers in the children's nursery and a full-time nurse at the plantation."

He shakes his head. "We have plenty of mission teams who come to help."

"You—you don't want the five million?" I stutter, stunned by his defensive tone. Most people are thrilled when they find out I'm with the foundation, trying to promote their organization's mission, not deter me from funding them.

"It's not that I don't want the money." He looks down at his dust-smeared hands. "We could sure use it to grow, but I'm always hesitant about the strings attached."

"Strings are minimal at our foundation, as long as you'll do what you—or your sister—says you'll do with the money."

He turns to me. "But yet you came all this way from . . ."

"Technically, I was in Amsterdam, but I live in New York. Upstate."

"I suppose you already know that I live in Portland half the year."

I nod, trying to smile. "It's in your bio."

"You're the stringer for this foundation?"

"Director, but I'm more of a reporter, I think. Double-checking the facts to make sure they are true."

He unbuttons the pocket on his flannel shirt and pulls out his phone.

"What are you doing?"

He punches several keys on the screen. "Texting my sister."

"Why—?"

"She should have talked to me first."

I reach for the proposal and slide it back into the green folder. "I sure hope you let her have it."

He doesn't say anything as he works on his text.

"Seriously," I continue, "she's a terrible sister, asking for money for your organization."

"It would be nice to know before she sends out my biography." He glances back at me. "And invites you to Uganda."

"She didn't know I was coming."

Perhaps it makes him feel better to check in with Kendall, more in control or something while he can't help Faith. I stuff the proposal into my handbag, and as he waits for a response, I lean my head against the wall, watching a patient speak with someone in the waiting room.

"I've never actually had to hard-sell grant money before."

"You don't have to sell me on anything," he says. "Did the bio say where I used to work?"

"Google. Systems analyst."

"So I know a bit about planning."

"You probably learned all about it when you got your MBA from Portland State."

He groans.

"Or when you graduated top of your class from Anoka High School in Minnesota."

"That's disturbing, Ava."

"All I'm saying is that you know all about the importance of due diligence before investing in a company."

He lowers his phone. "Bishara is nonprofit."

"But our foundation sees it as an investment. So the strings, in your case, are the return in how many people are given jobs as a result of your growth and how many children are cared for in your homes. We want you to be successful, Landon."

"That's one thing we can agree on." His gaze returns to the corridor as if he can see Faith behind the walls. "It's too much for me to process right now."

I nod toward the hall. "Let's focus on her first, and then we can discuss the grant."

"Do you pray, Ava?"

"I prayed pretty hard on the ride here."

"Then perhaps you'll join me in prayer twice today."

He bows his head, and for a moment, I think he might reach for my hand. Instead he prays for God's mercy, for help when he doesn't know what to do, and power seems to radiate off this man as he pleads with God to save Faith's life.

TEN

JOSIE

Spring flowers bloomed in pots along the rambling lane near Amersfoort's old town, church bells tolling in the distance. Josie strolled through the towers on the medieval gates, then down a lane of row houses, a forced smile on her face as if she were enjoying the warm afternoon.

She'd locked her suitcase at the train station an hour ago and meandered this direction, stopping along the way to make sure no one was watching. Under her arm was a loaf of brown bread, a delivery to a friend. If someone was following her, she hoped they'd lose interest soon.

Others were walking as well on this Sunday afternoon,

seemingly oblivious to those who occupied their country. The streets in Amersfoort were clear of policemen, but she still didn't ride a streetcar, afraid an agent might be patrolling it. Her forged identity card was back in Amsterdam—she hadn't known that Samuel would have a delivery for her on the way home. If she were stopped, the police would discover the resistance money along with her real name. It wouldn't take them long to find her parents and alert agents across the country to search for Samuel.

After wandering for an hour through town, she found the address that Samuel had made her memorize. A whitewashed brick house sandwiched between others, a park with tall, wispy birch trees across the street. The place looked as innocent as she did in her role as a courier.

According to Samuel's instructions, she was supposed to knock at a side entrance in the alley, ask to buy an egg. She slipped between the two buildings and found the small door, a window beside it with a curtain wide-open to signal all was well.

After checking the numbers beside the door, Josie lifted the knocker and pounded twice. A man answered, one of the curls from his blond hair slipping across his forehead, his smile wide.

"I'm pleased to see you, Juffrouw." The greeting was correct, spoken in a fluent Dutch, and the man was certainly friendly.

Perhaps too friendly.

She remembered well the man in Maastricht last weekend, his trepidation when she arrived. While the contents she carried were essential in their resistance, most people were quite ready for her to be on her way.

She recited her carefully orchestrated part. "My mother asked me to purchase an egg."

"Of course," the man replied. "Please come inside."

Josie didn't move. The man wasn't supposed to invite her in, not yet. He was supposed to say, "I can sell you two."

Or at least, that's how she remembered Samuel's instructions.

Her fingers crept down to her waist, pressing against the envelope under her garments as she tried to recall the details that she'd stamped in her mind.

Of the dozens of envelopes she'd delivered over the past year, no one had ever messed up the order of their greeting. The preciseness was critical for all of them.

Turning her head, she glanced at the curtain in the window again. Someone had inched the lacy material together. Not completely shut, but partially drawn. As if someone inside was trying to warn her.

Everything inside Josie screamed for her to run, but she took a step back casually, forced another smile.

"Please forgive me." She patted her skirt pocket as if she were searching for the coins. "I've forgotten my money."

"You can bring it later." He glanced toward the lane. "You must come in now."

Silly. That's what Samuel had commended her for. If she clung to her innocence, followed the unwritten rules, the Nazis wouldn't suspect she was working against them.

"I couldn't possibly do that." She giggled and then cupped

her hand over her mouth like an awkward schoolgirl. "Mama said I must pay you first."

The man looked concerned, as if he wasn't sure whether or not he should insist that she come indoors.

"I'll retrieve the money right away."

"Juffrouw—"

But still she turned away, doubts raging in her mind.

What if this contact was a gentleman? What if he was trying to protect her from harm? The greetings were seemingly mundane; perhaps he just messed up the words.

But the curtain . . .

Something shuffled behind her as she started walking down the alley.

Was the man following her?

She didn't dare run or even act scared. She was simply wandering back home to retrieve the coins from her mother, praying as she wandered that a policeman wouldn't stop her.

Whoever was behind her, she had to convince him that she wasn't afraid. That she'd done nothing wrong.

She whistled as she turned onto the cobblestone lane, glancing back over her shoulder. No one was following her now.

Several children played by a pond in the park, and Josie collapsed on a bench behind a shield of elm leaves that blocked her view of the house. She sat in that space and pondered, the envelope pressing into her skin.

Should she return to the house? Or would the Dutchman come looking for her?

She wanted to be rid of this envelope and its bounty, but she couldn't leave it here until she was certain this house was safe. If Samuel found her later, if he was angry, she would tell him about the botched conversation along with the curtain.

An hour passed, and she heard a rumble of trucks blistering the street, the squeal of brakes. Children raced away from the pond, to the arms of their parents, and these families seemed to vanish into the trees. Josie slipped to the edge of the bench, to a peephole between leaves.

Three canvas-covered trucks stopped outside the house—like the army trucks she'd seen on Plantage Middenlaan—and a dozen black boots hit the ground before soldiers rushed inside, rifles in their hands.

A *razzia*.

Her stomach turned, and she clutched a branch as if she might faint. The poor people inside. She wanted to help, desperately, but what could she do, a silly Girl Guide who was more of a carrier pigeon than a resistance worker, delivering her goods before finding her way back home. A pigeon couldn't go up against the *Reichsadler*, the Imperial Eagle of Germany. She'd get eaten alive.

Nothing she could do would stop this madness. Nothing to help save the people in this house or anywhere else, it seemed.

Minutes later, at least ten of her countrymen were forced outside, prodded forward by the barrels of the soldier's guns. These men and women had gone under, she guessed, or they'd been hiding others. Jewish or not, they would each be treated as a criminal.

As the prisoners were loaded into the trucks, the blond man who'd answered her knock stepped from the house. Instead of climbing onto the truck with the others, he watched the scene calmly as if it were the final act of a play. Hands in his coat pockets, he ignored the cries of those who begged for help.

Was this man a neighbor? Or perhaps a relative who had betrayed his family for a Nazi bounty? How else would he have known how to greet her today?

Perhaps whoever gave him the information had intentionally botched the words to save Josie. If she'd handed over the envelope, stepped into the house, she would be one of the people hauled away to a prison for those who resisted.

Perhaps this man was too embarrassed to tell the soldiers that she had walked away.

Before the trucks drove off, a German officer slipped something into the hand of the traitor. A dozen people, seven and a half guilders per Jew. A pittance, for what? A few dinners out and a change of clothes. And transportation away from this city on the next train. If any of the resistance members found this man, they'd probably kill him.

When she glanced through the trees again, the man was walking away, unscathed.

Why hadn't he grabbed her arm, forced her inside?

Perhaps he'd thought she would cause a scene before the soldiers arrived. Or perhaps he'd thought she would return.

Josie smoothed a hand over her skirt, pressing against her girdle. What would they have done to her if she hadn't walked away? This money, whatever it was meant for, would be in German hands. And she . . .

Samuel had told her multiple times that the risk was great, but until this moment, she'd never really believed the Nazis would take her, a naïve student who simply wanted to teach.

What was she supposed to do with this envelope and its twenty thousand guilders now?

She prayed on the train ride home that she would find a safe place for these guilders and that her brother would be as elusive as the wind in his work to hide people across Holland.

Thank God, Eliese was in England and Mrs. Pon was safe at Westerbork.

ELEVEN

Landon waves his hand, motioning for me to follow him back to Faith's room, but I hesitate, thinking he'll want to visit with the doctor alone.

"Please join me," he asks, and I hear the desperate undertone in his words.

We follow Dr. Daniel past four patient rooms, all of them occupied, and enter one with Faith resting on a narrow bed, an empty chair beside it. The space is tidy and clean, her arm hooked up to an IV. A mosquito net drapes down from the ceiling, covering the bed, and the pale-red marks on her face seem to glow in the fading sunlight that streams through a screen-covered window.

The doctor leans against the peeling plaster on the wall,

his sober face hiding any prelude to the diagnosis. "I'm afraid she has cerebral malaria."

Landon collapses into the chair.

"What is cerebral malaria?" I ask Dr. Daniel.

"Malaria parasites have blocked the blood vessels to her brain and made it swell."

I squeeze my hands together. "How do we stop it?"

"Quinine is our best defense. We've already started that in the IV, along with glucose to elevate her blood sugar."

My voice shakes with my next question. "Is it fatal?"

"It can be," he says slowly. "All we can do now is monitor her and wait."

Exactly what the EMT had said after the fire. He monitored, and I waited . . . and waited. And then both my mother and brother were gone.

Landon leans forward, his arms propped on his legs. "How long do we have to wait?"

"We'll know within twenty-four hours," Dr. Daniel says. "I'll call you first thing tomorrow—"

Landon shakes his head. "I'm not leaving her."

A bell chimes in the background, and seconds later, Willie steps into our room. "I got your text."

I blink, startled back into my reality. The plane to Amsterdam leaves at midnight.

"You said you would be ready at three," Willie says.

"I'm sorry." I study Faith's still face. "We had an emergency."

He looks briefly at the bed as if, sadly, this unconscious girl is a common sight in Uganda. As if the fight for her life doesn't really matter at all. "We should retrieve your things from the hotel before dark."

The heaviness of the jet lag, this long day, presses down on me. I so want to collapse on a decent bed, sleep a few hours, and then climb back into a first-class seat and fly far away from here. But across the room, Landon's strong shoulders are slumped in defeat from a disease he can't control. This man who has given up so much for others has nothing more to give.

"Do you have another chair?" I ask the doctor.

"You don't have to stay," Landon says.

I look him in the eye. "Neither do you."

"There's only one flight to Amsterdam tonight. If you miss it—"

"I'll take it tomorrow."

Willie eyes me as if I might be a little crazy. "So no ride to the airport?"

"I'll call you in the morning."

"*Mzungu,*" he mutters before leaving.

Landon offers me his chair, but I don't sit until Dr. Daniel brings him another one. The exhaustion from my day settles over me, brain fog stealing into every lobe.

"Malaria is one of the top killers in this country." Landon's gaze doesn't waver from Faith. "A disease we can cure, or at least curb, in the US steals away lives here every day, no real respecter of age because most people don't have the five dollars to purchase quinine."

"But you and Dr. Daniel are doing something about it."

He shakes his head. "A pebble chucked into an ocean of problems."

MELANIE DOBSON

"Or a stone thrown at a giant's head."

He turns to me now, studying my face a moment before he speaks again. "I suppose we all should be throwing whatever God has given us at our enemy."

In the distance, bright lights begin to shine, pods of them whitewashing the darkness. "What are those lights?"

"The locals are catching grasshoppers."

"Why do they want grasshoppers?" I ask.

"To eat."

My stomach rolls. I was hungry a few times as a child, while my mom waited for her next paycheck, but I've never been so hungry that I would eat an insect.

"It's a delicacy here," he explains. "Years ago some enterprising Ugandans saw the menacing swarms as an opportunity. People woo them with light and then trap them in oil drums so they can fry and sell in the market. Instead of smoke and mirrors, they use smoke and metal and electric lights."

And I can smell the smoke, permeating our screen. "Everything is so different."

"The way of doing life, perhaps, but not the people. Between Idi Amin's genocide and the terror from the Lord's Resistance Army up north, they've suffered their own holocaust in the past forty years. They are determined to be resilient in spite of all they've lost. They are rebuilding, and I . . ." He pauses. "I believe God has called me to be part of His redemption plan here."

His words startle me. I'd read about the genocide in school, but I never thought to equate what happened here with Europe's Holocaust or considered how God uses various people and their passions in His plan. Landon produces and

108

sells coffee—good coffee from what I've read. But can coffee really be part of God's redemption?

When his phone chimes, he glances down at it.

"I'm sorry, Ava," he says, looking back up. "My sister says I can be a bit, uh, bristly."

"You care deeply about what you do." The lights flicker across Faith's face. "And for the people you love. There should be no apology for that."

"Ten years ago God rescued me, when I was staring down the gates of hell. Then He put the many pieces of my brokenness back together again and invited me to help rescue others. It's . . ." He rakes his fingers through his hair, seeming to organize his thoughts. "God's radical grace shocked me and those who saw the change in my life. It's an honor to love others like He loves me."

I'm stunned by his words, this relationship he so clearly values. It reminds me of something my mom would have said in her last year of life. She, too, experienced God's radical grace.

"Then you rescued Faith . . ."

He glances back at the bed. "I found her, after a friend told me about a man who was trying to sell his niece."

I shiver.

"The state of her uncle's shack, the stench . . ." He reaches for Faith's still hand. "He'd thought I'd come to place a bid for her future, like the other men; and I suppose he was right in that sense. My bid, though, was a far cry from the prison called trafficking."

Tears soak his cheeks, and this startles me as well. I've never seen any of the men in my life cry.

"I'm sorry," he says. "Sometimes the grief here feels overwhelming."

"You're a hero—"

"No, I'm a disciple, Ava. And a lousy one at that." He stands, moving toward the window. "Too often I want to run back to Portland and hide away in the rhythm of our coffee business there, but every time I leave this place, I feel like I've left a bit of myself behind. And then God keeps inviting me back."

"Did you have to pay Faith's uncle?"

He shakes his head. "I reminded the local magistrate that parliament recently passed the Children Act to protect Ugandan children from predators. The Bishara home was granted custody of the child."

"You saved her life."

"There are thousands more like her who need someone to care for them." He sits back in his chair and glances over at me. "It was brave of you to come to Uganda on your own."

My mom called me brave once, but if anyone else has ever seen courage in me, they've never mentioned it. I certainly don't feel courageous. "Thank you."

"And brave of you to stare down that snake instead of topple the motorcycle."

"I was screaming, Landon. Not staring."

"I never heard you scream."

An attendant brings in a mat and sheet, handing them to Landon. I'm tired enough to sleep on the floor but am grateful when she returns with a wheeled cot, offering it to me. Landon remains in his chair while I collapse on the thin mattress that feels more comfortable in this moment than an airplane seat. The door is open to the hallway, but still it feels strange to lie down on this bed with Landon across the room.

Grasshopper lights flash through my head when I close my eyes, flames cresting and then snaking out like tendrils trying to tangle me. It feels as if I'm the one staring down the gates of hell.

Opening my eyes, I look back out the window, at the orange flickering in the distance. These nightmares have been tormenting me ever since I returned to live with Marcella, the cruel haunting of my past that won't let me forget.

The flames grow in the darkness again as I drift away, too late to return.

I hear my brother, with both of my ears, screaming in the fire. Craning my neck, I try to find him, rescue him from the flames, but I can't see his face. The heat seems to stick to my skin, searing through it, and everything around me is about to come down.

"No!" I shout, trying to climb through the debris. "Andrew—"

I must find him before it's too late.

The room fills with white fire. Smoke. I can't see, can't breathe, but I reach out, searching for Andrew until my hand hits something. Someone.

"You can't have him!" I yell, racing to find my brother.

He's crying, crying for me in the flames.

I can see my brother's face now, so close, and yet I can't reach him. A man catches my arm, pulling me away, and I struggle against him.

"No—"

"Ava?" I don't know who's calling my name, but I wrestle against him, swinging my hands to break free.

"Please, Ava." The voice is stronger this time, more pressing. "We'll find him together."

My eyes open, and Landon is sitting on the mattress beside me, my hand cushioned between his. And I feel terribly exposed having him see this part of me.

"The snake is gone," he says quietly and yet there is strength in his voice.

A child is crying, someplace nearby. I glance around the room, remembering where I am, remembering the girl beside us whose life is in peril.

"I'm sorry." If only I could crawl under this metal bed and hide. "Sometimes I dream . . ."

"You don't have to apologize."

"So now you've heard me scream," I say, my laugh raw.

He smiles at me as if I'm one of the children in his care. "The entire clinic heard you."

"Great."

He releases my hand. "There aren't any snakes in this room."

But the snakes in my mind, they follow me everywhere.

"Did I hurt you?" I ask.

"Just a flesh wound."

Landon waits beside me, giving me the opportunity to tell him about my nightmare, it seems, but this is mine to carry alone.

"Thank you for waking me."

"Go back to sleep." As he returns to his chair, a breeze

whispers through the screen, ruffling the sheet around me, cooling my skin. "No more dreams tonight."

I nod, as if together we can scare them away.

*Every experience God gives us, every
person He puts in our lives
is the perfect preparation for a
future that only He can see.*

CORRIE TEN BOOM
THE HIDING PLACE

TWELVE

ELIESE

Wind rustled through the open doors, creeping into the cavernous corners of the theater that had been emptied of its curtains and chairs, stirring up sawdust and the trailing stench of men who'd been employed to desecrate this beautiful space. Nine hundred seats had been uprooted, and even the gold-and-burgundy carpet inside the auditorium had been peeled away.

Soon the open doors of the theater would welcome guests who—like her—would rather be at home.

People across Holland had been rounded up and relocated to the Jewish ghetto several blocks away. Many of them had been relieved, she'd heard, to avoid being sent to one of the dreaded camps in Germany.

But tonight . . .

Tonight everything was about to change for those who'd been transported to Amsterdam, and she was powerless to help them. Her name would remain on Puttkammer's List, her father said, but only if she cooperated with Walter Süskind and the Jewish Council—*Judenrat*. If she didn't keep their records, she might be sent away like those from the ghetto. And she might never see her son again.

She had to remain strong. When this war was over, William would return, and she and Hein would sail with him to America to finally live as a family.

A flick of four switches, and darkness fell over the orchestra pit and two balconies above. Then she shut the double doors into the auditorium.

On the other side of these doors was the lobby with a ticket window, settee, and old piano, a place where people used to socialize before they watched a performance. The Nazis had left the carpet in this room as if the comfort of it would lure people inside.

It seemed to her that this was what their occupiers had been doing all along: slowly coaxing the Jewish people into their trap. When it snapped . . . no one knew exactly what would happen then.

Eliese shivered, her hand traveling across the star stitched onto the charcoal galaxy of her bolero jacket, the northern points of it covered by her hair. Her own identity card was in the handbag she carried over her shoulder, the stamp inside it her ticket to freedom. She had to cling to that hope or she had nothing. Without the stamp, she was no different from any of those about to be transported out of Amsterdam.

Two tables had been set up in the cloakroom at the side of the lobby, each table holding a typewriter. A beige filing cabinet was centered behind the tables, courtesy of the council, to hold hundreds of registration cards. Stacks of these empty index cards waited on each table to be filled out and filed neatly so the Nazis could account for every person who arrived tonight.

Walter Süskind walked through the open doors, his balding head glistening in the lobby, the collar under his wrinkled jacket damp from perspiration. Stitched near his lapel was a yellow star as well, and he wore a white band around his arm to show he was part of the esteemed Jewish Council.

Mr. Süskind, like her, had fled from the persecution of the German Jews almost a decade ago. Now he was leading the charge to persecute the Jewish people here in Holland, and she and the other registrars were required to assist him.

She hated this man for what he was doing to the Jewish people, hated herself for being forced to participate. Refusing was an option, of course, but only if she wanted to be shipped off to Kamp Westerbork without her son.

She'd never forgive herself—and neither would William—if she left Hein behind.

Fear was a powerful motivator, one that the Nazis had mastered.

"Two other registrars will be arriving soon," Mr. Süskind said. "Do you want some coffee?"

"No."

"It will be a long night."

"A long night in a frightfully long year."

His nod was sharp, dismissive. A truck engine roared outside, and then she heard footfalls, someone shouting for the passengers to step into queue.

The SS leader in command of this place, a vile man by the name of Ferdinand aus der Fünten, strode into the building. Mr. Süskind greeted the commandant with a *Heil Hitler*, and her stomach rolled. The two Germans—one Aryan with his blond hair and the other a Jew—were odd comrades in what she was starting to think was a crime.

Two other women joined her at the table, each wearing a yellow star. They introduced themselves, recent graduates of the university, and Mr. Süskind began instructing them. Every family must have a registration card filed in the cabinets behind the tables, listing the names and birth dates of each member. It was their responsibility as registrars to ensure that no one was overlooked.

Fünten motioned with his gloved hand, and one of his men accompanied a family with three children through the lobby door, each one except the toddler carrying a canvas bag and bedroll. Mr. Süskind nodded at Eliese, and she took one of the registration cards from the pile and threaded it into the typewriter.

"Good evening," she said to the husband and wife, trying to maintain kindness in the most trying of circumstances. "May I have your identity cards?"

The woman clung to her husband's arm as he produced a folded card for himself and his wife, each one stamped with a copper-colored *J*. Unlike the card she had stored in her own pocketbook, no special stamp exempted this family from being relocated.

She swiftly typed their names on the index card and then asked for the names of their children.

"Where are we going?" the woman asked.

Eliese pointed at the set of closed doors, a German soldier standing beside it as if he were an usher about to accompany attendees to their seats. "Into the theater."

"Not tonight," the woman whispered. "After the theater."

She eyed the queue forming behind them, Fünten watching over her and the other registrars to make sure they didn't make a mistake in their pristine keeping of records.

"I don't know what's next."

A lie, but how could she tell this woman that she was being sent out of Amsterdam? If the Nazis were going to steal people from their homes, they should be the ones to explain their destination.

The guard opened the door, and as the family shuffled into the auditorium, Eliese filed the registration card into the cabinet and rolled another blank card into the typewriter.

She worked for several hours, as Mr. Süskind had predicted, her fingers aching as she registered more than a hundred adults and their children. They were nearing the end of the queue now, in these hours before dawn, and she was ready to ball up like the others on a bedroll.

From her seat in the lobby she could hear crying outside, a child sobbing. When the boy's family entered the cloakroom, the cries seemed to balloon, echoing off the plaster walls, and pain shot through Eliese's head, splitting it in two.

"Quiet!" a guard at the back of the line yelled.

The mother bounced the toddler on her hip, trying desperately to keep him quiet. Eliese understood. She'd done the same thing with Hein when he was a baby, afraid he would disturb their neighbors, but often nothing would stop his cries.

The guard dug into his holster and wielded a pistol at the child. The older children in the lobby, the ones who understood, started wailing with him.

So did the mother.

"If you don't shut him up—" the steel barrel gleamed in the light, an erratic flash as he swung the gun—"I swear I'll shoot him right here—"

The lobby was erupting, but Mr. Süskind stood like stone beside her. Fünten didn't stop the guard either, didn't even speak to him.

A gunshot—and Eliese almost passed out on the floor.

The room quieted in an instant. When Eliese dared look up again, she saw the child in the mother's arms. And a hole that pierced the plaster wall.

The boy started crying again.

"Fräulein." The commandant pointed at Eliese. "Do something with that child."

She rose quickly to her feet, glancing at Mr. Süskind. He confirmed the commandant's words with a brisk nod, and she barreled through her thoughts, as erratic as the soldier's pistol. If she took this child, if she couldn't stop his cries, would the guard shoot both of them?

She had to get this child out of here.

"Across the street, there's a crèche," Eliese said in German. "Perhaps the workers can care for him until tomorrow."

"They will care for him as long as I say they will care for him." Fünten sounded as if he had a hundred concerns more pressing than the life of this child.

Her gaze fell to her feet. "Of course."

"Take him now!"

The mother didn't hesitate and neither did Eliese. When she stepped around the counter, the mother rushed toward her, handing over her son.

"His name is Clemens," the woman whispered.

Eliese nodded, not daring to speak. The crying boy bundled awkwardly in her arms, she rushed out the lobby doors, across the wide street that separated the theater from the nursery.

And she knew—she would have to keep Hein away from these men or they would hurt him as well.

THIRTEEN

Sunshine trickles like tears across the cement floor, the solution in the IV bag glistening in its light. I jolt up, tangling myself in a mosquito net that dangles from a hook above the bed next to mine.

I am in Africa. Sleeping in a medical clinic.

During the night, Landon must have draped the net over me.

He is asleep on the mat, and I almost close my eyes again to rest a few more minutes. But something moves on my left.

Turning, I refocus quickly on the girl next to me.

She smiles back.

"Landon," I shout, flinging back the net.

He sits up slowly, groggy at first, but when he sees Faith,

he hops to his feet, shouting for the doctor as he frantically digs through the net.

"Wait until Dr. Daniel looks at her," I say, stopping him before he sweeps her up, the IV still attached to her arm.

He kisses Faith's forehead instead, clinging to her hand as he did with mine last night.

Dr. Daniel races into the room, and the grim look on his face fades into relief when Faith looks up at him. How often, I wonder, do his critically ill patients make it through the night?

He speaks to her in another language, maybe Swahili or the local Luganda, and she nods in response before he checks her vitals. Then he turns back to Landon, resting his stethoscope on his chest. "She should recover just fine."

A blast of air, utter relief, escapes from Landon's lungs. "Thank you."

"Thank the Lord," Dr. Daniel says. "And thank you both for getting her here so quickly."

When Faith closes her eyes again, Landon lets go of her hand. "When can we take her home?"

"I want to monitor her a few more hours." He checks his watch. "If all goes well, she should be able to leave at noon, providing you take the return trip in an enclosed vehicle."

"Of course."

Dr. Daniel waves his arm. "Go get some coffee."

"We should wait—" Landon starts, but Dr. Daniel shoos us both toward the door.

"She needs to rest a few hours without interruption. I'll call you if you need to return."

"You need coffee more than we do," Landon insists.

"Bring me back some."

"Where do we buy coffee?" I ask and then decide how ridiculous that must sound to a man who operates a coffee plantation. "Coffee brewed in a cup."

The doctor laughs. "Landon knows a place."

A woman at the front desk hands both Landon and me a bottle of water. I promptly chug mine down, so she hands me a second one before we walk outside.

Landon eyes the motorcycle before looking down at my sandals. "It would take longer to ride to the shop than walk."

"Are there any cobras in town?"

"None that I've seen."

"Then we should walk."

Dust billows with every step as we hurry along the rock-strewn road, tiny yellow birds hanging from the trees, chattering as they work. Intricate nests from these birds—weavers, Landon calls them—hang from the branches, and watermelon-size fruit dangles over our heads.

I won't admit it, but I wish I'd taken Landon up on his offering of Crocs.

"What is that?" I ask, pointing at the spiked fruit.

"Jackfruit."

I eye it curiously. I've only seen cubes of jackfruit from a can before, but this one looks as if it could knock us both unconscious if it decided to plunge.

My escort opens the door into a small, terra-cotta building, and we find customers inside sipping drinks at three of the five round tables, a gallery of African artwork on the walls.

"Landon!" the man at the counter exclaims, reaching out his hand. "I've missed you."

Landon clasps the man's hand and shakes it. "We've been working overtime on the fields."

"The staff has been working overtime right here as well."

Landon turns to me. "Michael sells the best coffee in all of Uganda. A secret arabica blend that he roasts out back."

The man behind the counter laughs. "Not *me*, Landon. We sell the best."

That's when I notice the sign above him. *Bishara Café*.

I don't remember reading about this coffee shop in the dossier. How many coffee shops does Landon own?

"Landon is known around here as King of the Golden Bean."

"And Michael is known for talking way too much." The peppered stubble on Landon's chin shifts upward with his smile. "But he is one of my business partners and an aficionado when it comes to making any coffee drink you'd like."

"I actually prefer tea to coffee," I say, tapping one of my hands on the counter.

Michael laughs. "So do the majority of Ugandans."

"You must have never had a decent cup of coffee," Landon says.

"*Mzungu.*" Michael points toward a chalkboard of options. "What would you like?"

And I assume he's talking to me. "Black tea. And what exactly does *Mzungu* mean?"

The men laugh.

"What?"

Landon lowers his voice, placing his hand over mine. "It means someone who moves back and forth all the time, like a crazy white person."

I move to swat him, but he steps around the counter with Michael. And I escape into a modern bathroom at the side of the shop. After splashing tap water on my face, I knot my hair back with a band and pull a travel toothbrush out of my handbag, using the bottle of water to brush my teeth. Still I feel groggy, but perhaps a cup of African tea will revive my brain.

Landon's waiting for me at the table with two mugs of black coffee, along with plates of scrambled eggs and fresh mango.

He nudges one of the coffee mugs toward me. "Michael wants you to try his coffee before you drink the tea."

"I think you want me to try it."

"How can you research Bishara without at least sampling our product?"

He has a point. Tentatively I take a sip, my lips puckering together before I lower the mug.

He's watching me closely. "What do you taste?"

"Acid."

He waves his hand. "And?"

I take a long swig from the water bottle. "I need sweetener and cream to help me sort it out."

He sighs, picking up his own mug, and I inch my elbows forward, curious as he seems to savor the aroma from his cup, sniffing it as if it were a glass of wine. "What exactly are you smelling?"

"Honey and almonds and . . . bergamot."

"I think you're a *Mzungu.*"

He laughs again before taking a long sip. "And there's a hint of chocolate."

I decide to try one more sip, for the sake of the chocolate. "It's still acid to me."

"Every cup of good coffee carries a taste of its homeland," he says. "*Terroir* is what we call it." The word sounds like "too are"—the art of coffee.

"Milk and sugar have terroir."

He shakes his head. "The processing strips away every bit of home."

Still he heads back to the counter while I eat the slices of mango, relishing its African terroir.

When Landon returns, he's carrying a packet of raw sugar and some steamed milk. "We have powdered creamer for most of our guests, but I refuse to let you completely ruin this."

I dump the sugar and milk into my mug, and this time I can almost taste chocolate.

Several people are crowded around a table nearby, talking about something in a language I don't understand. "It's what I like most about coffee," he says. "No matter where you are, even if you don't like the taste, coffee brings people together."

I fidget with the handle on my mug, feeling exposed in front of this man I barely know. A man I'm supposed to be investigating. "Thank you for waking me up last night. My nightmares, they can be terrifying sometimes."

"You called for someone named Andrew."

I blink, not certain what to say. I haven't talked about Andrew for years, not even with Vi.

When I don't explain, he continues. "My great-grandmother has nightmares too. Sometimes she cries out in her sleep."

"Your Dutch grandmother?"

He groans. "Do you know everything about me?"

"No," I say slowly. "I'm discovering that I know very little after all."

"I know you're here to scrutinize me and my work, but I'm not looking to re-create myself into something that I'm not." He sweeps his hand across the room. "Something that we're not."

"I'm not asking you to." I pause. "What are your great-grandmother's nightmares about?"

"She seems to be searching for someone."

"Do you know who she's searching for?" I ask.

He shakes his head. "She doesn't talk much about the past, but she is a woman of prayer. She's prayed for me my entire life."

"You seem to inspire everyone working for you with your faith."

He sips his coffee again. "Many of the people here, they've experienced the grace and light of Christ in ways that few Americans have. They are some of the kindest, most gracious people I've ever met, and I like working with them to help bring order to this land and love to those who can't fend for themselves. To partner together as Jesus' hands and feet."

He finishes his cup and sets down the mug.

"The darker the evil, I think, the more brilliant are the flickers of light. And that's what I see here. These glimpses of heaven in the people and the land and the care of all who come to help. We don't need more money or a complex infra-structure to find it, Ava. All we need is the willingness of

God's people to follow wherever He leads them to bring good back into this world."

"Did your sister ask you to talk me out of this grant?"

"No." He sighs. "She asked me to be nice."

"You have an extremely smart sister." I lean forward. "Perhaps God is leading our foundation to you."

He raises an eyebrow, skeptical of my words. "I did a little research of my own last night, after you fell asleep."

I slowly rotate my mug in a circle. "And what did you find?"

"The Kingston family is a mess."

"To put it mildly." I decide not to tell him quite yet that I'm an intimate part of the mess.

He leans back in his chair, hickory-brown eyes studying my face. The man is five years older than me, and if he realizes how handsome he is, he doesn't show it. "Why do they want to invest in a mission organization?"

"Unlike the rest of the family, the foundation trustee wants to bring good into the world as well. Marcella is particularly enthusiastic about helping people with a Dutch heritage succeed."

"It's important to me to create partnerships. Not become a PR piece."

I swallow hard. I can guarantee them the money, if Marcella ultimately approves, but I can't guarantee their name won't be splashed across press releases and the foundation's website and social media. Most people want the publicity.

He takes another sip of his chocolate coffee. "Sometimes businesses use goodwill public relations to cover up something that isn't quite so good."

"This isn't a cover-up." But even as I say the words, I think of all the turmoil under the hood of the Kingston Corporation. It's a miracle that our engine still runs.

He shrugs. "I searched for information about an Ava Drake with the Kingston foundation but couldn't find much."

"I prefer to keep my life offline."

"Admirable," he says, but it's not as admirable as he thinks. "What is your story?"

I twist the mug again. While I spend much of my time researching other people, I'm not nearly as keen on them researching me. "I grew up in North Carolina with my mom."

"Where's your dad?"

"In Idaho. He left when I was young."

"No father should ever leave his child."

If only the world operated by Landon West's rules.

"When I was fourteen, my house . . ." I take a deep breath, my gaze dropping to my cup. "My mom was killed in a fire."

"I'm sorry."

"Her faith in God was unshakable, but it shook mine up pretty good." And shook up my foundation, one not made of money. "After she died, a social worker discovered that these messed-up Kingstons are actually my relatives."

His lips form an O shape as if he's trying to decide whether or not he needs to offer up an apology.

"You're right." I move on quickly. "Most of the family is a wreck, but Marcella— my grandmother—really wants to help people."

"So you stepped into their family after your mother died."

"Stepped into *my* family, Landon. Not theirs." I decide to change the direction of this conversation. "If you received money from a grant, what would you do with it?"

"Hire more people to work the farm and care for the children."

"Work to set them free?"

He eyes me curiously. "Work is freeing, but the truth is the only thing that can set us free."

"So you'll combine work and truth—"

Someone calls Landon's name, and he returns their wave. "I want to provide a sustainable income for our partners and then use the profits to educate and provide housing and food and medicine for everyone in our care."

And I want to do this for him and his sister and the children here so they can expand rapidly on their own. My visit to Portland, I hope, will confirm that God is clearly working through Kendall and Landon and their team on both sides of the ocean.

That afternoon Willie retrieves me—the crazy white woman—from the Mityana clinic along with Landon and Faith. I let Faith borrow my sunglasses in the Land Rover, worried that she'll get a headache from the sun, and hold her hand all the way back up the bumpy road. Then Landon lets me carry her into the nursery.

Ruth takes Faith into her open arms, snuggling her to her chest. "Thank the Lord."

I want to kiss Faith's forehead, like Landon did this morning, but it feels awkward. Faith takes off the sunglasses, holds them out to me, but I shake my head.

"For you," I say, and she flashes me a giant smile, replacing the sunglasses askew on her small face. Then she runs up the steps, and I'm sad. I wanted to at least say goodbye.

Seconds later, she's back, holding out something in her hand. "For you."

It's an old fidget spinner, splashed with all the colors of a rainbow. One of the arms is broken, but to her, it seems to be a treasure.

"I couldn't—"

"It's a gift," Landon says, his voice quite firm. And I realize that I have to take the toy.

I pull it to my chest. "I love it."

Faith makes a fist, and I look back at Landon. When he whispers something, I turn my head to capture his words.

"Bump it," he says again.

So I make my own fist and gently bump her hand.

"I can take you to the airport," Landon says as we step out of the nursery, into a breeze scented by lemon. The fidget spinner is secured in my hand.

"You don't have to—"

"I need to pick up some supplies in Kampala."

"Like Kleenex?"

He laughs. "I'll try and have some on hand the next time you come."

Next time?

Oddly enough, I like the thought of it.

"Do you grow lemongrass on your plantation?" I ask.

"Yes." He gives me a lopsided grin. "It keeps the snakes away."

I send Willie on his way, and an hour later, Landon drives me to the airport—not because of the millions that

I represent but because, it seems, he might actually enjoy spending time with me.

"I'm glad you came," he says as we stand outside security.

"Me too."

"Will you text when you land in New York?"

I smile. Landon isn't married, but I'm wondering in that moment if he's seeing someone back home. The research firm mentioned a fiancée at one time, but no girlfriend. "I'll need your phone number."

He sends his contact info to my Ugandan phone, and I reply with my iPhone number, hoping Claire has taken it back with her to New York.

"When do you return to Portland?" I ask.

"On Sunday."

"Perhaps I'll see you at one of your American cafés," I say.

"I'd like that."

He waves one last time after I walk through security, and then he's gone.

When I board the plane, I cling to the broken fidget spinner. Landon said that each time he leaves Uganda, he feels like he's left a bit of himself behind.

And I feel as if I'm leaving a small part of myself here as well.

FOURTEEN

JOSIE

Josie woke suddenly in her room, her forehead drenched in sweat as she lifted herself up on her elbows, listening. Did she hear a noise or was it the remnants of a dream rattling in her head?

She inched back the blackout curtain and propped her window open with a wooden stay, the night air cooling her room. The Allied planes had never dropped bombs on their city, but some nights, when the planes flew over, an alarm roused all of Amsterdam from their sleep. And in some way, the sirens comforted her. Even when she couldn't see them, the planes were fighting for freedom.

She didn't hear anything outside her window. Unless the air siren was raging, the nights since the Nazis arrived had been deathly quiet, as if the city was afraid to even breathe.

Had her brother somehow managed to steal into the courtyard below? Perhaps he'd been throwing stones at her window.

"Samuel?" she whispered, but no one responded.

Sleep had been fitful for the past week, ever since she'd knocked on that door in Amersfoort. After the delivery failed, she'd hoped her brother would find her, tell her what to do with the envelope of guilders.

She hadn't seen him or received any type of message, but a collage of pictures had glued itself across the pages of her mind. Of her and Samuel paddling back from the windmill. Of the Dutchman who'd opened the door. Of people being herded like animals onto the army truck.

She blinked in the darkness but couldn't erase the pictures in her head.

A reproduction of a Weissenbruch farmhouse hung at the end of her bed, the old watercolor dangling by a nail and wire on the plaster wall. Hidden behind the farmhouse, in a sleeve that she'd created out of sellotape and cardboard, were her fake identity card—the one that said Laurina de Jong—and Samuel's envelope. She wanted to pretend it wasn't there, but the weight of this money, the responsibility of it, hung heavy on her.

The money was needed someplace, but until Samuel returned, she didn't know what to do with it and she couldn't very well dump it into a canal like so many people who needed to hide their things. So she'd continue praying, late into the night, that Samuel would return soon—or send someone to take this money from her.

Another sound.

This wasn't a stone hitting the window. It was a cry, piercing the night.

She reached for her robe, hanging on a peg beside the bed. All the children and crèche workers, except the director, were supposed to be at home, but if one of the children had to spend the night, perhaps Miss Pimentel needed her help.

She padded to the staircase outside her room. Through the alcove window, she saw five trucks, like the ones she'd seen in Amersfoort, parked outside the theater, and a queue of people on the sidewalk as if they were waiting for a midnight show. Except these people weren't dressed for an evening out. They wore long coats in spite of the summer heat and clung to suitcases and the hands of their children.

Moonlight reflected off the white walls of the theater, a dim spotlight for those forced onto the stage out front. Then, for an instant, the light seemed to disappear as a cloud crossed over the splinter of moon. Almost as if God blinked.

Josie rushed down the steps and into the arched corridor that separated the college from the crèche, to the locked gate leading out to Plantage Middenlaan.

From the shadows, Josie watched another truck park across the street, guards unloading people from the bed. And she felt sick. Most of them were silent, stony as they waited, but several of the children cried in their parents' arms.

Had they been hiding, Josie wondered, or taken from their homes? They must be terrified.

Stars glowed in the moonlight, stitched onto the coats of those in line.

God hadn't blinked. He saw all of this. Every man and woman being herded like cattle. Every child crying. Every guard pointing the muzzle of a gun.

If only He would make the earth tremble under this sidewalk and send the guards running. Stop this madness.

"God help us," she prayed out loud.

Watching and praying. Waiting for someone to stand for all that was right and true and good. She felt like a girl again, hidden under the wooden quay, waiting until her brother had hung the flag.

She needed to pray, but she no longer wanted to wait. She wanted to help those like the van Gelders who were being taken away from their homes.

Light trailed down the path, and Josie turned quickly to see Miss Pimentel with a flashlight in hand, a pale-pink robe wrapped around her stout body and her gray hair pinned back in curls. She lived on the top floor of the crèche, alert to everything that happened both day and night in the building that housed her kids. The helpers at the crèche respected this older woman and her brisk style that kept them focused on the children.

Miss Pimentel turned off the light and shuffled up beside Josie at the gate, grasping two of the wrought-iron spindles. "It's started."

"What is it?" Josie whispered.

"Racial purity," Miss Pimentel said. "The Nazis plan to remove all the Jews from Holland, starting in Amsterdam."

Josie shook her head. "That's impossible."

Their country was home to more than a hundred thousand Jews.

Truck number seven arrived, soldiers unloading more people onto the sidewalk.

"Not in their eyes," Miss Pimentel said. "Hatred stops at nothing to destroy, but love can break through the root of evil. Grow something good instead."

"We have to do something to stop this!"

"We must fight in prayer, and we must fight together, arm in arm with those we trust."

The woman kept her gaze on the streets, watching the guards and people who stole silently through the theater's front doors. "This crèche, it's my kingdom, Josie."

"Kingdom?"

She tapped the flashlight on the edge of the gate. "We are here, the both of us perhaps, for such a rare time as this."

Josie thought back to the story in the Bible of a queen who risked her life to rescue her people from exactly where God had planted her.

Perhaps she didn't have to go away like Samuel to resist this enemy. Perhaps she could resist right here. Instead of sending angels down from heaven tonight, perhaps He had sent Miss Pimentel to her.

But what could they do in the face of the German guns?

"I see you playing with the children, Josie. You are a blessing to them."

"And they are a blessing to me."

Miss Pimentel placed a hand on Josie's shoulder. "We must pray now that we can bless those across the street."

Before Miss Pimentel began to pray, a woman rushed

toward them from the theater, another crying child in her arms.

"Step back," Miss Pimentel commanded, and Josie moved behind the bicycle rack.

"This boy needs a place to stay," the woman whispered from the other side of the gate. "Away from the guards."

A gruff voice shouted from across the street, presumably at the woman.

"His name is Clemens." She shoved the young boy through the widely spaced spindles, into the director's arms. "I must go."

"When should we bring him back?"

"At first light."

In this moment Josie knew exactly what God had called her to do, no matter what her brother had said about not being able to rescue those who were already detained. She would help the children whose parents could no longer fight for them.

"Hurry now," Miss Pimentel said, pointing Josie toward the door of the nursery. The boy's cries continued inside the crèche, where the guards couldn't hear him.

Miss Pimentel pulled one of the cribs the children used for their naptime out of a closet and situated it away from the front window. Then she retrieved a glass of buttermilk and a piece of potato-meal bread frosted in honey.

The boy began to calm his crying as he drank the milk. "Mama?"

"We've just brought you here to sleep," Josie said as she eased him under the covers. "You will see your mother tomorrow."

His breathing slowed and minutes later he was asleep, wet eyelashes curled on his cheeks.

Miss Pimentel peeled back the dark curtain, glancing outside before she turned back to Josie. "You must go to your room now."

"He shouldn't be alone."

"I'll sleep on a cot beside him," the director said. "We'll take him back to the theater in the morning."

Josie slipped back under her covers in her room, but she couldn't sleep. Instead she prayed for Clemens and his mother. For Samuel and Mrs. Pon. For Miss Pimentel.

And most of all, she prayed for the children and their parents who appeared to be spending the rest of their night in a theater.

FIFTEEN

"I was worried about you." Marcella places her fork beside a bowl of strawberries and thick cream, reaching for my hands when I walk into the breakfast room of the Kingston farmhouse, its wall of windows overlooking the Hudson River and maple-checkered hills on the other side.

Marcella kisses my cheek, and I collapse into one of the dining room chairs, the white linen slipcover tied neatly down its spine. It feels strange to be back in New York—no chickens clucking or grasshopper lights flashing or snakes trying to chase me.

"Did Claire pass along my email?"

"She did." One of the housemaids, a veteran employee named Leah, refills Marcella's coffee cup from an antique silver carafe, and Marcella sips her drink. "Claire tried to call the number you sent, but it didn't work."

"Does Claire have my iPhone?"

"Yes, she put it up in your room." In the west wing of this massive house.

The family has expanded the Kingston home for eighty years until it seems just as large, perhaps even larger, than all the buildings on the Bishara plantation combined. So strange to have more than fifteen thousand squares of space for one woman. And a few squares shared with me and the household staff.

Leah brings out a second bowl of strawberries, and I thank her.

"You must be exhausted," Marcella says.

"I slept some on the plane."

She takes another sip of coffee, and I'm fascinated by the ripples swirling in her cup, knowing now its journey to arrive at this table, a journey most of us take for granted. "Was there really a coffee plantation?"

"An actual working one, along with a small school and a home for children of the plantation workers and some kids who've lost their parents."

"You've written it up?"

"I took notes, but I'll format it after I speak to Kendall Stafford."

She dabs her cloth napkin on the sides of her mouth, signaling that breakfast is done. "How was your time with Mr. West?"

Laughter bubbles up inside me, rippling like the coffee, and this surprises me. I haven't laughed, truly laughed, in a long time. I stuff it back down lest I have to explain the details about spending the night with Landon in a medical clinic. Marcella wouldn't think that funny at all.

The hours with Landon as we drove to the airport, the time with Faith in the clinic, our early morning at the coffee shop. These memories, I think, are mine alone.

I admire Landon greatly for his work and even more so for not kowtowing to me when he found out I was from the foundation. Clearly he needs the grant money, but this didn't seem to change who he is at the core.

"He's a capable manager and completely devoted to their mission. A grant would help him grow his staff and provide some much-needed infrastructure."

The telephone rings at the side of the room, one of those old-fashioned rotary ones with a black receiver and spiral cord.

Marcella glances at her watch. "We have a lot to discuss, Emily."

"Ava."

Her lips press tightly together, as they always do when I remind her that I'm not my mother.

"Of course. Ava." She smiles at me. "I'm glad you are back safely."

"Thank you for giving Bishara a chance." Whether or not Landon wants the money, I'll do everything I can to help him get this grant.

"I have a meeting in Brooklyn this afternoon, and I'll be spending the night," she says. "We'll reconvene when you get back from Portland."

"I'm flying down to North Carolina in the morning." I've

been clinging to that hope for months now, ready to burrow into all that's familiar for a few days before I resume life here.

"I'm sorry." She inches back her chair. "You'll have to go later."

"But—"

"You need to finish the grant review."

I dig my bare heels into the mahogany floor. "I can go to Portland on Monday." After Landon returns home.

"The board of directors meets on Monday morning. They'll be ready to make a decision."

Words seem to be trapped, deep in my throat, capping off the laughter stuck there.

"It will be months before the board meets again," she says.

If everything is legit in Oregon, I don't want Landon and Faith and all the children at Bishara to wait months to receive their grant money. Or, perhaps, not receive it at all.

North Carolina will have to wait. Again.

"I read an old book about our family while I was in Africa," I say, standing up with her.

Marcella's face pales. "What book?"

"It's called *Darkest Before Dawn*."

"There's a lot of nonsense in old books."

"And some truth in them," I say, "or we wouldn't have stocked an entire library in Amsterdam."

"Did you get it from Amsterdam?" The book does matter to her, it seems, more than the information inside.

"Paul Epker found it for me, but that's not the p—"

"Please give it to Claire so we can return it."

"The book talks about your father spending his last years at a place called Craig House."

She reaches for the back of her chair, her fingers curling around it. "I have a phone meeting right now."

"Why won't you talk about Peter?" I ask.

"He was a troubled man." Marcella glances out at the river. "He needed a safe place to rest in his last years, so we found a good home for him nearby."

But why did Peter Ziegler, with all of his wealth, have to stay at an institution? If he needed rest, he could have checked himself into a resort for the rest of his life.

"Did he want to be there?" I ask.

Those lines, I see them forming around her eyes. While I've seen her explode at her sons, she's never raged at me. But like the oily smell of ozone right before a storm, I know the signs well. At any moment, a flash of lightning is coming.

"It didn't matter what my father wanted."

Claire whisks into the breakfast room with her briefcase, as if she's been listening outside the door. "Time for your meeting," she says, pointing toward a door.

Marcella brushes her hands over her straight skirt. "Of course."

Claire smiles at me. "Welcome back."

Back. Not home. As soon as I finish the grant review for Bishara, I'm going home, three states south of here.

I nod at Claire, but she doesn't seem to notice my discomfort as she reaches for Marcella's coffee cup, ready to carry it out of the room. "Henry Bradwell is on the phone."

"I'll take it in my office," she says, straightening her pearl necklace.

Marcella pats my shoulder, the lines on her forehead sanded away. Lost again in the safe world of business. As if these appointments, a frantic schedule, eradicate any conversation that would actually mean anything between us.

Perhaps that was why my mom, as hard as she worked to provide for Andrew and me, set aside time for us to simply be together.

Marcella cares about me in her own way, but I've been dismissed this morning, second to this newspaper editor and any other pressing Kingston business. My question about Peter, my plans for my weekend, they've been dismissed as well.

What am I going to tell Victoria?

Claire follows Marcella to the connecting office and I slip back into the hallway, passing artwork that has been collected in the Kingston family for generations, along with portraits of William and his wife, Abigail—my great-grandmother.

There aren't any portraits of Peter or Trudy Ziegler, but the hallway that leads past the library, the music room, and a banquet hall has multiple photographs of Marcella at different ages. Her wedding photograph with Randolph is the last framed picture, at the bottom of a carpeted staircase. Upstairs are the formal portraits of Randolph and Marcella with their three children, and like sprouted seeds, the beginnings of the next generation, including a studio photo taken of me during my college years.

My bedroom overlooks the manicured front lawn of the estate and a stone driveway that circles a water fountain imported from Rome. I fall onto the canopy bed with lavender-and-white ruffles that Marcella had designed for my mother when she was a girl. Leah stored most of my mother's things up in the attic after she left home, but the decor is the same.

In the weeks after I arrived, I found the attic boxes and perused through clothes, an entire collection of Boxcar Children books, and cassette tapes, but I couldn't seem to find my mom there. A piece of her is in this room, though, wrapped up in these cotton-candy walls. Her essence, the memory of her youth, gives me hope.

My cell phone is beside the bed, dozens of texts vying for space on the screen, most of them from Victoria. Her last one was sent around midnight, threatening to call Homeland Security if I didn't contact her right away.

I send her a short note.

I'm back.

Her reply is almost instantaneous. Thank God! I thought you'd left me for good!!

Marcella sent me to Africa.

Seconds later, my phone rings, and Vi's lovely face emerges on my screen. "You're in Africa?" she exclaims.

"No, I got back way too early this morning."

"I thought you were in Amsterdam, opening a museum."

"It was a library."

"I can't keep up, Ava. You're spending more time in the air these days than a migrating bird."

I open the French doors leading out to a terrace with a table, two wrought iron chairs, and a red geranium. Fresh air floods my room. "I had to check out another nonprofit. My mind—and body, for that matter—is officially shot."

"Good thing you're coming home tomorrow!"

"About that—"

Vi groans. "Her Majesty canceled your plans."

"Don't call her that," I whisper, stepping away from the terrace.

"Her Highness, then. Or supreme pain in the—"

"Vi!"

"Her royal hiney-ness?"

"Some respect please."

"She's not really royalty, Ava. You don't have to defend her."

I fall onto the bed, my head propped up on a lacy cushion of pillows. "She needs me to visit the organization's headquarters in Portland."

"And you need to come home. It's not like Marcella's going to fire you."

"It doesn't matter what Marcella thinks."

"Right," Vi clips.

"If I don't go, the board might not grant the money, and Landon needs it."

"Wait." Vi pauses. "Who's Landon?"

"Landon West. The owner of the coffee company."

"Married?"

"Oh, please—"

"This is important information."

I swing my legs over the side of the bed, looking out over the driveway again.

"Not married. And not any of your or my business."

"Not my business, perhaps, but it should be yours." Vi stops to talk to someone before returning to the phone. "I guess you won't tell me if he's cute."

"Nope." I pull Paul's book out of my bag, opting to change

the subject. "I found something odd about the Kingstons while I was away, in a book I was given."

"Everything about that family is odd."

I almost remind her that this is my family now, but she knows this. "It says my great-grandfather died in a mental institution about fifty years ago."

"Did you ask Marcella if it was true?"

"She doesn't want to talk about him."

"So what are you going to do?"

I think for a moment. "I suppose I'm going to find out what happened on my own."

"Let me know if you need me to help," she says. "I can do some research tomorrow night, when you and I are supposed to be at the beach."

"I'm sorry, Vi."

"I'm sorry for you, my friend. I don't want you to lose yourself while trying to find . . . well, I'm still not exactly certain what you're trying to find."

Someone knocks on my bedroom door. "I have to go."

"Please come home soon."

Monday. That's when I'll go. But I don't tell her this. I don't want to make another promise that I can't keep. "As soon as I can."

Leah opens the door, strands of her curly hair falling out from its twist, silver mist on the shoulders of her black uniform. "I thought you might still be hungry. Would you like me to bring up some lunch and hot tea?"

"Yes, please."

Her smile lights the blue in her eyes. "I'll be right back."

She starts to close the door, tiptoeing backward as if I might have forgotten she's here.

"Leah—" I call before she closes the door.

She inches it open again. "Yes, Miss Ava?"

I glance around at the pastels of the room, at the watercolors on the wall. Hardly the colors of a teen rebel. How had my mother gone from this to such a dark place in her life before she discovered God's light?

"Were you working here when my mother was young?"

Skepticism fills her eyes. Maddening. Marcella won't tell me about her father, and the staff aren't supposed to talk about Emily. "I was."

"What do you remember about her?"

She steps into the room and closes the door behind her. "Your mom brought life into this house when it sorely needed life. She was kind and gracious and had a keen mind for business. If Mr. Kingston would have allowed it, she could have run his company."

"Why didn't he allow it?"

She shrugs, but I know. Because she was a girl. Not even Marcella, I'm told, had an active part in the business until her husband died. When Randolph passed away, she stepped right into his place—much to the chagrin of her sons, who'd expected to take over. The Kingston boys were set solidly back into places they didn't want to be, in their mother's wake again.

"Did she leave home because she was pregnant?"

Leah shifts on her feet. "It's not my place to talk about your family."

"I suppose not." Marcella would have Leah's job if she said

something I'm not supposed to hear, as if I'm still too young at twenty-seven to hear the truth.

"I'll get you that tea."

After Leah leaves, I remove the worn fidget spinner from my bag and prop Faith's gift up beside the framed photograph I have displayed on the dresser, one of my mom and me when I was three years old, hand in hand as we strolled along the beach in matching sundresses, daisy chains threaded around our necks.

Someone from the church where Mom worked brought me this picture the week after the fire, along with her Bible and the other things she kept in her desk. The Bible is a treasure trove, her colored illustrations in the margins depicting the stories and lessons my mom learned in the last year of her life.

A fierce lion and a gentle lamb. A broken heart on the page where Jesus died. Teal ocean waves beside verses on peace. And golden gates blown open near the end, a woman in a sundress stepping inside, arms outstretched before a king.

It's the picture I cling to when my heart aches the most.

Opening my nightstand, I take out Mom's Bible and slip it into my handbag so I can read through it again on my trip to Portland. Then I lean back against the pillows, closing my eyes. My brain is fried after the long trip, but it keeps wandering back to Africa, to Faith and the man who cared for her and the other children as if they were his own kids.

We have much in common, that little girl and me. One day, Landon will tell Faith her story, how she was rescued from evil. One day, I hope someone will tell me the pieces of my family's story that have been hidden away.

Leah returns with a small tray and sets the egg salad sand-wiches, sliced tomatoes, and a pot of Darjeeling tea on my nightstand. Then she turns to me. "It's not my place to talk about your mother."

"I shouldn't have asked you."

"But your mom," she continues, "it's her place to talk about the past."

I sigh, pulling my legs to my chest like I am that three-year-old once more. "I wish I could talk to her one more time."

Leah steps back toward the door, but she doesn't leave. "Your mama, she was always writing in one of those journals of hers."

My head snaps up. "What journals?"

"The ones stored in my room so they don't get lost."

"Oh, Leah . . ."

Minutes later, this beautiful woman brings me a small bundle wrapped in brown paper and bound together with masking tape.

I practically leap off my bed. "Thank you."

"Things sometimes disappear upstairs. I didn't want any-thing to happen to them." Tears fill her eyes. "I miss your mama very much."

"Thank you." It's the first time anyone here has said they miss her.

"You remind me a lot of Miss Emily, wanting to do the right thing."

"Sometimes it's hard to know what the right thing is."

I slip out onto the terrace and sit on the cushioned chair before carefully unwrapping the brown paper. Inside are three journals, one cover designed with bright paisleys and another with plaid. The last cover is blue, a stormy color reminding me of the Hudson.

I open the paisley journal, and suddenly I'm lost in the world of a thirteen-year-old girl who doesn't feel like she belongs. On most of the pages are sketches, in colored pencil, but words are what I want now, written in a script that seems to pride itself on beauty.

As I read, a black sedan parks on the ring of drive below. Both Marcella and Claire walk out of the house and climb into the car. I can sit here all afternoon if I want and no one will bother me.

Minutes turn into hours as I read through the years of my mother's story. About the all-girl prep school she attended in Connecticut, about the brothers who pestered her in the summer, the horses she loved at school and home.

Then there's my father. Jeffery Drake. A stable hand she met at an equestrian competition. He was seventeen, a year older than her, and he planned to be a trainer one day. She convinced their head groom to hire him and began spending more of her weekends and holidays at home.

I skim through each entry, searching for answers about both my parents, but I don't find much more about my father.

Jeffery had planned to get a cut of the Kingston money after they ran away together. That's what Marcella told me after I moved here. When Jeffery didn't get the money—or the lifestyle—he decided to run again. This time, on his own.

And my mother moved on to another man.

The daughter of a king. That's what my mom used to

say when I asked about my father. A princess. After Mom became a Christian, she told me that we were both daughters of a king.

Near the end of the blue journal, penned when she was in her late teens, Mom writes about her own questions, wondering why she feels so out of place in this family. How Marcella dotes on her and Randolph ignores her and how her older brothers, Carlton and Will, mock her when no one else is around.

Will was drunk, stone drunk when he found me alone in the barn. The look in his eyes—I thought he was going to kill me at first. But he wanted to wound me with words. Mean ones that cut into my heart.

He told me what I suspected all along. Mom and Dad adopted me when I was a baby. I was left on the doorstep, he said, by gypsies.

Not even the gypsies wanted me.

I lower the journal, feeling the breadth of her pain. When I was younger, when I asked about her parents, she didn't tell me their names, but she told me that she was adopted. As if that explained everything.

But I learned in my teen years that it explained nothing really. Vi was adopted and she adores her parents.

My hands linger on the page even as my gaze wanders to the steeple of the old equestrian center among the trees on the north side of the property. The horses my mom once rode have been gone for about a decade, the building turned into a gym with a basketball court, weight room, and spa.

It's easy to renovate one's life and surroundings with

unlimited amounts of money. If you don't like something—a building, a lifestyle, a car, a spouse—you change it.

And if you aren't happy with your current family, you buy another child.

But no one, including a child, can cure an unhappy heart.

I'll never be a Kingston by blood, but Marcella has assured me that I belong in this family.

Did she ever tell my mom that as well?

My hand shakes as I turn the page, to the last one in her journals. I read the words quickly at first and then mull over them until daylight begins to slip away.

> *Marcella has paid them, still pays them, Will said with a laugh, to keep the adoption quiet. They would know what happened, of course. Will and Carlton were thirteen and fifteen when I was born.*
>
> *I'd hoped Marcella adopted me because she wanted to rescue a baby, but it seems she wanted to save herself. And the good name of the Kingstons.*
>
> *Money won't redeem the past, but I'm afraid Marcella will do anything to cover up the sins of this family.*
>
> *I'm afraid of my brothers. Afraid for my future. Afraid what will happen if someone else finds out the truth.*

I close the book quietly, her words resounding in my head.

The records for my mom's adoption are closed; I checked when I was eighteen. Was Marcella continuing to pay her sons, almost five decades later, to keep the adoption—or my mother's biological parents—a secret? And how did adopting my mom save the Kingstons' good name?

My phone buzzes and I see a text from Landon, checking to make sure I've arrived home. I send him a short note in return, apologizing for not texting him earlier. I am grateful for his concern. For his budding friendship. If only my family were more like Landon's. Normal. Then I wouldn't have to chase down the truth.

Tomorrow morning, before I go to Portland, I'll visit Craig House.

Perhaps there I'll find out what Marcella is trying to hide.

SIXTEEN

JOSIE

AMSTERDAM

JULY 1942

The square courtyard behind the crèche was surrounded by a fortress of buildings, the garden and patches of dirt partitioned off by hedgerows almost as tall as Josie. A mosaic window capped the door into the crèche, pieced together perfectly to create a stained-glass beach with seashells scattered on the sand.

This garden, Josie thought, was a haven where neither the children nor their attendants had to worry about whatever the Nazis were doing across the street. In the magic of this courtyard, it almost seemed as if there were no war waging beyond their hedge, as if play could cure any woe.

Here Josie could pretend as well—that she and Eliese were canoeing out to the peatery or skating down their canal during the winter months. That nothing else mattered outside a world they'd created on their own.

Josie bounced Clemens in her arms all morning as she tried to entertain the other children. He'd been asking for his mama since he woke, but neither she nor Miss Pimentel wanted to take him back to the theater yet. People had been queued up on the street for hours last night before the doors swallowed them, but no one except a guard was on the sidewalk this morning.

Josie glanced at the window of her room, on the other side of a hedge that divided the college and crèche. The building in front of her served as a place to care for children while the building to her right trained teachers to educate children in the future. Divided and yet they shared a common goal. No matter what happened in their country, they'd always have children, and these children would need teachers.

A girl stepped up beside Josie, tugging her arm. "It's my turn."

"You're right." With Clemens on her hip, Josie leaned down to help the six-year-old tie a string around her waist, a nail dangling from the end. The girl joined four other children, each hopping around a bottle, trying to deposit the attached nail into the glass.

Metal clanked inside one of the bottles and a boy named Dirk lifted his bottle so everyone playing the game could see. Then he bounded along a row of flowers like a rabbit, the string and nail trailing behind him. When she called his name, Dirk eyed a split in the hedge to their left like he might sneak through it; then he looked up as if considering whether or not to catapult over the top, landing in the college garden.

Josie rushed to his side, and he reluctantly untied the string around his waist and handed the nail over to her before joining another game.

The older children—more than twenty of them—raced with their flour sacks along the edge of the garden, kicked a football across the dirt, and dropped these nails into milk bottles while toddlers bounced in wooden playpens that the janitor had set up under the shade of trees. In the afternoons, the crèche workers took them on a walk around their block, pushing carriages with the babies while the older kids followed like ducklings close behind.

Josie and the other four nursery workers were dressed alike—ash-gray dresses, white aprons, and white handkerchiefs tied over their hair. The children in the crèche knew exactly who was supposed to be caring for them by the neat uniforms that Miss Pimentel required her attendants wear.

These morning hours had become the favorite part of Josie's day, soaking up the laughter and play instead of listening to the instructor in her classroom. One day, when she was a teacher, she would instruct her students outside, all day if she could. Let them dream and imagine and move their bodies to inspire their brains like she'd once done as a girl.

Another nail clinked in the glass, and the children clapped, laughing together.

Josie snapped her eyes closed and then slowly opened them as if she could capture this beautiful scene in the film of her mind, take it with her to replace the terrible ones from Amersfoort. Or, at least, add to the collage.

These children, they must know the fear that had inundated their country, but inside these walls was a respite for all of them. The light these kids brought each day offset some of the darkness that loomed on the other side.

A woman stepped out of the crèche's back door, into the garden, and Josie stared at her. She was dressed in a black skirt and jacket, two pins holding back her long hair, a star branding her coat. And in that moment, Josie felt as if she'd been transported back to her childhood in Giethoorn.

"Eliese?"

"Josie . . ." Her old friend looked just as startled as she did. "Why are you here?"

She nodded toward the hedge. "I'm a student at the teachers' college." Josie transferred Clemens to her other hip, a thousand questions surging through her mind. She focused on the most pressing. "I thought you were in England."

"I was, for a season." Eliese kissed her on the cheek. "I came home two years ago."

Right before Germany invaded their land.

"Why didn't you find me?" Josie begged.

Eliese shook her head, her eyes sad. "I couldn't."

"I've missed you."

"I wish I could have told you I was here," Eliese whispered. "But it was too dangerous."

"Does Samuel know?"

Eliese brushed her hands over the buttons on her suit, glancing at the other caregivers in the garden. "I'm here to retrieve the boy." She reached for Clemens, but the boy clung to Josie's shoulder.

"Have you been up all night?" Josie asked.

"Unfortunately."

Several of the caregivers were watching them now. Josie nodded toward the door. "Let's talk inside."

Together they stepped into the colorful crèche, a dozen tables already set to feed the children their lunch.

"What is happening in the theater?" Josie asked.

"The Nazis are registering the Jewish people before they transport them out of Amsterdam."

Josie looked into the brown eyes of the boy in her arms. "Even the children?"

"Yes." She leaned back against the wall, her face shadowed with exhaustion. "They don't want to separate the families."

"You're helping them."

"They didn't give me a choice."

Josie lowered herself into a rocking chair near the front window. Was it possible they might bring the van Gelder family here?

"How is Samuel?" Eliese asked.

Josie shook her head. "I don't know."

Eliese pulled one of the chairs out from under the table and sat beside Josie. "I have to tell you something."

Clemens squirmed, and Josie rocked back on the chair. Whatever it was, she suspected that she didn't want to hear.

"Do you remember William Kingston? He worked with my father."

She remembered. Samuel didn't like the man.

"William and I were married in London."

Josie's toes planted on the carpet, stopping her rock. How could Eliese have rejected Samuel, a man who loved her more than his own life? A man who would have done anything to protect her? "Samuel wanted to marry you."

"Much has happened since we were children."

Josie leaned her head back on the chair. "I don't want anything else to change."

"I wish we could stop it."

"If you married William—" Josie eyed her curiously—"why did you return to Holland?"

Eliese looked at Clemens again before meeting her eye. "I had to find a place to live . . . for me and my son."

Her words lodged in Josie's mind. Eliese, her childhood friend. A wife and now a mother. She couldn't process it all.

"Where is William now?"

"New York," Eliese said. "With the new laws, Samuel wouldn't have been allowed to marry me anyway."

"Samuel doesn't care much about the Nazi laws."

Eliese glanced at the front window as if their occupiers stood right outside. "We can't talk like that anymore."

"I really have missed you," Josie said. "I've missed how things used to be."

Eliese nodded sadly, reaching her arms out again. "We must get you back to your mama."

Clemens buried his head into Josie's shoulder. "He's terrified."

"Can you carry him over?" Eliese asked.

Miss Pimentel was in the kitchen, overseeing the lunch preparations, but she would tell Josie to go.

The two women waited for the traffic on Plantage

Middenlaan and then the tram to pass before they hurried across to the theater.

"It's crowded inside," Eliese said when they stepped into the lobby.

Josie shuddered as a guard unlocked the auditorium door. Not only were the Jews brought here, the Nazis had locked them up as if they were in prison.

The auditorium had been gutted and all that remained was a sloped floor surrounded by tall marble columns and balconies. Babies cried across the room—the acoustics carrying sound like they'd once done when an orchestra performed—and the children were shouting as they tried to play with each other, adults shouting back at them to stop the noise.

And the stench. For the rest of her life, Josie would never forget the smell in that theater or hundreds of people crowded together, no rows to separate their mats and bedding. She skimmed the heads, searching for the van Gelder family, but it would be impossible to find them in this sea of people.

"Mama!" Clemens shouted, struggling in Josie's arms.

A woman moved toward them, her own arms outstretched, and when she took her child, Clemens settled into her, content again.

The woman brushed Clemens's bangs out of his eyes. "Thank you for taking care of him."

"It was my pleasure."

The mother inched back, and while Josie was pleased that Clemens was with his family, she didn't want to leave him here, trapped in this squalor. This child, all the children in this place, needed space to play. Air to breathe. Perhaps they would be sent to a camp like Westerbork.

Eliese nodded toward the main door. "It's time to leave."

Josie glanced back, but Clemens and his mother were already lost in this crowd.

"Some days, I wish I could return to Giethoorn," Eliese said. "Paddle out to the lake again."

"Maybe one day," Josie said softly, "we'll take your son."

Eliese smiled.

Josie walked away from her old friend and all the chaos in this place, away from the noise and stench. Unlike the others in the theater, she was allowed to go out into the fresh air, the promise of morning, without anyone stopping her. She, with the thousands of stolen guilders hidden away in her room.

If the guard found out about the money, she had no doubt he and his friends would take her someplace much worse than this. She wanted to be just as strong, but some days it felt like she was the nail on the end of the string, bouncing about instead of landing safely in the glass. And if she landed wrong, the glass would shatter around her.

"Wait!" someone shouted behind her, and she froze between the rails of the tram, the word sounding more like "Halt!" in her ears.

Turning slowly, she saw a middle-aged man in a crumpled suit, sweat pouring down his forehead. What could he want with her?

"Mrs. Kingston says she knows you well."

Josie nodded. "We grew up together."

"My name's Walter Süskind. I'm in charge of registration."

She glanced at his star and then the white band around

his arm. How tragic for a Jewish man to be sending away other Jews.

He scanned the brick buildings across the street. "Where is this crèche?"

Josie pointed toward the windows in front of the tram stop.

"The Schouwburg is almost to capacity," he said.

"It seemed well over capacity to me."

The rail began to vibrate under her feet. In a minute or two, the streetcar would be dividing the crèche and the theater, like a curtain sliding across a stage.

"The children are too loud," Mr. Süskind said, rubbing his hands together as if he were cold. "We need to find a temporary place for them."

"Our director always has room for children."

Josie stepped off the rails seconds before the streetcar arrived. A minute passed, an eternity encased in those sixty seconds, before the streetcar followed the line of overhead wires away from the school.

Mr. Süskind was gone.

Hours later, someone rapped on the main door. Miss Pimentel scanned the room, seeming to make sure everything was in its proper place. Most of the children were playing in the garden while those inside were preparing for their naps.

Miss Pimentel smoothed her hands down the seams of her gray skirt, then opened the door. A German officer stood on the stoop, his honey-brown hair parted at the side and combed neatly back, the front pocket on his olive-green uniform coat gleaming from its ornaments of metal. Thirty children were lined up along the sidewalk behind him, the oldest children carrying the youngest ones.

The officer gave Miss Pimentel a brisk nod. "These children will be staying here until they are transported."

"They are welcome to stay."

He moved away from the door, but Miss Pimentel stopped him. "Of course, we will need supplies to care for them."

He turned back. "What sort of supplies?"

"Extra rations and nappies and rollaway beds with sheets for each child."

The officer nodded toward the line behind him. "They have bedrolls."

"Children cannot sleep on a bedroll," Miss Pimentel said, properly appalled, and Josie admired the strength in her voice, as if this really were her kingdom. "We keep order in this crèche, Herr . . ."

"Hauptsturmführer," he said, scanning her blouse as if searching for a yellow star. "Hauptsturmführer aus der Fünten."

"As an officer in the *Schutzstaffel*, you must understand the need for order. And supplies to care for the people in your care."

He shook his head. "These are children. Filthy Jews."

"Even the Jewish people need to sleep." Josie could hear the sarcasm in the woman's words, but if he realized she was mocking him, he didn't reprimand her.

"We will get you the supplies."

"Then you may bring us as many children as you'd like," she said as if she had a choice.

The officer ducked outside long before the children finished filing through the door.

Josie scanned their heads until she saw Clemens with one of the older kids. He reached his arms out to her, and she reached back, welcoming him and all the children into Miss Pimentel's kingdom.

SEVENTEEN

The top on my convertible down, my long hair blows in the wind as I cross the Hudson, passing by a Dutch Reformed church in the hills that looks as if it fell asleep around the same time as Rip van Winkle and never awakened.

The Craig House property is located behind a gate, outside the town of Beacon. Branches dip low over my car as I park, the wind puppeteering a dance of sunlight across the black hood and seat. After securing the gray top, I squeeze past the gate, through a space carved out for pedestrians, and walk up the overgrown lane.

The weeds transport me back to Africa, the motorcycle ride across that treacherous path to Mityana. I find myself scanning the path for cobras, as if the Hudson River Valley is a hotbed. At least the rattlesnakes here make some noise before they strike. All I need is one rattle, and I'll climb any one of these trees in record time.

The abandoned Craig House, I'd read online, is a Victorian mansion originally built by a Civil War officer. Where I grew up, Victorian homes were painted bright colors and hosted large front porches where one could settle in with a friend or two and a pitcher of icy lemonade. The brown bones of the house before me, with its crumbling bricks and dark spires, are gothic, the creepy sort that welcomes ghosts instead of friends through the front door.

Or perhaps its ghosts are imprisoned inside.

A hundred years ago, this house was turned into a posh psychiatric hospital, the residence of renowned people like Zelda Fitzgerald and Rosemary Kennedy. Whatever happened here with Peter, it seems Marcella wants to erase it from the Kingston family story.

I can't change the past now, but the truth—like Landon said—has the power to set one free. Does the truth have the power to set an entire family free?

I'll never know unless I keep digging.

The house is falling apart, weeds growing through the crumbling front steps, but the view from the porch is incredible, from the sprawling Hudson River Valley to the rolling Catskills in the distance. A golf course once traversed these green hills, I'd read last night, since the philosophy of this place had been to combine therapy with plenty of luxury and leisure to heal the mind.

My phone chimes and I look down to see a picture of

Faith, my sunglasses perched on her head, her smile lighting the screen.

She misses you.

I return a text to Landon. Tell her I miss her too.

And I wonder if Landon might miss me just a bit as well, because the truth is I wish I could fly back to Uganda to spend a few more days with him.

I hired someone to help at the nursery today. She's not a nurse but she used to assist the doctors at a clinic in Kampala.

I'm glad, Landon. That will be good for all of you.

It will certainly make me feel better when I come home. Or my second home . . .

Home. It's a strange word, especially looking around at this mansion and then the outbuildings where hundreds of people once lived and worked and played but probably never felt at home.

Or, perhaps, some of them found themselves in this eerie place.

Did Peter die here at the hospital or did he return home before he passed away? Marcella would have been in her twenties when he died, already a mother herself.

Back in Uganda, Landon spoke about the glimpses of heaven as home, and that still resonates with me. Perhaps we're not supposed to really feel completely at home anywhere in this world. Perhaps this longing in our hearts, in my heart, is for more than a glimpse of heaven. It's the longing for an everlasting home.

The hum of a motor breezes over the hill. Turning, I see a Rhino motor cart cruising toward me, an elderly woman at

MELANIE DOBSON

its helm. She hops out with a Tigger-like spring as she slides ruby-red sunglasses up to top off her short white hair.

Then both her hands slide down, anchoring themselves on her petite hips. "This is private property."

I move quickly down the steps. "I'm sorry—"

She tilts her head slightly, studying me as I walk toward her. "What are you looking for?"

The truth, I want to say, but it won't make any sense to this woman.

She turns back to the old house. "A lot of people who visit are just curious, but some people are searching for answers."

"My great-grandfather was a guest—a patient—here about fifty years ago. I want to know what happened to him."

"What was his name?" she asks.

"Peter Ziegler."

Something changes in her face, a tightening of her lips. "You're a Kingston."

"Yes," I say slowly, suspecting that she might not approve. "My name is Ava."

She checks her watch. "It's teatime. I don't have any fancy sandwiches, but you're welcome to join me for something to drink."

I climb into the passenger side of the Rhino as she introduces herself—Stella Martin—and cling to the roll bar as we bump over moss-covered rocks and sticks in our path, as if a storm has torn through this property recently and no one bothered to pick up the debris.

Set back in the trees is a row of small houses, most of

172

them the size of a double-wide, and we arrive at one painted white with a welcoming porch spread across the front, two wooden rocking chairs ready for company.

"The hospital closed in 1999," Stella says, parking the motor cart under a canopy. "I worked as a nurse, and now the people who own the house let me stay on as a caretaker of sorts."

"And a watchdog?"

The skin around her mouth crinkles into a smile. "Nothing happens on this property without my knowing it."

"Were you here in 1967?" I ask as we walk through the tall grass and up onto the porch.

She nods, holding the front door open for me.

"So you knew Peter . . ."

"Everyone here knew Mr. Ziegler."

Neat stacks of magazines— home decor, entertainment, medical journals—cover the glass coffee table in her small living room. She steps through a doorframe into the kitchen, and I hear the click of an electric pot.

Stella, I hope, doesn't have any reason to hide information from me.

Minutes later she delivers two mugs, tea bags steeping inside each one, and hands both of them to me. Then she returns to the kitchen for a plate with shortbread cookies, directing me back outside to the porch.

The pitched roof of the mansion slants over the hill above us, and when she speaks again, she sounds sad. "Dr. Slocum insisted that we stop every afternoon for tea, like we worked at Buckingham Palace."

"Do you miss the hospital?"

"Very much. Most of the patients who came here simply needed a friend."

"And you were their friend?"

"I listened, just like Dr. Slocum and the others who worked with us." She takes one of the mugs from my hand as we sit on rockers. "They probably wouldn't serve green tea to the queen, but I prefer it."

I take a sip and taste jasmine in it, like Landon can taste the homeland in his coffee. "The queen would drink it if she tasted this."

Stella lifts her mug.

"Do you know why Peter was admitted to Craig House?" I ask.

"I don't know the particulars, although he clearly needed a quiet place and a steady routine. He told the most outrageous stories that entertained the other patients. He was a kind man, but . . ."

I lean forward, waiting for her to continue.

"Mr. Ziegler was easily agitated when he wasn't painting. The art studio gave him a bit of solace until . . ."

"Until what?"

She eyes me curiously. "Your family didn't tell you what happened?"

"Most of my family doesn't like me, and those who do won't talk about him."

She glances down at the cookies and then back up at the mansion as if she's deciding whether or not to gift me with this story. "Some memories can be faulty."

My mind flashes back to the nightmare that haunts

me. My own faulty memories from childhood. "I want to understand."

"Some patients are impossible to forget, especially those who take their own lives."

The mug slips out of my hand, shattering into pieces on the floor, green tea splashing across the boards. I race inside for a towel, my hands craving a task, any task at the moment. Cleaning up this tea is at the top of my list.

"I'm sorry," I say, dabbing the floor as she collects the shards of ceramic and tidies them into a pile.

"I'm sorry that I had to be the one to tell you," she says. "He shot himself in the studio."

But I don't want her to apologize. I want my family to be honest with me, about the good and bad from the past. I want the truth from people who are supposed to be on the same side, not fighting against me.

"The residents were allowed to have guns?"

"No," she says. "But Mr. Ziegler was a brilliant and wealthy man. It wouldn't have been hard to convince one of the workers to buy it for him."

"He must have been extremely ill."

"His conscience, I fear, was his worst enemy." She leans back against her chair, staring at the broken ceramic. "Would you like to see his final painting?"

My heart begins to race. "Very much."

She accommodates me, driving me back up the hill in her Rhino, then between the mansion and an empty swimming pool green from algae.

The back door of the mansion is locked, but Stella slips a key out of her pocket and opens it. I was expecting broken panels and rotting furniture and a lacquer of dust, but the formal living room and library smell like lemon oil and pine. Each piece of antique furniture reflects a sheen from the gloss, the high-back chairs upholstered in cheery yellows and blues. Even the dining hall off the foyer, with its long table, looks as if it were prepared to host a banquet. I feel, for a moment, as if we've stepped back several decades in time.

"You've taken good care of this house," I say.

She gives me a sheepish grin, her hazel eyes gleaming like the furniture gloss. "Let's keep it between you and me."

"The owner doesn't know you're coming inside?"

She shrugs. "He's more concerned about the land than this house."

The memories that Stella must have accumulated here. No wonder she wants to keep it all in good order.

She points toward a wide staircase lined by dark panels. "The studio is upstairs."

We pad up the worn steps, like the hundreds of patients and staff before us.

"Dr. Slocum tried to display at least one piece from each resident who spent time here," she says. "But he refused to show any of Mr. Ziegler's work."

Stella opens a door on the top floor, and we walk into a gallery with dozens of paintings along the paneled walls, some landscapes, others portraits, some of strange shapes or chunky figures. She presses a wide panel between two of the paintings, and it pops out toward us.

I stare at the gap in the wall.

"Come along." She flips on a flashlight before turning

sideways and squeezing through a narrow corridor. The creepiness of this old house has multiplied exponentially, but one thing I've learned as the director of the Kingston Family Foundation is that I can't rely completely on someone else's account. I need to search for information on my own.

So I follow Stella and her light back about four feet behind the wall until the hall opens up into a room. She hands me the flashlight as she searches through the spines of at least twenty canvases, all of them resting in a bundle on the floor. Tall shelves frame this space, and on each one are cardboard boxes labeled with the names of medication.

Dr. Slocum, it seems, was a smart man to hide the medicine. But why did he keep my great-grandfather's artwork in here?

Stella slides one of the canvases out. "Mr. Ziegler used a pseudonym."

"Are you certain this is his work?"

She turns it slowly, no need to convince me anymore. It's a self-portrait of sorts, Peter's face a pasty white. And he's staring at something on the ground, a pile of what looks like leaves soaking in a puddle of blood.

Behind his shoulder is another man, his face partially obscured by the shadows. On the forehead of each man, in the same shade of red, is a swastika.

My stomach rolls.

Stella nods toward the blood-soaked pile in the painting. "Do you know what that is?"

I lean closer, studying what I thought were leaves. "It looks like money."

Stella turns the canvas quickly, but not before I see his

pseudonym inscribed in black. Daan Kooiman, that was the name Peter used.

The Kingston family, I suspect, would do almost anything to keep this artwork away from the public. And to keep my great-grandfather quiet.

EIGHTEEN

JOSIE

AMSTERDAM

JULY 1942

Josie tried to imagine silky threads of a cocoon woven around the nursery, protecting everyone inside. Tried to pretend that all was well. But when Klaas paid a visit to the crèche, the strands in her mind began to unravel.

They slipped out into the garden of the college, the hedge separating them from the fifty or so children who had taken up residence at the crèche. The Nazis had relocated their former children to another nursery so those waiting for transport could spend both day and night here.

Klaas looked handsome in his brown plaid suit, blond hair creeping down over his collar, while she wore her gray dress and apron. As plain as one of the buzzards who flew overhead.

"Eliese has returned home," she said as they sat on a bench together.

"A rotten time for her to come back." He twisted a tweed cap in his hands. "Does Samuel know?"

"I haven't seen him since we returned from Giethoorn." When she shifted on the bench, the white handkerchief slipped down her forehead, and she untied it quickly, letting it drop to her lap. Her brother would be devastated when he found out that Eliese was now Mrs. Kingston. "Have you talked to him?"

"No." His gaze wandered to the hedge before looking back at her. "He was supposed to take something to friends of ours, but . . ."

She squirmed as he searched her face.

She and Klaas had spent their childhood fluctuating between being enemies and the best of friends, but as adults, Klaas had been like a second brother to her. Had Samuel changed his mind and told Klaas about the delivery to Amersfoort? Her brother was keeping plenty of things secret from her—he hadn't even told her that she was carrying money until she'd found out in Maastricht.

Klaas leaned forward. "I thought he'd delivered it, but . . . neither our friends nor I have seen him. I'm worried about him, Josie."

She nodded. "I'm worried about him too."

"I went to see him at the bank, but his manager said they received a notice that Samuel had been relocated to Germany."

She didn't believe for a moment that Samuel had gone to work at one of the German factories. He would go underground long before he boarded a train headed east.

But then again, she'd heard rumors of men who were picked up when they were riding a train to another destination. Had the Nazis taken Samuel away while he was trying to hide?

"He didn't say anything about Germany," she insisted. "He—"

Klaas leaned forward. "What did he say?"

She almost told him about the envelope, to reassure him that everything was as fine as it could be, but something in the way he was asking, the urgency in his voice, silenced her.

"What did Samuel say when he left Giethoorn?" he repeated, snapping her back to their conversation.

"That he would see me soon."

Klaas crossed his legs, his wingtip shoe propped over the hem of his trousers. "I don't think he's in a German factory."

She glanced down at her hands. "Neither do I."

"This delivery," he said slowly. "It was paramount to our work."

"What work?" she asked, trying to maintain her innocence, but Klaas knew her better than almost anyone. She couldn't lie to him.

"You know, Jozefien." Not a question, a simple declaration that spoke volumes.

Several planes flew overhead, the black swastika scarring their sides.

"When will it stop, Klaas?" she whispered.

"I fear it hasn't actually begun."

Her gaze slid down to her hand, entwined in Klaas's. When had he reached for it?

Or perhaps she had reached for his.

"Did Samuel give you anything?" he asked.

They weren't children anymore, prone to childish pouting and rage. If she cared for Klaas, truly cared for him, perhaps she would have to trust him.

But if she told him the truth, the Nazis might come for him too. The contents inside that envelope were dangerous to everyone she cared about.

"I must go," she said as she shook her hand free. Then she fled for the door, a hundred emotions warring within her.

She couldn't sort through her feelings now, didn't want to feel anything if she was honest with herself. They had to survive this war first.

Later she and Klaas could sort things out between them.

The younger children slept in cribs, under the mosaic window of seashells that Miss Pimentel refused to cover. Lamplight crept out through the stained glass each evening, but no one in the courtyard had complained to the authorities. Josie suspected that the director would be just fine if the Allied pilots could see the glow as they flew over Amsterdam.

The older children, dressed in white nightshirts, crowded around Josie's feet as she prepared to tell them a story. A truck engine rumbled outside the front window, soldiers probably bringing more people to the theater, but the children couldn't see beyond the black sheet.

How long these children would be here, no one knew. Nor did Josie understand how the Nazis could possibly fit another adult inside the overcrowded theater.

One of the boys glanced toward the blackout curtain, reminding her of Klaas as a child, always in search of mischief. If light slipped out on this side of the crèche, the guard across the street might break their window.

Josie leaned toward the boy, smiling. "Do you like to explore?"

He nodded slowly, his attention diverted back at her.

"Who would like to go on an adventure before bed?" she asked the other children.

Some of them raised their hands; others watched with wide eyes in expectation for the adventure about to unfold. It was a grand adventure they would take together, she told them, about a little girl and boy who'd never seen the ocean.

About half the children raised their hands when she asked if they'd been to the North Sea. The Dutch hadn't been able to defeat the Nazis, but centuries ago, they'd conquered the threatening sea, reclaiming the land.

"The parents of this boy and girl were gone, so they were spending the night with their favorite auntie in Amsterdam. Long after midnight, she woke them up in a flurry, and they boarded a train at the central station. What they didn't know was that this was a special train, a magical train, that could fly up into the sky. Their noses pressed against the glass, the children whirled through the stars and circled the moon and then dove gracefully back down to the earth, splashing into the North Sea."

One of the children gasped, and Josie's voice lowered to a whisper.

"But they had to be quiet, very quiet, if they were to see what was underneath the ocean, for even the slightest noise would scare the sea creatures away."

The children at her feet grew still, none of them daring to squirm.

"The train plunged into the depths of the ocean, and they were just in time."

"In time for what?" a boy blurted.

His neighbor elbowed him. "You're supposed to be quiet."

National Geographic magazines packed her father's shelves in Giethoorn, one with illustrations of the Bathysphere's magical descent into the ocean. Josie decided to take the children at her feet on an imaginary dive, describing their very own parade of whales and squid and octopuses—all the creatures she could remember from her father's magazines, all in brilliant colors. As if God kept some of His masterpieces on display in this private gallery to show those who searched for Him in the depths.

No one knew fully what God was doing beneath the surface.

When Josie finished her story, Miss Pimentel stepped beside her. All the children folded their hands, and they repeated the familiar Dutch prayer together.

"We fold our hands, close our eyes, as we quietly say our prayer to You, Lord. Take care of me. Bless us all."

"Amen," one of the youngest girls shouted at the end.

The children slipped into their beds, their belongings tucked beneath the cots. Josie still kept her room in the college, but Dr. van Hulst had excused her from all her classes. Most nights she slept down here with the children.

Sometime during the night, she was awakened by a knock, the brisk sound on the front door a bitter one. Süskind or Eliese usually brought any new children to them in the morning, after they completed registration.

She waited on the edge of her cot as Miss Pimentel opened the front door.

"Guten Abend." Fünten didn't even attempt to muffle his voice at this late hour.

Several of the children stirred, but no one cried. They were silent whenever Fünten or one of his uniformed men visited the crèche.

Miss Pimentel stepped outside to speak with him, closing the door behind her, and Josie peered around the blackout curtains. Two trucks were parked outside the theater, the familiar queue on the sidewalk, except these people were moving out of the theater instead of going inside.

Seconds later, Miss Pimentel returned, a slip of paper in hand. "They are transporting some of the families out of Amsterdam."

"Where are they going?"

"I don't know." Miss Pimentel held out the paper with a list of names. "Their parents are waiting for them outside."

Josie nodded, unable to speak. How could she when she'd become part of this wicked scheme to rid their city, their country, of its children?

But at least the Nazis were keeping the families together. If they were being transported to Kamp Westerbork, these children would have plenty of space to play in the forests and heather fields and perhaps even a canal.

Miss Pimentel shone a flashlight on the list, and Josie skimmed the eleven names. She couldn't think, couldn't show the sadness that stirred inside her. A mask was what she needed, one of her own making. She needed to send these children off with the reminder of God's love no matter the wickedness of man.

Josie began to collect the older ones, waking the boy who'd been watching the window.

"Are we going to the sea?" he asked.

"Not tonight. You're going to a camp."

He didn't move.

She leaned down, whispering. "And your parents are traveling with you."

He reached for his knapsack under the cot and sprang to his feet.

While Miss Pimentel gathered the other children, Josie prepared a bottle for Clemens, the youngest child on their list. She mixed powdered milk with water and a paregoric tincture so he wouldn't cry, sweeping the bottle into his mouth before she lifted him from the crib.

With Clemens in her arms and ten other children behind her, Josie led them across the street, sheep following their shepherd. None of them were permitted to talk, their words stolen away by men who mandated quiet above all else. Order. Keet had told her never to cry, but tears slipped unbidden down her cheeks as she quietly handed Clemens back to his mother.

While the other children found their parents, she turned her face, wiped her tears.

Mr. Süskind counted the people—his people—one more time before they boarded, matching up the names on the registration cards. And she realized that she was no different from him or Eliese. They were working together to turn their fellow countrymen over to Hitler's men.

Mr. Süskind nodded to her, sending her on her way, but Josie didn't go far. She stood behind the gate, watching until the trucks carrying their children—*her* children for a season—were gone.

Ten empty beds and a crib stood inside the crèche now. She wanted to believe that the children who'd slept there an hour ago were going to a better place, a camp with much better conditions than the overcrowded theater, but even though they were with their families, she feared their parents couldn't protect them now.

If only they—she and her fellow countrymen—could work together to help these children find a safe place away from the Nazis. Instead of sending them away, she wished they could find a place where these children could thrive until the Germans returned home.

NINETEEN

ELIESE

At precisely 4:45 in the morning, an hour before the first train left Amsterdam Centraal, Eliese climbed into the front seat between Hauptsturmführer Fünten and the driver. One of six trucks in a convoy headed to the station.

For almost three months now, the Nazis had been escorting the Jewish people away from the theater, transporting them to Kamp Westerbork. This morning, the commandant—with help from the Jewish Council—was deporting more than a hundred people before curfew ended so only those citizens who awakened before dawn could see the trucks from their windows, if they happened to look beyond the curtains that blocked their view.

No one could see the people crammed together inside these trucks, enveloped by the canvas sides.

Even though Eliese wore a yellow star on her sweater, none of the inhabitants at the theater spoke to her beyond what was required at registration. She'd crossed a line in their minds, become a traitor like the NSB who supported their oppressors.

She would stop the Nazis if she could, but she was powerless to fight against them. All she had was Puttkammer's stamp—and this job—to save her and her family. If those crowded behind her on the bed of this truck had the opportunity to buy a stamp, they would do it as well.

Fünten leaned toward her, his leg pressed against hers on the seat, the silver skull on his visor dipping toward her. "You are a hard worker, Fräulein."

"Fräu—"

But the commandant didn't care if she was married. He was the cat and she was a mouse—or rat—to do with as he pleased.

"I have much admiration for those who work hard," he said. "This work will set you free. It will set us all free."

Eliese glanced toward the driver, the brim of his peaked soldier's cap low on his forehead. He'd be no help if Fünten tried to harm her.

The commandant's hand began to wander, and she lifted it off her leg. "Do you have a wife, Commander?"

He crushed her hand. "It does not matter."

"It would matter to her."

Fünten laughed at her appeal, as if she were a child.

The driver stopped the truck in front of the station's clock tower and hopped out. She scooted to the far side of the seat, but Fünten reached for her arm and she feared what might come next.

"We have work to do," she said.

Fünten was a man of work, a man of principle. He might hurt her later, in secret, but when someone rapped on the window, he released her and didn't speak to her again.

Eliese sat by herself on the musty passenger train to Kamp Westerbork, a designated escort who'd been chosen by the Jewish Council to ensure everyone on Mr. Süskind's list arrived safely, as if someone might attempt to jump off along the way.

A German commander oversaw Westerbork on the eastern edge of Holland, but like registration at the theater, the Jewish people were in charge of the day-to-day operations. Eliese was relieved to see that, unlike the Jewish theater, these people had plenty of space.

Soldiers guarded the encampment from watchtowers, but the residents could roam onto the heath and they had actual barracks and latrines inside the barbed wire fence. Some families even lived in wooden houses along the perimeter. It wasn't plush, but neither was it much different from the Girl Guide camp she'd attended with Josie.

At least they seemed to have some amenities here. A hairdresser. A theater. A home for the orphaned children.

Eliese handed the list of names to camp registrars, who began counting and registering the new residents. Those who'd arrived on the train pushed wheelbarrows filled with their luggage up to registration; then Dutch porters escorted them to their new housing assignments.

When Eliese stepped back outside, the passenger train was gone and a new train had arrived, this one with windowless cattle cars. Dozens of people congregated around the train's platform, but instead of wheelbarrows filled with their things, they carried only one bag each, helped along by the same stoic porters if they needed assistance.

"Where is this train going?" Eliese asked a porter.

"East."

As she eyed the bronze cars, her mind ticked through names on the ledger back home, the listings of all the metal, chemical, and oil companies her father had helped grow. "For supplies?"

"No," he said, nodding toward the waiting men and women. "To relocate some of our residents to a German camp."

"I thought they stayed here—"

"A few are permanent, but most are just guests, passing through."

"They are putting them into cattle cars?" she asked, horrified at the thought.

"All the other trains are being used someplace else."

A wind blew over the heath, and she rubbed her arms.

No wonder her father was so insistent that they were on Puttkammer's list. They'd already lived in Germany, and while she didn't remember much, Papa had said it was better to stay in Holland where the Dutch Jewish Council—instead of the Germans—oversaw the well-being of their people.

"I'm supposed to return to Amsterdam this afternoon," she said.

"You'll have to find a ride to the station in Hooghalen."

Eliese scanned the crowd until her gaze landed on someone she knew. Mrs. Pon, the kind woman who'd hosted her after she arrived from Germany. The woman had invited her back summer after summer, saying that Eliese was like a daughter since she didn't have any children of her own. Her pretty hair had turned wiry with gray since Eliese had seen her, three years past, and her face had aged from the sun.

This morning she was holding the hands of a boy and a girl, each about five or six years of age, both of them wearing wooden shoes on their feet.

Eliese hurried toward her and kissed her cheek, relieved to find a friend, but the older woman didn't return her kiss or her smile.

"I'd hoped they wouldn't send for you," Mrs. Pon said sadly.

"They didn't. I'm living in Amsterdam now, with my father and my son."

"You and Samuel—"

Eliese stopped her. "William Kingston is my husband. An American."

"Ah."

"Why aren't you in Giethoorn?" Eliese asked, wishing they could spend the afternoon sipping warm Chocomel inside her cottage, Mrs. Pon sharing memories of her husband, asking Eliese about her dreams for the future.

Mrs. Pon nodded back toward a two-story building separated from the rest of the camp. "I've been working at the hospital."

Eliese glanced at the waiting train behind them, an anchor sinking in her chest. "Are you leaving for Germany?"

The older woman shook her head. "They need me to stay here and work, but these two brave soldiers—" she smiled down at both of the children as if they were the best of friends—"they've been assigned to go on ahead."

"We'll be waiting for her at the next camp," the boy explained.

Mrs. Pon smoothed his wavy hair. "I'll be coming as soon as I can."

A man in blue overalls blew a whistle and people began to queue up on the platform.

Mrs. Pon kissed each of the children's cheeks. "Go ahead now. I'll watch you from here."

The children moved forward without her, each carrying a bedroll and suitcase.

Eliese glanced around them. "Who's escorting them on the train?"

"None of the orphans are accompanied when they leave."

A porter prodded the children toward an open door, and the tremors of a fracture, foreboding, crept across Eliese's skin. "Surely the Germans will have nurses or teachers waiting for them at the next camp."

"I'm not so certain. . . ."

Mrs. Pon waved one more time before the porter shut the door and scribbled *46 Pers* in chalk on the side of the train so whoever opened its door would know exactly how many people were aboard.

On the front of the train, someone had written *Auschwitz*. She knew the name of that Polish town from her father's work. I. G. Farben had built a rubber and oil factory there in preparation for a war.

"A train comes every Tuesday and then leaves with more than two thousand people to meet the German quota," Mrs. Pon whispered. "We're told they are going to a nicer camp, but no one's ever returned with a report."

Was Mrs. Pon lying to her about the camp on the other side, like Eliese had lied to the people coming into the theater? As more children were loaded onto the train, all of them without an adult, Eliese couldn't imagine that they were going to a nicer place. It seemed that it would be better for them to stay here in the care of a woman like Mrs. Pon.

"Who do they transport?" Eliese asked.

"A member of the Jewish Council submits a list. Those who've been caught in hiding are transported first. And the rest of them—there doesn't seem to be much reasoning over who else is taken away."

"Except those with a stamp," Eliese said. "They won't be transported."

Mrs. Pon tilted her head. "A stamp?"

Eliese nodded. "From Puttkammer."

"People arrive with all sorts of promises, but the Nazis don't care about things like stamps."

Eliese wanted to argue with her, but there was no sense arguing if her friend had never heard of Mr. Puttkammer and his executive list.

A shuffle nearby, and Eliese turned to see an older man being dragged by a guard. The man refused to walk, refused to board the train.

Eliese turned away when the guard reached for his gun, but she heard the shot, Mrs. Pon's gasp. Then a stillness reigned over the camp as one of the porters found a hand-cart and put the body on it. He didn't wheel it away—it was almost as if he wanted the others to see what would happen if they tried to resist.

Her hands trembling, Eliese stood with the crowd and waited until carriage doors clanged shut, bolted from the outside. Then steam poured from the engine as the train headed east.

She could hear the faintest sound under the clatter of wheels, people singing on the other side of metal walls.

"They always sing when they leave," Mrs. Pon said.

The mood was somber in the minutes after the train left, but slowly it began to change. As people trickled away from the platform, returning to their work, they began to sing as well, a wave of relief cresting on the tide. They all had at least one more week at Westerbork.

"I'd like to mail you a gift," Eliese said. "Perhaps clothing . . ."

Mrs. Pon studied her. "We need food for the children."

"I will send you food."

Mrs. Pon kissed Eliese on both cheeks before returning to the hospital.

Eliese reached for her purse and unzipped it, searching the folds for her identity card that she'd tucked into the inner pocket. She didn't take it out, but the prized green stamp signed by Puttkammer marked the inside. And Mr. Puttkammer promised to keep the people on his list safe.

She showed her identity card at the gate, and a guard waved her past the barbed wire to speak with the commandant about a train ride home.

The Nazis did care about these stamps. That's why she and Mr. Süskind and the members of the Jewish Council hadn't been deported like the other Jews.

TWENTY

Bishara Café, one of three stateside coffee shops that Landon and Kendall own, is located in Portland's upscale district called the Pearl. I've had enough surprises this week, so instead of just showing up, I scheduled a time to meet with Landon's sister.

A series of slate boards hang on each of the whitewashed brick walls, displaying Bible verses written in chalk. A rustic wooden bar stretches along an interior window, overlooking their roasting floor, and outside the front window are two tables, streams of drizzle traversing the teak slabs.

Whatever I find here, I hope it confirms that Bishara Coffee & Café is an organization that the foundation can support.

In lieu of coffee, I order a glass of the lavender kombucha they have on tap, a fizzy tea drink that Portlanders seem to have embraced along with their coffee. Sitting on a barstool, I watch two workers dump Ugandan beans out of burlap bags into a roaster, then weigh and package up the roasted beans into paper sacks. I like this bit of transparency, watching the coffee being roasted before it's served.

Last night, on my flight to Portland, I sent Paul an email, asking about the Kingston biography he'd ordered, but I haven't heard back from him yet. Instead of spending my plane ride researching another organization for the foundation, I dug for answers about what happened to Peter Ziegler and William Kingston. And to find out why Peter had painted a self-portrait with a swastika on his forehead.

According to *Darkness Before Dawn*, Peter had been a German Jew. Why would he embrace the Nazi cause?

The materials I found online celebrated the forward thinking of the Kingston-Ziegler conglomeration, demonstrating how they invested in dozens of industries that grew Europe and the United States after the Depression and then the success of their glass business after World War II, but information about their personal lives was lacking. In fact, the online history about the Kingston family sounded the exact same on a variety of websites, as if someone cut and pasted the information directly from Wikipedia. As if the family's version of events, backed by money and the endless resources of manpower and marketing, had overtaken the online world as well.

Was it possible for the Kingston family—the Kingston money—to rewrite history?

As I wait for Kendall to arrive, I google the Mori Men, the society where the author of *Darkest Before Dawn* said William and Peter met in 1932. The Order of the Memento

Mori—that was the full name of it. The meaning in Latin: *Remember that you have to die.*

I rub my hands over my arms. Who came up with that name?

A scary-looking building appears on the screen, the stone on its face blushing a pale red as if embarrassed by whatever secrets it holds inside.

The Crypt. That's what the students called their clubhouse.

The society was disbanded twenty years ago, but this was where the Ziegler and Kingston families were united. The Mori Men, I read, were an elite group of seniors at Cambridge University, their society more than a hundred years old with roots—according to legend—in the German Illuminati, but doctrines of this society seem murky.

Only twelve were picked each year to pledge, like they were disciples following a leader whose name I can't seem to find recorded online. After graduation, the men were released to succeed in the world, never straying too far from their brotherhood. Or from whatever they had pledged.

I sip the sour kombucha, then pull out my cell phone. Paul still hasn't answered my email, and the Kingston Bibliotheek closes in an hour, so I decide to call. If he's received the biography, I'm hoping he can overnight it to Portland.

A woman named Liesbeth answers for the library, and I ask to speak with Mr. Epker.

"I'm sorry," Liesbeth says. "He has resigned his position."

"But the library just opened . . ."

"We will be hiring a new curator soon."

My mind spins. It doesn't make sense that he would resign a week after the grand opening.

When I explain that I'm Marcella's granddaughter, Liesbeth is instantly willing to help however she can.

"Mr. Epker said that you would be receiving a rare book about our family's history. I was trying to locate it."

"Do you know the name of this book?" she asks.

"No—"

"I would be glad to search for it."

I thank her and end the call as I see a woman in a linen blazer and skirt walking through the doors. Her hair is piled back in a classic bun, and she is wearing chic tortoiseshell glasses over eyes that display no makeup except mascara.

"You must be Ava," she says, her hand outstretched, and I see a glimpse of Landon in her smile.

I decide right away that I like her.

She sits down beside me. "So you've already met my brother."

"Yes, it was quite an adventure."

"It seems you caught him by surprise." Kendall places her satchel on the bar top. "He didn't know I applied for a grant."

"I figured that out pretty quickly."

"I would have told him, if I'd known we were being considered for it." A barista sets a latte down beside her. "Not that you should have told us."

"You'd be surprised to hear the kinds of things we find when we simply show up."

"It's unfortunate for all of us working in the nonprofit world when people try to deceive."

"I agree."

She takes a sip of her drink. "I hope Landon didn't chase you off the plantation."

"No." I laugh. "He thought I was on a volunteer team arriving that day, so he put me to work."

"The fact that you're here . . . I hope it means it wasn't a colossal fail."

"It wasn't. You and Landon seem to have created a sustainable model to employ a number of people. I'm glad I visited." I pull out the dossier from my bag and set it between us. "Why did you apply for this grant?"

"I've applied for a number of grants over the years with no luck," she says. "My great-grandmother lived in Amsterdam during the war, and she inspired both Landon and me to be creative in how we help others. When I saw your foundation was opening a library in Amsterdam, I was hoping it might be a fit."

"I talked with your brother at length, but I wondered if you could tell me what your vision is for Bishara."

She nods. "Both Landon and I want to provide a regular income for our partners in Africa and use our profits to educate and provide housing and food and medicine for the children in our care. We are followers of Christ, so we try to line up our work with our faith."

"Your brother isn't very excited about the possibility of a grant."

"He's excited about the possibility of expanding Bishara. He'll just want to vet your foundation in his own way."

"Fair enough."

She pulls a narrow white binder out of her satchel and hands it to me. "Here's a copy of our most recent financials."

I tuck it into my bag. "Thank you."

"One of our top values is integrity, so we roast the coffee for this store right here." She points at the rain-soaked window leading outside. "But we do the rest of our roasting and distribution in Portland's Eastside. Would you like a tour of our operations?"

"Absolutely."

"It's too bad you're not staying for the weekend," she says.

"Why's that?"

"Landon comes home on Sunday night, and he gives the best tours."

Again I'm tempted to stay on until Monday, but I realize slowly that I wouldn't be doing it for the foundation. I'm supposed to remain unbiased as the director, but my neutrality, I fear, is slipping away.

Better that I'm gone long before Sunday.

After Kendall introduces me to her staff at this shop, we rush through the rain and climb into her hybrid Prius. Minutes later we're crossing the Willamette River.

She glances left, nodding toward the ribbing of bridges. "Locals call our city Bridgetown."

I like the concept of a bridge town. All these pieces of concrete and steel trying to mend a gap, bringing together two sides of a city divided by water so it can breathe.

It's easy to divide, but hard to sew a wound back together. Restore something that's been broken. A team of engineers and builders had to work together to unify this chasm for the people of Portland.

The industrial district on this side of the river is very different from the Pearl. Underneath the bridge are dozens of tents to house the homeless, and as we drive east, we pass rows of warehouses separated by boutique shops.

"Portland is a city of bridges, in more ways than one," Kendall says. "Bridges don't solve all our problems, but most people here try to understand each other."

"I think there is much to gain in the trying."

She nods. "Landon and I want to be a bridge of sorts between people who want to help and those who need a hand so they can begin to support themselves and their families."

Kendall parks in a reserved space behind a worn four-story brick building with arched windows that overlook train tracks and a row of other warehouses. Inside the front door is a renovated space that has been turned into another coffee shop with dark wood floors and about eight tables set up near two windowed garage doors that, I assume, open on a sunny day to expand their café.

She guides me around the main counter and an entire new world opens up. Boxes pack the massive shelves in their distribution center. Yellow utility vehicles buzz around like swarming bees, burlap bags and boxes balanced on their tails. Bishara is indeed as expansive an operation as Kendall portrayed in her proposal.

The smells of freshly roasted coffee—honey and butter and Landon's chocolate—seep out of these walls, permeating every crevice in this warehouse. A reminder, I think, of the greater purpose beyond their work.

Kendall waves at one of the employees and then directs me to a carrier built for two passengers, like an indoor Rhino. Stella Martin, I think, would like working here.

I climb onto the seat, and we spend the afternoon touring

the different departments, meeting the core of their team in the States, the people who deliver a taste of Uganda around the world.

At the end of the tour, I breathe the rich aroma of coffee one last time, remembering. "I don't know if I'll ever be able to smell coffee again without thinking about Africa." And about Landon.

"I've never actually been to Africa," Kendall says. The rain has stopped, but clouds have settled in low over this city.

"Why not?"

"I'd go if I absolutely needed to, but the stories that my brother tells . . ." She unlocks the car, and we climb inside her Prius. "If I went to Africa, I'm afraid the Ugandan people would have to take care of me!"

"It's a wonderful thing that you and Landon are doing, on both sides of the world." I close the door. "How did your great-grandmother inspire you to start this?"

"Oma inspires pretty much everyone in her circle." Kendall glances at her watch. "Would you like to meet her?"

"Very much."

Kendall presses the button to start her engine. "We'll have to hurry."

I click the seat belt into the buckle. "Where is she?"

"At the hospital."

I wave my hand. "We don't have to trouble her there."

"She's not *in* the hospital, Ava." Kendall grins at me. "I suppose you'll just have to see."

TWENTY-ONE

ELIESE

AMSTERDAM
SEPTEMBER 1942

The boy and girl from Westerbork—their frightened eyes haunted Eliese all the way back to Amsterdam. What if the Nazis—Dutch or German—loaded Hein onto one of their trains traveling east? What if she had to watch him ride away, alone, with the other children?

Her father was right. She had to do more than keep her son out of sight. She had to find a place for him to hide.

When she returned that afternoon, hours after she usually arrived home from the theater, Papa was gone. She found Hein asleep in his crib as if her father had put him down for a nap before leaving the house. His cheeks were stained red, his blanket damp from tears, his stuffed lamb crushed against his chest.

How long had he been crying?

His breathing was slow, steady, as if he'd exhausted himself.

She brushed her fingers over Hein's forehead, sweeping back a lock of his blond hair. More of it had fallen out on his collection of stuffed animals, leaving a brown patch above his left ear. A doctor should examine him, but there were no Jewish doctors left in Amsterdam and she refused to take him to one at Westerbork. They might have the tools to heal him, but not the power to save his life.

Instead of collapsing on her bed, Eliese ripped off the spread and a pillow, moving back across the corridor into Hein's room and arranging a place to sleep beside his crib.

The other registrars had been dismissed weeks ago, she and Mr. Süskind the only ones left to register those brought to the theater. Working these nights for the past three months, her hours often bleeding into morning, had drained her. Or perhaps it was the burden of her work. How she hated herself for what she had to do.

She kissed her son's cheek before covering herself with the quilt, terrified at the thought of those porters in Westerbork forcing him into a cattle car with other children. It was no longer safe for Hein to stay in their home, but she didn't know where to hide him.

If only William were here to help her, he would know exactly what to do.

Her eyes closed, the lines of William's handsome face etched in her mind, and she tried to escape with him to a happier place, back to their months together in London. He had captured her heart the first time she'd met him, when she was sixteen. He was a decade older and the most handsome man who'd ever expressed interest in spending time with her.

The next year William returned to Amsterdam and show-ered her with gifts from New York, including the turquoise ring she now wore on her hand. But it was more than the gifts that made her heart spin. He'd encouraged her with his words, charmed her with his smile, and then after weeks of working with her father, taking her to dinner each night, he'd asked her to join him in London, spending a few months with the Ziegler family. Papa hesitated at first, but he'd known Peter since grammar school. He trusted the man.

She'd never told her father that Peter and his wife didn't return to London until long after she arrived. But William had cared for her well in the time they were together. Papa wanted her to marry well, and William Kingston was a gentleman.

Hours later, when she woke, Hein was sitting beside her, a stuffed lamb in one of his hands, a ball in the other.

Had he been climbing out of his crib on the nights she was gone?

"I missed you," she said, pulling him into her arms.

Her body ached, but her heart filled with this smallest of pleasure, the joy of having her son at her side. She would miss him dearly, but he had to leave this city before the Nazis realized they'd left a Jewish child behind.

He reached for the ball, his brown eyes skeptical. Then he held up his little lamb as if she couldn't possibly turn down a request from his stuffed animal.

"Mama, play?"

Josie played with the children who were waiting in the crèche; she loved them like they were her own. Perhaps her friend could help her find a hiding place for Hein.

"Yes, little lamb," Eliese said, smiling at him. "Let's play."

"They're sending the children away from Westerbork," she whispered to Mr. Süskind as they waited for Fünten to arrive. "Alone."

The man had a daughter of his own, not much older than Hein. Unlike her father, Mr. Süskind might understand her concerns about leaving a child to fend for himself.

He removed a stack of index cards from the filing cabinet and placed them on the table. "What about their parents?"

"The children I saw didn't seem to have parents."

She waited for Mr. Süskind to reassure her, say the Nazis would never send away children without someone to care for them or that it was only a short journey, wherever they were going. A decent home and school awaited them at the camp on the other end.

Instead, he said nothing.

Fünten walked through the main doors, his tall black boots gleaming in the electric light. And in his eyes was that glint again, a sickening familiarity as he greeted her by her first name.

She wished she could run away with Hein.

Mr. Süskind directed the commandant toward the lobby, talking about logistics for this night. He must have said something funny because Fünten laughed.

How could this Jewish man laugh with a German commander when hundreds of innocent people were imprisoned behind the lobby wall?

While Mr. Süskind entertained him, she kept her head down in the cloakroom, dusting off her typewriter and then straightening the stack of registration cards. Tonight she would have to find a way to talk to Josie, ask her to find a hiding place for Hein.

And she prayed Josie would help.

The doors opened and a family of three—the mother clutching the hand of her young daughter—stepped into the cloakroom, canvas bags hanging over their shoulders.

The van Gelders, they said as Eliese took their identity cards. She fed a new card into the roller of her typewriter and began to type their first names.

Werner, Hanneke, and Esther.

After she typed their birth dates, she removed the card and placed it in her box to file.

"The children are housed across the street," Eliese explained.

Mrs. van Gelder pulled her daughter close to her side, fear raging through her eyes. "I want Esther with me."

"The children have good food and a bed in the crèche," Eliese explained. "And women who will care well for them."

"I still want her here."

Eliese shook her head sadly. "Unfortunately we don't have a choice."

When the little girl started to cry, Mr. Süskind stepped up beside her, urging the girl forward, but she refused to move. What had she seen to make her afraid?

"Take her now," Fünten directed before marching outside.

As Eliese picked up another index card, she turned toward Mr. Süskind. "May I escort her to the crèche?"

With no other registrars, the people in queue would have to wait, but someone needed to take this child across the street, and she wanted to speak with Josie.

"Please," Mr. Süskind said. Then he picked up a card and threaded it into the roller himself. If he continued with registration, she wouldn't have to hurry.

Eliese knelt beside the girl. "You will see your parents soon."

Esther glanced back at Mr. and Mrs. van Gelder and the guard who stood over them. "I don't want to go."

"I promise you will be safe there." Eliese held out her hand, and the girl took it. "We must hurry."

The door to the theater opened, and the commandant stepped back in, glaring at the child. "Why is she still here?"

The pierce of his gaze prodded Esther forward.

Across the street, Miss Pimentel answered the door, and Esther followed her willingly into the nursery for a cup of warm honey milk. Eliese followed as well, searching for Josie among the workers, but she didn't see her friend. The irony, she thought. Hein hadn't been allowed to attend a nursery months ago because of his heritage, and now the crèche was filled with Jewish children.

Miss Pimentel said that Josie was up in her room, resting. Eliese climbed the stairway in the college and knocked on her door.

"I need your help," Eliese said after she slipped inside.

Josie propped herself up on the headboard. "You need to ask the Jewish Council for help."

"I never meant to hurt Samuel." Eliese turned the desk chair around and sat in it. "When I met William, I fell deeply in love."

"You fell deeply into something."

"I'm not asking for help for myself, Josie, but Hein—he hasn't done anything wrong."

Josie's eyes flickered. "How old is your son?"

"Almost three, and he's an easy child." Charming—just like his father. "I'll pay someone handsomely for taking care of him."

"I'll make inquiries," Josie said.

It was all she could ask for.

Eliese glanced at the painting of a remote farmhouse that hung on Josie's wall. "I visited Westerbork this morning."

Josie leaned forward. "What did you find?"

As Eliese told her about the children, the trains, tears pooled in the eyes of her friend.

"I'll find a place for Hein," Josie promised.

"Thank you."

She trailed Josie back down to the nursery, and when they stepped into the classroom, Josie stopped by the door. Then she called out Esther van Gelder's name.

The girl didn't seem to recognize her, but Josie wrapped Esther in her arms.

TWENTY-TWO

Doernbecher Children's Hospital is perched on the side of a steep hill overlooking Portland and the river that cuts through it. Kendall motions me to an elevator and we find two women on the fifth floor, laughing together as if they don't have six or seven decades separating them. As if they are coconspirators in a crime.

The older woman—Landon and Kendall's great-grandmother, I assume—wears black leggings and a loose smock with cartoon tigers splattered across the blazing-orange front. Her silver-white hair is trimmed close to her neck in a short pixie cut, and she steadies herself on a cane striped red and white like a peppermint stick. The younger woman appears to be in her late twenties. Her hair is jet-black, cut short like Mrs. West's, and she carries a huge black tote over the shoulder of her T-shirt.

The older woman reaches for Kendall's hand. "What are you doing here?"

Kendall kisses her cheek. "I wanted to introduce you to a friend. This is Ava Drake, from New York."

Kendall turns toward me. "This is my great-grandmother, though she says the word *great* grates on her nerves, so consider yourself warned. We all call her Oma. And this is Suzanne. She is . . ." Kendall smiles at the woman beside Mrs. West. "Well, what are you exactly?"

Suzanne laughs. "BFF."

"Only if you're being nice," the older woman quips.

"I am always nice!"

"Except when you won't let me order a piece of chocolate cake after all the green stuff you force me to eat for lunch."

Suzanne rolls her eyes. "That cake was like a foot tall."

"And it needed to be eaten."

I try to clamp my jaw shut to keep from laughing. Now I know where Landon gets his spunk.

"Welcome, Ava. I'm Mrs. West," she says as she reaches for my hand. Her fingers are cold, gnarled in places, but her smile is warm. "Would you like to help us?"

"Help you with what?"

I see Landon in her light-brown eyes, except instead of holding out a child, she digs in Suzanne's tote and hands me a wig.

Not that I'm an expert on wigs, but this is no ordinary

hairpiece. It has long yellow tendrils like Rapunzel's though it's made of yarn, a garden of pastel flowers woven into it.

I run my fingers across the top. "What am I supposed to do with this?"

"Come along," she says.

Mrs. West is slightly hunched over her peppermint cane, but the prop does nothing to slow her speed as we follow her up the hallway. Kendall winks at me as if she's privy to a great secret. Even though I don't know what's about to happen, I'm excited to see what Mrs. West has planned.

We follow her and Suzanne into a carnival-colored hospital room, the walls undeterred by a gray mist outside. A young girl is sitting on her hospital bed, watching *Dora the Explorer* on TV. Her bald head glows in the lamplight; her arms are pencil thin.

"Oma!" she exclaims when she sees the woman in front of me.

Mrs. West leans over and gives her a hug. "I've brought friends with me today," she says. "And a gift."

Mrs. West nods at me, and for a moment, I feel like I'm back in Africa, completely out of my element, but perhaps this time I can actually help a child without wounding them in return.

Taking a deep breath, I hold out the wig. "I believe this is for you."

"Tangled!" the girl exclaims, reaching for it.

The other three women giggle with her as she tries it on, the yarn lying lopsided across her left shoulder, faux blonde hair pooling out over pillows.

"How do I look?" she asks, and I wait for Mrs. West to answer until I realize that she's asking me.

"Stunning," I say.

The girl's smile grows even larger, and I realize what a gift this is. Not the yarn and flowers as much as the gift of beauty. Dignity. She doesn't need the wig to be complete, but it makes her feel special. Strong, even, in her weakness.

"Where are your story beads?" Mrs. West asks the girl.

She reaches under her pillow and pulls out a long strand. "I've hidden them."

The colorful beads on her string are all different shapes of hearts and animals. One is a crown.

Mrs. West sits beside the girl on her bed, leaning over the strand. "Tell me about your stories this week."

She shows the older woman a crab bead. "I made Nurse Jenn laugh yesterday."

"Well done."

"And I got a panda for a shot."

Mrs. West points to a yellow emoticon bead, a sad face with a tear. "You had a bad day since I saw you last."

She nods. "They had to tap on my spine."

Mrs. West sighs. "I don't like people tapping on my spine either."

The girl glances at the peppermint cane. "Do you get memory beads?"

"No," she says, looking over at Kendall. "I have something else to help me remember."

"You should do the beads too. So you won't forget your story."

"Perhaps I shall."

And I think this is a grand idea, collecting beads to remember the good stories. But what about the panda bears and sad emoticons? I've spent much of my life trying to forget the terrible days. Was there any reason to remember those?

Of course, I can't help but remember, at least in the darkness. My nightmares won't let me forget.

"What do you think?" Kendall asks me as we follow Mrs. West and Suzanne down the hall, stopping at the different rooms.

"It's amazing." I nod toward Mrs. West. "She's amazing."

"She makes all of the hats and wigs by hand. Won't let anyone else help her."

"That's remarkable."

"It's her way to show these children they're loved."

Near the end of the hall, Mrs. West turns to Suzanne. "Our last friend asked for a green cap and feather like Peter Pan."

Suzanne pulls the cap and feather out of the tote, red tufts of yarn woven like hair underneath it, and hands it to Mrs. West. She holds it in her free hand as we walk toward the door.

But then Mrs. West stops, staring at the nameplate.

It's blank.

She looks back at Kendall, and I see the fear in her eyes. And I realize what an empty nameplate might mean.

Mrs. West's steps are slow as she walks toward the nurses' station, inquiring about the patient in room 203. I don't hear the nurse's response, but the shake of her head, the soft pat on Mrs. West's shoulder, speak of a universal sadness. The depth of it plunges inside me, and I can't seem to move.

I don't want to feel this sadness. Don't want to return, in this light of day, to the darkness.

Mrs. West wipes off her wet cheeks with the back of her hand, just like her great-grandson did. And it seems just as natural for her to mourn while others are watching.

Kendall places her hand on Mrs. West's elbow. "Let's get you some tea."

"I'm sorry." Suzanne tucks the Peter Pan cap back into the tote before kissing her on the cheek. "He was a really sweet kid."

"A warrior," Mrs. West says.

Suzanne leans toward Kendall. "I have to be at my other job in an hour."

"Go ahead," Kendall says. "We'll drive her home."

Mrs. West smiles, but the light doesn't quite reach her eyes. "If you'd let me borrow the keys, I could drive myself."

Kendall shakes her head. "I don't think so."

The three of us ride the elevator up to a small café with a view spanning the city of bridges, as if we're in a castle on a hill. After ordering tea, we sit on a covered deck, settling into the space as the rain drums gently on the roof. Mrs. West's eyes seem to follow the path of the rain soaking the streets and buildings below us.

"All he wanted to do was play with other kids, but he had to spend his life fighting cancer. And now . . ." Her hand shakes. "It doesn't seem right to say that God took him home."

Kendall glances at me, and I can see the concern in her

eyes for her great-grandmother. She reaches for Mrs. West's hand to hold, to stop the shaking.

"You can't save all of these children, Oma."

"I know that."

"But you give the ones who are slipping away such great joy. They see the love of God in your smile and in your gifts."

"I pray over each one," she says. "Every night before I go to bed. And every morning, I thank God for another day so I can pray for them again."

My heart warms at the thought of her prayers, loving these children like Landon did with both her words and her work. And I wonder at her story. A hundred questions pop up in my mind, yet I can't ask any of them right now.

Kendall nods at me. "Ava here was just in Uganda, touring the coffee plantation and children's home with Landon."

Mrs. West blinks as if she's forgotten I'm here. I admire how Kendall seems to bring her back. "Why were you in Uganda?"

"I'm with a foundation," I explain. "We're considering a grant proposal from Bishara."

"If anyone should receive a grant, it's Kendall and Landon. They are changing the world with their coffee beans."

"How long have you lived in Portland?" I ask Mrs. West as someone delivers a carafe with hot water and an assortment of Steven Smith tea.

"Pretty much my entire life."

"Kendall tells me you are from the Netherlands."

"A lifetime ago."

Kendall nods at me, encouraging me to continue our conversation.

"My great-grandfather spent some time in Amsterdam right after the war."

Mrs. West gives me a curious look. "Was he Dutch?"

"Oh no. He was from New York."

The curiosity in her eyes turns into something else, something I don't recognize.

"Not many Americans came to Amsterdam after the war," she says, "unless they were soldiers."

"He was actually a businessman who invested in the post-war efforts. He built windows across Europe."

Mrs. West's cup shakes as she sets it on the table, spilling tea over the sides. "What was your great-grandfather's name?"

"William Kingston."

She inhales sharply, blanching. "Oh, my . . ."

Mrs. West begins to list to one side—a sturdy ship ruffled by the wind.

Kendall reaches for her arm. "Oma?"

"I think . . ." Her eyes look almost desperate now. "Oh, Kendall, I need to go home."

I stand up quickly. "Should I get a wheelchair?"

"Yes, please," Kendall says, and I rush toward the café's front counter.

The man in charge summons an attendant, who wheels a chair toward us and carefully helps Mrs. West transfer. Once inside, she clings to the armrests.

"I'm sorry—" I say.

"It's not you, Ava," Kendall replies as we follow Mrs. West

and the attendant down the hall. "This afternoon—it was just too much."

When we turn, Mrs. West looks back at me as if I were a ghost, and I realize that Kendall, in spite of her intentions, is wrong. Perhaps Mrs. West's anxiety stems from the loss of the boy today, but it's more than that. Somehow I've managed to frighten this poor woman.

"Do you mind if we take her home first?" Kendall asks me as the attendant presses a button to summon the elevator. "She lives in a suburb just south of here."

"I'll take a taxi back to my hotel."

After the elevator door opens, Kendall thrusts her arm out so it won't close on Mrs. West's wheelchair. "Are you sure?"

"Of course. You need to take her—" Kendall said home, but I'm not sure, exactly, if the older woman needs to go home or to a hospital that isn't for children. "You need to care for her."

"Take the aerial tram down into Portland," Kendall says. "The light rail can drop you off at your hotel."

I don't dare kiss Mrs. West's cheek or even shake her hand, afraid of what might happen if I step back into her bubble.

"I'll check in later," I say before the doors close again.

The aerial tram transfers its passengers from the ninth floor of the hospital down the steep hill, sloping over the busy interstate and taking a sharp dive between two buildings, depositing us into a station near the riverfront.

The rain has stopped, at least for the moment, so I walk the mile to my hotel. Bicycles fly past me and a myriad of dogs join me on this path, all of them seeming to walk their owners. Several people are pushing carts with garbage bags that bulge over the top, and children race through the grassy plaza near the waterside, a set of parents sipping wine on a blanket underneath the bridge.

A breeze stirs up the water and mixes together a unique brew of its own, the aromas of food from the local restaurants along with the stench of fish and diesel and river water.

If only I could build a bridge to cross the divide in my family, put things back together again. The division, it seems, started with William and Peter, but until I can find out what divided them, where the brokenness started, I fear we'll never be able to mend.

My hotel is a block from the riverfront and its lobby looks like an Italian villa, everything pristine. So very different from the messy world outside. The messiness inside me.

If only I could ask questions about my family and get straight answers.

If only people would share their stories instead of locking them away.

TWENTY-THREE

JOSIE

AMSTERDAM

SEPTEMBER 1942

Josie slipped into one of the chairs at a sidewalk café and waited, sipping the hot drink made of chicory grounds and sketching in her journal. The message she'd received said to be at the café along the canal called *Entrepotdok* at half past four.

Someone had dropped this message into the pocket of her cardigan when she was escorting a group of children on their afternoon walk. She knew the moment she'd received it, but she didn't search for the messenger. Nor did she read the note until she was hidden away in her room.

An important errand—that's what she told Miss Pimentel

when she requested two hours away. The director didn't ask any questions. The Dutch—at least the innocent ones— asked very few questions these days.

People crowded around tables on the sidewalk, drinking their hot chicory and eating sweet *poffertjes* as if they'd forgotten their country was under siege. The Gestapo dined here as well, dressed in their charcoal-gray uniforms, but the aroma from their cups smelled like actual coffee.

A man sat down in the chair across from Josie, and her heart leapt. Even with the felt hat, a pair of clunky glasses, she knew immediately that it was her brother.

Relief washed over her. Klaas had come by the crèche several times, inquiring about Samuel, but she hadn't heard a word from her brother since he'd swept away in the family's motorboat. She'd begun to fear that he really had been forced to work in Germany.

"It's nice to see you, Fräulein," he said in perfect German as if he had nothing to hide.

"You as well." She lowered her voice, leaning forward. "I've been worried."

A truck rumbled past between the sidewalk and canal, and she knew exactly why Samuel had picked this place: so they could talk in the open, under the drone of noise.

"You don't need to worry about me." He leaned forward as if they were on a date, whispering to her. "What happened to our letter?"

"It's in my room. I visited the place you sent me, but the people—" She tapped her pen on the paper and began sketching one of the pictures from the collage in her brain.

The house in Amersfoort, the truck on the street, a woman being forced inside.

He nodded his head slowly, pointing at the man she'd drawn off to the side. "A neighbor."

"But not a friend," she said, turning the picture into a fury of dark clouds in case someone demanded to see her book.

"Not a friend at all." The Gestapo agents stood up and strolled down the canal without even glancing their way. After they left, the steady buzz of Dutch conversation resumed. Samuel switched to Dutch as well, his voice blending with the others. "I never should have involved you."

"I would have helped anyway." She didn't want him to feel guilty. She'd chosen to resist on her own, using what little she had to work against their enemy. "Where did you get the money, Samuel?"

He pointed across the street. "Walk with me."

The smell of brined herring permeated the air as they walked like other couples along the canal, as if they were enjoying the golden canopy of leaves. "When I was working with Mr. Linden, the bank was flooded with money from investors to fund the beginnings of Hitler's war. I transferred a portion of those funds to various resistance groups who needed the money to counteract Hitler and kept some to help them later."

"It seems that you kept a lot for later," she said. "Does Mr. Linden know?"

His sharp glance told her this secret was one he wouldn't tell.

"But the investors will know eventually that their money is gone."

"Not until after the war," he said. "And when the Allies win, no one is going to want to have money in Hitler's ring. They'll take any money still invested with Mr. Linden and run."

Something clicked in her brain, the flash of a bulb. "William Kingston is one of the investors."

He stopped. "How do you know about Mr. Kingston?"

"Eliese told me."

But she couldn't bring herself to tell Samuel that Eliese had married him.

"You've seen Eliese?" Samuel asked.

"She is working with the *Judenrat*, registering people for deportation."

His face grew sad. "I suppose I'm not surprised."

They began walking again, quiet as they rounded a corner.

"Did you know she has a son?" Josie asked.

"I'd heard a rumor."

"His name is Hein."

Her brother's gaze fell to his hands.

"I'm starting to hate her, Samuel. I don't want to, but I do. She's sending away people to save herself."

"We don't know what we would do if we were in her shoes."

Josie wanted to scream that she did know, but the truth was, she was the biggest hypocrite of all. She'd seen hundreds of people taken away now—*children*—and hadn't done anything to stop it.

Esther's face fluttered in her mind. The girl needed someone to help her, someone who cared, but Josie wanted to do more than care for these children before they were deported. She wanted to find them a safe place to live.

They circled back to the café, but the sidewalk chairs were empty now. The only people around them were the few who rushed along the canal's edge, probably coming home after work.

"I have a favor to ask," she said.

Samuel scanned both sides of the street, alert. "What is it?"

"I need you to find a home."

"You already have a home. Two of them if you count our parents' house."

"Not for me. I need a home, a family, that would be kind to a child."

"Ah . . ."

"He's an orphan," she whispered. "From the Rotterdam bombings."

"A lot of orphans need homes these days."

With so many families being rounded up at the theater, that didn't surprise her. "Can you find me a place?"

"It's Eliese's son, isn't it."

She wanted to lie, afraid he would reject her request, but she nodded slowly instead.

He paused before answering. "I can find a place."

"Even after what she did?"

"Josie—" his smile was gentle but strong—"I forgave her a long time ago."

"That's heroic of you." Josie didn't know if she'd ever be able to forgive Eliese for promising to marry Samuel and then disappearing with another man.

"We have to save whoever we can, as soon as possible."

She reached for the railing. "What have you heard?"

"That the people they're putting on trains will never come home."

"Why not?"

"The work camps in Germany are really death camps. According to Radio Holland, the Nazis are killing the young and old."

Her stomach rolled.

"I will meet you here again tomorrow at the same time, for the envelope."

She nodded, glad to rid herself of the guilders.

He stopped in front of the patio where they'd sat. "Actually meet me across the canal tomorrow, by the letterbox."

She glanced over at the red-painted box on the other side of the water, the crowns on its emblem gleaming in the sun. The Nazis had stripped most everything royal from their country, but they hadn't removed these.

Someone stopped near the letterbox, watching them. It almost looked like—

"That's Klaas," she said, waving at their friend.

She waited for Samuel to say something, and when he didn't speak, she turned back around.

Once again, her brother was gone.

The following evening Josie waited in the rain by the letterbox, the money pinned into the hem of her skirt so she could hand it off to Samuel. Her brother's words about the death camps had haunted her the past twenty-four hours. She knew the Nazis hated the noise, but she couldn't imagine them kill-ing the children. She trusted her brother, but this . . .

Surely he had received the wrong information from Radio Holland.

Raindrops soaked her gabardine coat, poured down the sides of her boots, and after an hour, she decided it was point-less to stay. She prayed that Samuel was only detained tem-porarily, wherever he was.

What was she going to do with the envelope of guilders now? And what would she do with Hein?

The bulky hood over her head, she turned and hurried back toward the college. A metal gate clanged in the wind, unnerving her, but even the Gestapo, it seemed, weren't out in this storm.

Someone joined her side, walking in stride, and she thought it was Samuel at first, his black fedora pulled low over his eyes to keep them from the rain.

"Hello, Jozefien," the man said.

She blinked. "What are you doing here, Klaas?"

"I'm on an errand."

"I saw you yesterday," she said. "Near Vers Café."

He shook his head. "It wasn't me. I managed to get a dinner date since you don't ever have time for a night out."

Irritation knocked against her chest. She was certain it had been Klaas standing by the letterbox. Why was he lying to her?

He lowered his voice. "Samuel sent me to find you."

She looked back at him. "Why didn't he come himself?"

"He was detained, but he said you have something he needs."

She shivered, but not from the evening air. How she

wanted to trust this man beside her, wanted to think they would all be friends for life, but something was off with Klaas, his jovial smile gone.

Would Samuel send Klaas if he was in danger? An alarm—like the chaotic beating of that gate—clanged inside her head.

"You have to believe me," he said, directing her into an alley, under the shelter of an awning. "Samuel and I have been working together for a long time, and now . . . now he needs our help."

Her hand hidden under her parka sleeve, she circled the lion bracelet around her wrist as if it would give her the strength she needed to find the truth. "Where is Samuel?"

Klaas glanced at the entrance to the alley, to see if someone had noticed them, but the sheen of raindrops seemed to wall them in. "The Nazis are asking him some questions, but they'll release him if we have enough money to bribe the agent in charge."

Did Klaas know about the guilders that she carried under her parka? She would give them to him in a heartbeat if it would set her brother free.

"Samuel needs you, Jozefien. He needs both of us."

Her entire body began shaking. She wanted to do the right thing, but Samuel had told her to trust no one, not even Klaas. Would he change his mind now? He'd done it when they were younger, but it was more about keeping the peace by letting Klaas win. Her brother had never changed the rules of their game.

A collage of pictures ticked through her mind again, stopping at the blond man in Amersfoort. The neighbor who'd exposed those who lived nearby. She'd known Klaas her entire life, but this wasn't a game. Stakes were much higher than the capture of a flag.

"I have to think about it," she said.

"He's your brother."

"I'm supposed to give the money directly to him."

It was a slip; she realized it the moment the words came out of her mouth, and she rushed out of the alley. Klaas didn't follow her back to the college.

It didn't matter if Klaas was angry at her—she was scared for her brother. What if the Nazis really did have him?

But up in her room, hidden under her pillow, was an envelope, a lion marking it. Relieved, she ripped it open and read her brother's note on contraband stationery, a picture of William of Nassau at the top—one of the soldiers who'd led the Dutch revolt against Spain.

I must move on again, but please take the envelope to our cousin—she will know what to do with it.

As for the other gift—a lady will meet our friend on Tuesday, along the pool outside the Rijksmuseum. She'll be wearing a blue scarf pinned with a diamond. Your package will be safe with her.

Strength and courage.

O zo.

O zo. The triumph of the orange.

Josie took her Weissenbruch painting off the hook and turned it over, sliding the envelope from her clothing into the pocket, beside the fake identity card. Then she shredded Samuel's note.

Klaas was wrong—her brother hadn't been detained by the Nazis.

She shouldn't have said anything about the money, even if he already knew. They were no longer playing the games of their youth where the victor hung a flag and the loser pouted for a day or two before the games began again. Those who didn't win now could lose their lives.

No matter how handsome he was, no matter if Klaas truly cared for her, she wouldn't play games any longer, for her sake or the children in her care.

If only she could take Esther down to Maastricht with her when she took the envelope, hide her at Keet's house.

If only they could tear up the deportation lists, the children in their care would be free.

She walked back downstairs and outside. Lights glowed in some of the windows down Plantage Middenlaan, in the hour before the blackout curtains would erase any light. Her shift at the crèche officially started at eight tonight, but every waking hour she tried to join Miss Pimentel and the others, the staffing short.

Right now she needed to speak with Eliese, before the trucks arrived.

Mr. Süskind and Eliese were sitting at the registration table inside the theater, sorting through cards, a soldier behind them smoking a cigarette.

God had forgiven Josie for a multitude of wrongs in her nineteen years. As she watched her old friend, the sadness in her eyes as she worked, Josie knew that, like Samuel, she had to rid herself of the hatred in her heart. Samuel had already forgiven Eliese for hurting him. With God's help, Josie would have to forgive her as well.

Josie caught her eye through the window and gave her the slightest nod before retreating back to the alley beside the crèche. Minutes later, Eliese joined her in the shadows.

"I found a place for Hein," Josie whispered.

"Thank you."

She gave Eliese the instructions, made her repeat the details twice to make sure that she'd memorized them.

"I've heard a rumor," Josie said, "about the Nazis killing children in their camps."

"I can't confirm that."

"But you fear it."

Eliese nodded her head.

"Do you think—?" Josie started, the words hard to say. "Do you think I could hide one of the children staying in the crèche?"

Eliese rubbed her arms. "It would be close to impossible."

"How close?"

"Life and death close, Josie. We have to count every person who comes and goes from here. The commandant personally checks the registration and then the deportation lists to make sure no one is missing. If he found one of the children gone, he would kill us both."

Josie pressed her hand against the brick wall. "If we don't save some of these children, they all might die."

Eliese looked down. "It's hard to think beyond the ones we love."

"We must pray for wisdom," Josie said. "And that God will expand our hearts."

Even if this expansion exposed everything inside them.

If only we could make these children disappear.

TWENTY-FOUR

ELIESE

A brown cashmere cap—that's what she placed on her son's head when they stepped out into the chilly afternoon. One day Hein could wear a black derby like his father, but dressed in his best trousers and coat, he still reminded her of a miniature William.

Hein pulled the cap low on his forehead, shading his eyes as they strolled down the block, Eliese holding firmly to his hand.

She used to walk with him almost every day, hidden under the canopy of his pram, but it had been months since Hein had been outside their house. Ever since they'd released their gardener, the courtyard in back had become completely unsuitable for play.

Hein's eyes soaked in everything around them—the white-and-red tram that carved a path through the cars, baskets that bloomed with autumn flowers and loaves of freshly baked bread, golden leaves dangling over houseboats in the canal.

But the crisp leaves under her boots, the dimly lit hours that bookended their days, reminded her this was a season of endings. Saying goodbye to Hein, even temporarily, felt like a death of sorts. An autumn of her heart.

How was she going to give him to a stranger?

Spring—that's what she needed to cling to this morning. The hope, renewal, after the darkest of days. Without the hope of spring, she couldn't bear to say goodbye.

Josie had said to meet the woman with a blue scarf in front of the Rijksmuseum, along a pool that reflected back the building's facade like a piece of art framed by a concrete wall. The Nazis had closed the museum, but its plaza was crowded this afternoon, hundreds of people sitting around the pool and on the lawn.

Hein dipped his hand into the water, lapping up handfuls and throwing them into the air, the droplets sprinkling back down on the pool, losing themselves again.

Now he needed to lose himself in this great pool of people.

"We're meeting a friend," she said. "You're going to visit her for a few days."

He glanced up. "To play?"

"Yes, to play."

Tears were coming, but she blinked them back before

someone—a policeman or soldier—noticed the crying woman with a star on her coat and a child by her side.

On one hand, Eliese hoped the lady was delayed, but on the other, she hoped the woman would hurry. Many of the stars had already been extinguished in this city, and those that remained seemed to glow brighter.

Minutes later, a college-age woman leaned her bicycle against the low wall of the pool, a turquoise-blue scarf around the collar of her button-down coat, a diamond pinned near the top. Attached on the back of her bicycle was a seat for a child.

As a group of students passed by, all huddled together, the woman knelt down to check her tire. "You must be Hein," she said quietly.

He nodded his head.

"I have a nice warm jacket for you." The woman slipped a plain black coat from the satchel in her basket, erasing his star.

"His clothing is in the bag." Eliese held out Hein's knapsack, but the woman shook her head.

"I have all the supplies we need."

"Of course." Eliese pulled the sack back toward her. "How will I find him again?"

"After it's safe, our mutual friend will find you."

Eliese lifted the tattered gray lamb from the knapsack and handed it to Hein. Then she kissed him on the forehead.

"Mama?"

"You're going to play," she reminded him.

"You'll need to walk away first," the woman whispered, "so we don't cause a disturbance."

Eliese had no choice. She had to put her trust in this woman, for the sake of her son.

A smile, shaky at best, when she glimpsed those pale-brown eyes for the last time, the tiny hands clinging to his lamb, trying to be strong.

Then she turned away.

Relief—that's what she felt at first, knowing that Hein was with someone who would care for him. Someone who could protect him from Nazis with guns.

But the relief quickly faded into a chilling coldness, her heart folding over itself to sustain an ember of warmth. And she couldn't breathe.

God, help me.

A step, her weary feet carrying the burden of her heart.

She had to keep walking. Had to take another breath. If the quaking in her heart surfaced, she could lose everything.

A diamond—that's what she'd pretend to be. Like the one on the woman's scarf. Like those stored in her father's vault under their house, hidden from their enemy. Strong enough to withstand.

Her head high, her heart in tatters, she walked away from her son. William would have wanted Hein to be safe. He would be proud of her for finding him a place to live.

William would be proud.

She whispered this to herself until she reached the corner. Then she looked back.

And she could no longer stand.

Her son—their beautiful boy—was already gone.

TWENTY-FIVE

Sweat soaks my hotel pillowcase and sheet, the flames flickering in my mind, heat burning my skin. If only I could see Andrew's face one more time, hold his hand. Feel his arms tighten around my neck, snuggling his face into my skin.

The fire stole away my brother's life, but this man keeps haunting my dreams, standing outside my window instead of helping me rescue Andrew.

After all these years, why won't this man leave me alone?

I fling back the covers and hop onto my feet as if I can outrun this nightmare that's lapped my mind again, taunting me wherever I sleep. Reaching for my phone, I find the photo of my mom, Andrew, and me tucked away on one of my apps so no one else will stumble on it, the three of us on a beach towel, me holding my brother.

Andrew used to be my shadow in those months before he died, following me all over the town house. Mom worked full-time at our church during the day and then served tables at a local restaurant most evenings to keep up with the bills, so in the summer months, I was in charge of Andrew both day and night.

Looking back, I wonder how our mother adapted to the overwhelming amount of work after growing up as a Kingston. If she ever wanted to return to the privileged life of her youth, she'd never mentioned it to me. The work, it seemed, was much better than living with her brothers.

I lower myself back onto the bed and lean against the headboard, slipping my phone back onto the nightstand.

My mom stopped working for a few years, after she met Andrew's father. A man who lived with us until my brother was born. Then a neighbor introduced Mom to Jesus and Andrew's father wanted nothing to do with God or the woman who'd decided to follow Him. I think we were both relieved when he left.

I still remember my brother's smile, the wonder in his eyes when the world opened up something new to him. I was twelve when he was born, and I adored him from the moment he arrived in our world. Over the next two years, I took my responsibility to care for him after school quite seriously, not letting him out of my sight until he fell asleep.

The night of the fire left me without a mother or brother. It also left me deaf in my left ear; a gas explosion ruptured the drum, stealing away my hearing. No cochlear implant, the doctors told me, would ever recover it.

After my mom died, a caseworker located my father—Jeffery Drake—in Idaho, paying intermittent support for two younger children there. When this caseworker contacted him, Jeffery made it quite clear that he wasn't interested in supporting another kid, so she began searching for my grandparents.

When she found Marcella, I rushed at the opportunity of having a family to call my own again. To belong. And yet, I don't really belong. Even Marcella, who has been my pillar for the past twelve years, seems to be retreating into her own world.

I check my clock. It's three in the morning on the Pacific Coast, six in New York. And who knows what time in Uganda. The fog in my brain seems to have thinned, but my internal clock is still upside down.

I brew a cup of black tea and sit down on a leather chair overlooking Portland's lights. A dotted stream of headlights and taillights flows across the bridge below my window, vehicles traveling both directions to reach the other side.

Perhaps it's time for me to stop evaluating the work of others, at least temporarily, and spend a few days evaluating myself. What I want to do with my life inside and out of the Kingston family. Where my heart wants to call home.

But before I start thinking about my future, I need to finish my current work, for Landon and Kendall and the hundreds of people under their care. For my mom, who would have celebrated the good this brother and sister are doing as they share Christ's love. For my brother, who never had a chance to help someone else.

Opening my laptop, I begin to fill in our grant template—detailing the history and goals for Bishara Coffee & Café, the interviews with Kendall and Landon, my experiences in Uganda and Portland, the work that God is clearly doing on their plantation.

The final section of the report is a scale, asking whether I would recommend the foundation offer grant money to this organization. I give them my highest recommendation and then add a note, suggesting that Bishara should not only expand its organization, it should work with other organizations to replicate its healthy mix of money and mission.

Scanning my words one last time, I realize it's a glowing report, but it is an honest glow.

One more click and my report is uploaded onto a private website for the foundation board members. Claire will print it out for Marcella so she can make notes, and if she greenlights this grant, the other directors will follow her lead.

Filling a to-go cup with tea, I slip on my tennis shoes and head down to a bridge reserved for pedestrians and public transport. No one else is crossing at this early hour, and I stop to watch the day's first light blooming in the soil of river, a production of its own as it flickers across the surface, illuminating the moored boats and sliver of an island.

Something about my grandfather frightened Mrs. West. Were others, like Peter Ziegler, frightened of him as well?

I could forget whatever William did—or might have done. Let it go. Instead of walking away like my mom, I could stay with Marcella and continue to help others through the foundation, using the grant money to mend whatever happened in the past. If I don't search, the truth might continue to be hidden for generations, perhaps forever with the history rewritten.

"The truth will set us free." That's what Landon said back in Uganda. And I remember those words from my mom's Bible.

I sit on a bench and retrieve her Bible out of my handbag to find the verses where Jesus speaks about the truth of His teaching, truth that could set people free. The father of lies wants to conceal the truth, He said, enslave people in their sin. Their shame. God sent His Son to set them—to set me—free.

Mom drew a chain beside these words, snapped in two.

Something happened in the past to ensnare my family. A lie, perhaps, that has made slaves of us all. I can't continue representing the Kingston Family Foundation until I learn what happened in my family long ago.

A picture appears on my cell, one that Landon has taken of him and Faith. He's swinging her on the playground behind the children's home, and she is smiling like the champion she is, the defeater of malaria and an overcomer of a childhood that must have been racked by pain.

I want to be just like her.

After sending him a note, I text Kendall, apologizing for anything I did to scare her grandmother. Seconds later, she texts back.

Would you be able to stop by Oma's house before you leave? She wants to apologize.

I type a quick reply. I'd love to see her, but she doesn't have to apologize. She didn't do anything wrong.

Several minutes pass before I receive another text. How about 9?

I'll be there.

As I turn back to the hotel, I call the airline and reschedule my flight. Then I text Claire and tell her that I'm staying another day to speak with Landon's great-grandmother.

Her story, I hope, will expand far beyond Bishara Café.

The truth, I pray, will set all of us free.

TWENTY-SIX

ELIESE

AMSTERDAM

OCTOBER 1942

Eliese inched forward in her chair to look at the boy on the other side of her registration table. He reminded her of Hein with his warm smile and small fingers that clutched a rabbit in lieu of her son's lamb.

Two weeks had gone by since she'd handed Hein off to the lady with the diamond pin. Two weeks of registering families who would soon head east; gathering food to send for Mrs. Pon to share with her wards; roaming the lonely corridors of her home as she tried not to think about her son.

But she couldn't help herself. In the evening hours, after dinner with her father, she arranged photographs into a baby album that she'd purchased, writing stories about all that was good in Hein's life. One day she would give it to him so he could remember their lost years.

But these nights in the theater's cloakroom, she couldn't think about Hein. She was judge and jury for every family who came through here, Fünten and Mr. Süskind the rules of law.

A diamond.

Stone.

She had to be strong for all of them now.

She took this family's identity papers and began to type their information onto a new registration card.

"What is your name?" Eliese asked, not daring to look at the boy again.

"Lars."

His parents had the same look in their eyes that most people did when they walked into the lobby. Resigned and terrified.

The unknown was terrifying for all of them.

If only she could rip this registration card into shreds so this family didn't exist anymore in the eyes of their occupiers. So Lars was never born. Erase their identity and let Lars ride away to freedom like Hein had done with the woman.

Names and addresses—the record of every person who lived in Amsterdam—fueled the Nazi Party. Fünten and his men lived by these lists, their meticulous record-keeping here and at the central Registry Office. Not the faces of the people they saw as a problem.

The sprout of an idea planted itself in her mind; then the roots of it began to grow.

What if she could revise their lists?

Fünten hadn't propositioned her again since her journey to Westerbork, but he rarely left his post near the registration table, watching her record every name lest she make an error.

But what if she didn't make an error? What if she simply eliminated a name?

Mr. Süskind laughed with the commander to her right, entertaining him while she placed the family's card on the table beside her.

She turned toward Mr. Süskind. "Should I take this child to the crèche?"

The family waited as he consulted with Fünten. Sometimes the man had Mr. Süskind take the children over by themselves; other nights the children had to wait in the theater and were transported as a group in the morning.

"Have him wait with his family in the theater," Mr. Süskind said. She directed the family to the door, then turned to file their card.

Fünten walked out the front door of the lobby, and her hands shook as she opened the cabinet. She'd registered Hein at the Registry Office when he was born, like they were all required to do, but in the eyes of their occupiers, she prayed he'd ceased to exist. That they would forget she had a child.

Without registering Lars and the other children, they didn't exist, at least not in the eyes of their occupiers. What if—like Josie had said—they really could make some of these children disappear?

"Eliese?" It was Mr. Süskind standing beside her, and he looked concerned.

The man might oversee the records at the Hollandsche

Schouwburg, but he had a Jewish daughter at home. Perhaps he would understand.

She quickly slid the card into place and then fed another card into the roller of her typewriter, registering an elderly woman who'd been waiting behind Lars's family.

Mr. Süskind sat down at the table beside her. "Fünten doesn't want you or me taking the children to the crèche anymore."

"But they must stay over there." They couldn't rescue any children once they were inside the theater.

"He'll have someone from the crèche retrieve them."

The next family in line waited by the table, but they weren't in any rush to enter the auditorium. The guard by the door looked as if he'd entered a comatose state, his boots anchoring him to the ground.

She remembered the girl that she'd taken over to the crèche weeks ago, the one Josie had embraced. Esther had been her name. Van Gelder.

Eliese retrieved the van Gelders' card out of the cabinet and glanced at the information. She could memorize the details, retype the card while Fünten was distracted, when he and his men thought she was registering someone else.

In order to make this work, she would need Mr. Süskind's help. She prayed he would understand, for his daughter's sake, but if he didn't, if he turned her over to Fünten, the only one who would suffer for this idea was her.

"What's wrong?" he asked.

She sat back down, her eyes on her typewriter. "I want to take some of the names off the registration cards."

"Which names?"

She looked up at him. "The children."

He turned quickly, rustling in the filing cabinet behind her, and she held her breath. Would he call for the commandant now? Or perhaps just shuffle her off to the auditorium with the others. Even Puttkammer couldn't help a traitor.

Mr. Süskind leaned over her shoulder, placing a card beside her as if they were reviewing it together. "They'll find the original cards."

Blood raced through her veins. If they could truly delete the names, hide the children away, the Nazis would never know they were gone.

She recovered her breath. "Not if I take them home."

"You'd have to burn them."

"Of course."

"Fünten checks the registration cards with the central office," he said. "So they won't miss anyone."

The roots of her idea began to wither. She might be able to manipulate these cards, but she had no authority in the Registry Office.

Mr. Süskind glanced up at the family waiting in front of them, a baby in the mother's arms, before turning back to her. "I have a friend who might help us. I'll ask tomorrow."

Eliese met his gaze. "Why do you laugh with Fünten?"

He took off his glasses, swiped the sweat off his brow. "I have no choice if I want to help those in our care."

And she wondered how many this man had helped.

"The parents must give us permission," she said.

He nodded as he opened another drawer in the cabinet, riffling through the cards again. "You speak to your friend at the crèche, and I will talk to my colleague."

Fünten walked back into the cloakroom in his pressed uniform, Josie at his side with her gray dress and white kerchief.

Perhaps they weren't powerless to fight for these children after all.

"Is there a problem?" Fünten asked, stepping up beside them.

"No problem." Mr. Süskind pulled out another card and placed it beside their stack. "We're preparing the list for tomorrow's transport."

"Later," Fünten said, pointing at the queue as if they hadn't noticed it.

"Eliese—retrieve the children who need to be taken to the crèche," Mr. Süskind said before sliding into her chair to continue with registration.

Eliese didn't ask for permission to invite Josie into the auditorium. She simply waved her through the theater doors as if Fünten had commanded it himself. And hope began to rise inside her when she saw Lars, holding the hand of his mother.

"Have you heard any news about Hein?" Eliese asked as they maneuvered between the bedrolls.

Josie shook her head.

She hadn't expected the woman to contact Josie, but still she'd hoped . . .

Eliese stopped walking, her voice low in the thundering sound of this room. "Mr. Süskind wants to help us save some of the children."

Josie's blue eyes swelled like the waves on the North Sea. "I thought he supported the Nazis."

"It's an act."

Josie glanced up at the balcony, at the hundreds of people crammed into this room. "I couldn't make the choice, between who stays and who goes."

"The parents will decide for us."

Eliese scanned the room. She hated coming in here, the very pores of this room seeping in despair. "The van Gelders are on the transport list to leave tomorrow."

Josie shook her head. "We can't let Esther go."

"If I can remove her name from the registration list, we'd need to find a place for her to hide."

Josie straightened the handkerchief that covered her hair. "I know where to take her."

Eliese smiled back at her. If they rescued another child, like Hein, it would be remarkable.

And even more remarkable if they could steal away more.

TWENTY-SEVEN

JOSIE

Clouds streaked the morning sky as Josie and Miss Pimentel bundled up eight of their children. Josie dressed Esther in three layers of clothing, but she left the girl's suitcase tucked under her bed. Dr. van Hulst had agreed to hide it later in the attic of the college.

Werner and Hanneke van Gelder had given the crèche workers permission to take their daughter to a safe place, and with the dozens of children coming and going from the crèche each week, Josie prayed no one would ask about one girl.

She eyed the man who guarded the theater's front door

across the street. He watched them in a bored sort of way, but he wasn't really paying attention to her or the children she and Miss Pimentel ushered outside.

At the top of the hour, this guard would change, a new man who wouldn't know how many children had left the crèche. Nor, she prayed, would he particularly care. They were banking on his apathy.

One toddler rode in the pram that Miss Pimentel pushed and the other seven children walked between her and Josie, their eyes wandering over to the theater where their parents were being held. None of the children spoke, as if the quiet would make them invisible.

Ahead was Amsterdam Centraal—the station where, hours from now, Esther's parents and dozens of others would board a train for their journey to Westerbork. Josie already had two tickets in her pocket, one for her and one for her niece, headed south instead of east. And she had her fake identity card with the tickets. If anyone asked for it, they would think her name was Laurina de Jong.

As the children rounded the corner, Josie pointed Esther toward a flock of geese landing on the canal, their orange beaks a beacon against the dark blue. After watching for a moment, Esther looked up, searching for her playmates. "They've left us behind."

"You and I are going to have an adventure of our own today."

Esther stared at the station's clock tower. "A magic train?"

"A train, but I'm not certain about any magic."

She glanced around. "Is Mama meeting us?"

"Not quite yet."

"Papa?"

"No, but your parents asked me to take you on this journey."

Tears puddled in Esther's eyes, but she blinked them away.

Hanneke van Gelder hadn't wanted her to take Esther, but after almost a month in the theater, she understood the need. Josie promised she'd take her to a safe place. And she prayed Keet would agree.

With her garden and farm, her cousin wouldn't need ration coupons to feed another child, and she was out far enough from town that she and Erik could easily hide Esther if someone came to check on them. Only God knew who was choosing good and who was choosing evil these days, but she prayed this girl would be safe with them.

Esther stopped walking several meters in front of the train station, frozen in the midst of a crowd.

"Please come with me," Josie said.

The girl's gaze traveled one more time. Searching, perhaps, for the other children or for her mother, but no one was looking back at her.

"We'll pretend we're taking a magic train." Josie knelt down beside her. "And we must pretend something else."

Esther was listening now. "What?"

Josie looped her arm through the girl's. "I am going to be your auntie, and you must call me Tante Laurina."

"Can my name be Hanneke?"

"No, you are still Esther." Josie smiled. "Esther de Jong. And just for today, let's pretend that neither of your parents wear a yellow star."

"I like this game."

"We're going to visit a friend," she said, inching the girl forward. "I have tickets in my pocket for both of us."

Esther smiled bravely as they walked into the station and boarded a passenger train. Smiled bravely as they traveled out of Amsterdam. Smiled until one of the Grüne Polizei stepped into their car and broke the silence with his stern voice, barking the order to see everyone's identity papers.

Esther grasped Josie's hand, her smile gone. Josie eyed the door, but the train had already begun moving. There'd be no escaping this man.

Esther's hand was shaking. Or perhaps that was her own hand trembling, clasped around the girl's fingers.

Cool air seemed to steal up the aisle as the policeman drew closer, his heels clicking against the metal floor, the smell of his cologne mixing with the raw stench of fear.

She released Esther's hand, and as she reached for her purse, she whispered, "Don't stop smiling."

Tears came in spite of Josie's warning, gurgling up—she feared—from the depths of a geyser. And these tears could ruin everything.

The policeman stepped up to the passengers seated behind them. *"Ausweis."*

Even with the wheels rattling along the track, Josie could hear the crisp turn of pages as he studied the papers. And Josie thought about the commandant in the theater—Hauptsturmführer Fünten. The only thing he feared—or, at least, disliked—were tears of a child.

Perhaps she could use the tears to their advantage.

"Esther de Jong," she said sternly, just loud enough for

the policeman to hear. "I told you to stop kicking the seat in front of us."

Esther's bottom lip trembled, unable to reply, and Josie leaned closer, scolding her even louder. "You are going to make fools out of us."

The geyser exploded, tears flooding out now. God forgive her for making this scared child cry.

"Ausweis," the policeman said, eyeing both Josie and Esther. Esther's cheeks were streaked with red and she struggled to catch her breath in between sobs.

"Esther—" Josie presented their identity cards to the policeman with a smile as fake as her papers before turning back to the girl—"you must hush."

"Where are you traveling?" the man asked, the oil on his mustache gleaming in the light.

"Maastricht. To visit our cousin." Then she wished that she hadn't said anything about Keet. The less information, Samuel always told her, the better.

"And how long will you be there?"

"Just for the weekend."

He glanced at Esther but didn't seem to really see her. He was all business, searching for an enemy, or at least a perceived enemy, when one was right in front of him.

He looked at the two of them again. "You are sisters?"

"She's my niece," Josie said as the man glanced again at her paperwork. It felt like those eternal seconds when she was a girl, holding her breath underwater so Klaas wouldn't find her.

"What is your name?" the policeman asked the girl.

"Esther," she whispered before looking back at Josie, panic in her swollen eyes.

"Esther de Jong," Josie scolded like she'd done moments before, "tell this man your full name."

Her gaze fell to her knees. "Esther de Jong."

The policeman handed Josie back her paperwork. "Perhaps Miss Esther didn't mean to kick the back of the chair."

The trapped air surged out of her lungs when the man moved on, checking the papers of a man in his twenties. Her brother's age. Every moment, every breath, seemed to bring anxiety or relief these days. As if they were all living in the constant state of in-between. This fear drained her strength like marrow seeping out of her bones.

At the next station, the policeman directed the man off the train. Either the officer was going to take him to the police station, or he would be forced to work in the east, the place where all the Dutch men seemed to be headed.

Josie reached for Esther's hand when the man left and enveloped the trembling fingers in her own. "I'm sorry."

Esther wiped away her tears with her sleeve.

"Together we'll be strong," Josie whispered.

Esther knew—oh, Josie hoped she knew—that she'd only scolded her so the man wouldn't suspect they were frauds. That she'd had to hurt Esther in order to help her. Wounding her to save her life.

Everything was upside down.

When the train stopped in Maastricht, they stepped off quickly and shuffled over the bridge to the town center. Planes swept low overhead, Allied ones flying east.

Esther held her hand as they passed by the old Roman ruins in town and then walked up into the hills, between mine openings that scarred the vineyards. Two children she didn't recognize were playing with her nephews and niece outside, playing music with their stone and stick instruments. They greeted Josie, but she didn't join in their game.

"What is your name?" Keet asked, studying Esther's chestnut-brown braids.

"Esther . . . Esther de Jong."

"Her parents were lost in the Rotterdam bombing," Josie said.

All three of them knew she was lying, but the truth was too dangerous to reveal.

Josie continued. "She needs a place to stay for a month or two."

Keet glanced at the other children playing before leaning down to Esther. "I was just saying that I'd love to have another guest."

Keet introduced Esther to the children outside, and they added her to their orchestra.

"Thank you," Josie said as the children began to make music together. "How is Erik?"

"Worried," Keet whispered. "Our brood continues to grow."

"You have others?"

"Seven with Esther, and it's not just children."

Josie looked up at her cousin's brick farmhouse, the thatched roof that capped two stories. A diver's inn, Samuel would have called it. A place that harbored people like the house in Amersfoort.

Who else was Keet hiding and where?

"If we could, Erik and I would take everyone who needed a home, but even with our gardens and woods, we have to buy ration coupons and supplies. The money for both seems to be running out."

Josie stepped into the house and retrieved the envelope with Samuel's guilders from where she'd pinned it under her skirt. Then she handed it to Keet. "This should be enough for supplies. And perhaps help a few others in Maastricht as well."

When Keet opened it, her eyes grew wide. "I can't take this."

Josie refused to take it back. "Samuel told me to give it to you."

"It's too much."

"You and Erik can use it to keep helping those who don't have homes."

Keet glanced at the children playing their faux instruments and slipped the envelope into her pocket. "I wish we could do more."

"I wish I could do more too," Josie whispered, the eyes of the children back home haunting her.

TWENTY-EIGHT

Kendall welcomes me to Mrs. West's bungalow along Oswego Lake's shore, leading me through the living and dining room space, into a sunroom with impatiens blossoms dripping from the ceiling, potted geraniums anchoring the tile floor.

Mrs. West sits in a white wicker chair in quiet elegance, a scarlet scarf knotted around her neck, and she smiles when I walk into the room, extending her hand to shake mine. "I'm sorry I had to leave yesterday without saying goodbye."

I sit down in the chair beside her. "I'm sorry if I offended you."

Mrs. West begins fiddling with her silver wedding band, looking out the window beside her at the branches of fir trees shivering in the breeze. "I've lived ninety-eight years, Ava. I stopped being offended a long time ago."

"That's a gift," I say, wishing I could brush off offenses so easily.

Kendall brings me a cup of tea; then she seems to disappear.

"You said that your family used to build windows," Mrs. West says.

"They still build them—" I sip my tea—"around the world."

Her eyes don't waver from the trees, her hand reaching out to touch the pane framed in white. "Windows are a curious thing, aren't they?"

"I've never really thought about it."

"The stained ones transform the light but not the transparent glass. These windows allow us to see what's on the other side, but what we're seeing—it's counterfeit."

My mug cradled between my hands, I lean forward. "What do you mean?"

"We can watch the wind or even a fire but not feel it. We see the trees but can't smell their pine. The windows give us perspective, but it's not the entire picture."

As I watch the wind rustling the branches, I can almost feel it, but she's right. Sitting in this sunroom, I don't know if it's hot or cold, not like the heat I felt coming through the open window in Uganda.

"Our eyes can deceive us sometimes," she says. "We think we are seeing something accurate, and yet they are like windows: they can camouflage the truth. In a moment, the glass can shatter . . ."

"And the fire can rage inside." My words seem to surprise both of us, and she slowly nods.

"Fire. Wind. A flood of rain. A good window can mask all of it."

"Mrs. West . . ." I pause. "How did you know about my great-grandfather?"

"Most of the Dutch knew about Mr. Kingston after the war." Her voice sounds far away, as if masked by a window. "He was a philanthropist as well as a businessman."

"Did you ever meet him?"

When she doesn't answer, I venture another question, presumptuous maybe, but I want to know what happened. "Did he do something to hurt you?"

Light flickers across the tile, and she watches the waltz of sun and wind. "I can't say."

"After the war—" I stop. If I don't tread lightly, this conversation could end as quickly as it did yesterday. "When did you first come to the United States?"

"In 1946."

"You weren't in Holland very long after the war ended."

Her nod reminds me of a water pump, the slow cranking of a handle that's expelling its final drops. "I was there long enough to remember."

I want to hear her story, every word of it, but she seems to have layered it with her own glass, stained perhaps, these windows built over the past for herself and her family to view.

"What do you remember?" I ask with trepidation, afraid that she'll dismiss me again.

She redirects my question in one sweep. "Where are you from, Ava?"

"North Carolina."

"Any brothers or sisters?"

The simplest of questions yet one of the hardest for me to answer. "One brother, but he is gone."

She reflects on this. "It's hard to lose someone you love. Part of you seems to die with them."

And I wonder at her words. Did a part of me die that day I lost Andrew and my mother? The confidence in who God made me to be, what He had planned for my life?

"Kendall and Landon don't know much about my time in Holland."

"Why haven't you told them?"

"The memories are hard." She twists the wedding band again, twice around her finger. "After the war, a lot of people didn't believe the horrors of what happened to those who'd been taken by the Nazis. It was too much to process, I suppose. I wouldn't have believed it either. . . ."

She looks out at the pine trees again, at the coat of needles that conceal the cones.

"Those of us who lived through it tried to stuff our memories deep inside, but they seem to filter out no matter what we do."

"In your dreams?" Landon said she had nightmares about someone she lost.

"In dreams and how I treat other people, I suppose. Many of us who survived have tried desperately to live what we deemed to be a normal life, free from the horror, but then— something unexpected stirs it up again."

The branches dance again outside the window, the wind

rustling their gentle sway. "Did you lose your family?" I ask softly.

"I left behind a child."

The words are unexpected, and my heart tumbles in sorrow for her. "I'm sorry."

"Many people died. Six million, I'm told. I can't remember all of them, but I can remember the one—the ones—I lost."

I want her to share more of her story, but she's clearly setting the pace. I won't run ahead, lest I trip her.

"Come with me?" she says, carefully standing.

I follow her across the tile and then the white carpeted floor, to a small room at the front of her cottage with a suede recliner and a shelf filled with antique bottles of different shapes and sizes, the sunlight burnishing their colors, rustling them like branches along the wall. I don't dare touch them, but I study her collection closely, wondering why she's kept them.

"What happened to your child?" I ask.

"My husband—" Her voice breaks, and she turns to sit in the recliner.

"Was your husband Dutch?"

"No, but we met in Holland. I helped rescue him, and then he—" She closes her eyes, leans her head back against the chair. "He rescued me."

There comes a time for forgetting,
For who could live and not forget?
Now and then, however,
There must also be one who remembers.

ALBRECHT GOES
DAS BRANDOPFER (THE BURNT OFFERING)

TWENTY-NINE

ELIESE

Singing—that's what Fünten and Süskind were doing, gathered around the lobby's piano with an SS officer and the soldier who'd been guarding the door. The men belted out *"Das Lied der Deutschen"* as if they'd been invited to entertain on the stage of this theater, smoke from their cigars a backdrop to the performance.

Eliese had learned the words to this anthem as a child, the reminder that Germany was above all, but she'd also learned that its lyrics were a lie. The men sang about their brotherhood, about unity and rights and freedom for all, but Germany didn't protect the rights of all its citizens. Only those deemed worthy.

The men downed the wine reserves that Süskind had brought from his home, though no one told her what they were celebrating.

Could the people on the other side of the doors hear their song? What must they think, these drunk men who'd imprisoned them now celebrating as victors in their hunt? The quarry hadn't even tried to run.

No one lined up on the sidewalk in the early hours of this morning, but a handful of people remained in the theater, behind the locked doors. A fraction of the tens of thousands who'd filtered through here since last summer. She'd heard rumors of *razzias*, soldiers now taking Jewish people directly from their homes in Amsterdam and putting them on a train to Westerbork or the notorious SS camp called Vught. A purge, according to *De Telegraaf.* The Nazis had increased their reward for a Jewish person to thirty-seven and a half guilders to spur hunters into finding everyone who'd been hidden away.

Soon it would be light outside and Fünten and his officer would fade away, their work done under the cape of darkness. Usually Eliese walked home at first light—it wasn't safe for her to walk in the dark, even with the white Nazi-issued armband that permitted her to be out at night—but this celebration frightened her even more than the soldiers who wielded their guns. She wanted to run across the street and hide the remaining children from whatever Fünten had planned.

All of the children at the crèche were precious in God's sight, but their network hadn't been able to save all of them from the Nazis. Some parents made the decision for them—they didn't want their sons or daughters to leave with strangers. Other children weren't fit to travel. And some days those working underground couldn't find housing for anyone else.

During this past year, each person in their network had played his or her part impeccably, hundreds of Jewish children disappearing in the shadows, behind the curtain of the tram. They'd vanished in metal milk cans, burlap bags, and barrels loaded into wagons. Tucked away in prams and replaced by a doll before the children returned from their daily walks. Couriers then transported these children to homes across Holland.

The Nazis never even knew they were gone.

But the parents knew, and their hearts must have ached terribly, just as hers did whenever she thought about her son in these same shadows. They were all grieving the loss of their children even as they had to pretend nothing was wrong.

Even as she had to pretend tonight that she wasn't afraid.

Fünten poured another glass of the wine and held it out toward her. "Drink, Fräulein."

"It's Frau," she reminded him. "Frau Kingston."

He scrutinized her, the drink pulled back to his side. "Your diligence has been admirable, Eliese."

Her stomach turned at his familiarity, her name spoken in a drunken haze. If only she could turn and run the two blocks to the safety of her home.

"Your husband is American," he said.

She nodded.

"Is he fighting with the Allies?"

"No," she said. "He's an investor with the Holland Trade Bank."

He held out the drink again. "Then we shall drink to your husband."

She shook her head. "No thank you."

The commandant lowered the drink slowly, his eyes narrowing. Mr. Süskind swept in, grabbing the glass from Fünten's hands. Then he handed it to Eliese.

"Drink," he ordered as if her life—and perhaps others'—depended on it.

"To William," she muttered, and the others followed.

The wine forged a trail of fire down her throat, burning her stomach. Fünten clapped once, pleased at her submission, and then he began to sing the German anthem again, the other men following him.

When Süskind glared at her, she joined them, and she marveled at this man, walking the tightest of ropes over hell itself.

Fünten leaned close to her, the steam from his breath suffocating.

It was clear what he wanted. A drink, she could barely stomach. But this . . .

The only man she'd ever slept with was William, and she'd done it because she loved him. Would she sleep with this man to protect herself? Her son?

Oh, Hein.

If only she knew where to look for him. She'd somehow find a boat back to England. Or a ship to America. Take her son far away from here.

The lobby door opened, and the men stopped their singing. She could see a truck on the other side and she rushed into the cloakroom, grateful for the reprieve. Mr. Süskind followed close behind her while Fünten and the other men resumed their singing.

"What are they celebrating?" she asked Mr. Süskind.

"The Jewish Council will be closing the theater tomorrow."

"They're stopping deportations?" Perhaps Puttkammer's list had saved her and her father after all.

"The work you've done has been good, Eliese," he said. "Never forget that, no matter what you are told."

Mr. Süskind knew exactly which cards she'd slip up her sleeve and take home each morning, which cards she typed again the next evening, which names were missing each time. He knew how to distract Fünten when he needed to and how to pick the children he thought would be strong enough to live with a stranger.

She hadn't burned the index cards like she'd told Mr. Süskind—the ones with the names of parents and all of their children. They were stowed in her father's safe so one day the hidden children could return home.

"Is my work finished?" she asked.

"Not according to Fünten, but you and your father need to hide until the war is over."

"But what about the children in the crèche?"

"I fear we've saved all that we can."

His words pierced like an arrow to her heart, but she had nowhere to take the remaining children on her own. Her role was to make their names disappear. "Are the Allies winning?"

"I believe so," he said, his voice drowning in the music. "We must remain strong until they do."

And she would hold on—for her and Hein. For William. When this madness ended, their reunion would be sweet.

Then William could help her and Mr. Süskind reunite all the children with their families.

A soldier stood outside the door, but no one had entered to register. She folded her hands in her lap, silently praying for strength.

"Did you know I have a son?" she asked Mr. Süskind.

"It's not my business—"

"He's been hiding for almost a year now. I don't know where he is."

"A lot of people are hiding," Mr. Süskind said, simply stating this fact, but after a year at the theater, she was well aware that she was not alone.

"My father thinks we'll be invited to stay at the castle in Barneveld."

He glanced back at the lobby, but all they could see was the edge of the piano. "Do you think Fünten and his men will let you stay for long, in a castle?"

When she didn't answer, he turned toward her. "You and your father need to go under like your son."

"Thank you for protecting me," she said. "Others would have looked the other way."

"I can't protect you if you come back here."

She nodded.

"Make sure Fünten never finds those cards," he said.

Hiding and forgetting—they must do both to survive.

Another soldier escorted a gentleman into the theater, dressed in a black suit and tie, carrying a girl who wasn't more than two. The child's thick hair curled to her head, a ribbon tied around it. Had the man fixed her ribbon or had she been with her mother hours before?

When Mr. Süskind saw the child, he returned to the lobby, and she prayed silently that he would be able to distract Fünten one last time.

The gentleman opened his identity card, flat on the table. Inside she saw his name—Sjoerd Asch—and the black *J*. Then she saw familiar green letters on the ivory paper, the E.A.P. from her own card. The mark of Puttkammer.

Her voice trembled. "You have the stamp."

"It's rubbish," he snapped.

This stamp, the thirty thousand guilders he'd paid, was supposed to keep him safe, but perhaps it was as Mrs. Pon said. Perhaps Mr. Puttkammer and his colleagues simply took the money and then laughed behind the backs of everyone who joined this list.

Puttkammer wasn't going to keep her safe and neither was her job. She was pretending like all the others.

She lifted an index card from the stack and threaded it into the typewriter. "What is your child's name?"

"She's not mine," Mr. Asch said quietly.

"Then we will call her—" Eliese paused. "Let's not call her anything."

A flame sparked in the man's eyes. Understanding. The child's only hope of survival was if she remained nameless.

Eliese typed one card with just the man's name, the tapping of her keys muted by the men's song. "I have a safe place for her to stay."

When the singing stopped again, she quickly filed the registration card before Fünten stepped into the cloakroom. Mr. Süskind trailed close behind, a bottle in his hands. *Oude jenever* instead of wine.

The gin might have dulled the commandant's senses, but she doubted it would alter his focus.

"Is there a problem?" he demanded.

"No problem," she said, but her hands shook as she rolled a new card into the typewriter cylinder and began typing again as he looked over her shoulder, the stench of stale wine and smoke stifling her. She couldn't tell him about the card she'd filed lest he ask about the empty line.

Quickly she made up a name for the girl. Margot—the name of Eliese's mother. Margot Asch.

When Mr. Süskind filled Fünten's glass, she slipped the registration card with Margot's name up her bolero sleeve and then reached for the toddler, pretending to file the card with the girl in her arms.

The soldier escorted the man into the auditorium, and when he was gone, the commandant offered her his arm as if he were a gentleman, ignoring the baby who'd settled against her. "I'll drive you home, Eliese."

She hated the way that he said her name, clipped and broken. Hated the desperation that made her search for Mr. Süskind's help.

In the man's eyes, she caught a glimpse of her own desperation.

"It's only two blocks home," she said.

"And even closer to my rooms."

Mr. Süskind slapped Fünten on the back as if they were the best of friends. "I promised Eliese's father that I would drive her this morning."

"Her father means nothing to me."

Mr. Süskind glanced at Eliese as if he were passing an unseen torch and she must run with it for her life.

She'd asked Fünten about his wife before, to no avail. Perhaps he had children.

"Do you have daughters, Hauptsturmführer?" she asked, glancing down at the girl in her arms.

His gaze flickered, a light sparking on and then off again. A glimpse of humanity blackened quickly by the curtains of his soul.

Mr. Süskind handed her another glass, and the drink blazed inside her, emboldening her.

"You must take good care of your daughters, like my father does me."

"Sentiment doesn't deter me, Fräulein."

Mr. Süskind lifted the bottle of gin and filled the commandant's glass. Then he poured a glass for each of the men. "Good drink bleeds away all sentiment."

"I must take this girl to the crèche before we leave." Eliese inched the child up on her hip as if they might have forgotten about her.

Fünten swayed on his feet. "She can stay here."

"All the children are—"

"Of course the child can stay," Mr. Süskind interrupted her. "But it will be easier to count them if they are together."

"We're done counting," Fünten said. "They are all leaving on Thursday."

Tomorrow morning.

None of the children who remained had parents left to travel with them. She would have to warn Josie. Somehow they would have to steal these children away before Fünten and his men came for them.

"I will escort her over." Mr. Süskind took the girl from her arms, whispering in Eliese's ear, "And you will go home."

Fünten lifted his glass. "To *Judenrein*."

Eliese shivered, but even as Mr. Süskind lifted his glass for a toast, she saw the twitch in his eyes. Amsterdam wasn't free of all its Jews. She and her father and Mr. Süskind and the esteemed Jewish Council, the orphaned children who remained in the crèche and the adults left in the theater. They were still here, tainting the city.

The Nazis no longer needed the council to round up the Jews; her or Mr. Süskind to register them. Amsterdam wouldn't be free of the Jewish people until they were all gone.

But Mr. Süskind had no choice.

He lifted his glass and drank.

As the enemy drank with him, she backed out the door.

THIRTY

The answers I'm seeking are in Amsterdam; that's what Mrs. West said. Speaking William's name again seemed to darken even the lights that danced on her walls. It certainly swept the light out of her eyes.

Whatever she knew about my great-grandfather, she refused to tell me, so I called Claire from the Portland airport and left a message, asking why this Dutch woman who now lived in Oregon would be afraid of a man who'd died decades ago. Marcella called me back in minutes, but instead of answering my questions, she begged me to stop digging. Then she told me to come home.

But I'm not going back to New York. Not until I find out the truth of what William Kingston did.

The plane descends over the North Sea and then slips of plowed fields, each one chalked off by canals. The foundation may not pay me a salary, but the board has issued me a perfectly good credit card for personal and business expenses. This morning I'm going to use it to track down Paul Epker and his book.

A taxi takes me from the airport to the edge of the Jewish Quarter. To the library on Nieuwe Keizersgracht. Claire has left two voice mails on my phone and a text, demanding that I call, but I haven't returned her messages. It's the middle of the night on the East Coast, and if I'm really honest, I'm not prepared to face Marcella's wrath for flying to Amsterdam instead of New York.

The people pleaser in me is weary. I wish I could be more like Landon and not care so much about what people think, but I still care deeply.

"It doesn't matter," Mom whispered to me once, after a brood of girls ganged up on me in middle school, pecking at me with words that scarred. Later Mom told me that I should care only what God thinks of me, but I cared more, at the time, about what those girls thought.

What does God think of me now?

I've spent a lifetime trying to make others like me, trying to be good, but I have never felt good enough. Perhaps, in hindsight, I've spent a lifetime trying to be God.

A picture of Faith and two girls appears on my screen, a caption from Landon under it.

Don't you want to come back?

I do want to see him and Faith, but I can't tell him that.

I was only there as a delegate, not one of his team members who will return to Africa again and again.

I type back a quick response. I thought you were on your way home.

In a few hours, he writes.

Through Amsterdam?

Yes. Then direct to Portland.

What if I return to the airport? Surprise him?

I shake my head, pushing the crazy thought away. Unless I bought a ticket for this afternoon, security would never let me through to his gate.

People are huddled together at the library's tables when I arrive, Marcella's favorite quote about knowledge and power inscribed above them all.

As I watch these people turn pages, searching for information, I begin to wonder something else: Is Marcella trying to do more than provide knowledge through this library? Is she somehow trying to control it? I thought my family had built an entire library to find truth, but perhaps it was to filter the truth instead.

Knowledge is power, but knowledge can also be healing. It can be the key to fixing something broken.

A young woman approaches and asks if I need assistance. "Are you Liesbeth?" I ask.

She rings a strand of blonde hair behind her ear. "I am."

"I'm Ava Drake. I spoke with you on the phone about a book that Paul Epker was planning to send me."

"Mrs. Kingston left a voice mail," she said. "She asked that you contact her directly."

"Were you able to find the book he ordered?"

Liesbeth points at the phone on her desk as if I should pick it up right now. "Before I can give you any information, you need to speak with Mrs. Kingston."

"Perhaps you could give me Mr. Epker's mobile number instead. He'd know the answer to my question."

"I'm sorry," she says, shaking her head. "You'll have to talk to your grandmother."

I've learned plenty from Marcella in the past decade. The first thing is not to waste one's time fishing for answers among bottom-feeders if there are none to be found. So I step outside the library and call the mayor's office. After I introduce myself, his assistant gives me Paul's cell.

I leave a message and glance down at the photo Landon just sent me. What would he think if I invited him to join me for the day in Amsterdam? Our family stories seem to merge here. Perhaps we can bridge them together.

Instead of texting, I decide to call.

"Hey there," I say.

"Ava?"

"It's me." I smile, glad to hear his voice.

"Are you at the Entebbe airport?"

"Almost," he says. "I'll wave when I fly over New York."

I follow a canal away from the library, turning onto a busy street divided by a tram. On my right is the city zoo, and through an opening in the fence, I see coral-colored flamingos wading in a pond.

Landon continues, "Kendall said that you and Oma had a long talk."

"She told me a little about her life in the Netherlands."

I don't mention the lost child—this is something that she needs to tell him on her own.

"I suspect you know more than I do about her years in Amsterdam."

"You should ask her about it."

"I have, but she says she doesn't want to burden our family."

"I wonder why her memories are a burden . . ." But even as I say the words, I understand this burden. I've carried the memories of my brother for most of my life, and it's a tremendously heavy load.

Static garbles his response, and I fear I've lost him for a moment.

"I'm actually in the Netherlands," I say.

"I thought you were going to North Carolina."

"I am, but first—" I take a breath—"would you be able to extend your layover in Amsterdam for the day?"

His silence, even for a moment, the rejection—it worries me. "Your *oma* knows something about my great-grandfather that seems to frighten her. I was hoping you could help me search—"

"It's part of her light years," he says.

"Her what?"

"The gap years that she won't talk about. She remembers them through the light on her walls."

"She showed me her collection of glass."

"Oma loves to help others, but it's rare for her to invite someone into her world."

A pedestrian light flashes in front of me, and I step off the curb. "I'd better let you go."

"I'll change my flight," he says before disconnecting our call.

Ahead of me is Amsterdam's Holocaust Memorial, housed in a theater with white Renaissance columns that make it look like an ancient temple. Inside the lobby is a glass wall engraved with thousands of surnames, Dutch citizens who were transported from here. One hundred and twelve thousand Dutch Jews were deported during the Holocaust, I read. Five thousand survived, but nothing was the same for those men and women who came home.

What happened back then, it seems, continues silencing people today.

The auditorium in this old theater has been demolished, leaving behind a paved courtyard outside with brick walls in memory of all who'd been held here and then taken to a place called Westerbork.

My phone chimes, and I look down to see a text from Paul. It's an invitation to join him at his house tomorrow morning, just south of Amsterdam. I readily accept and ask to bring a friend.

The other walls of the lobby are lined with black-and-white photographs of the deportation center, photographs of some of the families who'd been transported to camps.

One picture captures my eye and I study it.

A middle-aged man and a petite woman are standing beside a typewriter—both wearing white bands around their arms, stars on their chests. His name is Walter Süskind, a German Jewish man in charge of registering everyone brought to this theater. The woman is one of his registrars.

I lean closer to read the caption beside the photo, and goose bumps ripple across my arms.

A network of people, including Walter and his assistant, rescued hundreds of children from this place before they were sent to concentration camps.

Across the street, another placard reads, was a nursery and a teachers' college. The theater was too small to house all the Jewish people taken from their homes, so the commander relocated the children to the nursery until they were sent east with their families.

With a parent's permission, the registrars began secretly deleting children's names from the registration cards so the Nazis no longer had a record of them. In spite of the Nazis' strict oversight, a team of nursery employees and college students were able to hide these kids.

Walter was sent to Westerbork in 1944. He received permission to return to Amsterdam, but his wife and daughter did not receive an exemption. When he learned they were about to be deported, he joined them on the train.

Walter's wife and daughter were gassed on arrival at Birkenau, but he survived four more months. No one knows exactly how he died, but some think he was killed by Dutch prisoners at Auschwitz who thought he had collaborated with their enemy.

The placard doesn't say what happened to the young woman who helped him rescue the children.

THIRTY-ONE

ELIESE

The heavy bolt groaned as Eliese turned the key, unlocking the front door.

"Papa!" she called in the foyer, breathless after running home.

Fünten had been consumed by the gin when she left, but he wouldn't be distracted for long. She and her father had to go under like Hein, someplace where Fünten and his men wouldn't find them.

Three envelopes from the Central Office for Jewish Emigration rested on the hardwood floor at her feet, slipped through the mail slot during the night.

The first letter, addressed to her father, stated that he was supposed to report to *De Schaffelaar*, the castle in Barneveld reserved for deserving Jews, the elite few who were still exempted from deportation.

In lieu of an invitation, she'd received a summons, *OPROEPING!* emblazoned across the top.

She must report to Amsterdam's Centraal Station by noon with a suitcase, prepared to work. The items to bring were listed below: a blanket, woolen sweater, pair of sturdy shoes. She knew the items well—the Jewish Council sold them in prepared deportation sacks for those who didn't have time to pack. Thousands had brought these canvas bags to the theater.

Were the Nazis planning to send her to Westerbork first, or would the train continue straight on to a work camp, men like Fünten waiting at the other end? It wouldn't matter where she or her father went—the Nazis wouldn't see a respectable investor and his daughter. They would see two filthy Jews needing to be transported east, and those in the east, she suspected, wouldn't want them either.

It didn't matter—she wasn't going to the train station today.

The third letter and list was a copy of hers, addressed to Hein, as if her three-year-old son needed a pair of sturdy shoes and wool sweater when he reported for work.

Grateful—she was so grateful—he was already gone and, she prayed, safe in a province like Zeeland, far from the border their country shared with Germany.

"Papa!" she called again as she rushed toward the steps, all three letters in hand.

When she reached the second floor, she pounded on his door. "Papa?"

He opened the door slowly, his bare toes creeping out from under pajama bottoms, his spectacles smeared where he'd jammed them onto his face.

She held out the letters, but he didn't reach for them.

"We received our notices," she said. "You're being sent to Barneveld."

"And you?"

"I'm supposed to register at the train station."

He took the letters from her. "We'll go to Barneveld together."

"Don't you see?" she begged. "They'll take you to this castle now, but it's only a farce. They won't keep you there forever."

"You don't know that—"

"We have to find a place to hide." The registration card crept down her arm, and she inched it back up her sleeve. "We'll wait."

"Wait for what?"

"For this war to end."

His laugh was harsh. "Hitler won't let it end, not until he's taken over the world."

"Mr. Süskind said the Allies are winning."

"Perhaps, but Hitler's men will find us long before the Allies arrive. Better to wait at a place like Barneveld, where we'll be protected."

"No one will protect us there."

"They need me," her father insisted. "To access the money."

She shook her head. "They've already taken everything they need."

"But there's so much more . . ."

Gerrit Linden and his investors helped Hitler launch this war, but the Nazis had more loot now than they could ever use in Holland, stuffed in the basement at Liro. They didn't need her father's money anymore.

"We're going to Barneveld." He stepped back into his room. "Go pack your suitcase and bring your warmest coat."

As if they'd be there until winter.

She couldn't stop her father's surrender, but she wouldn't go with him either, even if she thought the Germans would spare her life. She would help Josie with the children and then somehow—when the Allies finally arrived—she would be reunited with her son.

The ring of their doorbell echoed down the hall, reverberated through her skin.

Were the Gestapo planning to escort her to the station? What would they do when they discovered her son was gone?

Hurrying into her room, she swept Hein's baby book out of the bureau and stuffed several items of clothing into a knapsack. Papa stepped back into the corridor the same time she did, wearing his Sunday coat over the pajamas and carrying a giant ball of bedding in his arms.

"I'm not going," she said.

He blinked, studying her face for a moment. Then he kissed both of her cheeks.

She fled down the back steps, but before she stepped into the courtyard, she heard Fünten's voice in the foyer.

"*Guten Morgen*, Herr Linden." The commander, it

seemed, had overpowered the effects of his drink long enough to visit her home. "We are searching for your daughter and grandson."

Had Fünten just learned that she had a son or had he known it all along?

"You're too late," Papa said. "They've already gone—"

"Then you won't mind if we look around."

Eliese fled out to the gardener's shed. Inside, behind pots and tools, was an iron grate and wooden steps that led into the depths of their basement. In decades past, before it was boarded up, a servant would load the coal furnace through the cellar entrance inside the house, but she and her father were the only ones who used these stairs in the shed.

She lowered herself through the grate and slid an iron bolt into the lock. Light seeped through the coal chute at the far end of the cellar and pinpricks on the ceiling, a constellation shining through the kitchen drains.

Voices filtered down as she hurried across the rugged floor, scattered with cinders, and around a clunky furnace and shelves once filled with tinned herring and Gouda wheels. The baby book in her hands, she slid into the darkness of a corner, wishing she could hide herself in the mortar between the brick walls.

Something scratched her arm, startling her. And she remembered the card beneath her sleeve, Margot's name typed neatly on it.

Mr. Süskind had promised to take that little girl over to the crèche, but he wouldn't warn Josie and the others about *Judenrein*, afraid they would endanger the lives of those left in Amsterdam if they fled. How she hated this weighing and measuring of life, but Mr. Süskind had a family to protect at home and probably others directly under his care.

Instead of warning Josie herself, she had run back to her house, to hide away with her father. What had become of her, choosing to flee instead of helping her friend? Leaving those children—Margot—to be taken away.

She'd become another Dutch coward.

Unrolling her sleeve, she removed Margot's card to store with the others.

The safe was located at the far end of the room, hidden behind a wall of bricks and mortar that her father had built when they first moved into this house. He kept a flashlight on top of the wall, and she clicked it on before inching away two of the bricks to reveal a silver dial lock.

The treasures inside the safe's belly were vast—diamonds and money and gold—but the most valuable to her father were the ledgers with all of their investments. The registration cards, to her, were worth more than anything else.

Someone shouted above, the words muffled, and she quickly placed Margot's card inside with the others. Then she kissed the edge of Hein's baby album and set it on top of the ledgers.

Reaching deep into the vault, she retrieved a bottle filled with the diamonds that her father had gathered over the years, an investment that wouldn't lose value like Reichsmarks or guilders. She slipped the bottle into her pocket, then relocked the safe and placed the bricks carefully over the opening before ducking between the iron bins that once collected coal pouring in from a truck on the street.

Upstairs she heard stomping of boots, more shouting. Then all was quiet overhead.

Climbing up one of the bins, she pushed on the chute's metal door and peeked onto the sidewalk. A troop of heels—black pillars on shiny jackboots—stomped by. Then her father's brown oxfords, trapped between them.

An engine rumbled, and seconds later, the shoes were gone.

She slumped down with the cinders.

Had Fünten taken her father to Barneveld or one of the camps?

She'd never be able to help him now.

Leaning against the wall, she closed her eyes. Instead of Hein or her father, she saw Margot looking back at her.

Tomorrow morning—that's when Fünten said they would be taking the last transport to Westerbork. They'd leave for the station at 4:45 a.m.

Her hand slipped into her pocket, the diamonds hidden deep inside. Tonight she would return to the crèche to warn Josie about the roundup. Perhaps with these stones, they could bribe a soldier or two to look the other way. And bribe someone else to help them hide the children.

THIRTY-TWO

JOSIE

AMSTERDAM

SEPTEMBER 1943

Children were scattered around Josie's feet, listening to the story about a fairy and an enchanted arrow—an arrow that could kill an entire army of Ossaerts who'd been tormenting the gnomes in her forest. It was a contraband book, one she'd read dozens of times to the children who spent the night at their crèche.

The back door was open to the courtyard so they could hear the soft drum of raindrops on the pavement, breathe the last of the evening air. And in her arms was Margot, the girl that Mr. Süskind had brought them early this morning. The only child left who wasn't on the Nazis' registry list.

The other children—sixty-seven of them—who remained

didn't have parents left to care for them, but Fünten ensured that each one had registered when they arrived in the ghetto's final roundup. She and Miss Pimentel wanted to hide all of these children, but Fünten had their names in his registry. If they hid any of their wards, they'd risk losing them all.

Several of the children inched closer to Josie as she read about the rabbit hole in the deep woods, the hiding place that protected the gnomes from harm.

The gray light was fading into black, but neither she nor Miss Pimentel moved to close the door. They could pretend for a few more moments that they were in the forest, protected by magical arrows and a shield of rain.

When they finished their prayers, each child returned to a cot. Miss Pimentel placed a baby in one of the cribs, and Josie pulled the covers over Margot as if the blankets the Nazis had provided would protect her as well.

It had been days since the trucks lined up outside the crèche to transfer the deportees. She'd prayed that Fünten had forgotten them, that the children left here would stay.

But the Nazis refused to leave these little ones alone.

A brisk knock, moments after Josie slipped under her blanket, shot like a bullet through her soul, paralyzing her until Margot began to cry. A lamp flickered on, and as she lifted the child, Miss Pimentel motioned for Josie to step into the shadows, near the cots along the back wall.

The director squared her shoulders and answered the knock.

Fünten marched swiftly into the room and swore. As if he'd forgotten how many children were here.

"We're leaving," he announced.

At first she felt relief; the Germans were finally leaving—

"Who is leaving?" Miss Pimentel asked.

His hand swept in front of him as if it were the cruel broom of a witch collecting bits of dust. "Them."

"But they have no parents—"

"They don't need parents to ride in a truck."

"We must prepare them for this journey," Miss Pimentel insisted, her worn hands pressed together.

"Everything they need will be provided."

The director shook her head. "The younger ones must have their bottles."

Rain trickled down both sides of his cap, onto his face, water falling off cold stone. He handed Miss Pimentel the final list. "You have ten minutes."

Ten minutes and all the children would be gone.

If only she and Miss Pimentel could open the doors and set these children free. But Fünten and his men, she feared, would shoot them as they ran.

Miss Pimentel rushed across the room, her usually knotted hair lying across her shoulders, and began preparing bottles. Josie fled out the back door with Margot, through the break in their hedge.

A rabbit hole.

Dr. van Hulst was in his office, and he blanched when he saw her and the child, Josie in her robe, Margot's curly hair soaked with rain. "What is it?"

"The Nazis are taking all the children, but this girl—she's not on their list."

Margot went to Dr. van Hulst willingly. "We will find a place for her," he promised.

"Godspeed," she whispered as he rushed from the office. And a good place to hide.

"You must leave," Miss Pimentel said when Josie stepped back into the nursery, closing the door behind her, "before Fünten comes back."

"What will you do?" Josie asked as she buttoned her gray dress.

"I'll escort the children to camp."

Josie took a deep breath, her resolve growing. She'd been cowering for the past three years, sneaking around with her letters and then the children, watching thousands being taken away. This time she would stand with her wards.

"I'm going with you."

Miss Pimentel shook her head. "You must continue helping others."

"God has called me to help these children."

"No—"

"I can't stay here."

Miss Pimentel started to speak again, but she was interrupted by Fünten and two of his dark-cloaked men, marching through the door.

Fünten lifted a clipboard and began reading the names of those who remained. The older ones lined up with their bedrolls by the door. Miss Pimentel lifted a baby out of his crib.

He finished the list and then looked up. "Where is the other child?"

"What child?" Josie asked, her voice trembling.

"The girl," he said. "The one brought over earlier today."

"We don't have another girl."

Fünten removed the gun from the holster and raised it.

She thought he would shoot her, but he lifted it and shot the mosaic window behind her, shards of seawater and shells filling the cradles below.

Several of the children screamed. Then everything was still.

Josie wanted to join the boys and girls in their quiet tears, but she held her face firm for Margot's sake.

"Get in the truck," Fünten shouted.

They emptied the crèche in seconds, herded like animals onto the street, through the downpour of rain.

One of the older girls began to whimper, and Josie reached for her hand. The girl burrowed in close to her on their journey to the central station, in the train car headed east.

She didn't let go until they arrived in Westerbork.

THIRTY-THREE

Landon smiles at me when he steps into the inn, and my heart does a strange flip. I don't move, but when he crosses the small lobby, when he hugs me, I don't want to let go of this man who loves children and coffee. A man who honors his commitments.

My phone buzzes, and I step back, catching a breath full of roasted coffee and sandalwood and a hint of lemongrass, warding the snakes away.

I don't answer the call. Uncle Will has already left me four voice mails, blotting them all with an assortment of colorful words, calling my journey here a witch hunt.

"Thank you for coming," I tell the man in front of me. "How is Faith?"

"You'd never even know that she had malaria. She's keeping all the children entertained with her new song about rainbows."

I smile at the good memories from my time in Africa. And I want to be there again, singing with her, as long as the snakes leave me alone.

"I sent my report to the foundation," I say, "giving Bishara my highest recommendation, but I'm afraid—"

He looks offended. "I'm not here about the grant."

"I know, Landon."

The offense in his eyes dissolves into relief. "That's out of the way, then."

"Do you want coffee?" I ask, grasping for something familiar.

"Later," he says. "I'm worried about Oma. Kendall said she won't leave her room with the glass."

I study this man in his faded sweatshirt and rugged sandals and jeans. Landon and I have already been in the trenches together, racing to save Faith's life, and I greatly admire his devotion to those in his family. I can trust him, I think, with my own suspicions that something happened long ago between Mrs. West and my great-grandfather.

I tell him what I've read and then I tell him about Paul Epker's book. "I'm supposed to meet with him in an hour."

He glances at his phone.

"Would you like to go with me?" I ask.

When he pauses, I think I've overstepped the boundary of our friendship again until he looks back at me. "Are you certain?"

Certain of what, I'm not sure.

Certain that I want him to go with me or certain that I want this friendship that we've established to grow.

"Yes, I'm certain," I say.

And he smiles.

Paul lives in a lovely old villa along the Amstel. He's waiting for us by the front door, his face somber, a satchel in hand.

Instead of inviting us inside, Paul asks me and Landon to take a walk on the path beside the river. The clouds have emptied themselves, cleansing the stones and sprinkling the wildflowers.

Water separates this city like Portland, the many bridges mending their divide, but we stay on Paul's side of the river this morning.

He glances at me. "Did you know my godfather once worked for William Kingston?"

I shake my head.

"After the war, William hired him to expand his window business across the Netherlands. My father also worked for the Kingston Corporation for a few years, but he left in his twenties." Paul's voice cracks. "All this time, I didn't know . . ."

"What didn't you know?"

He continues walking, his hand gripping the satchel at his side. Then he pulls out a small book, the cloth cover a chocolate brown. "Mrs. Kingston asked me to find this for her. As far as I know, it's the last copy in existence, and I'm afraid she wants to destroy it."

When I shiver, Landon takes my hand, steadying me.

"I don't want to give it to you either," Paul says. "But not because I think you'll trash it."

I glance at the worn edges of its cover. "Part of me doesn't want to take it."

"The facts are hard to read, even if knowledge is power. The Dutch publisher recalled this book days after the release."

"Are you certain it's true?" I ask.

"We may never be able to confirm all of it, but I've done enough digging to confirm the worst parts. I don't know how the author got this information. He or she used a pseudonym."

We've reached an enclosed gazebo at the edge of his property. A tearoom, Paul calls it. Inside is a wicker couch with cushions and two chairs and a glass table that holds a pitcher of water, garnished with lemon slices.

"I thought you might want to read it here." He hands me the slim book, and I stare down at the title.

Hitler's Bank by . . .

The author's name blurs for a moment before I read it again.

Daan Kooiman.

The name Peter Ziegler used to sign his paintings.

"Kooiman," Paul says, "means 'man of the cage.'"

Had Peter spent his time at Craig House writing as well? Trying to break free?

Perhaps this book will tell me what exactly held him and his mind in chains.

"Are you okay?" Landon asks, his hand curled around my elbow.

"I don't know."

He reaches for a chair. "I'll stay."

"No." I take a breath. "I suspect I need to read this alone."

"We'll stay on the property," Paul says. "Just text when you're done."

I glance at Landon and see the concern in his eyes.

"I'll be okay."

Landon closes the door, but the men don't walk far, just to the edge of the river.

My hands tremble as I open the first page.

Inside the cover is a laminated newspaper clip, an article from 1968 saying the book was written by a madman, the story a farce. The Kingston family had done and continued to do a world of good, William Kingston was quoted as saying. They'd helped rebuild Europe after the war, their focus on the future, not the past.

The book released a year earlier, in 1967.

The same year that Peter Ziegler died.

THIRTY-FOUR

ELIESE

Her neighbors, it seemed, had been waiting on the fringes
for the Nazis to finish their dirty work. Then they began to
plunder the Linden home.

In the hours Eliese had been hiding, people had removed
pieces of furniture from their sitting room, valuable paintings
from the walls. Even the clock that her father had carried so
carefully from Germany, to remember her mother, was gone.

She hurried up to her bedroom and changed into a black
skirt and gray blouse before affixing the white band around
her arm that allowed her to break curfew.

Rain poured out of the dark skies, pelting her windows.

Somehow, in the next few hours, she and Josie would have to steal the children out of the crèche, find them hiding places before Fünten arrived with his trucks.

Any that remained could return to her house, hide in the basement with her and Josie and Miss Pimentel until they found families who could care for them.

The streets were empty as she battled the winds of this storm, the guards who usually patrolled them gone. A rumble of thunder startled her as she walked—no, it was a different kind of sound. A roar of engines barreling up the road.

Eliese slipped into an alley, a cavern of shadows, as two army trucks rushed past her, driving away from the theater. The same kind of trucks that transported the Jewish people to Amsterdam Centraal.

But they never transported people from the theater at this hour. They always left at 4:45, an hour before the train departed.

Lightning flashed as she hurried down the street, rounded the corner. The sidewalk in front of the theater was empty, the door into the crèche unlocked.

The room was usually warm during the night, the children's beds crowded together in neat rows, but when she opened the door tonight, all she felt was cold.

Lightning sparked again. The stained-glass window in the back was gone and so were all the children.

She felt as if she were in a trance, gliding across the floor. As if the ghosts of these children were asleep on their cots, Margot resting among them. But instead of children, the beds were filled with glass.

Eliese collapsed onto the scuffed hardwood, shards cutting the bare skin on her legs. The weight of this day, this year, pressed down on her, more than she could bear. She'd wanted to help these children who'd lost their parents, find them a safe place like they'd done for so many others. Like Josie had done for Hein.

But she'd never be able to put these beautiful broken pieces together again.

"Eliese."

Someone whispered her name from the side of the room, but she didn't move. It was only the ghosts whispering to her.

"Eliese," the voice said again—a man—and then he was at her side. It was Samuel, but not the man she remembered. His face was gaunt, covered in stubble, ragged clothes hanging loosely on his frame. In his arms he held the girl she'd registered early this morning.

"Margot," she whispered.

Samuel held out the child, and Margot slipped into her arms. Eliese wouldn't let go of her again.

"You have to leave this place," Samuel said.

She brushed the rainwater off Margot's face before turning back to him. "What are you doing here?"

"I came to warn Josie—"

"Did Fünten take her and the children?"

When he nodded slowly, the weight of it bore down on her. If only she'd left the house before dark. Just an hour earlier she might have saved them all.

Samuel stepped toward the door. "Now we have to find a safe place for this girl."

Eliese edged a shard of glass out of her palm and dropped

it onto the floor, the girl clinging to her neck like Hein had once done. "You've been the one helping these children."

"Many of us helped."

"But you led them."

He took her hand, pulling her and Margot away from the glass. "Fünten is searching for you, Eliese. He's doubled the reward to seventy-five guilders."

"Are you going to turn us in?" she asked as they neared the front door.

"Of course not, but you can't stay here."

"They took my father this morning."

One hand still secured around hers, Samuel lifted the edge of the blackout curtain, peeking out before he turned back to her. "Did they find his books?"

She shook her head. "You and I are the only ones in Holland who know where he was investing his money."

Samuel released her hand. "Your father regretted what he did. He tried to make amends."

"But he didn't stop, even after the Nazis invaded. He continued funneling money to those German companies as collateral."

"I fear we all have blood on our hands."

She looked down at her hands, two silhouettes in the ring of shadows. So many had been sent away after she'd recorded their names with these fingers. So many, she feared, had died. Adults and children alike, registered by her.

"Did William and Peter know what my father was doing?" she asked, her voice shaking.

"Your father kept them informed of everything that

was happening until the war began." He paused. "Then he poured some of their investment back into the resistance."

She nodded slowly. William would be glad that he'd used this money to fight the Nazis.

Samuel reached for the doorknob. "You can hide at my cousin's house in Maastricht."

She looked at the girl, her heart aching. "I can't leave Amsterdam without Hein."

"Oh, Eliese—"

When she heard the sorrow in his voice, she felt herself sinking, down to the floor again. Samuel reached for Margot even as he kept talking, telling her that they had to leave now, but she shoved her fingers into her ears, rocking back and forth as if she were a child again, as if she could shut out this cruel, dark world.

His hand was on her shoulder, trying to comfort her, but grief soaked through all that had begun to callous. She wrapped her hands over her legs, wishing she could roll herself into a ball. A cocoon from this pain that ripped through her heart. All this time she'd been working, her son needed her. She was safe while he—

She rocked back again, looking up. "Josie said it was a safe place."

"It was safe . . . until their neighbor turned them in."

"Where did the Nazis take my son?"

"They took everyone they found to Kamp Vught." A place much worse than Westerbork.

"I must go—"

"It's too late," he said. "They've already been transported east."

Closing her eyes, she turned away from Samuel.

"Get up, Eliese," he commanded.

She didn't stir, nor would she. She'd been the worst of mothers, helping the very men who'd taken her son.

"For Hein's sake, you must save yourself."

She choked on her words. "Hein is gone."

"Then do it for William."

THIRTY-FIVE

Terroir.

That's what I long for when I finish reading *Hitler's Bank*. The warm beaches of North Carolina, where I can bury my toes and perhaps my head in the sand, run away from the wicked truth of what my family has done.

Closing my eyes, I lean back against the glass of this gazebo.

Even if I ran home, I wouldn't be able to bury my head for long. No matter where I go, the past will follow me. Even when I try to fight, it haunts me in my dreams.

Somehow I have to confront what happened long ago or I fear it will destroy me as well.

The beginnings of this story I already knew: the

introduction of Peter and William at Cambridge, a forged bond that would last a lifetime. What I didn't know was the wellspring of their wealth. That portion had been omitted from our family's history—the worst kind of a lie.

Near the end of the Great Depression, these men—like other American and European investors—latched on to a politician named Adolf Hitler, who was uniting German business leaders to rebuild after the destruction of the Great War. It was a risky investment that became solid as the years passed. Before the Allied Forces entered the Second World War, William and Peter had already begun partnering with a Dutch bank to funnel the money back to Germany. Holland Trade Bank invested in oil and automobiles, coal mines and zinc, and IG Farben, a company that produced a pesticide called Zyklon.

The poison that Nazi Germany used in their gas chambers.

William and Peter invested an enormous amount of money into financing the preparations for Hitler's war, and they made an enormous amount through the slave labor at concentration camps, producing cheap goods.

The Kingston money is tainted, every dollar of it. My family's money, used to kill and destroy. The money more important than the people who were fighting for their lives.

According to this book, Peter Ziegler didn't learn until 1944 what happened in the concentration camps, but Hitler had never tried to hide his intent to persecute the Jewish people. Both Peter and William continued to invest through Holland Trade Bank, even after the war began.

No wonder William poured so much money into recovery after the war. He'd wanted to lose the family's sordid investments in the shuffle of all their good work so neither he nor Peter would be tried as a traitor.

Peter—the man in the cage—was dead less than a month after the publication of this book. His guilty conscience, it seemed, had spilled out on paper through his stories and on that last canvas. He, a Jewish German man, had betrayed his own people.

Was he truly ill or did the Kingston family have him committed when he threatened to tell the truth? And would William kill his business partner in order to keep their secrets?

Tears begin falling down my cheeks. Landon was right when he'd said that some businesses use goodwill public relations to cover up something that isn't good at all. Kingston Family Foundation, started decades ago, is a massive PR operation to cover up the truth about our legacy. It's a facade, like the headquarters office in Kenya, built to camouflage.

I don't want any part of it. Not the cover-up or the fortune or this culture of hurting others.

A glimpse of heaven, that is the *terroir* I need right now, a place where evil can no longer hide, the supreme light of Christ blasting away the shadows.

The phone buzzes in my hand, and I decline Claire's call again.

My mother was adopted into this family, and I stepped into it at the age of fifteen, desperate for a family of my own; but the deception, the lies—this isn't what I want.

My mother ran away from this madness, but I don't want to run. I want to find out the truth so no one else gets hurt.

At the end of the book is a photograph of three men and a young woman, a caption underneath. It's the owner of Holland Trade Bank—Gerrit Linden and his daughter, Anneliese, with William and Peter. William has his arm around the girl.

I lean closer. It's the same woman I saw in the theater, the one in the photograph with Walter Süskind, but in this picture, she's younger. And she's smiling.

In her smile, I see Landon.

The book in my hand, I leave the gazebo and find Paul and Landon standing beside a creek fringed with daffodils. When Landon sees my tears, he grasps my hand in his, like he did with Faith when she lay on the hospital bed. One more person who needs to be rescued.

"You know who wrote this?" Paul asks.

"I believe so, but it's much too late to prove it." I brush my hand over the cover. "Is this why you resigned your position?"

He nods. "My godfather worked for the Kingstons his entire life, but I—I'm afraid I can't work for them any longer."

"What is your godfather's name?" I ask.

"Klaas." He pauses. "Klaas Schoght."

He waits as if I might say that I've heard of Mr. Schoght, but the Kingston Corporation has employed tens of thousands of people in the past seventy years. And I know only a handful of the executive team now.

"Is your godfather still alive?" I ask.

He shakes his head. "He died more than a decade ago."

"What about Anneliese Linden?"

"I don't know what happened to her."

Opening the book, I show Landon the photograph of

Anneliese and her father. He takes a long breath as he studies the woman standing next to William.

"Oma," he says slowly.

Mrs. West did know my great-grandfather. Quite well, it seems.

Paul may no longer work for the library, but he still has the key to a side gate. And as a representative of Kingston Family Foundation, I request an after-hours tour.

After a long phone conversation this afternoon, Mrs. West told Landon that she had been known as Anneliese, a lifetime ago. She also suggested that he visit the cellar under the house where she'd lived in Amsterdam. On Nieuwe Keizersgracht.

According to Paul, the Nazis confiscated the Kingston Bibliotheek canal house from a Jewish family during the war, before William Kingston purchased it, but Paul didn't realize that Gerrit and Anneliese Linden had once lived here.

Access to the cellar is through a glass garden house behind the library, tiny bulbs strung low across the ceiling. Paul doesn't turn on the lights. He uses a flashlight instead, directing us to a set of stairs sectioned off by a half wall, then down a short corridor until we're back under the house.

The cellar is dank, the dirt floor stubbled with fragments of stone. Along the wall are bricks, each one stitched together by a seam of mortar.

Landon uses a screwdriver to inch out the bricks that Mrs. West told him to remove, and behind them is the rusted dial of a safe, engraved with numbers from zero to seventy-five. He doesn't need to use the combination Mrs. West gave him. Someone has left it open.

The floor creaks overhead, and we all freeze. Maybe it's just the groaning of old bones, but Paul turns off his flashlight. The only light left is what steals in through the cracks from the streetlamps outside.

Landon sweeps his arm inside the safe, collecting whatever he can find. Then he slips it into his pocket.

More creaking above, footsteps on the wood. A watchman, I hope, is simply checking on the building, but like my mother, I'm beginning to fear what her brothers might do.

The glow from my phone is dimmer than Paul's flashlight, but it's bright enough for us to find our way around the cellar's posts and walls, to the steps on the other side. Silently we walk out of the garden house and gate, taking a car back to Paul's villa.

My heart is still pounding as Paul makes us cappuccinos. Landon places the sole item that he found in the safe on the kitchen table, a worn index card with names typed on it.

Werner, Hanneke, and Esther van Gelder.

After their names is an address in Amsterdam, the ages of the parents and their daughter—aged four—Werner's occupation as an interior decorator. Landon looks up the address on his phone; it's now home to a bicycle repair shop.

I've been hoping for answers, the connection between my family and Mrs. West, but there's nothing on this card to link us.

Paul returns with two cappuccinos and lifts the card, studying it. "Remarkable."

"What is it?" Landon asks.

"A registration card," Paul says. "We know the registrars helped rescue Jewish children from the crèche, but no one knows exactly how they erased their names."

"Oma stole it?" Landon asks.

"Perhaps."

Landon sips the cappuccino. "I wonder what happened to the other cards. . . ."

I sigh. "William probably found them when he bought her house."

"Or maybe Oma brought them to the United States with her."

Paul's cat wraps itself around my leg, and I reach down to pet it. "How exactly did she get to the United States?"

"My great-grandfather's plane was shot down over the Netherlands," Landon says. "She found him before the Nazis did, and they escaped together."

"Klaas used to say those planes swarmed like bees over this city."

"What was your godfather like?" I ask.

Paul leaves the room and returns with a frame that holds dual photographs, one in color and the other black-and-white. The older photograph is of a handsome young man laughing in the wind, his necktie blowing over his shoulder. The other picture is of a stern gentleman in a chair, his hand curled around the arm. On his finger is a gold ring, speckled with jewels, and beside him is a handsome young man in a striped suit, his smile stretching across generations.

"That's my papa." Paul points to the smiling man. "Klaas never had any children of his own, but he spoiled my father."

"What is your father's name?"

"Hein." Paul traces his hand across the edge of the photograph. "His parents died during the war, but he was adopted by a couple in Maastricht."

"I wonder if Klaas knew Anneliese."

Paul lowers the frame. "I never heard him talk about anyone from those war years."

"So many were silent," Landon says.

Paul looks back down at the photographs. "A story untold never seems to heal."

"We'll never be satisfied in here—" Landon pounds his chest—"by relying on someone other than God to heal us. He desires redemption, not pain, for His children."

I've been digging through books from the past for pieces of my heritage, but perhaps I need to look through another old book to find it. Perhaps I need to turn my heart, my soul, back to where I'd searched for answers as a child.

As I settle into my bed that night, my mother's Bible in my hands, I start at the beginning, in the Garden of Eden. My mother drew a tree with golden fruit, a man and woman holding hands. And then she drew a black snake, encircling the tree.

Like the cobra I saw in Africa.

I'm not hunting witches on this trip, but snakes perhaps. The past seems to be lurking like that spitting cobra in the grass, ready to blind anyone who startles it.

What had William Kingston done when he became afraid?

Near the bottom of the page, marked in purple ink, is a reference to another verse in Romans.

"Do not be overcome by evil, but overcome evil with good."

My mom drew a picture of a hand, nailed into wood, a single drop of blood spilling out onto the world below.

In this book, instead of sorrow, perhaps true healing can be found.

THIRTY-SIX

JOSIE

WESTERBORK
SEPTEMBER 1943

Heat sweltered the crowded registration room that smelled like cabbage soup and sausage. Albert Gemmeker, the commandant at Westerbork, scanned the heads of the sixty-seven children, including the baby in Miss Pimentel's arms, and waved them to the front of the line.

"Where are their parents?" he barked as Josie tried to calm those who'd lost their battle against tears.

Miss Pimentel replied calmly to Gemmeker's demand. "They no longer have parents."

He checked his watch. "Their train leaves in an hour—"

"But we've only just arrived."

The man's eyes narrowed, the silver braids on his cap dangling over them. "All the orphaned children are being sent east."

Josie pulled one of the boys close to her, quickly wiping his tears lest the camp commandant ridicule him.

The children had been transported here via train in the night hours, spread out among cars filled with those captured in the latest roundup and a host of workers who'd been summoned for a party at Gemmeker's home tonight, on the other side of the barbed wire. Supplies for the commandant's event were piled in boxes and barrels at one end of this narrow building while the children had been crammed into the other.

The registrar glanced at Josie's identity card and handed it back to her with an exemption paper so she could escort the children to their train before returning home, but she wasn't planning to go back.

"Henriëtte Pimentel," the registrar muttered as her typewriter keys transcribed the director's information.

All this time that Josie had been working at the crèche, she hadn't even known the woman's first name.

Miss Pimentel wouldn't ask for an exemption either. She would go in strength and dignity, no matter what men like Fünten did.

The two women escorted the children out into the dusty yard, the youngest ones clinging to their hands. The pinks of dawn settled across the white barracks on this heath, and the camp's residents began emerging, many with knapsacks over their shoulders, a steady rhythm of footfalls from those who wore wood for shoes.

A new train, this one a chain of cattle cars, crept into the center of camp. On the platform was another woman surrounded by children, many of them wearing casts or bandaged with gauze. She wore a white apron over her blue dress, and she was holding the hand of a boy about three or four. His scalp was almost bare, splotched with patches where he'd lost clumps of hair, his cheeks ruddy. In his other hand, he held a faded lamb.

Josie stepped toward the woman, a surge of relief in the midst of the turmoil. "Mrs. Pon?"

"What are you doing here?" Distress instead of relief raged in her former neighbor's gaze.

"I've come with children from Amsterdam."

Mrs. Pon eyed their group. "Did they put you on the transport list?"

"No, but I'm going with them."

"Do you want to play?" the boy asked with a smile, as if they could kick a ball or play hopscotch before boarding this train.

Josie leaned down next to him. "What is your name?"

"Hein," he said proudly. "Hein Kingston."

Josie's mouth gaped open. Only a moment, but Mrs. Pon saw and the woman nodded back at her. "The surname hasn't done him any favors here."

"I thought he was—" She stopped herself, her heart plunging. She'd promised Eliese that he would be safe in an Aryan home. "How did he get here?"

"He was shipped up from Kamp Vught," Mrs. Pon said. "Where is Eliese?"

"I don't know."

"She sent me packages for months, and then they stopped." Mrs. Pon lifted Hein; then she handed him to Josie. The boy's arms felt warm against her skin.

"Come with me," Mrs. Pon said.

Josie promised Miss Pimentel that she'd return.

Hein looped her long hair in circles as they maneuvered around oak barrels and crates—more supplies, she assumed, for the commandant's soiree—until they reached a building with a makeshift sign that read Children's Ward.

Two rows of empty bunk beds stood three high, straw from the mattresses sticking out of the sides, toys instead of children scattered across the lumpy tops. An assortment of medical supplies had been piled on a central table and on the wooden floor was a galvanized tub, filled with murky water.

Mrs. Pon reached for a washcloth and wiped Hein's forehead. Then she prepared something in a glass for him.

"Drink this," she said kindly, and Hein grimaced as he sipped it.

Josie glanced again at the empty beds. "Were those your patients on the platform?"

Mrs. Pon nodded. "They usually don't deport the children who are ill, but it seems things have changed again."

Something chimed outside, like the church bells in Amsterdam.

"It's time for me to leave." Mrs. Pon leaned forward and kissed Hein's cheek. "The valerian will help him sleep so you can hide."

Josie stepped to the door beside her, Hein in her arms. "I'm going with you."

Rain began falling, soaking the windows between bunks.

"You don't belong on that train, Josie."

"None of us belong on it."

Mrs. Pon glanced at the window. "After every transport, the people here begin to celebrate and then the commandant will dine with his friends. During the cabaret performance, you and Hein must leave."

"I'm already leaving—"

"We have a cutter to snip the bolts off containers. It will snap right through the wire fence."

A guard shouted into a megaphone outside, calling Hein Kingston's name. The boy burrowed his head into her shoulder.

"You're not on their list, Josie."

"But he is."

Mrs. Pon snatched a doll from one of the beds and wrapped it in a hospital blanket, holding it up to her shoulder so the top of the doll's head was exposed. "We will save him, for Eliese. So she and her husband can find him after the war."

For Eliese—the woman who had been her best friend as a girl. The woman who had betrayed her brother and left with an American.

The woman who had helped her rescue hundreds of children even when she didn't know what happened to her son.

Mrs. Pon opened the door to a small closet, waving Josie inside. "Hurry."

Still she didn't move.

"Please, Josie."

Miss Pimentel, all the children, they would think she

abandoned them. But then she could almost hear Miss Pimentel whispering in her ear.

"We can't save all of the children, Josie, but you can save one more."

Miss Pimentel and Mrs. Pon, they would care well for the others.

With Hein in her arms, Josie ducked in beside a mop and bucket. And she wished it were all a game, hiding like she'd done with Samuel and Klaas when they were children.

Mrs. Pon whispered through the narrow slats of the closet door. "L'chaim."

To life.

Hein began stirring in her arms.

"Let's play a game," Josie whispered. "It's called cat and mouse."

"I don't know that game."

"We are mice and no matter what the cat does, we mustn't make a sound. If we do, we'll both lose, and I hate losing."

One noise, and they would lose everything in this game.

A guard stomped into the room, and through the slats, Josie saw the grim resolve in the man's face. "Hein Kingston?"

Hein opened his mouth, but Josie pressed her fingers on his lips. He collapsed against her, burying his head again.

"He's here," Mrs. Pon said, rubbing her hand over the bundle of blanket and doll. "He has scarlet fever."

The guard backed away, his hands raised as if she'd drawn a gun. For a moment neither Mrs. Pon nor the guard spoke.

Josie held her breath, praying that Hein wouldn't break their quiet.

"What is your name?" the guard demanded.

"Margot Pon."

"You will take him on the train."

"Of course," she said sadly.

Josie's former neighbor didn't hesitate. She hurried out the door, the guard following her.

"Very good," Josie whispered to Hein. "You won the game."

"Mrs. Pon wasn't quiet."

Nor could she be. The cat wouldn't leave this room without a mouse.

Hein slept as they waited for the train to leave, the collage in her mind flashing the pictures of all who would be boarding. She prayed that God Himself would care for the women who were loving His children. Send angels to soothe all their tears.

Music filtered into the empty room, and she inched the door open. Rain continued to fall, but it didn't seem to diminish the revelry outside. As Mrs. Pon predicted, some people were singing and others were dancing between the barracks.

She had to escape with Hein before one of the guards found them, but even if she was able to cut the fence, she feared the perimeter was being watched after dark. If he weren't medicated, Hein might have been able to scoot underneath and run before a guard spotted them, but he was barely able to walk right now. It would be impossible to carry him under the wires.

Josie eyed the galvanized tub on the floor, another idea taking form. After setting Hein on a bed, she tipped over the tub, and dirty water flooded the room.

"Have you ever played the game where you drop a nail into a glass?" she asked.

Hein nodded slowly, wiggling his hips as if preparing to play.

"In this new game, you get to be the nail." She pointed at the steel tub. "But instead of lowering you into a bottle, I'm going to cover you with this tub."

He eyed it skeptically. "Will I break?"

"I won't let you break."

Still he didn't move.

"Would you like to see your mama, Hein?"

He nodded.

"Then you must play this game with me."

He folded his knees into his body and the tub enveloped him like the tight space under the quay when she was a girl. Outside she found an abandoned pushcart, the wooden platform plenty large enough for a tub. No one stopped her as she maneuvered the cart around the corner to the children's ward.

She filled the cart with several boxes from the hospital and then lifted the tub off Hein's head. "How is the nail?"

"Hot."

"You won't be hot for long," she promised before reiterating their rules. "Do nails talk?"

He shook his head.

"Do they squirm?"

"No."

"They bump and turn inside the glass. Then they wait patiently until someone pulls them back out to play again."

No matter how hard you shake them, they won't break the glass.

Josie draped a borrowed poncho over herself as she lifted the tub with Hein inside. Then she turned it over on the platform, covering him.

Rain pinged against the steel, dripping down the sides as she started to push the cart toward the entrance of Westerbork.

Someone called for her, and she turned, startled that anyone knew her name. "Mr. Linden?"

The man was dressed in the same blue overalls as those who'd been transporting carts, but he also wore a black bowler hat as if he were reporting to the bank this evening. "Mrs. Pon said my grandson is here."

"Is Eliese with you?" she asked.

He shook his head.

Josie nodded toward the tub, surrounded by boxes. "Do you want to see him?"

"I can't." His voice broke before he spoke again. "But perhaps I can help you get him to the other side."

Mr. Linden took the handles of the cart and followed the train tracks toward the camp's entrance, the opening etched between barbed wire. On the other side was a two-story home, painted white and green.

The guard at the entrance eyed them and their supplies.

Mr. Linden nodded at the house. "It's for Gemmeker's party."

"Who are you?" the guard asked Josie.

She handed over her identity card. "The caterer."

As he hunched over her card, a human umbrella so the print wouldn't smear, her eyes filled with tears. It was too much—the heartache, the fear, the possibility that she could lose Eliese's son right here in the shadow of the commandant's house.

But she couldn't cry now. Even with the rain, her tears would betray her. She had to be a nail as well, strong inside the glass.

When the guard didn't find a *J* on her card, he handed it back to her.

"If you have any extra food—"

Josie forced a smile even as she blinked back her tears. "We'll bring a meal back to you."

He waved them both around the barbs.

Mr. Linden pushed the cart to the far side of the commandant's house. Josie heard a band playing, and her anger flared. How could this man—how could any of them—celebrate after sending so many children away?

When they reached the trees, Mr. Linden stopped.

"Come with us," she offered.

He shook his head. "I deserve to go east, more than anyone here."

"No one deserves that."

Doubt flickered in his eyes. "Your brother knows what I've done."

"We'll escape through the woods. No one will see us."

"The barrack leader will discover I'm gone; then they'll search with dogs until they find me. And when they find me . . ." In the dim light, he caught Josie's eye and she saw the weariness in them. "Mrs. Pon said the guards don't know about Hein."

"They think he's already on a train."

"I don't want my grandson to ever find out about his father."

"I won't tell him." Josie pointed at the tub, the rain soaking its sides. "Do you want to say goodbye?"

Shaking his head, he backed away slowly.

"I'll take good care of him," she promised.

Then Mr. Linden fled back toward the gap between wires.

When she lifted the tub, rain fell over Hein and she quickly covered him with the poncho.

"Did I break the glass?" he asked.

"No," she said. "You won that game."

His eyes drifted closed again as he leaned back against the boxes, his face flushed red. "So tired . . ."

She eyed the gray forest in front of them, the walnut boughs that shuddered in the wind. "We have to play one more game, Hein."

"I'm tired of the games."

"I'll race you to the canal on the other side of these trees."

Thunder crashed above them, rousing him awake.

He didn't run exactly, but he shuffled into the forest.

She cried as she followed him, the rain washing away her tears. The Germans would never see her cry, but God, she suspected, wept alongside her.

THIRTY-SEVEN

"Ava!" Claire shouts, chasing after me as I breeze through the dining room of the Kingston farmhouse, straight toward Marcella's office.

Leah is cleaning up dishes from the breakfast table, and when she looks up, she smiles. At least one person in this house seems glad that I'm home.

My grandmother is talking to someone on the landline, and when I collapse into a stiff chair, she hangs up the phone. Leaning back, she presses her fingers together, an unflappable tent over her desk. With Claire standing in the doorway, there is nothing except Marcella's hands bricked between us.

This time I don't deposit my phone into its proper bin. Nor do I wait for her to challenge me. Instead I decide to speak the truth, for the redemption of us all.

"I found something in Amsterdam," I say.

Marcella leans forward. "What exactly did you find?"

Reaching into my handbag, I pull out the book about Hitler's bank and place it on the desk. She recognizes the title—I can tell from the way the lines splay out from her eyes.

"Where did you get this?"

"From the Kingston library."

"Paul was supposed to send it to me."

I inch it forward. "Do you know what's inside?"

"A compilation of lies."

Marcella's view of the past is all polished, I'm afraid, like the tabletops at Craig House—to hide the wounds inside.

"But why would your father lie?"

Marcella glances at Claire and her assistant reaches for the door handle, closing the door behind her when she leaves.

Marcella pushes the book away. "My father has nothing to do with this."

Standing up, I pace to the sliding-glass door that overlooks the Hudson. Whatever my family did in the past does not reflect who I am today. Nor is Marcella responsible for what her father or father-in-law did. But she is responsible—we are responsible—for the choices we are making right now, the choice to deceive, or at least omit, what really happened.

"Your father wrote this," I say. "Perhaps to make amends for what he did."

"You can't prove that."

"Why do you want to cover up the truth?"

Her hand is shaking when she lifts her coffee cup, but she doesn't actually take a sip. "The truth will destroy us."

"Or not, Marcella. Maybe it will set this family free."

"My father," she starts, but her next words are muffled. Turning my head, I lean closer to hear.

Her cup crashes onto the desk, splashing coffee across her papers, but she doesn't seem to notice her spill. Instead she is looking at the window, squinting.

"I can't—" Her voice shreds into fear. "I can't see."

"Claire!" I shout, running toward the door.

She's back in an instant, someone else behind her. My uncle Will rushes into the room, the sleeves on his white dress shirt rolled up to his elbows, and when he looks at me . . .

My mind flashes back more than a decade before. I've seen that look in his eyes before, the pure hatred in it, the night of the fire.

The face outside my window.

"You were there," I whisper.

I didn't mean for him to hear, but his eyes narrow. I've already been wounded by his words, his disdain, but I've never been afraid. Marcella has always protected me.

If William Kingston killed Peter, would one of his descendants kill my mother, my brother, so they wouldn't inherit the Kingston fortune? If so, why hadn't he tried to hurt me?

I turn swiftly around and race toward the desk. Marcella's skin has sagged on the left side of her face, her mouth crooked as she searches for words.

"Call 911," I say, but Claire is already on the phone.

Marcella pushes back from her desk and moves to stand as if she can run away. She teeters on her feet and I lean in to capture her before she falls, resting her against my side.

I search for Will, but he's gone. The sick thought runs

through my head that he is out checking on their accounts. Or texting his offspring. This is what he and the other family members have been wanting—Marcella's death. They're ready to celebrate instead of mourn.

Claire balances the phone on her shoulder, telling the operator what's happening as she helps me move Marcella to the sofa.

Marcella's looking at me, trying to say something as I hold her shaky hand in mine. I turn my good ear toward her, but I still don't understand her words.

As her frustration escalates, I pat her arm. "Tell me later."

Will is back in the room. "The car's ready to take her to the hospital."

"An ambulance is on the way," Claire says. "Ten minutes."

"This will be faster," he insists. He's yet to really look at his mother or offer any assistance to her needs.

My mind is jumbled—I don't know for certain that he was at the fire. But I'm no longer that little girl anymore—I am a daughter of a King, filled with His courage even when I don't feel brave. And I can't cower now. The police—they thought the fire that killed my brother was an accident, that I'd left something on the stove.

What if it wasn't an accident after all?

Everything within me is screaming now: Don't let Marcella get into that car.

"We're waiting for the ambulance," I say as Claire steps in front of Marcella, shielding her.

The rawness in my uncle's laugh makes me cringe. "You don't have any authority here."

"Neither do you, Will." Claire flips out her phone to show him something on the screen. "Power of attorney."

He swears.

"I have her advance directive too, if you'd like to see it. She's spelled everything out clearly, so there really shouldn't be any questions about health care, but if something comes up, she's appointed me to make her medical decisions as well."

Of course she has. Claire's loyalty to Marcella goes far beyond money.

I'm relieved that Claire has all of this information, but my guilt bears down again. What have I done, telling Marcella about this book?

She has stopped trying to talk, but her eyes are still open, watching her son. I can't imagine how it must feel to watch a grown child who's supposed to love you thinking only of himself.

Leah opens the door. "They're here."

Seconds later, two EMTs and their stretcher are beside the couch, asking us questions as they prepare to wheel Marcella away. Claire lifts the briefcase from beside the desk. She and the advance directive go with her into the ambulance.

While Will is on his phone, texting someone, Leah hands me the keys to the Mercedes. I hurry to the hospital before my uncle arrives.

"She had a stroke," I tell Vi as I step outside the waiting room, onto a patio overlooking a Japanese garden.

"Is she okay?" Vi asks.

"They started her on alteplase right away to get the blood flowing to her brain, but they don't know when she'll be able to walk or talk again."

Something buzzes on her end. "I'm coming to New York."

"Thank you." I close my eyes, the warmth of sunshine washing over me.

"I'll even be nice if we visit her."

"I don't know if she'll be in much of a place to see anyone except family."

VI's typing on her keyboard. "I can fly out of here in three hours."

A nurse steps onto the patio, an iPad in hand. "Ava Drake?"

"That's me."

"Your grandmother is asking for you."

Claire is the only one besides Marcella in the hospital room, sitting on a chair in the corner with her phone. Marcella is awake, an IV line running fluids into her arm, but the left side of her face is anchored down and she still can't talk. Claire must have been the one looking for me.

She opens her briefcase and takes out a leather portfolio, turning to a page stored inside.

"'I, Marcella Ziegler Kingston, appoint Claire Fields as my health care agent.'" She looks up at me. "She appointed me to oversee her health care proxy and her living will."

"You don't have to convince me."

Claire lowers the paper. "There are things you don't understand, Ava."

"I'm afraid there's a lot that I don't understand."

"Marcella wants to protect you, even more than she wants to protect the secrets of your family."

"Protect me from my uncles?"

Claire nods. "After what happened in North Carolina, Marcella revised her will and notified your uncles and cousins. If you die before she passes away, the Kingston fortune will be donated to a multitude of charities instead of being divided among the family."

"And if I die after?"

"You need to go on another trip, Ava. Just until we can sort out what's happened to her."

I rub my arms. "I'll go to North Carolina."

Claire shakes her head. "They'll find you there."

"Then I'll go—"

She stops me. "Don't tell me where."

I kiss my grandmother's forehead. Her father might have failed her, just like mine did for me, but we are both daughters of a King.

"You make her happy," Claire tells me.

"She didn't seem very happy today."

"You remind her of Emily. It's a mixed bag of emotions." Claire nods toward my handbag. "Do you have that book with you?"

I nod. It's stored in my handbag, alongside my mother's Bible.

"It's the book that Peter wrote, isn't it?"

"I believe so. It details how he and William invested in the Nazi Party and how their investment in what became the Holocaust made them millionaires, but I don't know if anyone can prove it."

332

"What happened during the war may threaten the Kingston reputation, but what's happening now is threatening the well-being of the entire family." This time Claire doesn't look at Marcella. "I think the best way to protect this family's future is to be honest about their past."

"But who do we tell?"

"May I borrow the book?" she asks.

I take it out of my bag and hold it close to my chest. Paul made a copy but I still don't want this one to disappear. "What will you do with it?"

"Give it to Henry and tell him not to hold back at the *Times*. Those who want to dig up more dirt will hit rock instead, and then, if you want, you and your cousins can begin building a new legacy for the Kingstons."

Her phone flashes, and she glances down. "You'd better leave."

"Is Will coming back?"

"And Carlton," she says. "They're on the elevator."

I thank Claire and hand her the book. Before I leave, she digs into a pocket on the outside of the briefcase.

"At the west end of the attic is a gray filing cabinet." She tosses me a key. "It contains a few things you'll want to see."

THIRTY-EIGHT

ELIESE

MAASTRICHT

NOVEMBER 1943

Cold air breathed out of the mine entrance near Maastricht, and Eliese feared the darkness might swallow her.

"We must hurry!" A lantern swung in the hands of Eduard, their guide, as he motioned her and Nathan forward.

Hurry—that's all she'd been doing for weeks now as she'd rushed down to Keet's house with Margot, helped when the Allied airmen appeared at their back door, cared for the children who cried in the night.

She could keep hurrying, but for what? Everyone she loved was gone. Except William, but he was a lifetime away now. The knotted corridors in these tunnels wouldn't lead her back to him.

Wind rustled the branches around them, coaxing out strands of hair that she'd secured in pins. Then Nathan West—the navigator from America—was beside her, taking her hand, urging her forward with whispers in case the Nazis were near. She inhaled once more of fresh air, as if it were her last breath, then ducked into the black chasm. Eduard closed an iron door behind them, and it clanged before he locked it from the inside.

Lamplight danced on the rugged stone passage. Marlstone—that's what the caramel-colored walls were made of in these ancient mining tunnels, thousands of them webbed together between Maastricht and the border of Belgium.

These arteries, Keet had told her, channeled both Allied airmen and underdivers out of Holland. The Dutch also stored an entire gallery of art down here, hundreds of valuable pieces from across their country. The Nazis knew about the collection, but in lieu of confiscating it now, they were preserving the art for plunder after the war.

If they turned the wrong way in these mines, Eduard told them, they'd be lost in the maze. While the Nazis were vigilant aboveground, they hated coming down here, afraid of getting lost without a map, afraid of what those desperate enough to hide might do if found. They patrolled the main channels though. If she and Nathan took a wrong turn, the Germans would eventually find them.

The damp chill of the cave seeped through her thin coat and skin, into her bones, the corridors fanning out like a claw in front of them. Eduard pointed them to the second passage on their left. Even though she wore a pair of men's mountain boots, she struggled to find steady footing.

"You're too cold," Nathan whispered as they followed the spray of Eduard's light along the rugged path, their hands tracing the wet stone as if they were drying its tears.

"No more than anyone else." A fever had plagued her since she'd left her home in Amsterdam—each time Keet thought her cured, it would rage again—but they'd all been battered in one way or another by this war.

Nathan started to take off his leather flight jacket. "Wear my coat."

Eliese shook her head, but he insisted that she take his gloves, just like he'd been insisting for the past weeks to help whenever possible with her daily chores. He'd grown up on a hazelnut orchard in a place called Oregon and work, he'd said, helped him survive.

Eliese had been planning to stay at Keet's house until the end of the war, helping her with Esther and Margot and two other girls in her care, but an NSB officer came to their home yesterday, a casual inquiry about a B-26 that had been shot down nearby. He was looking for survivors.

The officer stayed a few hours, sipping Keet's tea and searching her barn. He didn't pay any mind to the children—everyone in the area knew that Erik and Keet had welcomed in orphans after the Rotterdam bombing. Keet was more concerned about the questions their absence might bring if she sent these children away.

An Allied airman was a different story and so was Eliese.

They'd hidden together inside the mouth of a mine on Keet's property until the officer left, but Keet said he would return soon, probably with others to help him search. Like the children at the crèche, she and Nathan had to be transported away.

Instead of wiping their names off a registration list, members of the resistance offered to guide them as they'd done with so many others to a safe place where they could recover their identities . . . or what was left of them after this war.

Her new identity card read Eloise—a strong German name with no *J*. And, she hoped, a deterrent for anyone searching for Anneliese.

They passed a grotto to the right, a garden of plants sprouting from the dirt someone had hauled down here. Endive and mushrooms grew in these tunnels—far away from the oversight of their occupiers.

Several hours passed and Eduard stopped, pouring chicory coffee from a thermos to sustain them. The damp air glazed her forehead and cheeks, and she wiped them off with Nathan's glove. Her body was warm from the walking, but the cold had settled into her skin, mixing with the weariness.

This was the end of Eduard's tour. Nathan had a lantern and a map with markings that explained which passages to take from here and how to cross the canal into Belgium so they could be evacuated up to England.

England.

So much had changed since she was there last. If she made it through these mines, through this war, surely the Zieglers would welcome her back until she and William were together again.

Someone had stacked firewood against the tunnel wall and nearby were crates stuffed with blankets and food supplies. They were close to another entrance now, Nathan said, one that bordered Belgium. He checked his watch, said they needed to wait here four more hours until it was dark outside, and she was grateful for the strength left in him to take the lead.

She eyed the blackened ceiling charred from the woodsmoke. "Should we build a fire?"

"No," Nathan said. "The Nazis will smell it."

When she shivered, he put his arm around her, and she sank into him for warmth. It was the first time in what seemed like forever that she felt safe. He extinguished their lantern, the darkness enveloping them. Darkness she'd come to hate.

"What are you going to do when we get to England?" Nathan asked, his voice low.

"Find my husband." The lie slid easily off her tongue now. In her mind, William was her husband, the license a mere formality that this war didn't afford.

"Ah . . ."

"Do you have a young woman waiting for you back home?"

"Two sisters who dote on me." She heard the smile in his voice.

"Your family will celebrate when you return, Nathan."

He started to ask something else, about her family perhaps, but she was drifting off. Time passed, she didn't know how long, before he woke her.

"We need to keep moving," he said.

They used a flashlight to find the opening. The dry air outside was welcome relief, but a bitter cold had anchored itself in her body, making her tremble even in the warmth.

By the time they reached Belgium, she could hardly stand. Pneumonia, Nathan said, refusing to leave her behind.

Nathan carried her across a plateau, through tunnels on the other side of the border, until they reached an abbey in the hills. For months, Nathan and the nuns cared for her. For months, they told her that God was offering her a cord, one stained crimson through the blood of Jesus Christ, a cord washed clean though the hope of His resurrection. She had only to cling to this thread, and He would rescue her.

By the time she was well again, the south of Holland had been liberated and the Allied forces had entered Belgium. The Nazis refused to release Amsterdam and the northern Dutch provinces, but she and Nathan were free.

Before he left for America, Nathan gave her a piece of paper with an address and telephone number.

"If you ever need anything—" Nathan paused as if he was struggling to find the words. "Please find me."

She nodded, taking the paper from him, but when she finally crossed the Atlantic, she'd find William in New York. After they married, they would search together to discover exactly what happened to their son.

THIRTY-NINE

Sunlight slips through the round windows in the attic of the Kingston farmhouse, veils of light trailing across the dusty floor. With the flip of a switch, an overhead light illuminates the vast room. Cavernous, really. And I hope nothing that slithers or scampers is hidden away in the corners.

Half the room is empty and the other half is jammed with filing cabinets, cardboard boxes, furniture draped with ivory sheets. The poor servants in decades past must have pushed and prodded all of these things up the winding stairs.

Or perhaps in the last eighty years, the house has been built up around some of these things, left over from the generations.

Marcella, I pray, will recover from the stroke, but after Claire speaks with the newspaper editor, nothing will ever be the same for this family. My uncles will be irate at me for bringing home Peter's book and at Claire for contacting the *Times*, but perhaps we can truly find power in knowledge. In our case, the power to start over.

Leah met me at the front door a half hour ago and promised to text if any member of the Kingston family returned to the house. I have no intention to linger, but when I pull three worn ledgers out of the filing cabinet—*HTB* inscribed on the spine—I open one.

Inside are the accounts for Holland Trade Bank.

Each entry is handwritten in Dutch, the sums marked as guilders in increments of thousands. Money invested first—according to Peter's book—in the New York branch and then transferred through Amsterdam to Berlin.

Two small filing boxes are on top of the ledgers, their lids slightly crushed but intact.

I stack all of it in my arms, and once I'm in my bedroom, Leah helps me fit all the pieces into a carry-on suitcase and oversize handbag so I don't have to check them at the airport.

"Please come back," she says as we wait for a taxi, tears in her eyes, "after this is done."

"I'm not sure what's going to happen next."

Leah hands me the suitcase as a taxi turns into the drive. "The Kingstons need you, Ava."

She looks as if she might say something else, but she hugs me instead, her tears dampening my shoulder.

It takes only twenty minutes to reach the airport outside New Windsor, and I arrive in the terminal just as Vi's plane pulls into the gate. The frantic pace of my heart calms when she rushes out of the Jetway, an orange-and-fluorescent-pink beach bag strapped over one shoulder, a half-empty bottle of Diet Coke in hand. A mass of curly brown hair has declared mutiny on the top of her head, escaping its messy bun.

She gives me a giant hug. "I've missed you."

"I'm pretty sure I've missed you more."

Vi spins around once, arms outstretched. "Hello, New York."

Several people—okay, an entire crowd—look at her as if she's lost her mind, but she doesn't care one whit what they think.

Her spin stops abruptly. "How's Marcella?"

"Awake when I saw her last, but still not talking."

Curiosity dawns in her eyes. "How exactly did you get through security?"

"Special mission."

"To make sure I don't get lost?"

I take her beach bag and loop it over my arm. "We have to hurry."

"To the hospital?"

"No."

She falls in beside me. "Ava?"

With a quick glance at a screen, I direct her to the corridor on our left—in five minutes, they're closing the gate.

"You've said hello to New York. Now it's time to say goodbye."

Kendall and her husband, Jay, live on the same property as Mrs. West, in a beautiful Craftsman-style home surrounded by bigleaf maples, the land between trees stippled with licorice fern. We've shifted the living room furniture to create plenty of space on their cherrywood floor, the couch and chairs spreading out toward a picture window and fireplace.

Landon retrieved Vi and me from the Portland airport an hour ago and drove us here, Vi entertaining him with story after story from our middle school years. Then she flashed me a not-so-subtle thumbs-up when we reached the house.

Minutes after our arrival, Vi disappeared into the kitchen, taking over the reins from Kendall, who seemed quite pleased to give them up. Vi's buzzing around now with a fruit and cheese tray, making sure everyone has something to eat and drink.

A cool breeze steals through an open window, maple leaves dusting the screen. Kendall and Jay are together on the leather couch, and I decide to sit near Landon on the floor. Mrs. West is eating a slice of Brie on a chair beside me, a large suitcase at her side.

Snippets of conversations whirl around us until Landon begins telling his family about our time in Amsterdam, the safe we found almost empty. Then I pull the accounting books out of my bag.

Mrs. West's eyes lock on them. "You found those in the safe?"

Landon shakes his head. "All we found was an index card."

"The ledgers were stored at my family's house," I say.

"The Kingstons?"

A shadow crosses her face when I nod, but she doesn't say anything about William. Instead she turns toward Landon. "Which card did you find?"

He hands her the one with the van Gelder family names, and after reading it, she clutches it to her chest. "Esther van Gelder was one of the most courageous girls I've ever known."

Kendall leans forward. "What happened to her?"

"Her parents were taken to a camp during the war, and she was the first—" Mrs. West lowers the card to her lap and smooths her hand over it. "There used to be hundreds of these."

I open the lid to one of the filing boxes and display stacks of index cards like the one we found listing the van Gelder family, bundled together with rubber bands. They are all typed neatly with the names of parents and children, addresses, ages, and occupations.

Mrs. West takes a stack, but she doesn't skim through them. Instead she studies the top card as if it might tell her its story. "Were these in the safe?"

"No," I say. "They were stored with the ledgers."

"William knew about them?"

"I don't know."

Mrs. West lowers the stack of cards onto her lap. "The Nazis were sticklers about their lists, but they never found out what we were doing. . . ."

Landon looks at me, his eyes an ebony brown in the dim light. We're both thinking about the placard hanging in the Holocaust Memorial, remembering the woman who helped Walter Süskind.

"You were a hero, Oma."

"I wasn't a hero." Her lips are grim. "I did many things wrong."

No one speaks for a moment, uncertain what to say.

Landon taps my hand gently and I realize that he's been talking to me, I just didn't hear. "I'm sorry—"

"Tell them about the book."

And so I tell Kendall and the others what we discovered about William Kingston and Peter Ziegler and Gerrit Linden, how they partnered together to finance Hitler and his party. About Gerrit's daughter, a woman named Anneliese, who worked at the deportation center.

Kendall reaches over from the couch and takes Mrs. West's hand. "Why won't you talk about it?"

"I don't want to remember."

"But we want to know your story," Kendall says.

"There's more to it." Mrs. West looks toward the window. "I lost someone during the war. Someone dear to me."

Vi squeezes in between Landon and me, cradling a glass of white wine. "Like your brother."

I shoot her a look, the one that usually silences her when she's said too much. This evening is about Mrs. West's story, not mine.

"What brother?" Landon asks.

"This isn't about me—"

Vi takes a sip of her wine, ignoring my look. "Her brother who died in the fire."

Landon is watching my face now. "Andrew . . ."

"Yes," I say quietly before looking out at the storm clouds. It's been a long time since anyone said his name.

"How old was he?" Mrs. West asks, releasing Kendall's hand.

"Almost two."

"So many children lost before their time." She leans her head back against the chair, the cards scattering down to the floor. "So many that we should have saved."

"What are these cards?" Kendall asks.

"The names of the children who were hidden away."

Kendall's eyes widen. "You hid the kids—"

"Many of us helped. We knew something bad was happening in the east, but we couldn't comprehend . . ." Her voice breaks. "I stored the cards in our safe so I could reunite these children with their families after the war, but their parents were gone."

"My great-grandfather purchased your house," I say.

"He must have been searching for the contents of the safe." Mrs. West opens one of the ledgers. "William and Peter both made a fortune from the war, and he probably didn't want anyone to find out how they made this money."

"They invested in Zyklon," I say. "Among other things."

"What's Zyklon?" Vi asks.

Mrs. West reaches down for her suitcase. "The poison used in gas chambers."

This quiets the room.

"Thousands were killed in those concentration camps," Mrs. West says, fumbling with the latch. "Many of them had friends and family to preserve their memory, but the orphans who left on the last transport from Amsterdam—they didn't have anyone left to remember."

Landon opens the suitcase and Mrs. West reaches for an amber-colored bottle, one of the many she displays in the front room of her cottage. She unwraps the paper around the glass and cradles it for a moment before handing it to me.

"And so you remember," I say.

She nods. "I'll never forget. I was hiding in the cellar while those children were stolen away. A coward . . ." Her voice breaks, the sorrow still raw after all these years.

Kendall leans toward her. "There was nothing you could have done, Oma."

"I should have done something, anything, to help the last children on their list." She tries to sip her wine, but it spills on her sleeve. "When I returned to the nursery, all that was left was glass from a window, crushed on the floor. . . ."

I clutch the bottle to my chest as if it were a child.

"Sixty-seven orphans were transported that night, each of them killed at Auschwitz." She pauses, reaching for another bottle. "At first I wanted to forget, but even though we didn't know their names, Nathan thought we should remember what happened to them. He started buying antique bottles in their memory, and for years we would watch the light pour into each one, filling what had been broken, their legacy living on in both of us."

Landon lifts a cobalt bottle out of the suitcase and studies the intricate design, tiny cuts etched into the sides. "A unique glass to remember every child."

"In my way . . ."

"That's beautiful, Oma," Kendall says, trying to sponge up the wine on Mrs. West's blouse with her napkin.

"They're my story beads." Like the beads at the children's hospital, to remember both the good and the bad.

"Each of the children who came to the nursery had a story," I say. "And you saved hundreds of them."

She shakes her head. "It wasn't enough."

Landon removes another bottle, the color a green mist. "You gave them all a second chance."

"I wonder what happened to the children who lived?" I ask.

"They were taken to safe places across Holland."

Landon hands me the glass. "Did you ever look for them?"

"No, their parents were gone. What good would it do?" She sighs. "The younger ones wouldn't remember hiding. They probably never even knew."

But I think it might have done a world of good for her to know what happened to these kids.

"Most of the caregivers were practically kids themselves. My friend Josie—she was only nineteen when she began stealing the children away."

Vi scoots closer to her. "What happened to Josie?"

"I don't know," Mrs. West says. "Nathan and I searched for her name on the lists, but we could never find it." Her hand drops to the suitcase beside her again, stroking the handle. "I longed for her courage when I was younger. She sacrificed so much for those kids."

"You said sixty-seven children," Kendall says.

Mrs. West nods.

"But there are sixty-eight bottles in your room." When Mrs. West flashes her a look, Kendall shrugs. "I counted them years ago."

"One child wasn't in that transport, but I'll never forget him. His memory is forever alive in my heart."

Landon leans forward. "Which child?"

Instead of answering, she reaches back into the folds of sheets protecting the glass and picks up an intricate perfume bottle, the color a dark red. She turns it twice in her hands before showing Landon the etched letters on the top.

He reads the initials out loud. "H. K."

"William's and my son," she says, her eyes on the engraved lid.

"Your son . . ." I can't tell who says the words first, but we all feel the weight of them.

"What happened to him?" Kendall asks.

"He died in Auschwitz like the other children, from the gas that my father and William helped manufacture."

The bottle slips from her hand, shattering on the cherry-wood. She stares at the floor for a moment, but none of us rushes to clean it. These shards, a thousand memories from a life now gone, are scattered around us.

Together we remember.

FORTY

ELIESE

NEW YORK
FEBRUARY 1946

Eloise Kingston. That was the name on her new passport.

The only thing her old name garnered was shame.

Here in America she would start anew. If only William would forgive her for losing their son. And forgive her father for funneling his money to Hitler and the German companies after the war began.

She wrapped her arms around her satchel as the ship docked in New York Harbor, but they still felt empty. Her heart was an enormous void that had emptied itself, a void she longed to refill.

She'd purchased this satchel and a trunk with one of her

father's diamonds and filled them with everything she needed for her journey, but the one thing she wanted most was gone.

After the war, she'd returned to Amsterdam to search for Hein, in case Samuel was wrong, but she'd found her son's name on the list of those who'd been sent to Auschwitz, a victim of her father's investments in what he'd once called *Geld*.

She'd known Hein was gone, but seeing his name—it was the last page of a book she wished she could shelve forever. A book whose pages kept fluttering open in her heart.

No one was compelled to return the items they'd ransacked from her home in Amsterdam, and she couldn't even get back inside to open her father's safe. Someone else had purchased the house.

But the items inside the safe were no longer important to her. She would never show Hein his baby album. None of the adults listed on her cards would be returning for their children. And those ledgers—she hoped they would stay buried forever.

People across Europe were hunting for the perpetrators of what was being called a crime. The information in these ledgers would incriminate her deceased father and the man she'd promised to marry and would probably incriminate her as well.

If only they had known . . .

Her father never would have invested in Zyklon, no matter how bright the gold.

Months after the war ended, she'd received a letter from William. He'd sent it to Klaas Schoght, the boy from her youth, and Klaas found her in Amsterdam.

After years of silence, William told her that he still loved her, wanted to marry her, and then he'd asked her to wait for him in Holland. But when she received the papers to immigrate, she couldn't bear to wait a moment longer. She sold another diamond and used the money to buy passage to New York.

The address she had for William, the place where she'd sent her many letters and telegrams over the years, was wrong. The residents said that William Kingston had never lived in their house. They also said that everyone—everyone, it seemed, except her—knew where the Kingston family lived.

The next morning, dressed in her nicest apparel—an emerald dress with a slender belt and wedged heels that sparkled with rhinestone buckles, William's turquoise ring on her hand—she took a train north and checked into an inn near the Kingston farm. Instead of transporting her trunk from the city, she carried only a small suitcase and the handbag with what remained of her father's diamonds.

A taxi delivered her to the Kingston home—a mansion along a broad river, grand columns ribbing the porch. Unlike the mansions in Amsterdam, it stood alone, and horses and cattle roamed on the riverbank below, partitioned off by a white fence.

They would have more children, she and William, and together they would live and work on this beautiful property, forgetting what they'd lost under a regime of horror.

The doorbell chimed, and a woman answered, wearing a modern floral dress, her arm ringed with colorful bracelets as if she were part caterpillar.

Eliese stood taller, dwarfing the stylish woman who was at least a decade older than her. "I'm here to see William."

The woman scanned her slowly, from her satin shoes to the black velvet hat she'd purchased in New York City. "We have no *Villiam* here."

"William," she repeated, trying to be clear.

"I can't understand you—"

Eliese took a deep breath. "I need to find William Kingston."

"Who are you?" the woman asked, glancing down at the ring on Eliese's finger.

"His—" She searched for the right word—*girlfriend, fiancée, wife*? "An employee from the Holland bank."

"Then he is Mr. Kingston to you."

He was so much more than Mr. Kingston, but she wouldn't argue. This woman in all her arrogance would find out soon enough.

"William!" the woman shouted over her shoulder, a shrill echo through the corridor.

And then he was there, standing in front of her. More than six years had passed since they were together, but he looked just as handsome, just as strong. His dark hair was salted with gray, but it only made him look more distinguished, like the successful businessman that he was.

She waited for the stirring in her heart, the thrill that once charged through her skin whenever she saw him, but the feelings were gone. In fact, she felt nothing at all.

The face of an American navigator stole back into her mind, as it often did these days, and she blinked it away. She'd promised herself to William, gave herself to him long ago. She would be faithful to her vow.

The blankness in his eyes filled with recognition. Then

he smiled, but not the kind of smile that had captivated her as a young woman. It reminded her of Fünten when he was drunk. When he demanded to drive her home.

Eliese stepped back, shivering as she studied him and the woman who stood by his shoulder. A boy joined the woman's side, his hair smoothed back except a cowlick near the front that stood on end. With his blond hair, confident gaze, he looked, perhaps, like Hein would have if he'd survived the war.

William kissed the woman on the cheek. "I'll take care of this."

He moved out onto the patio beside Eliese and closed the door.

She'd pictured this so differently in her dreams, him exuberant to see her and then devastated when she told him about Hein. They were supposed to mourn the death of their son together before they started a new life.

"You're married," she said, words bitter on her lips.

"Of course I'm married." His voice bristled with disdain, as if she'd been the fool for thinking otherwise.

The ground shifted under her feet, and she reached out, steadying herself on a column.

"How long have you been married?"

When he didn't answer, she sealed her thumb over the doorbell. "Should I ask your wife instead?"

He sighed. "For ten years."

The number pounded inside her head.

He'd been married when he first met her in Amsterdam, married when he'd invited her to stay in London, married when he'd slept with her.

This man was married when he proposed the idea of marriage to her.

Her father had been right; she was nothing but a whore.

William pointed toward a narrow path in the woods. "Let's walk, Eliese."

She didn't move—after her escape through the mines, she couldn't bear enclosed spaces. And for the first time, instead of security, she felt fear at William's side.

He'd deceived her, said they would marry. What else was a lie?

When she turned back toward the drive, he reached for her arm, caught it in his hand. "Where are the records?"

"What records?"

He squeezed her wrist. "The ledgers from the bank."

"You don't want those."

"I do. Very much."

"Father was investing in Nazi factories, William. Using your money to fund the war. Make poison."

"I know—"

"Poison that killed our son."

He dropped her arm. "Our son?"

"If you'd given me your correct address, you would have known about him. I even sent photographs—"

"What did you name him?"

Hein Kingston—she almost said but kept it to herself, the name sheltered in her heart.

When she shook her head, he stuck his hands into the pockets of his jacket. "Where is your father?"

"He died in a train car." On the way to a camp called Theresienstadt.

"So there's only a handful of us left who know—"

A flash of blue sparked in the window above them, and she saw the face of a girl, watching them through the screen. When Eliese caught her eye, the girl ducked. And then she saw the face of Peter Ziegler, visiting New York, she supposed, like William when he went to London. During the months she spent with the Zieglers, they knew William was already married, that he had a son, and they never told her.

"I'm choosing to forget, William." The ledgers, the war, the hundreds of children she couldn't save. Even the names she'd worked so hard to collect, it all brought sorrow.

He shook his head. "We can't forget."

But she had to in order to survive.

"Your father took my money," he said.

She glanced through the columns at the rolling hills of his property, the trees and barns. "And he made you a wealthy man."

"He has no use for the money now."

And, she realized in that moment, William Kingston no longer had any use for her.

He pointed toward the woods again. "Let's walk together, Anneliese, so we can talk in private."

"There's nothing left for us to say."

William turned and reopened the door, leaving her on the front steps. She'd been on her own for a long time now, living as Mrs. Kingston, the title offering a glimmer of hope for her future, but never had she felt more alone than right now.

She'd already sent the taxi away, but it wasn't far to the inn. She'd walked much farther when she lived in Amsterdam.

Partway down the drive, a girl ran up and reached for her hand. "Lady?"

"Yes—"

"You'd better hurry."

Eliese knelt beside her. "Why?"

"They're awfully mad at you."

"You're Peter and Trudy's daughter . . ."

The girl nodded.

"I stayed with your parents before you were born."

Someone called for the child—Marcella—and she dropped Eliese's hand.

Instead of returning to the inn, Eliese walked around the small town until dusk, her handbag tucked securely under her arm. It felt as if the darkness was closing in on her, as if she couldn't breathe. She'd expected, after receiving William's letter, that he would welcome her here, but he didn't care about her. He only wanted her father's ledgers.

Would he destroy the books so no one would uncover his investments or use the information to find where her father had hidden the rest of their profits?

Those ledgers would stay buried in that safe, the combination seared into her brain. No one else would make money off the chemicals that killed Hein and all those who'd been housed at the theater.

Her breath slowly began to return, along with the face of a pilot who'd walked through fire with her. Nathan might have gotten married in the months since she'd seen him, but as she stood in front of the inn, she realized her heart had moved beyond William. To the man who wanted to help, not hurt her.

By the time night fell over the hills, she wasn't angry at William anymore for lying to her. No, she was relieved. She would do what Marcella said and leave here right away.

The colonial inn was three stories, the brick walls reminding her of her home in Amsterdam. After climbing to the second floor, she slipped her key into the lock, but her door was already cracked open.

A familiar chill traveled up her skin as she pressed against it. Several people were inside rummaging through her things, whispering in the dark. And Marcella's warning echoed between her ears.

Light swept into the room from behind her, a spotlight to whatever they'd staged. A man shouted, and she yanked the door closed, instinctively turning the key.

"Eliese!" It was William calling her name, his feet thudding down the steps behind her before she flung open the front door.

One thing she'd learned how to do well these past years was hide.

Trees flecked the sprawling lawn and to her right was a dormant garden, an old shed, a block of clapboard houses, their light seeping onto the street. Instead of running, she crouched between evergreen bushes nestled against the inn.

The door slammed, and William swore as he rushed past. Then two men ran out the door behind him, as if it would take a small army to subdue her, fanning out in different directions to search.

William didn't just want her for the ledgers. He wanted her dead. So no one else would find out how he'd made his money.

Foolish—she'd been so foolish for trusting this man.

She couldn't stay here. The men would return soon to search every inch of this property and perhaps the town. She'd have to leave her satchel in the room.

Inching through the shadows, her purse at her side, she waited hours before she dared to try a pay phone. Then she retrieved the piece of paper that she'd carried for more than a year, crumpled and worn, the paper still smelling like marlstone.

She dialed the number, collect. Perhaps she could still shed the skin of her past, start anew.

"Eloise," she told the operator.

A man answered, and when the operator gave her name, he accepted the call.

"Nathan?" she whispered.

Silence.

Had he hung up? Perhaps his wife was standing beside him, wondering who was on the telephone.

She breathed deeply, panic rising again. She could sell her last diamond, get a return passage to England perhaps. She would never go back to Holland, of that she was certain.

"Where are you?" The words came through the phone garbled, but she recognized his voice.

"I'm in New York."

Her heart stilled, waiting for his response. She didn't know the future now, but this man on the line, he'd offered her a thread of hope back in Holland and then Belgium. And she desperately needed hope.

"Are you alone?" he asked.

"Yes," she said. "My husband—he isn't really my husband, Nathan. I'd thought that one day . . ."

Another moment of silence before he spoke again. "Do you want me to come to New York?"

"I'm not certain—"

"I need you to be certain, Eloise."

Months ago, Nathan and the nuns had offered a crimson cord to rescue her from all that she'd done. All she had to do was cling to it, he'd said, and God would forgive her. She could have a new life in Him.

She glanced up the street, several automobiles traveling up the road in these morning hours. At the end of the block was a red-and-silver bus, preparing to stop by the phone, offering her a way out.

She would cling to that scarlet thread.

"Don't come here," she said.

"Okay," he replied, disappointed.

She tucked the paper with his number and address back into her handbag and slipped off her ring, leaving it on the ledge. "I'm taking the next bus to Oregon."

FORTY-ONE

After I've spent a week in Portland, Claire assures me that my grandmother is recovering and wants me to read the contents of a green folder overnighted to Kendall's house. The paperwork from my mother's adoption journey.

The *New York Times* article ran today, so there's nothing left for our family to hide. No PR agency will be able to clean up this mess, but the Kingstons, I hope, can redeem it.

Instead of returning to New York, I fly to Greenville with Vi. Landon comes too, and Vi transports us from the airport to the tip of Hatteras in her vintage VW. Then she says I need to finish this journey alone.

Except I'm not alone. After hugging me, she dumps both Landon's overnight bag and mine in the parking lot of the ferry terminal and drives away. Then she texts ten minutes later, saying she'll pick us up whenever. A day. A week. A month. She doesn't care.

And I suppose I love her for dumping me.

Landon picks our bags off the asphalt. He doesn't seem the least bit upset about being stranded.

A pod of bottlenose dolphins escorts our ferry toward Ocracoke, and as we get closer to the island, my heart begins to race. This place holds fourteen years of my best and worst memories.

The battering wind makes it too hard to talk on deck, but Landon takes my hand as we near the terminal and I breathe deep. Today is about remembering both the good and the bad.

After storing our luggage at an inn, we step out onto a patio overlooking the harbor. The ocean breeze salts the veranda, and the smell takes me right back to my childhood on this beach: building sand castles with my mom, dodging waves with our dog, watching my baby brother bury his toes in the wet sand.

And then the fire, the details soot-laden in the smoke of my mind.

"My brother loved playing in the sand," I say, dipping my own toe into uncharted waters.

Landon faces the oceanfront, his elbows on the railing. "When you had your nightmare in Africa, you shouted for Andrew."

"I was trying to find him."

Ocean water sprays over us, cooling our skin.

"How exactly did you lose him?" he asks.

I show him the picture on my phone—of Mom, Andrew, and me at the beach—and the pieces of my story, broken and worn, begin to spill out. I tell him about the night my mother was waiting tables at a local restaurant, how I'd been left to watch over my brother—a job I'd taken quite seriously since he was born. My mother had come home early that night from work, but I didn't even know she was in the house until it was too late.

I tell him about the explosion that threw me off my bed, how I'd tried to rescue my brother in the next room, but the smoke was too thick, the doorknob too hot.

And then the face from my nightmares emerges in my mind. Eyes of hatred outside the window. Eyes that remind me of my uncle.

"That's all I can remember."

His eyes are still focused on the ocean, as if he might frighten me away by looking over. "Do you think your uncle set the fire?"

"My grandmother said it was an accident, but—" I take a breath—"I don't think she was surprised that it happened. Looking back, I wonder if she almost expected it."

"What's your next memory? After the fire?"

I close my eyes. "It's strange, the things you remember."

"What do you see?" he asks.

"Two daisies. They were in a mason jar beside my hospital bed. When I saw them, I wanted to make a chain like my mom used to do with me." I open my eyes again. "That time in the hospital was agony for me. No one would tell me about my brother or my mother, and the explosion had stolen away the hearing in my left ear."

Landon glances at me. "I thought you were just ignoring me."

"I was ignoring you when you told me to wear the Crocs!"

He smiles. "How about when I told you there was a snake ahead?"

"I didn't hear that."

"What happened to your dad?" he asks.

A twinge in my chest, the same one whenever I think about the man who was supposed to take care of me. "He'd left years before the fire and moved to Idaho. When my caseworker contacted him, he wasn't interested in having another daughter and his income was already divided among several other kids, so there was nothing left to support me."

I run my hands over the green folder that Claire sent with my mother's name, my emotions mixed. I want to know what's inside, but I'm afraid.

"I spent a year in foster care, until my caseworker found Marcella." I lift the thin folder, but I don't open it. "Marcella offered me a new life and what I thought would be a family."

I flew eagerly into her nest, and those first years were a mirage for a thirsty soul. But even more than its craving for family, my heart craved healing. A reminder of who I truly was in Christ.

"She wanted someone she could mold and shape into a proper Kingston, but I fear I'm more like my mother."

"A blessing, I think."

My smile is shaky, but I'm grateful.

"Do you want to open that folder?" he asks.

"Let's visit the cemetery first." I want to remember my

mother and brother in my own way, before the world shifts again.

Landon directs me to a floral shop and orders two dozen daisies. The bundle in hand, we follow a footpath to a picket-fenced cemetery, the graves tucked between wax myrtles and ancient oak trees.

My brother's name is etched in a small stone; my mother's grave next to his.

Andrew Drake

The epitaph under my brother's name verifies what I already know. He lived a year and eight months. And he was much loved, taking on my mother's and my surname after his biological father left.

I place the flowers beside by his grave and we remember him in the silence, the salty wind tangling my hair.

Then I turn to my mother's plot, rubbing my hand over her name.

Emily Kingston Drake

The woman who'd loved me fiercely even as she worked to provide for us. The woman who'd thought I would be safer growing up in a small townhome in North Carolina than the halls of a mansion up north.

Tears well in my eyes. "They are together."

"Together, but hardly alone," Landon says. "God welcomed them both home."

"I heard something outside that night, before the fire, but I didn't call for help."

"If your uncle started it, there was nothing you could have done."

"When I was younger, I begged God for forgiveness . . ."

"For your sins?" he asks.

"Yes . . . and for not rescuing my brother. I should have grabbed him and run."

"We've all sinned, Ava, and God forgives us when we ask. But what happened that night isn't sin. It's shame. You didn't do anything wrong."

I hear Landon's words, the truth in them, but they struggle to make it down into my heart.

He picks a bouquet of daisies off my brother's grave and slides one of the flowers out of the rubber band.

"What are you doing?" I ask.

He hands the flower to me. "Let's make them daisy chains."

Mrs. West has her glass bottles to remember and the children at Doernbecher have their story beads. I want something other than a photograph to remember Andrew and my mom.

Landon and I visit the place where my family's little home once stood, but there's nothing for me here, so we walk out to the beach and find a seat on the wind-polished limb of a fallen tree. Sand crabs scurry around us as the waves ebb and flow, seawater brushing wide strokes near our toes.

This burden of my memories, the extra weight of guilt, has almost crushed me. But long ago soldiers nailed up the burden of my sin on a cross, the depth of my shame, when they crucified Christ. Perhaps I can remember now without the weight of sorrow.

In my mind's eye, instead of Will peering in through a window, an angel steps into that fire with me. He sweeps Andrew and my mother into his arms, carrying them away, and me . . .

He carries me as well but straight out the front door.

My brother is gone, but maybe it's not my fault. God doesn't need to forgive me for what happened. I need to forgive myself.

Landon reaches for my hand as my tears fall, the breeze whisking them away. And the weight that I've borne for so long seems to be whisked away as well, rolling and crashing until it's swept into the sea.

This is where I'll remember the good and the bad from this island. Through the shedding of an old life. Through strength and beauty that have been stained by heartache and chiseled by the tide.

When the sea moves out, I find two shells in the soggy sand—an elegant pearly-gray one and a fragile shell streaked with purple and an iridescent color that's tinted blue in the sunlight.

Like Mrs. West's bottles, I want these shells to harbor my memories.

With Landon beside me, I slowly open the green folder and find a contract with a woman named Olivia Parker from New Jersey. My biological grandmother, I assume. The contract details a closed adoption, saying Olivia would never attempt to visit her daughter nor would she tell anyone about the biological father of her baby.

A check accompanied the contract, an enormous sum signed by Marcella and then cashed by Olivia in December 1975.

Landon studies the papers over my shoulder. "I've never heard of an adoption costing this much."

"It seemed that Olivia was paid a significant sum for her silence."

"Why would Marcella want her to stay quiet?"

But I know the answer, even before I look at the birth certificate. My mother—Emily Kingston—was the biological child of Olivia Parker and William Kingston. Born when William was in his sixties and Olivia was working as a maid in the Kingston farmhouse.

Emily was Randolph's half sister, which means Kingston blood flows through me too. I could step away from the members of this family, run as far as I'd like, but I'll always be a Kingston.

Randolph and Marcella adopted Emily to protect William's reputation, I assume. And perhaps to protect the baby.

If anything, this made Marcella a hero. Like Mrs. West.

No wonder my uncles hated my mother. She was a Kingston, by adoption and by blood. After Randolph died, she was William's only child, and they were terrified that she might inherit more—and perhaps all—of the Kingston fortune.

Then their hatred trickled down to Andrew and me.

I call Claire from the beach, and she quickly hands off the phone. My grandmother's voice is shaky, but I thank God that she's still alive and wants to talk to me.

"I'm sorry, Ava," she says.

"For what?"

"Not being honest with you."

"I forgive you," I say slowly. "Truly. You've always wanted what was best for me and my mother and the entire Kingston family."

"My father and William's partnership was founded on corruption," she says. "The pillars were bound to collapse."

"And we will begin building again."

"I've changed my will," she tells me. "You don't have to worry anymore."

"I'm not worried—"

"If you die before anyone in the family except me, the entire family loses their inheritance. An inheritance, I might add, that has been capped at a modest sum for each of my children and grandchildren. The rest is going to charity."

"My cousins will rush me to the ER if I sneeze."

"They may not care for the right reasons, but I want them to focus on something other than the money." It's too late to make them truly care, but at least none of them will try to hurt me. "The directors are going to give Bishara a grant."

I glance at the man beside me and my heart soars for him and his work. "Thank you."

"I'd like you to continue with the foundation," she says. "With a salary so you can find a home for yourself."

"I'll think about it."

And she respects my words.

Landon and I begin walking back toward the inn, the seashells secured in one of my hands, my other wrapped in his. And it just feels right being back on this island with him, telling him about Marcella.

"It seems that your grandmother has spent a lifetime trying to protect everyone in her family."

"Her fears have masked her love." Water trickles over my toes. "Instead of being honest, she tried to make everyone in the family happy by hiding what others had done wrong. Perhaps so she wouldn't lose them like Emily. Her sons took full advantage of her fear."

"I hope she'll choose a legacy of honesty," he says. "A way to remember the good and the bad . . ."

Like seashells and glass bottles and old index cards.

A boat soars past us, its brilliant green-and-white sail harnessing the wind.

"Do you think any of the children your *oma* rescued are still alive?"

"Probably . . ."

I stop walking. "I wonder if they remember what happened."

"Does it matter now?"

"I think it does," I say slowly. "They might find healing in the good and bad of their story as well."

FORTY-TWO

So much fuss, and for no reason at all, except a birthday she'd already celebrated ninety-eight times.

Eloise checked the pearl buttons on her blouse and shifted in the upholstered chair propped up like a throne on this miniature stage. Marcella had chartered a plane from Portland for the entire West family, and Eloise spent the ride stitching together another wig, this one for a girl at Doernbecher who loved the courageous princess in *Brave*. She glanced down at the yarn in her lap as she waited for the party to begin, the auburn color reminding her of Ava's beautiful hair.

Never in her life had she imagined she'd reconcile with a member of the Kingston family, let alone two, but she adored the young woman who'd found her, especially when she realized that Landon adored her too. She'd spent a lifetime being afraid of William Kingston and his family, even after William was gone, but she no longer wanted to be afraid.

Before they reached Amsterdam, the airplane made a stop in New York, and she'd been able to visit Marcella at the farmhouse Eloise had run away from long ago. The woman had asked for her forgiveness. The sins of her father-in-law weren't hers to bear, Eloise told her, but Marcella said she had done plenty of damage on her own.

Then Eloise told her about the crimson cord that God offered her. A thread to rescue those who sought after Him, even when the walls around them were crumbling down. Back all those years ago when she'd visited New York, Marcella Kingston had saved her life. And now, she prayed that God would save Marcella.

Ava and Marcella wanted to give this canal house back to Eloise as a gift, but she preferred that their family keep it as a library so others could learn the truth about the war. So that maybe, in remembering, they could keep others from being hurt.

Her glass bottles, lined up neatly again on her shelf back home, were all she wanted as a memorial to the past. The life she chose to celebrate was the one she'd built deep in the Pacific Northwest with the man who loved her and with the three children they had raised in the wide-open spaces of his family's orchard. As the years passed—more than fifty of them together—he'd helped her remember the children that she'd left behind, even as they protected their own children and then grandchildren.

Landon had bought her another red bottle to replace the

one for Hein, but she'd left it in a box. From now on, they would remember Hein as a family.

The interior of her old home here in Amsterdam had been gutted and redesigned. For that, Eloise was thankful. Landon had asked if she wanted to go down to the cellar after this ceremony, and she most certainly did not. Sitting here among the books, with a giant backdrop draped in orange behind the stage, was hard enough.

Below the platform were about thirty chairs, filled with her and Nathan's three children and their offspring, all of whom had flown in from around the world to celebrate her year. One of them had brought in this overstuffed chair. Those hard seats were no good for her anymore.

Instead of sitting before the festivities, her family clustered together across the library, chattering among themselves, and that made her heart the happiest of all. Then Landon and a man she didn't know—Paul Epker, he said—stepped up to a podium, complete with a microphone as if this small crowd couldn't hear him.

It was sweet of them to make her feel special, but all she really wanted was time visiting with her family. And dessert— it wouldn't be right to celebrate without butter cake.

But when Paul began speaking, he didn't say a word about her birthday. Instead his words transported her back to the war. Back to the days when she and Josie and so many others tried to help the children.

As he spoke about the theater and then the crèche, she closed her eyes and smelled the ink on her typewriter ribbon, heard the keys clacking in her head. The gauntlet of her fingertips to protect those she could, the power to make them invisible. A sword to slay those they couldn't remove from the list.

Paul called a name—Mr. Meijer—and she opened her eyes, worried that they thought she might have been sleeping.

An elderly man joined them on the platform. He was dressed in gray trousers and a white dress shirt, the silver knob of a cane in his hand.

Mr. Meijer took the card from Paul's hand. Smiling, he walked toward her.

"Thank you," he said, kissing her cheek. "I was just a baby when you saved my life."

He handed her a worn index card, stored now in a plastic sleeve. On it was his full name, *Lars Meijer*, highlighted in orange. One of the children from 1942.

Ava joined Mr. Meijer on the platform, and together they reached for the edge of the orange drape. The fabric tumbled to the floor, revealing a galaxy of stained glass, the window climbing three stories up to the roof.

Most of the panels were shaped like diamonds, hundreds of colorful jewels soldered together to filter the light. Star-shaped panels, larger than the others, were sprinkled among the diamonds.

Mr. Meijer moved slowly up to the glass, kissed one of the panels, and something inside her seemed to bloom. This boy from the crèche had made it through the war.

Her daughter Anne retrieved a chair for Mr. Meijer and he sat in a row with her family.

On every diamond, Paul explained, was the name of a person who'd been rescued from the nursery. Six hundred and forty-two of them. And then he began reading the names on a plaque below the window, dozens of people who had helped with the rescue. Walter Süskind. Henriëtte Pimentel. Jozefien and Samuel van Rees.

Josie.

Eloise closed her eyes again, for the briefest of moments, fighting the breeze across the peatland as she and Josie paddled toward their windmill. The friend that she'd failed in the end.

She didn't deserve this honor. Josie and the others—they should be here instead. All of them lined up together on a row of chairs.

But everyone in their network was gone now, it seemed. Everyone except her.

She bundled up the yarn in her lap, trying to be brave herself.

Paul called another name, and a woman rolled herself up in a wheelchair. She kissed a panel before moving across the platform to thank Eloise.

And the tears began to flow.

She wasn't a hero, but instead of hiding behind her own shame, Eloise decided to join the others in honoring the names on this plaque, honor Josie and their courageous friends for all they had done to save others instead of themselves.

And today she would celebrate the life of each person who'd been hidden away.

Over the next two hours, survivors kissed the panel with their name and then handed Eloise a card, most of them kissing her cheeks as well. Some of them paid their tribute on the balcony of the second or third floor, reaching across the railing to touch their window panel when their name was called.

The main floor began to fill with people. Never had she imagined that so many of these children had survived the war. Or lived more than seventy years after it was over.

She didn't remember any of these children except Lars—she'd typed thousands of cards during the war—but the older ones seemed to remember her. And it didn't matter. Her heart blossomed with each kiss until it felt as if she had a whole garden growing inside her. From the platform, several of these grown-up children said that she'd given them a gift, but today she was the beneficiary of their kindness.

No one tried to touch the colorful stars, glistening in the middle of the diamond frame, and her mind stole back to her own wall of light in her house, to the memory glass.

Delft blue, amber, the maple green—these stars were the exact same colors. Sixty-eight of them.

No one knew exactly how many Dutch children had been killed in the Holocaust, but among all who were saved on this wall, the Kingstons had remembered those who had been lost on that final transport. And they remembered Hein among them.

This tribute from the Kingston family was the greatest honor of all.

Anne reached across her chair to take Eloise's hand.

"They found the list of those orphans from the nursery," her daughter whispered. "Every star has a name."

A name to remember.

Her eyes focused on the crimson one, just to the right

of the platform. After the ceremony, she would kiss the star herself.

Paul was speaking again, and this time he seemed to stumble over his words. "I'd like to welcome my mother to the stage."

Mrs. Epker was lovely, wearing a pale-blue dress and double-stranded pearl necklace that dropped almost to her waistline. In one hand she held a card and in the other a red rose. Tied tight around her neck was a tattered orange scarf.

The woman kissed one of the diamonds and then she stopped beside the crimson star, kissing it too.

If Eloise had been a few decades younger, she would have sprung out of that chair, but she was bound to it instead.

Why was Paul's mother kissing the star for Hein?

Mrs. Epker placed the rose on Eloise's lap where the yarn had once been. Then she handed her the index card.

"'Margot Asch,'" Eloise read out loud. Her eyes widened, but she couldn't speak again.

Anne retrieved another chair from the corridor, but this time, instead of joining those on the floor, Margot sat down beside her.

"You took me down to your cousin's house," the woman said. "You hid me . . ."

Eloise grasped her hand. "I'm so pleased you were safe."

"Keet treated me like a daughter," she said. "Do you remember Esther van Gelder?"

Eloise nodded.

"Erik and Keet adopted both of us. Esther became a teacher in Maastricht and taught for almost fifty years."

"Were you a teacher as well?"

Margot shook her head slowly, gracefully. "I married when I was seventeen to a man I loved dearly."

Eloise's eyes fixed back on the glass. "Why did you kiss the crimson star?"

Paul invited the crowd to join them for a reception in the courtyard, but Eloise didn't care about butter cake now. After the people shuffled out, gracing her with the kindest of words along the way, all that remained were her and Margot, beneath this tower of glass.

"Why did you kiss his star?" she asked again.

"Mrs. West—" Margot covered Eloise's hand with hers, a shell around her fingers—"Hein didn't die during the war."

"He was killed in Auschwitz." Eloise had seen his name— Hein Kingston—on one of the many lists.

Margot's mouth pressed together as if she wasn't certain what to say next.

"How do you know my son?" Eloise asked.

The woman smiled. "He was my husband."

Eloise's eyes grew wide. "But the gas chamber . . ."

Margot shook her head. "Josie saved him from Westerbork."

FORTY-THREE

JOSIE

GIETHOORN
MAY 1946

Josie and Hein laughed as they paddled back to the house in the flicker of twilight, pink-and-white blossoms sprinkled like confetti across the canal. They'd spent the evening picnicking at the windmill they'd adopted as a playhouse, and it felt so good to laugh, good to play the games they both enjoyed.

Laughter had eluded them for so long. Even after the Canadian soldiers liberated the northern provinces, Josie hadn't been sure about their future. After they left Kamp Westerbork, she and Hein had been hiding—in the woods and meadowland at first, ducking when the swastika-tagged planes skimmed low over the ground, and then in this house. The only one who asked questions was a former teacher from her father's school. She'd told him that Hein was her son.

Back at Westerbork, she'd thought Mrs. Pon had been lying about scarlet fever, to scare the guard, but then a rash had broken out around Hein's neck and traveled down his arms. Josie had risked so much already to save Eliese's son. She wasn't going to lose him to a fever that Dr. Schoght could cure.

They'd returned to Giethoorn long enough to visit Klaas's father. The only questions Dr. Schoght asked were about his symptoms; then he'd given her morphine to calm the fever and food to help them both survive while thcy waited out the final months of war.

When the Nazis had finally been driven out of Holland, a year ago, she had brought Hein home with her. Their country was still in turmoil, people trying to regain some semblance of normalcy even as they punished those who'd been oppressing them. But she and Hein were free. They'd both lost much to this war, but at least they were together.

Her brother was gone. Near the end of the war, he'd been killed for stealing identity cards to use for those who'd gone under. Samuel had stayed true to exactly what he believed in, and she would remember him always as a man of integrity.

Her parents had been sent east like so many after the NSB found three Dutch men up under the eaves of their home, hiding away so they wouldn't be sent to a work camp in Germany. A local policeman—her father's friend—had taken the underdivers and her parents away weeks before she and Hein returned.

Josie had gone into Amsterdam once since the liberation to visit the Linden home, hoping to find Hein's mother, but neither Mr. Linden nor Eliese had returned. A large padlock barred their front door and neither of their names were on Westerbork's survivor list.

She would do what she must to find them, but the thought of giving Hein away now, after all they'd been through, seared her heart. He wasn't family, but after caring for him for almost three years, he felt like her nephew or even a son. And she wouldn't send a letter to William Kingston—Mr. Linden was very clear that he should never know about his child. Hein didn't even seem to remember that he'd once used the name Kingston. Like Esther on their train ride to Maastricht, he'd adopted her faux surname of de Jong.

Stories had flooded back from Germany, from survivors who were returning, and they were beyond comprehension. Many people thought the stories about cattle cars, the death and despair in the camps, had been fabricated, but she'd had a glimpse of the cars leaving Westerbork, saw the children being taken away. She'd seen Fünten and his men and their disdain for the people they'd imprisoned in the theater. And she believed these stories were true.

Some days—some hours—her heart ached from all that she'd lost but it quickly refilled with this boy's love. Hein still wanted nothing more than to play, and each time they played together, her heart flooded with joy. The only games they no longer played were ones that involved hiding. He didn't like tight spaces or dark rooms, preferring to sleep on the cot she'd set up in her room instead of the cushioned bed in Samuel's room. He liked to watch the moon through her window.

She and Hein maneuvered the canoe left, into the narrow *slootje* by their house.

"*Tante,*" he shouted, the name they'd chosen for her after they left Westerbork.

She laughed again when he splashed the water, dousing the orange scarf that she'd used her Girl Guide skills to knit after the war, a token she continued to wear in spite of the season. She fanned her paddle under the surface, soaking him back.

It was a gift—this laughter after so much sorrow.

But her laughter quickly faded as they paddled toward their covered slip along the water, the blues of night sponging up the color. Something moved inside the front window of her house, a shadow of a person in the dark room.

Her heart leapt in the stillness. Had her parents returned?

She hadn't really believed it possible, but she'd hoped in the past year that they might find their way home. She wanted nothing more than to sit on the porch with her mother and Hein and drink hot chicory together, hear her father's stories.

But if her parents were back, her mother would have turned on the lights and opened the windows, basked in the spring air.

Her hope began to fade with the sunlight. Whoever was inside, it seemed, didn't want them to know.

Was someone from Westerbork still hunting for Hein? Or had a remaining member of the NSB discovered her part in stealing away children from Amsterdam?

It might not be someone wanting to harm them. Perhaps Eliese or even Mrs. Pon had come home, hoping to surprise her. If it was Eliese, Josie would be sad, but pleased for her and Hein. Too many families had been broken apart in this war. Families that needed to be reunited.

She began paddling backward from their *slootje*. Instead of going home, she and Hein would cross the village canal to visit Dr. Schoght. He would find out who was in her home.

Hein didn't see the shadow—he'd spotted a flock of orange-billed geese and reached for one like Samuel and Klaas used to do, trying to catch it.

The canoe began to rock. "Hein—"

She reached for the slip, trying to steady the boat, but it was too late. The canoe tipped over, plunging both of them into the water.

When Hein emerged, he shouted with glee, but she cringed from the cold, from the growing worry about the intruder in their home.

"Hush," she said, desperate to quiet him. Just until they knew who was inside.

He shook his head, droplets of water flinging across the surface. "What's wrong?"

She hurried up the metal rungs of the slip's ladder, reaching down for his hand to pull him up, and in seconds, he was standing beside her.

Glass shattered inside their home—a window, a lamp, she didn't know. Hein spun toward her, worry flaring in his young eyes.

"Someone's here," he whispered.

"We'll find out who it is."

A man ran out onto the lawn, scanning the water. A man she didn't recognize. And in an instant, she stepped back more than ten years, to the days when she and Samuel fought against the Spanish ruler named Fernando. When she hid among her mother's flowers and under the copper sheen of canal.

Her hand on her wrist, she circled the lion bracelet around her skin. Years ago, she'd been able to distract the governor—Klaas—until Samuel pinned their Dutch flag on his door. She needed another distraction today, something that would lead this man away from the house. For Hein's sake.

In the far corner of the boat slip, under the wooden roof, she knelt beside Hein. "You must hide."

He shook his head. "I don't want to play that game."

"This time—" her voice trembled when she spoke again—"we're no longer playing a game."

"*Tante?*"

"Promise me that you'll hide."

He nodded, a crop of wet hair falling over his eyes.

The man outside shouted and then someone else said her name. How did they know her?

Evil, she feared, hadn't ended with the war.

"You are going to grow up into a gentleman, Hein." She kissed his cheek. "God is going to use you to bring people together instead of tear them apart."

"Josie . . ."

She unwound the orange scarf from her neck and strung it around his. "You are His son."

A lamp along the canal flickered on, spreading light across the platform, and she scooted him back against the wall.

The man by the water turned. A stranger in a black suit coat. In the lamplight she could see the glint of hatred in his gaze, and he reminded her of Fünten, the night he'd sworn when he saw the Jewish children still in the crèche, the night he'd almost killed her.

What had she done to make this man angry?

"Stop!" he shouted as he raced toward the slip.

If he came any closer, he'd see Hein.

Stepping onto the quay, she breathed deep, capturing the life inside her, but she left a bit of her heart here with the boy.

The water embraced her when she dove, and she kicked as fiercely as she'd kicked as a girl, like a frog fleeing from a heron. The heron, she prayed, would follow her all the way into the village center, far away from Hein.

She swam by Klaas's home and under the bridge where she'd carved their initials. Then she emerged for the briefest of moments for a breath, near the gap in the pilings where she used to hide.

The sound of a motor rippled up the canal, and she trembled. A whisper boat or a canoe, those she could out-swim, but she'd never beat an engine. This chase, she feared, wouldn't last long.

When they found her, would they force her back to the house? What if Hein was still waiting there on the boat slip?

"Run," her lips begged, even though he couldn't hear.

Run far away from these men.

The boat would be here any moment now. She couldn't outswim it, but maybe she could still duck under the quay, burrow between the posts.

She found the familiar ledge, but her shoulders were too wide to fit between the pilings now. Another breath and she ducked back under the water, hoping the boat would pass by, but when she emerged again, it was right beside her.

She started to dive again.

"Jozefien, don't."

This voice she recognized as an old friend, not a stranger. A friend she hadn't seen in years, since that evening in Amsterdam when he'd asked for the envelope of guilders.

Klaas hung over the side of the boat, his arm outstretched. "Hurry."

Her hand reached back for the platform instead. "What's happening, Klaas?"

"He will find you here."

"Who?"

"William Kingston."

Hein's father.

"Why does he want me?"

"It's not you—he wants the money that's missing from Mr. Linden's bank. He knows that Samuel took it, and now that your brother is gone, he thinks you know where it went."

"But why would he think that Samuel—?"

She stopped talking, everything sliding neatly into place. Mr. Linden had taken the money from the American investors, given some of it to Samuel to use for the resistance, and then she'd transported it across Holland for them. Klaas, it seemed, knew about their scheme.

She shivered again in the water. "You told him that Samuel was delivering money."

"Samuel had already been killed by the Gestapo."

"And now you're working for the man he despised."

"William is going to reinvest in Holland. To help us all."

Klaas reached under her arms and lifted her from the water, dragging her into the boat. Her entire body felt numb from the chill.

"You were never part of the resistance, were you?" she asked.

He didn't reply.

"The money is gone, Klaas. The resistance used it during the war."

"Surely some of it is left," he said, his voice desperate. "In your home."

"If so, I don't know where it is."

A loud noise—a gunshot—blasted from the shore and her shoulder burned.

"Stop shooting!" Klaas shouted, swearing at someone near them. William, she assumed.

Klaas pressed a towel against her shoulder.

"We don't need her anymore," William said.

"Yes, we do—"

"She's the only one left in Holland who knows."

Except Klaas, she wanted to say, but it wouldn't matter. At least William was looking for her, not Hein. He didn't know what happened to his son.

But what if he returned to search her house again? Even if William didn't know about Hein—what would he do if he found the boy?

She prepared to jump again, to hide in the shallows of this water. Perhaps he couldn't see her in the dark.

Another gunshot, and she crumpled into the bottom of the boat.

"Enough, William!"

Pain spread across Josie's chest, to the cavern that once held her heart.

"You were only supposed to ask about the money," Klaas said.

Another light flickered over the boat. A lamp brighter than any she'd ever seen in Giethoorn. A lamp that flooded her soul.

Klaas knelt beside her, holding up her head. "I'm sorry, Jozefien."

"There's a boy," she said, forcing the words out. "On my dock."

"Whose boy?" He held her head higher. "Josie—"

"Don't tell William . . ."

"I won't."

"Take him to Keet." Her eyes closed. "She'll care for him."

The light grew bigger, warmer. And another man appeared in the boat beside Klaas, fury raging in his brown eyes. But it wasn't her he was angry with. The fury faded into kindness as he bent over, lifted her in his arms.

"Well done," a voice said in the distance, the words cruel.

The kind man pulled her closer to his chest as he whispered the same words. "Well done."

Then he took her home.

FORTY-FOUR

Memories in Holland aren't contained in glass. They're spilled out across land reclaimed from the sea, narrow canals that eventually seep back into the ocean.

Margot took her mother-in-law to the village of Giethoorn first, the place of everything good from Eloise's childhood. They rented a whisper boat and cruised past Mrs. Pon's cottage, tying the boat up on a metal ring beside the house where Josie and Samuel had once lived.

The two of them sat on a bench surrounded by flowers, overlooking Klaas's house across the village canal, the algae-clad bridge still intact between them. It was as if the tragedies of the war never struck here.

"Do you remember Klaas?" Margot asked.

Eloise nodded. "We were friends as children, but his mother wasn't very fond of me. I don't think she liked Jews."

"I think she was less fond of you because you were German."

Eloise glanced at her, surprised. "Did you know Mrs. Schoght?"

"No, but I knew Klaas. He became Hein's godfather after the war."

Leaves blew across the path, reminding her of that day long ago when she took Hein to the woman in Amsterdam with the diamond on her scarf. Her entire life she'd regretted that day, wishing she could have accompanied him to Auschwitz instead. It wasn't rational, she knew, but often she'd wondered if she could have saved him from the gas chamber.

"Klaas Schoght was a complicated man," Margot said. "He never had a family, but he loved Hein like he was his own son."

"How did Klaas find Hein?" Eloise asked, one of a thousand questions.

Margot paused. "Klaas never wanted to choose sides, not during the war or after it. He tried to align himself with—"

"Whoever would benefit him the most."

Margot nodded. "Hein's death broke him. After years of my asking, Klaas finally told me his story."

The wind ruffled Eloise's sweater, and she cocooned herself with her hands. "Hein's death certainly broke me."

Margot linked her arm through Eloise's. "According to Klaas, Josie saved Hein from Westerbork."

"I don't understand—"

"Klaas found them together after the war," Margot began to explain. "Before William Kingston found the ledgers for Holland Trade Bank, he wanted to know where his money had gone. Gerrit Linden and Samuel van Rees had both been killed and you had disappeared, so he hired Samuel's best friend and paid him a significant amount of money to search for Josie. Klaas knew Josie had helped Samuel with the resistance, but he had kept her secret until William offered him a job.

"I think he loved Josie, in his own strange way. He thought she'd be safe after she told him what happened to the money, but sadly William killed her instead."

Eloise remembered well running through the fields and forest in New York, trying to escape from the man she'd once loved. "I'm afraid that doesn't surprise me."

"William never knew that Hein was still alive. When Klaas found him, he took Hein across the bridge to stay with his father at first and then down to live with Josie's cousin in Maastricht."

———

The next day, Margot and Eloise traveled down to Erik and Keet's old farmhouse. When Hein arrived in Maastricht, Margot told her, Keet had already adopted Margot and Esther. Unable to house another child, she found a place for Hein to live, a cottage near her home. Mr. Epker had lived there his entire life, an active member of the resistance. At the end of the war, he'd married a Jewish woman.

The Epkers had welcomed Hein as a son, and Margot assured Eloise repeatedly that they'd loved him well. She and

Hein were married after he graduated from the University of Amsterdam with a degree in engineering.

The two women strolled slowly by the cottage where Hein had been raised, on Schutterij—Civic Guard—Weg. Then they found the mine entrance where she and Nathan had escaped long ago, cool air escaping between the secured iron slats.

"He built bridges," Margot said, and Eloise laughed, pleased with this news. "Across water and land, but also between people. In his last years, he worked as a diplomat and secretly distributed Bibles to those who were locked behind the Iron Curtain."

"How did he die?" Eloise asked.

"From an autoimmune disease that plagued him for his entire life, causing his hair to fall out in patches when his immune system attacked the follicles. He always wore a cashmere cap to cover it."

The memories of his cashmere cap made Eloise smile.

"Did Hein remember?" Eloise asked quietly. "Josie or . . . ?"

She supposed he had been too young to remember her.

Margot lifted a book out of her purse. A colorful sketch on the cover showed a woman holding her baby son, surrounded by a toy lamb and sailboat and small windmill.

Eerste Levensjaren.

The words inscribed on the cover. A baby's first years.

Her hand shaking, Eloise brushed her fingers over the top. "It's his album."

"Klaas discovered the safe in your cellar and hired someone to break the lock. Most of the contents went to William, but he kept this." Margot handed the album to her. "When Klaas found it, he knew that Hein was your and William's son. Eventually he gave the album to Hein, but my husband never knew he was a Kingston. It wasn't until both Hein and William were gone that Klaas told me the truth."

"And you never told anyone—"

"Klaas wanted to protect Hein, and I didn't want to jeopardize Paul's work with the Kingston Corporation."

Inside were the pictures Eloise had taken of her and Hein together, the stories she'd written about his first years. The only thing missing was the Kingston name. The two places where she'd written Hein's last name had been blotted out with ink.

"He didn't know what happened to you or Josie, but he remembered you both."

"I'm grateful . . ."

"I'm sorry you didn't know Hein was alive," Margot said quietly. "You could have taken him to America with you."

Eloise took her hand again, comforting this woman she'd traveled with to Maastricht long ago. "If I'd brought Hein with me, I fear his father would have killed us both."

The Savior had redeemed her, made the broken places whole. Forgiveness she had received with open arms, the cleansing power to wash away her shame, and now she needed to forgive William for what he had done to her.

Hein had lived a full life in Holland. The crimson blaze of his legacy lived on through Margot and the Epker family and the many bridges that he'd built.

And his memory would remain always, an ember in her heart.

FORTY-FIVE

"We're practically cousins," Landon says as we cross over the thundering Multnomah Falls outside Portland, mountain water soaking our shorts.

"We are not cousins!"

"Like a dozen times removed."

I jab his shoulder. "Not even close . . ."

"Well, that's a relief," he says, reaching for my hand.

He's returning to Uganda tomorrow, and I don't want to say goodbye. God has used our months together as balm for my soul.

"Do you miss Marcella?" he asks as we hike around the waterfall.

I reach into my coat pocket, feel the three shells inside. "Very much."

She laid down her boxing gloves when she passed on, but she'd fought hard for our family, in her own way, spending her final months trying to mend what those before her had torn apart.

The last time I saw her, Marcella said that she loved both my mother and me, words I've stitched to my heart. She'd known all along where my mom lived, but her sons didn't. Not until Will saw Andrew's birth announcement. It took him months, but according to Marcella's attorney, he had indeed started the fire.

Marcella hadn't known about the fire until my caseworker tracked her down.

I've given my testimony, and now it's up to the courts to decide whether or not Will is guilty. I'm grateful that Marcella doesn't have to watch the courtroom drama as both my uncles fight against multiple charges.

Before Marcella died, she confirmed that William was my biological grandfather. My head spins, trying to sort through all the messiness of it, but William and Mrs. West were Hein's biological parents, making them Paul Epker's grandparents. And according to the family tree that I drew, Hein is an uncle to both Landon and me.

But all that really matters is this: no matter how much Landon teases me, we are not related to each other. Not. At. All. We're from two separate families who merged in the past, and with Marcella's blessing, our families will merge again as partners in our foundation work.

Paul Epker and I are descendants of a man who'd made money his god, and we've both received a significant portion of the Kingston estate. Neither of us contributed to what happened back in World War II, but the money is stained, I think, like the picture that Peter painted before he died.

After many discussions, Paul and I have agreed to give our inheritance away as directors of the revamped Kingston Family Foundation. We've both inherited a new family in the process. No matter what happens with Landon, I've decided to adopt the Epker and West families as my own.

I wish Marcella could see what was happening with Bishara. An entire complex is being constructed on their plantation with a dormitory, school, and medical clinic, paid for by the foundation. Marcella's House, we're calling it, but I hope the children will simply call it home.

The floor of this Columbia River Gorge is scarred black, the tree limbs charred from a recent fire, but new life is pressing through as buds in some of the branches. And I feel this same new life budding in me like it had in Mrs. West. My nightmares have stopped, but I still dream sometimes about Andrew and my mom. Those I cherish.

Vi tracked down Olivia Parker several months ago, and Landon and I visited her in Vermont. Marcella had kept track of her as well, sending regular payments for silence.

Olivia was more interested in talking about the end of these payments instead of a relationship with me, but I'm okay with this. My roots have grown much deeper.

Landon's phone makes a ticking sound, and he skims a message.

"Who's texting you?"

He smiles. "Faith is asking if you can come back to Uganda with me."

"Just Faith?" I quip.

"No." He stops on the path, facing me. "I'm asking too."

"Landon . . ."

He gently puts his hand under my chin, coaxing me to face all my fears. "Please?"

Part of me wants to weld armor back around my heart, warding off any intruder, but this man doesn't want to harm me. If nothing else, he's cared for me well as a friend. A gentleman.

"I'm falling in love with you, Landon," I finally say, no holds barred. "If you are meaning for this, for *us*, to be a casual thing, I need to bow out now. You can keep the grant money—"

"Oh, Ava." He turns my head slightly, making sure I can hear. "I wouldn't dream of messing with your heart."

Then he cradles my face between his hands and kisses me.

"Okay then," I say when I can breathe again.

He smiles. "Okay?"

"I'll come back to Uganda."

"I'm glad."

"And I may not leave—"

He kisses me again, and this time I taste home.

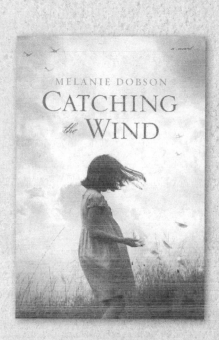
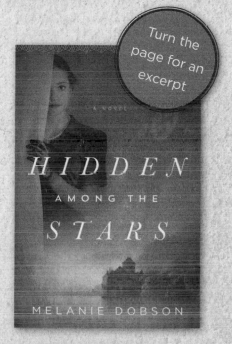

CHAPTER 1

ANNIKA

LAKE HALLSTATT, AUSTRIA
MARCH 1938

The blade of a shovel, cutting through frosted grass. That's what she remembered most from the spring of 1938. In the year that followed, on the darkest of nights, she could almost hear the whisper of digging again. The sound of Max Dornbach calling her name.

"Annika?" His confident voice bled into the fluid sounds of that evening, but her heart took on a rhythm of its own, twirling like the feathery seeds of dandelion caught in an Alpine storm.

How did Max know she was hidden behind the pines?

When she peeked between the branches, he was looking straight at her. Reluctantly, or at least attempting to appear reluctant, she stepped out from her haven, into the cast of blue moonlight, Vati's winter coat buttoned over her calico chemise.

Temperatures had dipped to near freezing again, but Max wore a linen shirt, the sleeves rolled up to his elbows. Strength swelled under those sleeves, arms that had rowed a wooden *fuhr* boat around Lake Hallstatt nearly every summer of his seventeen years, carving his muscles like the fallen birch her father liked to shape into benches and chairs.

"What are you doing out here?" he asked, though she should have been the one questioning him. He'd awakened her when he snuck by the cottage she and her father shared in the woods.

At first she'd thought it was Vati who crept by her window, on his way to the tavern, but then, in the beam of light, she'd seen the threads of blond in Max's brown hair, the shovel resting against his shoulder as if it were a rifle readied for battle. She liked to think he'd purposely rustled the branches because he'd missed her these winter months as much as she'd missed him.

"You woke me." Annika took another step toward him. "I didn't know you'd returned from Vienna."

"My parents wanted a holiday."

The Dornbachs visited at Christmastime, but rarely in the spring while Max was studying in *Gymnasium*. Unlike Annika's father, his parents thought an education with books and such was important.

"I'll tell Vati you're home," she said. "He can light the furnace."

"It's not necessary." Max stomped the heel of his boot onto the shovel to remove another pile of earth. She imagined the rust-colored clumps yawning after their hibernation this winter, shivering in the frigid air. "My father already lit it."

She hadn't realized Herr Dornbach could do such things on his own, but then again, even after living fifteen years—her entire life—on this estate, Annika knew little about Max's parents. Neither Herr nor Frau Dornbach bothered to befriend someone beneath their rank. Certainly not their caretaker's girl.

Annika scanned this knobby plot of land, harbored between the pines. "Why are you digging at night?"

When he shook his head, refusing to trust her with this, her heart wrenched. She'd never told another soul any of his secrets. Not about the dent in Herr Dornbach's motorboat four summers past or the gash in Max's leg that she'd helped wrap or the evening he'd cried when he lost Pascal, the pet fox he'd rescued from the forest.

Pascal now rested peacefully in this piece of earth along with numerous rabbits, four cats, two squirrels, and a goldfinch, each grave marked by a pyramid of stones that Max collected from the cliffs on Hoher Sarstein, the mountain towering over his family's estate.

When they were younger, Annika had helped Max conduct a service for each animal, solemnly crossing herself as they transferred the care for these animals over to *Gott.* Once a laugh slipped from her lips, as they'd been reciting the words from Job.

"But as for me I know that my Redeemer liveth, And at last he will stand upon the earth: And after my skin, even this body, is destroyed, Then without my flesh shall I see God. . . ."

They'd been burying a beetle named Charlie in the dirt, and the thought of this creature standing before a heavenly being, his six spindly legs trembling in awe, made Annika laugh. Looking back, it wasn't funny—irreverent, even—but she was only eight and quite nervous at both the thought of death and the unknowns surrounding the afterlife. All she could see was a frightened Charlie, feeling as small as she would feel under the gaze of the almighty God.

Max hadn't invited her to another funeral since that

summer, seven years past. She thought he'd stopped burying his pets, but apparently he'd been burying them in the night, when no one would ridicule him.

She moved closer to the hole. A cloth seed bag rested near the shovel, partially hidden behind Max. "What are you burying?"

"Oh, *Kätzchen*," he said, shaking his head. He'd called her *kitten* since she was in kindergarten. As if she were one of his pets.

Annika's hands balled into fists, and she buried them deep in Vati's pockets. "I am not a kitten."

Max resumed his work. Blade against earth, determined to conquer the soil. When she lifted the bag, he swatted her away. "That's not for you."

"Did you lose another animal?" she asked, still holding the cloth rim. It was heavier than she'd expected.

He shook his head again, this time more slowly. "I fear we're about to lose everything."

This new tone frightened her. "I don't understand."

He scooped out two more mounds of dirt, and she dropped the bag into the hole. Then he pushed the dirt in and smoothed his shovel back and forth over the ground as if he were trying to iron out the wrinkles. "Come along," he finally said, hiking toward the wall of pine trees that separated this plot from Schloss Schwansee, his family's castle.

"What's wrong, Max?"

"The parliament approved our annexation into Germany."

"I know," she replied, glad she was already privy to this bit of news. "Vati is pleased."

"The German Reich is no longer willing to tolerate the suppression of ten million Germans across the border."

That's what Hitler had said on the wireless last month. Salvation was what he promised, the rescue of Austrians who'd been mistreated. *Anschluss*—as he called it—was prohibited by the Treaty of Versailles, but their new Führer didn't seem to be daunted by treaties or the fact that the Austrian chancellor wasn't interested in a union between his country and Germany.

Her father had celebrated the *Anschluss* at the beer hall. He'd fought as a foot soldier in the Great War, and this new union, he thought, not only would revitalize Austria, it was reparation for their empire's bitter losses twenty years ago. This time, Vati said, no one would defeat a unified Germany.

Max stopped at the edge of the trees, light from the castle's windows filtering out onto the lawn, erasing the blue haze of moon. "Your father's pleased because he isn't Jewish."

Annika shrugged. "None of us are Jewish." Except her friend Sarah, but Hitler would hardly concern himself with the Jewish Austrians who lived back in these Alps. Only summer tourists—and the occasional skier—visited their mountains and lake.

Max planted his hands on her shoulders, anchoring them so she couldn't shrug again. She tried to focus on his eyes, but his touch electrified her, a jolt that ricocheted between her fingers, her toes.

"Adolf Hitler isn't a savior. He's the devil incarnate." Max's eyes flashed, the fierce edge in his voice frightening her. "And he won't be satisfied with the devotion of our country, *Kätzchen*. He'll want the hearts of our people, too."

She'd heard the stories about Hitler and his thugs, about

the years Hitler stirred up trouble in the streets of Austria, but still she protested. "Hitler's home is in Berlin now."

Max released her shoulders and stepped out from the mantle of pine. "It won't stop him from trying to build his Reich here."

Annika shivered as she followed him toward the cottage she shared with her father, though she tried to pretend that the trembling deep inside her, flaring across her skin, was from the cold. She'd never heard Max speak of politics before. Usually he talked about his animals or school or the music he loved in Vienna. She, his devoted audience, listened to his stories every summer and in the winter weeks when he came to ski.

To her right, the gray slate on the castle's turrets glowed in the moonlight. Back in the seventeenth century, the owner of the local salt mine had built this place as a fortress between the mountains and the lake. The upkeep and expansions kept her father and now her employed year round, though one day she dreamed of being the mistress of this castle, sipping tea in the parlor instead of scrubbing its floors.

Max tucked his shovel into the large shed where Vati kept his tools and equipment. "You'd best go home. Before your father begins to worry."

Annika dug her hands into the coat pockets. "I'm glad you're here."

"It's only for a day."

"Still, I'm glad."

He lifted her right hand from the warmth of her pocket and pressed his lips against it. "Don't let one of Hitler's men steal your heart, Annika."

He released her hand, but it stayed before her, suspended in the air.

Shouting erupted inside the main house, Herr Dornbach swearing. And then the voice of Frau Dornbach stole through the open library window, yelling back at him. Max moved quickly through a side door that led into the castle, and then he closed the window to silence the fight, at least to her ears.

Annika shuffled across the ice-glazed grass, to the lakeshore. Birch benches were scattered across the property, but this bench near the reeds was her favorite.

Sitting, she pulled her arms out of the large sleeves and wrapped them tightly over her chest. Tiny clouds rose with her breath, each one climbing in the air as if it wanted to scale the mountain ridge that curled around the lake, a glorious sea creature guarding its den.

Moonlight shimmered on the water, and several lights flickered on the other side of the lake in the village called Hallstatt. When they were children, she and Max had dreamed about one day swimming across this expanse of lake together, racing to see who would win. They'd never done it, of course. Vati wouldn't have cared if she tried, but Frau Dornbach took great care in keeping her only son safe.

Why had Herr Dornbach been yelling tonight? The arguing between him and Frau Dornbach had escalated this past summer, their words escaping through the windows and finding Annika in the garden or hammering nails into a board as she helped Vati build a bench or fix a wall.

Herr Dornbach yelled at Vati last summer as well, though usually because Vati didn't arrive early enough for work, too sluggish after a night in the beer hall.

Sometimes she wondered if her parents would have fought like the Dornbachs if her mother had lived. Or perhaps Vati wouldn't drink if her mother were still alive. Sometimes her father still called out to Kathrin—her mother—in his dreams, his sorrow a storm that shook the cottage rafters and pine walls.

When her father woke, he often called Annika's name, but only because he wanted her to bring black coffee to chase away the fog in his brain.

She closed her eyes, the cold settling over her face as her thoughts returned to the young man who'd been digging in the forest. If only Max could have seen her with her hair properly curled, dressed in the pale-pink summer frock she'd sewn for his return, instead of lumped up inside Vati's ragged coat.

Her gaze wandered back over her shoulder to the light on the ground floor of the castle, to the library where Max enjoyed reading one of the many books that trimmed its shelves. Was he looking out at the lake like her? Or perhaps he was missing whatever he'd buried.

The thought of buried bones made her stomach roll, but these animals were important to Max, so they were important to her—just as important as keeping his secrets.

A breeze rustled through the branches, stirring up the depths of this lake before her and the longings in her heart. And her mind wandered back to Max's hands on her shoulders, his lips pressed against her hand.

No one else could steal her heart because it had already been stolen. And nothing could ever change her love for Max Dornbach.

Nothing at all.

AUTHOR'S NOTE

A network of heroic men and women risked everything to rescue more than six hundred Jewish children from the Dutch theater, Hollandsche Schouwburg. Among them, Henriëtte Pimentel, Walter Süskind, and Johan van Hulst courageously confronted an unfathomable evil during World War II and worked tirelessly in their leadership roles to save as many children as they could. While Mr. Süskind and Miss Pimentel lost their lives near the end of the war, the Nazis never discovered their scheme.

The Nazi invasion, the persecution of the Jewish people, was a shock to most of the Dutch population. In 1940, after promising not to attack, Hitler swept furiously across bridges and borders, overtaking most of their country in five days. Dutch citizens had fortified their land against the sea, but they hadn't been able to protect themselves from their neighbor.

During the occupation, Nazis partnered with prominent Jewish citizens and used superiority, rank, and more false promises to deliberately, secretly begin expediting Hitler's final solution. The Dutch were forced to choose sides—often a life-or-death decision—and it took years to build new bridges among neighbors who'd turned against each other during and after the war, many of them refusing to welcome the Jewish people back home.

But Holland began blossoming again, the lush fields along with her people. And as a country, they began remembering the many who sacrificed their lives to fight the evil that invaded their land.

This novel was written to commemorate the many Dutch men and women who chose to use the gifts God gave them—talents that Jesus talked about in Matthew 25—to battle for good. To remember the bravery of Walter Süskind, Henriëtte Pimentel, and Johan van Hulst; registrar Felix Halverstad; child care workers Virrie Cohen, Sieny Kattenburg, Fanny Philips, and Betty Oudkerk; and the many resistance members and caregivers whose names we will never know.

I also wrote this story to celebrate those who continue rescuing children today.

Six years ago, my nine-year-old daughter Karlyn decided that she wanted to use her gifts to love orphans in Uganda. Neither my husband nor I had ever been to Africa, but we decided to go as a family for three weeks, and God used this experience to change all of our lives.

As I wrote this novel, two of the people who inspired this story slipped through the thin veil that separates our world from eternity. Susie Stewart was a passionate follower of Christ, and as the president of True Impact Ministries, she helped us organize our trip to Uganda. Her legacy to care for orphaned children continues on through her family and thousands of others that she inspired, including my daughter, who just returned to Africa to serve both children and their caregivers.

Johan van Hulst lived to be 107, and it has been a deep honor to weave a story around the journey of this heroic man. He passed away the month before I visited Holland, but the afternoon I spent at his grave was a powerful experience for me, the remembering of a life well lived. In the past months, I've often imagined Jesus embracing both Susie and Dr. van Hulst in His arms, welcoming these two faithful servants who committed their lives to loving Him and those in their care.

Most of the Dutch who rescued children didn't think they were heroic, and Dr. van Hulst was no exception. In fact, he once said in *Het Parool*, "I actually only think about what I have not been able to do. To those few thousand children that I could not have saved."

The six hundred that he helped rescue, I suspect, think of him often.

During my week in Holland, I visited the former deportation center in Hollandsche Schouwburg and the teaching college across the street, cruised the picturesque canals through Giethoorn, toured an old windmill at Kinderdijk, climbed almost five hundred steps up the medieval Dom Tower with my friend and editor Daniëlle Heerens, spent the night a block from Corrie ten Boom's safe house, and rode to Westerbork with a gracious bus driver who was thrilled to learn that I wanted to tell the story of people who'd been imprisoned at this camp.

In Maastricht, I explored the marlstone tunnels and

what remains of an underground town that citizens built during the war; then I walked five miles through vineyards and a lovely castle estate to cross the bridge into Belgium.

So many people shared the gift of their stories with me along the way, about the evil during World War II but also about the resilience and sacrifices of many men and women who risked everything to help others. When the military couldn't defeat the enemy, an army of Dutch citizens pressed into their God-given talents and unique occupations to resist in their own way.

Sadly only five thousand of those deported from Kamp Westerbork survived the war, but of the twenty-five thousand Jewish people—including more than four thousand children—who went into hiding, more than fifteen thousand remained hidden until liberation. I couldn't capture all of their stories here, but I hope *Memories of Glass* collectively honors the many who were lost and the many heroes who risked their lives to help someone else.

As I delved into this story, I also discovered that a handful of American businessmen invested in Nazi companies before and—secretly—during World War II. An anonymous writer, using the well-known name Warburg, wrote a book about Americans who'd profited from financing Adolf Hitler in the 1930s, filtering millions through an Amsterdam bank. The Dutch publisher recalled *The Financial Sources of National Socialism* soon after the release, but many years later one of three surviving copies was translated into English.

The greediness of Hitler's financiers was the antithesis of

those who sacrificed everything. I wanted to write a novel that reflected both the corrupt and heroic stories, especially those of people who chose not to profit off the rescue of children. Thank God, many of them chose to stand against the evil.

As a historical novelist, my desire is to research well and then create an accurate reflection of history through a compelling story. In order to do this, I had to consolidate some of the dates in *Memories of Glass*. Also, the accounts of what happened inside Hollandsche Schouwburg are conflicting, but I tried to reflect the facts as closely as possible through my fictional characters.

I've been blessed to partner with a number of supersmart people who shared their stories and their expertise with me. Any errors are mine alone. A very special thank-you to:

The incredible staff at Tyndale House, including my editors Stephanie Broene, Kathryn Olson, and Elizabeth Jackson, who graciously helped me wrangle my wandering ideas. It's an honor to partner with them and Tyndale's talented marketing, design, and sales teams.

My amazing agent and friend, Natasha Kern, who encouraged me to dig deeply for a story that reflected how God is working in my life. My dear friend Ann Menke, who told me about the mines scarring the Maastricht hills. Something must have happened there during World War II, she said, and she was exactly right. Once the largest labyrinth in the world, those tunnels were an escape route during the war and a refuge for thousands.

The many people who answered my questions and shared their stories about occupied Holland, including Nel

Kulyman, Wouter van Haaften, and Santine de Roover-Baaij. My Dutch friends who graciously welcomed me to their beautiful country and spoiled me with their kindness—Daniëlle Heerens, Anniek Soppe-Woltman, Suzanne Smith, and Frony and Femke de Sain.

Eline Simantel and Daan Hoekstra, for sharing the memories of their courageous mother Eline Hoekstra Dresden, who hid her blond Jewish son in plain sight during the war and wrote about her heartbreak and then the harrowing months at Westerbork in *Wishing Upon a Star*. And for sharing the beautiful baby album that Daan's war mom kept for him.

Tosha Williams, Andy and Susie Stewart, and Mike McDonald, who encouraged our family to serve in Uganda years ago. And our many Ugandan friends who continue to invite us to work alongside them.

The following Portland-based coffee shop owners and roasters for a crash course on the industry and giving me a greater appreciation for the *terrior* in each cup: Paul Thornton at Thornton Family Coffee Roaster, Mike and Caryn Nelson at Junior's Roasted Coffee, Kevin and Amanda Bates at Symposium Coffee, and Ben Reese at Lionheart Coffee Company.

My critique partners and friends Julie Zander, Dawn Shipman, Tracie Heskett, Nicole Miller, and April McGowan for reading early chapters and helping me polish them. Michele Heath, Sandra Byrd, Ann Menke, Wayne Vandekraak, and Gerrie Mills for insight that is absolutely priceless to me.

My husband and best friend, Jon, for his faithful love

and encouragement, and our two beautiful girls—Karlyn and Kiki. Karlyn's passion for Uganda and her fight against injustice inspires many people, and Kiki's love of life and literature makes this mama's heart happy.

To our Lord, who shines light into the secrets of darkness, wipes away the tears of the wounded, and honors those who care for His kids.

DISCUSSION QUESTIONS

1. Many of the heroes from World War II never shared their stories. Why do you think they kept their past quiet? How has hearing someone else's story changed or inspired you?

2. Instead of telling her family about Hein or the other children in Amsterdam, Mrs. West remembers them through her collection of glass. Do you think it's important to remember both the good and hard things from your or your family's past? If so, how do you remember?

3. Ava desperately wants to rescue Faith from her pain, just like she wanted to rescue her brother long ago. Have you ever felt overwhelmed by the pain of other people? How do you navigate when to help and when it's necessary to let go?

4. Landon uses his gifts to serve children and adults in Uganda, but we don't need to go to Africa in order to help and serve others. Have you had the opportunity to serve people in your community in an unusual way? How do you use the unique gifts God has given you?

5. Marcella is desperately trying to rewrite her family's past and control the Kingston family's future. What do you

think is the best way to redeem a tragic situation that continues impacting a family? And how does the truth change Marcella and the other characters in this story?

6. Like Eliese, real-life hero Walter Süskind was in an impossible place of having to work with the Nazis while rescuing Jewish people. Have you ever been in a seemingly impossible place? What did you do?

7. Eliese and Ava both needed to forgive themselves even more than they needed to forgive those who hurt them. Why is it sometimes harder to forgive ourselves than other people? How can we get rid of the shame?

8. According to Landon, even if you don't like the taste, coffee brings people together. What other things bring people together around the world? And where do you find *terroir*—a taste of home—in your life?

9. After World War II, many people didn't believe the experiences of Holocaust survivors, and these men and women often spent a lifetime silently battling PTSD. What is the best way to honor those who have been victimized or experienced painful things in their past?

10. In *Memories of Glass*, evil didn't end with the liberation. Nor did the kindness of people who wanted to help others. Where do you see good working today in the midst of evil?

ABOUT THE AUTHOR

Melanie Dobson is the award-winning author of nineteen historical romance, suspense, and time-slip novels, including *Hidden Among the Stars*, *Catching the Wind*, *Chateau of Secrets*, and *Shadows of Ladenbrooke Manor*. Four of her novels have won Carol Awards, *Catching the Wind* won the Audie Award for inspirational fiction, and *The Black Cloister* won the *Foreword* magazine Religious Fiction Book of the Year.

Melanie is the former corporate publicity manager at Focus on the Family and owner of the publicity firm Dobson Media Group. When she isn't writing, Melanie enjoys teaching both writing and public relations classes.

Melanie and her husband, Jon, have two daughters. After moving numerous times with work, the Dobson family has settled near Portland, Oregon, and they love to hike and camp in the mountains of the Pacific Northwest and along the Pacific Coast. Melanie also enjoys exploring ghost towns and abandoned homes, helping care for kids in her community, and reading stories with her girls.

Visit Melanie online at www.melaniedobson.com.

TYNDALE HOUSE PUBLISHERS IS CRAZY4FICTION!

Fiction that entertains and inspires

Get to know us! Become a member of the Crazy4Fiction community. Whether you read our blog, like us on Facebook, follow us on Twitter, or receive our e-newsletter, you're sure to get the latest news on the best in Christian fiction. You might even win something along the way!

JOIN IN THE FUN TODAY.

 www.crazy4fiction.com

 Crazy4Fiction

 @Crazy4Fiction